TELL ME NO SECRETS

Maggie Hudson was born in Bradford and now lives in London with her husband and three dogs. Writing under the name Margaret Pemberton, she is the author of many successful novels including the bestselling *The Flower Garden*, *White Christmas in Saigon* and *A Multitude of Sins*.

MAGGIE HUDSON

Tell Me No Secrets

HarperCollins*Publishers*

HarperCollins*Publishers*
77–85 Fulham Palace Road,
Hammersmith, London w6 8jb

A paperback edition 1999
3 5 7 9 8 6 4

First published in Great Britain by
HarperCollins*Publishers* 1999

A catalogue record for this book
is available from the British Library

ISBN 0 00 651153 8

Set in Sabon by
Rowland Phototypesetting Ltd,
Bury St Edmunds, Suffolk

Printed in Great Britain by
Clays Ltd, St Ives plc

For Joe

With fond memories of good
times and dangerous times
in sunny Rio.

ACKNOWLEDGEMENTS

I sincerely thank:

Joe, without whose help, advice, anecdotes and hospitality in unforgettable Buzios, *Tell Me No Secrets* might not have been written.

Linda Britter, far too many things to itemise but, above all, for unstinting support and friendship.

Carol Smith, agent *extraordinaire*, and her wonderful cohorts, Petra Lewis and Zoe Waldie.

Rachel Hore at HarperCollins, for constant encouragement and endless patience.

Lucy Ferguson, who was there in the beginning and whose enthusiasm was invaluable. Anne O'Brien, who picked up the reins and saw me through to the end with unruffled diligence and good humour. Yvonne Holland, for her care and eagle-eye.

And lastly, but by no means least, my husband, Mike Pemberton.

Chapter One

1963

The day President Kennedy died was the day Jock Sweeting walked out of Pentonville nick a free man. The warders and his still incarcerated mates knew it was a freedom unlikely to last for long, but if Jock was similarly aware he gave no indication.

'Stuff it, yah ponce,' he said in a hard Glaswegian accent, with a vulgar finger gesture to the warder who, having opened the gates for him, had thoughtlessly wished him a civil goodbye.

'And the same to you, matey,' the warder retorted with sarcastic pleasantness. 'Be back in time for Christmas, will yer?'

Jock hitched his duffel bag higher on his donkey-jacketed shoulder, his lips thinning against his teeth. Screws. He hated every last one of them to the depths of his guts. Eyes glittering, he spat back a word that succinctly summed up his feelings and turned into the petrol-fumed mayhem of Caledonian Road.

Usually, when fresh out of the nick, he made his way to whatever flea-ridden hostel was nearest. This time was different. This time he had an address in his pocket.

'Shack up wiv me an' the old gel,' Albie Rice, his former cellmate, had said generously before his own release a month earlier. 'We could pull a few stunts together. There's rich pickings dahn the docks and I can get you in there easy-peasy.'

'I'm no' working for a living no matter what the pickings,' Jock had growled, running his hand over close-

1

cropped grizzled hair, and richly rolling his Rs. 'I have a reputation to mind.'

Albie knew all about Jock Sweeting's reputation. It was one of the reasons he wanted to work a few tickles with him. It would take him and his brother-in-law, Smiler Burns, up a league in the thieving stakes, for Jock was an expert with gelignite, blowing safes anywhere a suitably stuffed one could be found.

'Whatever yer want, mate,' he had said placatingly. 'Yer don't 'ave a struggle and strife to keep 'appy, do yer? Lil likes the pickings from the docks. She says me doing casual dock-work makes us 'alfway to respectable.'

Jock came to a halt at a bus stop and swung his bag down to the ground. Albie – respectable! That was a laugh. Albie had been born a petty crook and now, in his forties, he was still a petty crook. He felt in his jacket pocket for his tobacco pouch and Rizlas. That Albie was after hanging on his coat-tails was clear as day. He rolled his ciggie, chewing the corner of his mouth thoughtfully. Maybe it wouldn't be a bad thing to let Albie and his brother-in-law ride shotgun with him for a while. He couldn't go back to Glasgow – he was too well known. The Bill would be on his heels every time he so much as sneezed.

A number 91 bus roared down the road towards him and he hitched his bag onto his shoulder again. A comfy billet in Bermondsey would be just the ticket – at least for a little while. And if Albie and Smiler Burns wanted to make themselves useful to him, why not?

Jock grinned, displaying an intimidating-looking cracked front tooth, as he swung himself aboard the bus. A couple of sidekicks, a place to kip and, if he ran true to form, a bit of nookie before the day was over. What more could a grafting villain ask for?

''E ain't sleeping wiv me and Johnny!' Seven-year-old Kevin Rice kicked the table leg, spots of angry colour in his

2

grubby cheeks. 'I 'ate it when people sleep in our room wiv us! That last geezer snored somethin' rotten.'

'That last geezer was your granddad, you cheeky young bugger.' Lily Rice slapped a loaf of sliced white bread down on the table together with a block of margarine and a knife. 'Now are you having jam or Marmite? I ain't waiting on you hand and foot all bleedin' day, and where did this penknife come from? You didn't have one when you went to school this morning.'

'I know I didn't but I got one now, ain't I?' In the triumph of his accomplishment Kevin forgot about the camp bed that had been squeezed into his and Johnny's cramped bedroom. 'It's a smasher, Mum. There's even a thingy for getting stones out of 'orses' 'ooves.'

Over at the kitchen sink where she was dampening her hair and winding it up in rollers, Pearl Burns, Lily's young unmarried sister, gave a gurgle of full-throated laughter. 'That's just what you need in Bermondsey, Kev. Place is full of bleedin' horses, ain't it? You can't move for 'em.'

Kevin, aware he was being made fun of, kicked the table leg again. His mother clouted him round the ear with one hand and slammed a jar of Marmite down beside the bread with the other. 'How many bleedin' times have I told you? You get caught thieving again at school and the old Bill'll be round here like greased lightning. Your dad's got fourteen crates of Johnnie Walker stashed in the cellar. If the Bill get their mince pies on 'em he'll be back inside sooner than it takes to spit.'

Kevin shoved his hands deep in the pockets of his short shabby trousers. He didn't want his dad to go back in the nick again. His dad was a great bloke – 'a proper family man' was how he'd heard their neighbours describe him. He never took his belt to either him or Johnny. Other dads in Creek Row belted their kids, though. His uncle, Smiler Burns, who lived next door to them, was always laying into their cousin Eddie. He used the buckle-end of his belt, too. Sometimes Eddie's shoulders and backside were a mass of purple weals. No one ever said anything about it, not even the teachers at school when he had to strip to his vest and shorts for PT. 'A man has a right to deal with his kids how he sees fit.' That was what he had once heard his own dad saying to his mum, though he hadn't sounded very happy about it. It was, however, an opinion the teachers at school obviously shared. Either that or they didn't want a late-night visit from Smiler.

'Come out of your bleedin' trance, Kev, and go and find Johnny.' His mother's voice was still fraught with tension and Kevin thought he knew why. She was worried his dad's ex-cellmate would turn out to be more trouble than he was worth. 'Tell him his tea is on the table. I want him in and out again before your dad's mate gets here.'

Kevin, well used to rounding his five-year-old kid brother up from wherever he'd roamed off to, dug his hands a little deeper in his pockets and mooched off in the direction of the back door. Seconds before he reached it, it was flung open and slammed back on its hinges with such force the whole house reverberated.

'*You'll never guess what the bleedin' Americans have gorn and done!*' His Aunty Flo, Smiler's wife, stood on the doorstep, steel curlers bristling hedgehog-like all over her head, a wraparound floral pinafore covering her ample girth. '*They've only gorn and shot their President!*'

Lily dropped the sugar canister she'd been lifting down from a cupboard shelf Pearl screamed, clutching at her heart.

'President Kennedy?' Kevin was instantly all bloodthirsty attention. 'Who did it? Is 'e dead? Is . . .'

'It's on the telly now!' Ignoring Kevin's questions Flo was lumbering even as she spoke down the passageway into the Rices' sitting room. 'He's bin shot in the head and rushed to hospital . . . How the hell do you put yer telly

4

on, Lil? Where's the bleedin' switch? It'll be over before the telly's warmed up.'

Hurrying past her, Johnny's whereabouts and the imminent arrival of Jock Sweeting forgotten, Lily turned the television on. With the back door still open Kevin could hear the distant sound of people shouting the news to each other in the street and over garden walls.

'Kennedy's been shot!

'He's dead!'

'No, 'e ain't, 'e's alive.'

'He might be alive but he's brain-damaged.'

As Pearl, who had always fancied Jack Kennedy something rotten and had a photograph of him in her bedroom next to a pin-up of Richard Burton, stared in stupefied disbelief at the images now coming up on the television screen, Lily sank down on the sagging sofa saying over and over again, 'Oh dear, oh dear. How did such a thing happen? How *could* it happen?'

'President Kennedy is dead.' The words filled the room and for a moment it looked as if the almost shell-shocked news broadcaster was going to be unable to continue. Fighting for control he rallied only with the greatest difficulty, saying, 'Five minutes ago, at one p.m., Central Standard Time, President John Fitzgerald Kennedy died in Parkland Hospital, Dallas . . .'

There were no voices calling out in the street now. The whole world it seemed was, like them, glued to their television screens.

All except Jock Sweeting.

Striding down Creek Row from its Jamaica Road end he noted he would be living in a slum, but a slum that would hardly have counted as such in Glasgow's Gorbals, his own home turf. There were no front gardens, only paint-scratched doors opening straight on to the narrow cobbled street. There was no one about either but it was November, dusk, and too cold to make being outdoors a pleasure. Ducking under a line of forlorn-looking washing Jock came to number 26.

The door was half open and he knocked on it loudly. There was no reply, probably because no one could hear over the incomprehensible blare of what sounded to be a television commentary.

Stepping inside, his booted feet scrunched on spilled sugar. Wondering if there had been a barney and a bag of Tate & Lyle had been thrown, he strolled through the house, heading in the direction the still incomprehensible news commentary was coming from and where, presumably, he would find Albie.

The sitting-room door, like all the other doors in the house, was wide open. What he saw from the threshold were three women, two of them middle-aged, one a little younger, and all quite obviously crying.

'Jock Sweeting,' he said succinctly, lowering his duffel bag on to pink linoleum and then, as the younger of the three women spun round to face him full on, and he received a favourable impression of green wide-spaced eyes and an exceedingly well-filled scarlet sweater, he added, 'What's the matter, then? Somebody snuffed it?'

'So that's what you've been doing?' It was two hours later and Jock was seated with Albie and Smiler in a corner of the public bar in the Manley Arms. 'A bit of hoisting and kiting and working some ringers?'

'I never said me and Smiler was the Krays,' Albie retorted defensively. 'And what's wrong with shoplifting and passing forged cheques, and stealing cars and selling 'em on? It keeps the wolf from the door.'

'It isna' worth being nicked for,' Jock growled richly. He felt in his donkey-jacket pocket for his tobacco pouch. 'I'm a peterman, you know that, Albie. Safes. That's ma game. If you're interested in coming in with me, fine and dandy. If not . . .' He shrugged.

If not he'd find two other professionals to do the business with him. Two was the absolute minimum. One to act as a lookout and to be at the wheel of a getaway car. One to act as a heavy-handed backup man. He ran his tongue across the edge of his Rizzler and rolled it down over his tobacco with one-handed practised ease. From what he'd seen of Albie's brother-in-law, Smiler would make a very handy heavy. Taciturn and built like a brick shit-house he was obviously as thick as a navvy's sandwich. Which was fine by him. It meant he'd do as he was told no questions asked. He also had unnervingly pale blue eyes. It was a colour Jock had seen before – and always the men in question had been capable of going the limit where violence was concerned.

'Come off it, Jock,' Albie said as drifts of conversation from the main body of the bar indicated that President Kennedy's death was still the only subject of conversation and likely to remain so for days to come. 'Yer know we're happy to throw in with you. I even have a job all lined up. A mate of mine is the night cleaner at the local flicks. He says the manager only banks the takings once a week, on a Monday morning. '*Cleopatra*'s on at the moment. The place'll be packed to the gunnels over the weekend and the dosh'll be grand.'

'And will your mate let us in?'

'Natch. He'll have to say he was forced into doing it, of course, but if we tie him up nice and tidy and he says we were masked and threatened him with a cosh, he'll swan it. All he wants is the usual little percentage.'

Jock grunted. All everyone wanted was a little percentage. Cops. Beaks. Screws. The so-called 'straight' geezers, always on the look-out for making something on the side by tipping a villain off about their employer's security arrangements, just as long as they didn't take any real risks themselves.

'And what kind of safe is it?' he asked, reaching for his pint of bitter. 'A Milner or a Chubb?'

'A Milner.' Albie was leaning forward in his seat, his

knees splayed, his hands clasped between them. A lot was riding on Jock Sweeting's response. For twenty-five years, since he'd been fifteen, he'd been thieving and ducking and diving. But he'd never blown a safe and he'd certainly never robbed a bank. If Jock decided to work with him and Smiler Albie knew he'd soon be doing both.

A Milner. Jock took a deep draw of his roll-up. With a bit of luck it would be an old one. Old Milners were a piece of cake.

'Will I be able tae look at it?' He wouldn't do the job if he couldn't. He hadn't come out of the nick to go bouncing back in again for a piddling cinema job. 'I'll need your pal to let me in so that I can check exactly what kind of a Milner it is.'

'Natch.' Albie was all tense anticipation. 'He'll slip us in the back way while the cleaners are in. Are yer sure you can do it, Jock? There won't be a problem?'

Jock looked at him pityingly. 'A Milner? Sweet Christ, Albie. An old Milner with a riveted back I can open as easy as blowing ma nose. We lift the back edge wi' a hammered chisel and we clamp in the jaws of big bolt cutters and roll back the rear plate like opening a tin of sardines. Then it's simply a hammer and chisel job through the asbestos and inner box of sheet metal. But you'd better make sure your mate's information is spot on. I'm nae risking ma fucking liberty for money that isna' there.'

'It'll be there.' Albie could hardly control his elation. He and Jock and Smiler were going to make a great team. He could feel it in his water.

Jock made a noncommittal noise deep in his throat. There'd have to be another meet with Albie's inside man. He'd never taken anything on trust yet and wasn't about to start now. 'Ma glass is empty,' he said, turning his attention to a matter of some importance. 'It's your round, Albie. Get 'em in.'

*   *   *

8

''Lo, Aunty Pearl. What are yer doin' sittin' on Ma Perkins' garden wall in the dark?' Five-year-old Johnny Rice sauntered up to her with interest, a mongrel on a length of string trailing behind him.

'I'm minding me own business, which is what you should be doing.' Pearl's voice was tart. Buried deep in a black and white checked jacket, her peroxide-blonde hair now backcombed to within an inch of its life, she hadn't particularly wanted to be seen. 'And it's half eight. You should have been home long ago.'

Johnny shrugged, his elbows poking out of his holey jumper, his hair an angelic gold in the glow of the sodium streetlights. 'I go home when I like,' he said in a take-it-or-leave-it manner. 'Are yer waitin' for me dad to come out o' the pub?'

Across the road the Manley Arms saloon door was closed against the November cold, the noise of conversation from within high and abnormally passionate as the dramatic events of a few hours ago were hashed and rehashed.

'No, I'm not, you cheeky bugger. Now sod off and take that apology of a dog with you. Your ma won't let you have it in the house, you realise that, don't you?'

'Dad will,' Johnny said nonchalantly, beginning to saunter on his way. He looked back over his shoulder. 'And if you're waitin' for dad's mate, me muvver says he's far too old for yer and he probably has a wife tucked away in Scotland.'

Pearl said a rude word and hugged herself even deeper into her jacket. Jock Sweeting had better not have a wife tucked away in Scotland because she, Pearl, fancied him. She fancied him something rotten. He wasn't very tall, but he was thickset and moved with boxer-like, springy precision. His face, too, hard-boned and uncompromising, excited her.

She couldn't just walk into the Manley Arms to waylay him, though. Not if he and Albie and Smiler were having a meet. What she *would* do was to be off the wall and strolling up the road the moment the three of them stepped outside. Then, when they overtook her and she began walking back to Creek Row with them all, she'd manage to have a few words with him. He might even suggest they returned to the pub together for a nightcap. If he didn't she'd make the suggestion herself.

'Can you get any gelly down here or will I need tae send up the road for it?' Jock was asking as Albie and Smiler followed him from the pub.

'Wot d'yer mean? Up the road?' Smiler was completely lost. 'Do yer mean Jamaica Road? The Old Kent Road?'

'I mean Scotland, you wally.'

'Going north for it might be best.' Albie tried to sound casual, not wanting to say that neither he nor Smiler had a clue where they could put their hands on gelignite.

Jock sighed. He might have known his new team-mates wouldn't be spectacularly helpful. 'We'll take the rattler tae Stirling at the weekend then.' He'd no intention of hitting a stone quarry in the Glasgow area. 'And we'll take all we can and store it. There's no point in taking only enough for a couple of jobs.'

They stood on the pavement, Smiler blowing on his hands to keep them warm. 'Where do quarry works keep their gelly, then?' he asked between puffs. 'Is breaking in dodgy?'

'Naw.' Jock turned up his jacket collar against smog-laden air. 'It's a piece of cake. Magazines are always sited for safety in the middle of a field, generally in a brick hut wi' a wall round it for extra protection. There'll be two doors. The first'll be padlocked and we can cut the padlock off wi' bolt-cutters. The inside'll be steel-covered wood and we just jemmy it off – and don't bleedin' well ask me how, Smiler. We just get a start wi' a hammerhead wrapped in cloth tae keep down the noise and then keep popping the rivets. When it's off we cut the lock out of the wood. OK?'

Smiler nodded. It sounded OK to him. He couldn't think why he and Albie hadn't been snaffling gelly yonks ago.

'What about detonators?' Albie asked as they began to walk away from the pub. 'Will they be stored with the gelly?'

Jock nodded. How Albie had made a living from thieving when he was so green he couldn't for the life of him think. 'We need tae rake up some large biscuit tins. One for gelly, one for detonators. And we need tae find a safe burrow for it. A wood, preferably. It needs tae be somewhere it willna' sweat. Gelly's only dangerous if it sweats.'

'So what do we do when we've got it? Bury it and mark the spot?'

Jock nodded again, trying to suppress his exasperation. Christ Almighty, couldn't Albie work out anything for himself? Was he even going to have to spell out the ground rules – no chickens, no loudmouths, no big spenders and, above all, no grasses? 'And when we've got a nice little supply tucked away we can make plans for a better bit of work,' he said, putting his acolytes out of their misery. 'A bank vault. How's that suit you and Smiler?'

Smiler's pale eyes gleamed. All his life he'd wanted to do a vault but he'd never had the brains to work out how to go about it.

Jock was well aware of Smiler's enthusiasm but had no intention of indulging it by jawing any more. A blonde walking a little way in front of them had attracted his attention. Dressed in a checked jacket, a provocatively short black skirt and stiletto-heeled patent shoes, there was something familiar about her and she was walking as if she knew full well they were behind her and was hoping they would catch up with her.

'Wotcha, Pearl!' Albie called out, and as the blonde turned, a look of affected surprise on her face, Jock grinned. Surprise, my arse. Pearl Burns had known damn well who was behind her. Loitering with intent, that's what Pearl had been doing – and he knew enough about women and the way they often reacted to him to know exactly what her intention was.

'Where've you been, gel?' Albie asked as the three of them drew abreast of her. 'The flicks?'

'What, tonight? With all the hoo-ha over President Kennedy?' Pearl's voice was genuinely incredulous. 'Course I ain't. I've been with a girl friend.' Though she was talking to Albie she was looking at Jock. 'She's ever so upset. Crying her eyes out she was when I left.'

Jock's eyes held hers. He wasn't usually a pushover for women but this one was very convenient. She knew he was a villain and so he wouldn't have to make an effort at pretending to be anything he wasn't. Being part of Albie's family she could be trusted to keep her trap shut about anything she overheard or saw. She was certainly a looker and, if she was nearer to her mid-thirties than her mid-twenties, so what? He could still give her fifteen years or so. Last, but by no means least, unless he was very much mistaken she was handing herself to him on a plate and he hadn't had a little bit of you-know-what for longer than he cared to remember.

'Doesna' sound much of a fun evening, hen,' he said, aware that, as she wasn't a West End tart, he wouldn't have to dig too deep in his pocket to keep her happy. 'How about our having a wee dram together? There's still ten minutes tae closing.'

'Don't mind if I do,' Pearl responded with feigned nonchalance. She slid her hand into the crook of his arm. 'G'night, Albie; 'night, Smiler. See yer.'

Albie gave a nod and Smiler grunted and then, as Jock's surprisingly light footfalls and the tip-tap of Pearl's high heels receded in the direction of the Manley Arms, Smiler said heavily, 'Do yer fink yer should tip 'im the wink that Pearl's 'usband-'unting?'

Albie considered for a moment or two and then, as they turned into the cobbled confines of Creek Row, said, 'Nah. I 'ope Pearl does get 'im to the altar. A bloke like Jock in the family could be a real asset, know what I mean?'

Smiler nodded, not too sure of the word 'asset' but getting the general drift. If Jock Sweeting was linked to him and Albie by marriage they wouldn't have to worry he'd soon be off looking for other backup men, leaving them in the lurch.

'Let's 'ope Pearl does 'er stuff, then,' he said, rocking unsteadily on his heels as he came to a halt outside a door with the words 'Up Millwall, screw Tottenham' penknifed into it. Albie, walking the further few yards to his own front door, made a noise of agreement. He, too, hoped Pearl would do her stuff and bring Jock Sweeting into the family fold.

In a chemist's doorway, conveniently deepset and three doorways short of the Manley Arms, Pearl was doing her stuff to the very best of her ability. Her panties were stuffed in one jacket pocket, her tights in the other, and her skirt was rucked as high around her thighs as it would go. With her arms wrapped around Jock's neck, his tongue deeply past hers, she was standing legs apart, tippy-toes in her stilettos so that he could enter her.

Jock, failing to do so despite an erection that would have done a bull proud, lifted his head from hers and, panting with a mixture of passion and exertion, cupped her buttocks, lifting her so that she could wind her legs around his waist Chinese tree style.

'*Do it*! *Do it*! *Do it*!' Pearl's urging, as with the doorway wall giving them support he thrust deep inside her, was frenzied. She'd already heard the bell being rung for time in the Manley Arms and knew that at any second customers would be spilling out of the pub and into the street.

'*Christ Almighty, hen*!' Jock, who hadn't copulated for

five years and hadn't attempted to do so in a standing position for a good deal longer, didn't know which of his fears was the most desperate: that she was about to slither from his grasp; that his legs were going to give way, or that the Manley Arms' regulars were about to appraise his performance.

Grunting and groaning he forged ahead to an explosive earth-rocking climax. He was aware of Pearl mewling as she hung on to him; he was aware of light flooding the street as the Manley Arms' saloon door opened and people began to spill out into the street; he was aware of Pearl hurriedly regaining her balance, frantically tugging her skirt down as she did so. And he was aware that knee-tremblers weren't the piece of cake they'd been in his ill-spent youth. His knees weren't trembling. They were bloody crippled.

Chapter Two

1969

'Good morning, new children!' Miss Cullin said brightly to her Easter intake who were sitting in a cross-legged group in front of her. 'Welcome to St Margaret's Infants' School. My name is Miss Cullin and now I want you to tell me, and the rest of the class, your names.' She beamed at them encouragingly. 'So, who have we here, right at the front?'

She was looking straight at Jackie and Jackie beamed back at her. 'Jackie, Miss,' she said, eager to please. 'Jackie Sweeting.'

Miss Cullin's encouraging smile faltered. The Headmaster had warned her that one of her pupils was cousin to the Rice boys and to Eddie Burns. Kevin Rice had attended both St Margaret's Infants' and St Margaret's Juniors' and was now, to the vast relief of St Margaret's staff, wreaking havoc in a secondary school on the far side of the borough, as was his cousin, Eddie. Johnny Rice was in his last year at St Margaret's Juniors' and rumour had it that junior-school teaching staff were counting off not only the days to the end of the summer term but the hours also.

Not that Johnny Rice, or Kevin either for that matter, fell into the same category as Eddie Burns. Though the Rice boys were tearaways and obviously intent on following their father into a life of crime, they had redeeming features and were reasonably likeable, Johnny especially so.

The same could not be said of Eddie. Eddie was not only disruptive and aggressive and a flagrant thief, Eddie was evil. Remembering the incident with the hamster Miss Cullin shuddered. Harry the hamster had served the purpose of being both a pet and a teaching aid for the first year infants. Eddie, by then in Junior School, had broken in to Class One after school hours, lifted Harry from his bed of wood shavings and, with the aid of a fiercesomely efficient homemade catapult, had lobbed him over the Infants' School roof in the direction of the Junior playground. It was the school caretaker who had scraped the pathetic remains of bloody impacted flesh from the Tarmacked gravel.

And now, closely related to this nightmare in human form, was a child who would be in her class for the next year at the very least.

'Jacqueline,' she corrected Jackie, pinning a smile in place with effort. 'We don't use shortened versions of names in class, Jacqueline. And you, little boy,' with undue haste she transferred her attention to the child seated on Jackie's left. 'What is your name?'

Before the boy seated next to her could answer Jackie shot her hand up to regain Miss Cullin's attention. 'Please, Miss,' she persisted, perplexed. 'My name *is* Jackie, Miss. It's always been Jackie. On account of President Kennedy being shotted, Miss.'

It was a statement too startling to ignore. Miss Cullin paused, turned her head slightly, and looked again into Jackie's upturned face. It was framed by short straight dark hair and was disarmingly earnest and surprisingly well scrubbed. 'Your mother named you after Mrs Kennedy?' There was dazed disbelief in her voice. She'd had an Elvis in a previous class and a Tippi, named after Tippi Hedron, and even a Ringo, but she'd never come across a child being named after Jacqueline Kennedy before.

'I don't know, Miss.' Jackie was beginning to feel uncomfortable. Why was Miss so interested in her name? Everyone was looking at her and the pasty-faced boy next to her was sniggering. 'It's just that I was borned the night President Kennedy was shotted and 'e was called Jack and mum called me Jackie.'

There was no doubt at all in Jackie's voice but Miss Cullin was more perplexed than ever. Hastily she looked down at her class register. Was Jackie Sweeting a year late in beginning school? Was she nearly six, not going on five? Neatly printed against her name was her birth date: 24 August 1964. She hadn't even been born when Kennedy had been assassinated. 'But you weren't even . . .' she began and then stopped short. November 1963 to August 1964 was exactly nine months. As realisation dawned as to why Jackie had been named after the late President or, if not the President, his wife, scarlet colour flooded her thin cheeks. How typical of the Sweeting, Rice and Burns tribe! How atrociously and monumentally tasteless!

'In my class,' she said with such sudden venom that Jackie flinched and the boy next to her ceased being amused, 'you will answer to the name of Jacqueline. Is that understood?'

'Yes, Miss. No, Miss.' Jackie was totally bewildered. She knew Johnny and Kevin and Eddie didn't like school but they were boys. *She* had been looking forward to school. She liked learning and already knew her two and three times tables. All the excitement she'd felt at starting school was rapidly turning to anxiety. She didn't think Miss liked her very much and, though she didn't know why, knew that it was all to do with her name. If Miss wanted to call her Jacqueline perhaps she should let her do so. It wouldn't be much different to her little sister, Raquel, being called Kelly all the time. It would just be the other way round, that was all. Having sorted things out in her own mind she breathed a sigh of relief. She'd be Jacqueline at school but not anywhere else – and she wouldn't tell her mum about Miss calling her Jacqueline. She knew enough about her mum to know that her mum wouldn't like it.

'So our next fill-in job is going to be a jack-in-the-box at Crawley, is it?' Albie, Smiler and Jock were having a meet in Sid's Dining Rooms, Plough Way, and it was Albie who was doing the asking.

'I dinna' see why not. It's worked a treat before and Crawley should be a guid haul.' Jock ran a hand over his close-cropped hair. 'We'll need a big square car, a Zephyr or a Zodiac.'

Albie nodded. The last jack-in-the-box they'd done, the car boot was so small he and Jock had nearly died from cramp and suffocation before Smiler, acting the part of a blind pedestrian, had tapped the boot with his stick, signalling that it was time for them to burst out. The job had been a success, though. Jack-in-the-boxes usually were. When security vans parked up the crew, prior to ferrying money sacks into or out of a bank, meticulously checked the street up and down. A parked car with three men in would immediately attract their attention. A seemingly empty car would not. The minute the money was unloaded and about to be transferred into the bank Jock and Albie, balaclavaed and with coshes at the ready, would seemingly spring out of thin air. Smiler, no longer 'blind', would leap into the car, revving the engine, and within split seconds, the robbery would be over and they would be away with the loot.

'Cash delivery tae the bank is ten o'clock, Monday mornings,' Jock continued, wondering when banks would wake up to the fact that staggering days and time might be a sensible security measure. 'Last week there were three big sacks.'

'Who'll lift the third one?' Albie knew it would be either him or Jock because Smiler would be doing the driving. A moment's hesitation over such a matter, once the job was underway, could mean disaster. In a jack-in-the-box every fraction of a second counted.

'I'll pitch it but only if time's on our side. It's better tae get away with two sacks than tae get caught with three.'

Albie's eyes met Smiler's and quickly slid away. Jock's reputation for reckless effrontery was mixed with a cautious canniness that was becoming a source of contention. If, on the job they were now planning, a sack of cash was left on the pavement behind them it wouldn't be for the first time. Smiler didn't like it and, in his heart of hearts, Albie didn't blame him. There was no point in causing a stir about it, though. When it came to planning jobs Jock was boss and, since the three of them had become a family concern, none of them had spent so much as an hour in the nick.

Aware that it was time to change the subject and diffuse the sudden tension, Albie said affably, 'Sod me if these eels aren't some of the best I've ever tasted. Bugger if I don't go another lot.'

Jock made a noise deep in his throat that could have meant anything and that Albie took to mean he, too, could go another lot of eels. Jock had meant nothing of the kind. He knew damn well Albie and Smiler didn't like his canniness – not when it came to a question of leaving dosh behind – but dosh was no use to man nor mouse if the extra few minutes spent in grabbing it meant security men or filth all over them. He and Albie were, after all, family men. What would his Pearl do if he queered up a job and got nicked for it? Although Jackie had just started school Kelly was only three and a bit. If Pearl had to get a job to make ends meet who would she leave Kelly with? She couldn't leave her with Lil – not if Lil was having to work because Albie, too, was back in the Ville. No. Like it or lump it his canny method of working was going to prevail. He might have come relatively late to family life but now he had his girls he wasn't going to be parted from them.

But there was no sense in putting the wind up Albie by telling him that he'd long ago determined he'd commit murder first.

'Course they'll let us in to play snooker,' Eddie said scornfully. 'Yer've only to be sixteen. Yer can pass for sixteen, can't yer?'

Kevin wasn't sure he could. He was tall for a thirteen-year-old but he didn't have Eddie's shoulders. Eddie had the shoulders of a boy of eighteen. He had big hands, too. When Eddie threw a punch – though throwing punches wasn't his favourite way of fighting – the poor bugger on the receiving end was knocked into the middle of next week.

'I could give it a try,' he said doubtfully, 'but Johnny'll never get in. He's not yet eleven and he only looks eleven.'

'Leave it out, will yer?' Johnny drummed his heels against the wall he was sitting on. He hated it when Eddie and Kevin ganged up on him, treating him as if he was still a snotty-nosed kid. He knew he wouldn't be able to get in at the snooker hall because he'd already tried once and been thrown out on his ear. He didn't think Kevin would be able to get in either but there was no point in saying so and starting a barney.

'Come on then.' Eddie didn't give a toss whether Johnny could get in or not. He knew *he'd* be able to get in and if he could, then Kevin would too. He'd make sure of it. He fingered the flick knife in his jacket pocket. He didn't take crap from anyone and, like a growing number of people in Bermondsey, the bloke who ran the snooker hall knew it. With a swagger that had been perfected by long hours in front of a mirror Eddie sauntered off, Kevin hard on his heels.

Johnny knew he had two options. He could either go with them and hang around the snooker hall entrance, or he could try and find someone else to pal up with. As most of his dad's mates' kids lived Deptford way, and as the other families in Creek Row, apart from his and Eddie's and his Aunty Pearl's, were straight, he was unlikely to find anyone to mate up with for the evening. Straight kids were a pain in the arse. Their mothers created hell if they were seen with him or Kevin or Eddie. Especially Eddie. They were always whinging on about having homework to do – and he had to mind his mouth whenever he was with them in case he let slip anything about his dad's or his uncles' activities that they could go home and grass about.

With a sigh of weary acceptance he slithered down from the wall. Rather than mooch about on his own for the rest of the evening he'd go with Eddie and Kevin to the snooker hall. There'd be bound to be other kids hanging around the doorway and some of the punters, those who knew his dad, would probably give him a free ciggie or a bottle of Coke.

'I don't think I heard yer right, mister,' Eddie was saying menacingly. 'I thought for a minute yer said my cousin didn't look sixteen.'

'He doesn't.' The snooker hall manager was well used to trouble and to handling it but he was beginning to feel an edge of unease. He'd had a run-in with Eddie before and it hadn't been pleasant. Also, he was mindful of the fact that Eddie's old man was Smiler Burns and he didn't want a visit from Smiler. He liked his face just the way it was and didn't want Smiler rearranging it for him.

Eddie leaned towards him fingering the knife in his pocket. He smiled. It was a smile that didn't reach his eyes. 'That's 'cos he had an illness as a kid,' he said, aware that several people were now looking towards them and enjoying himself hugely. 'It stunted his growth. Now which table are we goin' to play on?'

The snooker hall manager knew very well what Eddie

was toying with in his pocket. He was only a kid, of course, but he wasn't built like a kid and, if he was anything like his dad, he'd go the whole way once he lost his rag – which was one good reason for helping him not to lose it.

'Table twelve,' he said grudgingly, switching on table twelve's overhead lights and hoping that now he'd made this concession Eddie and his cousin would keep themselves to themselves. 'You pay when you've finished playing.'

'Yeah.' This time Eddie's smile was genuine. 'Course we do. Come on, Kev. Let's get a couple of cues.'

Kevin shot the manager a look of smug triumph and, thumbs hooked nonchalantly into the pockets of his jeans, sauntered in Eddie's wake across to the snooker table.

The boys playing on table eleven watched their approach in bad humour. They hadn't been allowed in the snooker hall until their sixteenth birthdays and still revelling in this recent rite of passage didn't like seeing others bypass it.

'That kid's only thirteen,' one of them said about Kevin in a loud voice as Eddie corralled the red balls into a frame and Kevin began setting the others out on the table. 'He goes to the same school as my sister. He's in her class.'

Kevin grinned, unabashed. It was the fact it was so obvious he was underage that made his being there such a blast.

'I fink you're being talked about, Kev.' Eddie lifted the frame free of the balls. 'They must be friends of yours. And if they're friends of yours, they'll be buying us a drink, won't they?'

There was derisive laughter from the other snooker table. 'Only in your dreams, man,' one of the other youths said, not even troubling to look towards Eddie.

Eddie applied chalk to the tip of his cue and, taking his time, blew the residue away. The boy who had just spoken was black. Eddie didn't like blacks. He didn't like blacks so much, he was thinking of going into politics and joining the National Front.

'Come on, Ed.' Kevin was getting a mite apprehensive.

A snooker hall wasn't the street or a piece of waste ground. If they pitched into a fight here they wouldn't be able to scarper quickly from it. Not only that, even with Eddie at his side he didn't fancy fighting youths three or four years his senior. There was also no telling who else in the snooker hall might pitch in against them and, though the Sambo hadn't been in the front of the queue when shoulders were given out, he had a dangerous slim and supple whippy look about him. 'Let's get on with the game,' he said, wishing Eddie wasn't always so ready to show he was a chip off the old block. 'Who's going to break? Are we going to toss for it?'

'I fink we're going to wait until your friend buys us a drink before we break.' Eddie, still with the cue in his hand, walked around to the side of the table adjacent to number eleven. His eyes were on his own table and the balls Kevin had so carefully set out but his thoughts weren't on them. He was savouring the feeling of excitement building up inside him. The excitement he always felt before lashing out with his fists and his feet – and whatever weapon there was to hand.

This time, with an opponent so much older than himself and with so many blokes nearby who would, no doubt, try to break it up, he would be running a real risk. What if the blackie gave him a pasting? His growing reputation for being someone it was better not to mess with would be shot to pieces.

Holding the cue in one hand he fingered the knife in his pocket with the other. Kev didn't know about the knife – which meant that Kev was in for a big surprise. Eddie liked surprising his cousin. It kept him one step ahead of him.

One thing Eddie had long ago decided was that, unlike his dad, he was never going to be a follower. He was going to be a leader. He was going to be like Jock Sweeting and call all the shots and have everyone running around doing what *he* said. And he was going to make sure people were frightened of him, too. Making people frightened of him was a good feeling. It made him feel he was somebody. It made his heart pound and the blood sing in his ears. And it made his cock big. He hadn't told anyone about that. Not even Kevin.

He could feel his cock getting big now as he anticipated the expression on the blackie's face when he pinned him down on the table, the cue hard across his throat.

Kevin saw the expression on Eddie's face and, in increasing nervousness, flicked a coin in the air. 'Heads,' he called, eager to divert attention from the stupid git goading them and to start the game. He wasn't chicken. When circumstances demanded it he had all the bottle in the world. This wasn't one of those circumstances, though. This was unnecessary. They were only thirteen years old, for Christ's sake, and everyone around them was sixteen or over. Plus the manager would have the old Bill in the place if Eddie went haywire and things got really out of hand.

The coin came down tails. 'It's your break, Eddie. Let's get on with the game, eh?' All Kevin could think of was that the game would be his first in a proper snooker club and that, unless Eddie snapped out of his present mood, it was a game that wasn't even going to get started.

To his relief Eddie gave an acquiescent shrug and bent over the table, lining up his cue. His back was only a foot or so from where the black youth was standing, waiting his turn to pot.

The black youth grinned. He was extraordinarily good-looking in a teenage Harry Belafonte kind of way. 'Decided to buy your own drinks, have you, man?' he asked mockingly.

It was the last time he spoke for a very long time.

Eddie spun round, kicking the youth's legs away from him and, at the same time, slamming the snooker cue lengthways across his throat. With a choked-off cry of agony the youth fell back on the table he'd been playing, balls skittering in all directions. Eddie leaped on him, pinning him to green baize, ramming the cue as hard as he could against his windpipe. As his victim bucked and struggled, choking in agony, he brought a knee up fast and hard, smashing him in the balls with all the force he was capable of.

'*What the fuck . . .?*' The disbelieving expletive from one of the other youths was all Kevin heard. The next minute the world and his brother seemed to be on him and he was savagely punching and biting and kicking – and being savagely punched and bitten and kicked.

It was bedlam. Lights over snooker tables were smashed. The manager was on the phone yelling for the police. Blokes who had come running from the far side of the snooker hall didn't know who was being set on and who was doing the setting-on and, as Kevin was obviously only a kid, assumed he was the one being victimised, and launched into an attack on those knocking the hell out of him.

What Eddie's situation was Kevin didn't know. All he knew was that he wanted out while he was still capable of getting home under his own steam. There were plenty of people only too happy to help him.

'Get that little wanker off my premises!' the manager was yelling to anyone who would listen. 'Mind those fucking tables! That fucking baize costs money! Stop breaking those bleeding cues!'

Someone had Kevin by the scruff of the neck and was dragging him over to the stairs that led down to the street. 'Eddie!' he shouted, only too willing to be hauled out of the mayhem. 'EDDIE!'

'He's got a blade! He's bleeding knifed Dexter! He's a fucking maniac!'

Kevin didn't know who was doing the yelling but he had a damned good idea who they were talking about. From somewhere in the distance there came the piercing screech of a police siren. A knife, for Christ's sake! What if Eddie had committed murder and he was roped in as an accessory?

He tumbled down the stairs, battered and bleeding. As he picked himself up at their foot and staggered out into the street a police car swerved to a halt at the kerb, lights flashing, and siren still going.

Johnny was running towards him, the stupid dog that followed him everywhere charging at his heels.

'Kev! *Kev*! What is it, Kev? What's happened? Where's Eddie? Is he in trouble? Is . . . ?'

As three coppers leaped from the car, heading with all speed towards the stairs leading above Burton's shop to the snooker hall, Kevin slung his arm around his kid brother's shoulders. He had two reasons for doing so. One was because if he hadn't he would have fallen to his knees. The other was that Johnny made a perfect blind. Alongside Johnny he looked what he was, a thirteen-year-old. Even with his jacket torn, his shirt almost ripped from his back and with blood pouring from his nose and a cut above his eye, the police made no attempt to detain him. They weren't after kids who had been caught up in the mêlée; they were after the instigators of it.

As the policemen sprinted up the stairs to the snooker hall Johnny said again, his voice raw with urgency, 'What the bleedin' hell happened, Kev? Why are the cozzers on the rampage? Where's Eddie? Are you hurt as bad as you look? Why –'

'Yes,' Kevin said, answering the question that was pre-occupying him most. 'I fucking am hurt as bad as I look. Just let's get home. I've swallowed a tooth, I'm gobbing blood, and I think Eddie's got himself into real trouble this time. Big trouble. The kind of trouble there's no walking away from. We need to get home and tell Uncle Jock.'

Johnny, still in the dark about what Eddie had actually done but aware their cousin must by now be in police hands, took as much of Kevin's weight as he was able. That it was their uncle Johnny wanted to tell first, not Eddie's dad or their own, came as no surprise to him. If the Rice, Burns and Sweeting families were a clan their Uncle Jock was the clan chief.

'He ain't goin' to be pleased,' he said as he laboriously heaved Kevin into Creek Row. 'It'll mean Eddie's house bein' visited by the cozzers an' they'll use it as an excuse to have a good old poke around.'

'Which is why we have to let Jock know what's happened sharpish.' Kevin wiped his bloody nose on the tattered sleeve of his jacket. 'Mum ain't goin' to be pleased about the state of this jacket, either. It didn't fall off the back of a lorry, yer know. She bought it cash in Deptford Market.'

'I think,' said Johnny, 'yer jacket 'll be the least of her worries.'

'Your nephew's divvy, hen. I hope you know that?' Jock was steaming. In his credo to draw police attention unnecessarily was an act of the grossest stupidity.

It was three hours later. The police had been and gone at the Burnses' house and, though they had been exceedingly unwelcome, hadn't used the incident as an excuse for a search. Eddie was being held overnight in Deptford nick and Jock had seen to it that it was Flo who had gone down to be with him, not Smiler. As a juvenile he was to be brought before a magistrate at ten o'clock the next morning on a charge of grievous bodily harm. His victim, with a knife wound to his chest, was undergoing emergency surgery at St Thomas's.

'I suppose he was defending himself,' Pearl said staunchly, though without much conviction.

'I doubt it.' Jock was scathing. 'The trouble with young Eddie is that he's like his old man – backward, fearless and violent. He turns for nae reason. And when he turns he's dangerous. Smiler's never been one tae just use his fists, has he? He always wants tae pick up a tool as well.'

They were in the kitchen, and though it was going on for eleven o'clock at night Kelly and Jackie, in nighties and dressing gowns, were seated at the table drinking mugs of Horlicks.

'Smiler just takes a bit of understanding, that's all.' Though she wasn't overfond of Smiler Pearl wasn't about to rubbish him. He was her brother, after all. 'The only thing wrong with Smiler is that he ain't very bright.'

Jock gave a crack of mirthless laughter. 'Too right he isna' very bright, hen. Smiler's between Dagenham and East Ham. He's Barking.'

Despite her anxieties Pearl gave a splutter of laughter and Jackie stared at her, not understanding how she could laugh when such a terrible thing had happened. Pink spots of colour burned her cheeks. Didn't her mum know that by the morning the whole of Creek Row would know Eddie had been arrested for hurting someone? And then school would know and the teachers would be talking about her again. Jackie hated it when Miss Cullin and the other teachers looked at her as if there were something wrong with her; as if she weren't like the other girls in her class; as if she were different. She didn't want to be different. She wanted to be like everyone else. It was difficult, though, when her friends at school didn't invite her to play in their homes and when her mum didn't like her bringing anyone to number 28 in case they were what her mum called 'them' and not, like the children of the blokes her dad and uncles did jobs with, 'us'.

Kelly didn't share her sister's inner anguish. Kelly was merely puzzled. What had her dad said to her mum that was so funny? And what was going to happen to Eddie now that nasty policemen had taken him away?

'Eddie will come home, won't he, Dad?' she asked, stirring the skin that had formed on top of her drink with her finger. 'He won't be locked up for ever and ever, will he?'

Jock ruffled her red-gold curls. His own hair, before it had become so salt-and-pepper, had had a mahogany cast to it but Kelly's hair wasn't mahogany – it was a glorious glowing titian. 'He's going to be locked up for longer than he's going to like, princess.' He swung her up so that he was carrying her in one well-muscled and tattooed arm. 'It's going to be borstal for Eddie-boy,' he said, stretching out his free hand towards Jackie.

As he took them upstairs to bed Kelly wrapped her arms tightly around his neck. When she was as old as Eddie she wouldn't let nasty policemen nab her. She'd be like her dad. She'd lead them a right merry dance, all the way round the houses and back again and they'd never catch her. Never, never, *never*!

Chapter Three

1972

'Now Jock's been nicked what are you goin' to do, Pearl?' Lily was pegging washing out. It was July and as well as being sunny it was also breezy. Her sheets and pillowcases would be dry in no time at all. She took a peg out of her mouth in order to speak more easily. 'The boys'll be doing a whip-round for you, of course.' By 'boys' Lily meant the extended network of south-east London villains who were Smiler, Albie and Jock's mates. 'They'll do it pretty reg'lar, too. Envelope through the letter box every Saturday night. Jock's well thought of. No one'll want it getting back to him that you and the kids ain't being cared for.'

'A charity whip-round ain't necessary, Lil, and you know it.'

It was a statement Lily couldn't argue with. Though their extended family still lived in Creek Row, it did so out of choice, not necessity. 'Never flash readies,' Jock had said in the early days when he, Albie and Smiler had carried out their first bit of work together. And so, instead of ostentatiously flashing it around in a manner that would have drawn attention, they had spent it on very exclusive and exceedingly discreet holiday homes on the Isle of Sheppey.

The compromise suited all three women. None of them wanted transplanting into a hoity-toity area such as Blackheath or Chislehurst. Bermondsey was familiar. It was where they'd been born and bred and where they felt comfortable. They felt comfortable on the Isle of Sheppey, too. A little way from their own select second residences was a giant caravan park and acres of chalets and those who holidayed there were nearly all, like themselves, from south-east London. The entertainment facilities on the camp site, all open to non residents, couldn't be bettered. There were bars and social clubs, fish and chip shops, and pie and mash shops, even a bingo hall. 'It's a little bit of 'eaven on earth,' Flo had said, revelling in the fact that she could spend weeks on end there if she wanted, leaving her miserable-faced other half to his own devices in Creek Row.

'And before you suggest I hang out at Sheppey for a while don't bother.' Pearl was sunk in bitterness. 'Flo's down there at the moment and I don't want her bleating on to me every hour of the day.'

Lily pegged out a nightie big enough to shelter a troop of boy scouts. Pearl and Flo weren't on the best of terms at the moment, which wasn't surprising seeing as it was Smiler's fault Jock was now in the boob. It hadn't been one of Jock's bigger jobs and he hadn't been tooled up, thank God, but even so, because of his record he'd been given six years. Smiler had copped for four.

'He should have been sent to bleedin' Broadmoor,' Pearl had fumed as he and Jock had been driven away from the court in a Black Maria. 'He's bleedin' crackers. Jock told him never, *ever* to leave the car on a jack-in-the-box. Not even if he and Albie were being beaten to smithereens. And why does he leave it? Because he sees there's more dosh than Jock and Albie can get away with. How Albie wasn't caught as well is a bleedin' miracle.'

'The coppers know he was the bloke that gave them the slip,' Lily had said, no happier about Smiler than her sister. 'Only as he never had his Balaclava ripped from his face, and Smiler and Jock ain't talking, they can't prove nothing, plus he was up and over the wall next to the post office like greased lighting. That post office motorcyclist must have wondered what had happened to him when Albie sent him flying and did a runner with his bike.'

'If Smiler had stayed with the getaway like he was supposed to they'd all have been able to do a runner.' Pearl hadn't the slightest intention of visiting Smiler in the nick. She wasn't sure if she'd even write to him.

With her arms folded across a bosom that was now as ample as her sister's she said, a different note in her voice: 'I'm goin' to get myself a little job, Lil. Something that will take my mind off things. I've seen a charring job advertised that might suit. It's in Blackheath and sounds as if it could be a nice little doddle.'

'Charring?' Lily tucked her now empty laundry basket beneath a mottled arm. 'You must be out of your head. And Blackheath's a funny place for office-cleaning, ain't it? All the Mrs Mops I know do for offices in the City.'

'And they get up at the crack of dawn to do 'em.' Pearl shuddered. 'No way, Lil. I just want something to take my mind off Jock being locked away. A couple of hours a day, two or three days a week, that what I'm after.'

Lily chewed the corner of her lip, not at all happy. 'There's an awful lot of high-falutin filth live at Blackheath – police superintendents, judges, magistrates. You don't want any of 'em cottoning on to who your old man is, do you?'

'Wouldn't make much bleedin' difference now he's already inside, would it?' Pearl could contain her resentful anger no longer. 'All that would happen is that they'd give me the sack – though why they should when *I* ain't never done no thievin' I don't bleedin' know, do you?'

She flounced off before Lily could retort that though she may not have thieved herself she'd lived off the proceeds for long enough – angry with Jock for having been nabbed – angry with Smiler for being responsible for his being nabbed – angry with herself for not being more stoical about things; angry with the world.

'Come on, Jackie! Kelly!' she shouted, storming into the house. 'Move your arses! We're goin' for a bus ride to Blackheath. Your mum's goin' to get herself a job!'

'I would like it if you could clean two hours a day, two days a week,' Lavender Pulfer said in a pleasantly cultured voice.

They were seated in a room Lavender Pulfer had described as the drawing room. It was very large, very high. The walls were papered in a magnolia wallpaper and there were several pictures on the walls, all pale water-colours and all in narrow gold frames. The carpet was oatmeal, the heavily swagged curtains cream. Pearl thought it colourless to the point of screaming monotony. She'd have had some bright floral curtains up and a cheerful flight of plaster ducks on the wall in no time at all. She reminded herself that she wasn't there to criticise the fur-nishings, but to get herself a job that would show Jock how miffed with him she was.

'Two hours a day, twice a week, will suit me fine,' she said, hoping that Jackie and Kelly, playing outside on stone-lion-flanked steps, were behaving themselves.

Mrs Pulfer had invited Jackie and Kelly inside but it was an offer Pearl had turned down. Jackie would have been all right. Jackie was always good as gold. Kelly, however, was another matter. Kelly would have been asking ques-tions and touching things and making a little nuisance of herself. Also, it wasn't beyond the realms of possibility that some small objects might have found their way into Kelly's pockets.

When she, Pearl, had stated in angry frustration to Lily that she'd never thieved she'd been telling the truth. Jackie was the same. Jackie would never take anything that wasn't hers. Kelly, however, was a different cup of tea. Not that she got her habit of petty pilfering from Jock. Jock was a thief but he never thieved anything *personal*. He thought

33

housebreakers the scum of the earth. What Jock thieved was money from banks, post offices and wages departments. Individuals didn't suffer when Jock thieved. It was a point of honour with him that it was institutions and insurance companies that were left uncomfortably out of pocket, not the average Joe in the street.

'How old are your little girls?' Lavender Pulfer's question broke in on her thoughts in such an unexpectedly friendly manner Pearl didn't know how to stop her surprise from showing.

In her experience well-to-do middle-class women were all the same – snooty and patronising. Mrs Pulfer, however, was proving to be an exception. From the moment she had opened the door to her she had treated her with utmost courtesy; asking if she'd like to bring Jackie and Kelly into the house; taking her into the drawing room, not the kitchen; even offering her a cup of tea.

'Jackie's eight and Kelly's six,' she said, sure there must be a drawback to the job somewhere but not being able to see where.

'When it is the school holidays, as now, perhaps you'd like to bring them with you?'

The suggestion was so considerate Pearl's eyes opened even wider.

'My daughter, Rosamund, is Jackie's age,' Lavender Pulfer continued, for all the world as if Pearl was a new-found Women's Institute friend. 'The three of them can play in the garden and will be quite safe. You won't have to worry about them wandering on to the street.'

Pearl refrained from explaining that the offer was unnecessary as Jackie had been navigating the streets of Bermondsey unaccompanied ever since she'd been old enough to go to school. As for Kelly – Kelly went where she wanted, when she wanted. Sensing this careless freedom wouldn't be much approved of, she said: 'Thank you. Much appreciated, I'm sure, but my sister'll most likely be looking after Jackie and Kelly when it's school holidays.'

'That sounds a happy arrangement.' With another friendly smile Lavender Pulfer rose to her feet. The little chat was clearly over.

As she followed her from the room Pearl wondered as to her age, judging her to be in her late forties or early fifties. If her daughter was only six she'd had her quite late in life. Whatever Mrs Pulfer's age she was well-groomed in a manner not dissimilar to her drawing room. Her hair, swept high in an immaculate French pleat, was tinted beige; her short square nails were buffed to a high sheen; her blouse was of ivory silk; her tailored skirt caramel and her sensibly heeled court shoes were of soft nut-brown leather.

'My son, Raymond, is home at the present moment,' she was saying as she led the way across a large square-shaped hall towards the front door, 'but I doubt he will get under your feet, Mrs Sweeting, and he'll be back at his boarding school the first week in September.'

Pearl had never understood boarding schools. Why have kids if you didn't want them around? It would be just as if they were away in a borstal. The thought reminded her of Eddie. Eddie had been in a borstal for two years and, now home again, was busy carving himself a reputation as a thug of the first water. She thrust the thought of Eddie and his possible influence on Lily's boys to the back of her mind. There was nothing she could do about it and, Jock being in the nick, nothing he could do about it either.

'Ta for everything,' she said cheerily at the door. 'I'll be here Monday morning ten o'clock sharp.'

'Lovely.' Lavender Pulfer looked across to where Jackie and Kelly were waiting for their mother, wondering what the younger girl's full name could possibly be. Coralie, perhaps? Cordelia? Neither name seemed very likely. Jackie, however, was quite obviously short for Jacqueline. With her jaw-length straight dark hair and smoky-blue eyes she possessed an air of shy diffidence that was immensely appealing. She was neat and tidy, too, in a way Lavender doubted had been parentally imposed.

The younger girl, dancing up and down in a fever of impatience to be off, had cheeky impudence exuding from every pore. She was also extremely pretty; her untidy mop of curly hair a glorious shade of red-gold. Her eyes, like her mother's, were distinctively wide-spaced and green as a cat's, and there was an air of fizzing buoyancy about her that indicated she'd be a handful to look after.

She watched Pearl Sweeting walk down the long pathway to the gate, her daughters skipping along beside her, questioning her as noisily as a couple of little starlings. Then as the gate clicked to behind them she reluctantly closed the door, shutting out the sound, the empty silence of her home pressing in on her like a physical weight.

Rosamund was at piano practice. Raymond was at Lords on the second day of a five-day course of schoolboy cricket practice. Though they would eventually return home her husband would not do so. She braved herself to say the word 'widow' aloud, wondering if she would ever become used to it; wondering if anyone ever became used to it.

The photograph she took out of her bureau drawer had a highly polished silver frame. She tried to nerve herself to set it back where it belonged, on the drawing-room mantelshelf, and failed. With Henry's photograph on the mantelshelf she wouldn't be able to forget about her loss for a single second.

Gently she touched the glass with her fingertips. Henry, in police uniform, had been a handsome man; an imposing figure. A slight smile touched the corners of her mouth. It would have been hard for any man to have looked other than imposing with the insignia of deputy commissioner emblazoning his chest.

'So what does her old man do, then?' It was five days later and Lily, brewing up a pot of tea in her kitchen, was curious. 'He must have a high-falutin job if the house is as big as Jackie and Kelly've been telling me.'

'He pushes up daisies,' Pearl said crudely. 'She's a widow. She's also very nice. She's older than me – about your age – and what she does all day with me doing her cleaning for her I can't begin to think. No one ever pops in for a chat and she never seems to pop out. Even though she's got two kids the house is like a bleedin' tomb. The boy is a stuck-up bit of work. Treats me as if I'm part of the furnishings – or he would if I let him get away with it. The little girl is Jackie's age, though you wouldn't think it the things Mrs Pulfer won't allow her to do. She can't go to the shops by herself, can't go to piano practice by herself, doesn't play outside other than in the garden. I ain't surprised Mrs Pulfer's always asking me if I'd like to take Jackie and Kelly with me. Poor little sod must be desperate for someone to play with.'

'I don't know why you bother with it.' Lily didn't like Pearl jaunting off to snobby Blackheath twice a week and didn't care who knew it. 'I bet you haven't told Jock you've taken up charring, have you? He won't like it when he gets to know of it, I can tell you that straight.'

'He's inside and I'm out and I have a life of me own to lead.' Pearl felt rebellious enough to spit. 'It ain't as if I'm going out with another fella. I've simply got myself a nice little cleaning job and I'm very happy with it, ta very much. So happy that next week I'm going to take Jackie and Kelly with me again. It ain't as if any trouble can come of it, is it?'

'Me dad's not very happy about Uncle Jock.' Eddie was holding court at the corner table of a coffee bar in Jamaica Road. 'He says it was Jock's fault he and him got nicked and he doesn't like Jock saying differently.'

Kevin and Johnny groaned in unison. That their Uncle Smiler was busy putting it around to his fellow inmates

37

it was Jock who cocked up, not himself, went without saying. What also went without saying was that no one believed him and that he wouldn't be mouthing off in such a manner if he and Jock were in the same nick. It was only because he was in Wandsworth and Jock was over a hundred miles away in Winson Green that he was mouthing off at all.

'It's all right you two bleedin' groaning!' Eddie's nostrils whitened with angry resentment. 'You fink he's Mr Wonderful, don't yer? Well, he ain't. You ask your dad where the Barclays dosh went to. Your dad and my dad never saw hide nor bleedin' hair of it. "I'm the banker" – that's what Jock bleedin' told 'em. Now he's in the nick and no one knows where the hell the dosh is. Aunty Pearl obviously doesn't else she wouldn't be goin' out charring.'

'Aunty Pearl goes out charring 'cos she wants to, not 'cos she needs to,' Johnny said with a perceptiveness beyond his years. 'She's tryin' to make Uncle Jock feel bad for bein' inside.'

'I shouldn't think he needs any help for that.' Kevin, seeing that two likely girls had entered the coffee bar, flicked the collar of his denim jacket up to give him a cool Elvis Presley look. 'Point is, what's goin' to happen now? No one's goin' to see the Barclays dosh until Uncle Jock's out again – and no matter what you may think, Eddie, that's not because he's squirrelled it away for himself. It's because he squirrelled it to fund a bit of work. A bit of work that can't be pulled without him.' He hesitated for a moment and then added placatingly, 'Or without your dad.'

Eddie grunted, knowing Kevin was flannelling him. Heavies were always expendable and his dad was no exception. That was why he, Eddie, wanted to be far more than a heavy. He wondered what the job was that Jock had been planning. Kevin and Johnny didn't know, that much was obvious, and he doubted very much if their dad knew either. Jock always kept things close to his chest. It was the thing about him Eddie hated most.

Kevin, still waiting for someone to answer his question as to what was going to happen now that their Uncle Jock and Smiler were in the nick, resumed his scrutiny of the girls. They were standing in front of the jukebox, giggling and posing the way girls did when they knew they were being eyed up. The distinctive opening chords of Marvin Gaye's 'I Heard It Through the Grapevine' assaulted his eardrums, sending tingles of pleasure down his spine. He gave them ten out of ten for good taste, grateful they weren't Donny Osmond fans.

'Well, Dad's going to have to lay low for a bit.' Johnny, being thirteen and not sixteen, hadn't had his attention diverted the way Kevin had. 'The filth are narked at not getting him for the post office job and, as they suspect him of the Barclays job as well, wherever he goes at the moment, they go too.'

'Which is one good reason why the Barclays dosh is best left wherever Jock stashed it.' Kevin decided one of the girls had too many spots and that the other looked suspiciously flat-chested. He returned his attention to Johnny and Eddie. 'So . . . like I said. What happens now?' His eyes held Eddie's.

Eddie hated it when Kevin did this to him – apparently deferring to him yet in a way that always undercut him. How the bleedin' hell did he know what happened now? The only thing he knew for sure was that with his dad away for a few years, he wouldn't have aggro to put up with at home.

Though he wouldn't have admitted it for the world he'd been pleased as punch when his dad had gone down for a four-year stretch. With Jock Sweeting serving time as well it meant the way was clear for him to take over as the dominant male in Creek Row. Albie certainly wouldn't be doing so. Albie was an old softie. It was a family joke that the last time Albie had done more than threaten anyone with a cosh he'd helped the bloke he'd hit back on to his feet.

'I dunno,' he said now to Kevin, trying to give the impression that he was thinking the problem over deeply and would, any minute, come up with the goods.

'I'll tell you what I think.' Johnny flicked a tumbled lock of blond hair away from his forehead and leaned across the table towards Eddie and Kevin so that, now he had lowered his voice, they would be able to hear him. 'I think it's time we did a few jobs ourselves.'

Eddie looked at him with pitying contempt. 'Oh, yeah? An' what do yer fink me and Kev have bin doin' since we were out of nappies?'

Johnny regarded him patiently, well used to Eddie never immediately cottoning on. 'I ain't talking about demanding money with menaces and fleecing tourists in Soho and nicking a little bit here and a little bit there. I'm talking about heavy jobs. The kind of jobs our old men pulled.'

'Armed robbery?' Kevin looked at his thirteen-year-old brother with a startled expression, uncertain as to whether or not he was taking the piss.

Johnny shifted his position, sitting sideways on to the table with an arm hooked around a bent knee, a plimsoll-shod foot resting on the bench-seat, his other leg dangling free. 'Why not? Uncle Jock and Smiler may be in the nick now but think of all the blaggings they got away with. And if they got away with them, why shouldn't we?'

'Because we ain't got the gear, that's why.' There was sneering contempt in Eddie's voice. It was bad enough Kevin making him feel a divvy without a kid like Johnny doing so as well.

Over on the jukebox the spine-tingling tones of Marvin Gaye gave way to the mind-numbing inanity of Mungo Jerry's 'In the Summertime'.

'We could use their gear.'

The effrontery and simplicity of Johnny's logic took Kevin's breath away. That their dad and Uncle Jock and Smiler had a varied range of weapons safely locked in a slaughter somewhere was common knowledge to all three of them. Just where the slaughter was, though, none of them knew.

'Dad must know.' Johnny had always been able to read his brother's thoughts clear as a bell. 'And as Uncle Jock and Smiler are inside he'll have the key.'

Excitement was rising in all of them. What Johnny was suggesting was that they took over where their dads had left off – and unsaid but understood was that they would be far more reckless and far more daring than their old men had been.

'Uncle Albie ain't goin' to hand over guns and gelly just fer the askin',' Eddie said, for once making an astute observation. 'How are yer goin' to persuade him to do it?'

Johnny grinned. 'I'm goin' with Aunty Pearl and the girls to visit Uncle Jock Saturday. When I come back I'll tell Dad it's what Uncle Jock wants. I won't let him know I'm goin' to be in on things as well, though. He might think thirteen's a bit too young to be holding up banks!'

Kevin cracked with laughter and even Eddie sniggered. They would be the youngest mini-gang doing heavy numbers in the whole of south-east London. They'd have the reputation of being right tasty merchants in no time whatsoever.

'We can do safes as well.' Johnny couldn't remember when he'd last had so much fun. 'I know exactly how to blow them and I've had a lot of practice.'

'Oh yeah?' Eddie had had just about enough of Johnny playing it big. 'And I suppose you're Batman as well, are you?'

Johnny remained unruffled. Eddie was family. Allowances had to be made. 'Uncle Jock brought an up-to-the-minute Chubb home so he could make sure I knew exactly

41

what I was about. The only thing we need apart from the gelly is a pack of three.'

'A pack of three?' Even Kevin was beginning to look dazed. 'Do you mean Durex?'

Johnny nodded. 'When you blow a safe, the way Uncle Jock blows a safe, you pack the gelly – a quarter-ounce will do it – in the keyhole. If the locking mechanism jams you use a French letter to blow the door off.'

'How?' Eddie said derisively.

'You slip the rubber in the lock, open end on the outside, and then pack it with gelly, squeezing it out in a thin line like you'd do if you were icing a cake. That way the gelly is held inside the safe in the French letter and when it's detonated it acts like a bomb. The detonator is attached to a nine-volt battery or a torch battery. You shove it in, wind it round the handle, pack Plasticine over the keyhole and then run Plasticine round the edges of the door.'

'Why?' Eddie interrupted again, this time not quite so jeeringly.

'So that the safe is airtight and the blast is controlled inside it. When you've done that you heap coats or carpets onto it to muffle the bang, cross the circuit and Bob's your uncle. One explosion and one safe with its door busted off.'

'Blimey.' If Eddie wasn't going to let on how impressed he was, Kevin had no such scruples. It should have been him, of course, not Johnny, who had been having secret confabs with their uncle. That it hadn't been was no one's fault but his own and he certainly wasn't going to sulk about it. 'As far as over-the-counter bank jobs are concerned,' he said, regaining something like control of the conversation, 'if we're going to pull them we're going to have to check them out just as carefully as Jock always did. We need to find one with a side turning and then, when we've found one, we need to decide who's going to go in to change a note and recce it out.'

'Like, seeing where the drawers are?' Eddie asked, forcing his brain cells into action.

Kevin nodded. 'And we'll need to check it isn't a bank with a new-fangled protective screen.'

Johnny's grin deepened. Their Uncle Jock swore blind it was because of the raids he, Albie and Smiler had carried out that some banks had now put a foot and a half or so of protective glass between cashiers and customers.

'Who's going to be on the door?' Kevin asked, determined it wasn't going to be he. He wanted to be in at the sharp end, vaulting over the counter and causing as much mayhem as possible.

'Well, it ain't goin' to be me.' Eddie didn't like the way Kevin was taking so much on himself and he certainly wasn't going to be palmed off with a job that traditionally went to the most unfit member of any bank-robbing team.

'We're going to need a couple more pairs of hands,' Johnny said, knowing full well Kevin wouldn't want to stay by the door and that, as well as a doorman, they'd need someone to be at the wheel of their getaway. 'Dad and Jock and Smiler usually took on a couple of extra hands when they did a bank job. We could see if any of their old cronies are up for coming in with us.'

'They won't want to take a chance with us. We're too young,' Kevin said baldly.

'An' they'll want to call all the shots.' Eddie had had enough of that when his old man had been at home.

'Then we'll have to build a team of our own.' Johnny was undismayed at the thought. It would be easy enough to do, especially if they did it on an *ad hoc* basis. 'And for our first few jobs I think we should leave the hardware at home. We don't want to risk really heavy sentencing if we come unstuck.'

'So what do we go in with, then?' Whatever it was, Eddie knew he wasn't going to like it much. What he wanted in his hands was a gun – the bigger the better.

This time it was Kevin's turn to grin. 'We go in mob-handed with pickaxe handles. What bank do you think we should hit first? Lloyds, Barclays, or the Midland?'

Jackie was exceedingly unhappy. She had a best friend at school, a new girl, Karen Trotter. The trouble was, Karen's dad was a policeman and she was forever having to lie to her.

'My dad's at sea,' she had said when Karen had asked why her dad never came with her mum to parents' evening. Another time, when Karen had asked why she couldn't come and play at her house, she had invented a fictional gran. 'My gran lives with us,' she had said, not liking herself one little bit. 'She's ever so ill and so I can't invite people home. She has to be quiet, see?'

That Karen was immensely understanding only made things worse, for she was continually asking her when her dad's ship would be coming back to England and if her gran was feeling any better, which meant that she had to make up yet more lies to explain why the answer to both questions was 'no'. Making her even unhappier was the way the teachers looked at her whenever they overheard these conversations, for they knew very well that she hadn't a gran and that her dad wasn't at sea, but was in the nick. There were other lies she found herself having to tell as well. One of the worst had been when Karen had invited her home to tea and she had had to lie to her mum in order to be able to go.

'So where does this friend of yours live and what does her dad do?' her mum had asked, sorting through a pile of Cellophane-wrapped shirts Uncle Albie had brought home to Aunty Lil after they had conveniently fallen off the back of a lorry and that Aunty Lil had passed on to her mum so that she could sell a few of them next time she went to bingo or to the pub.

'She lives in Slipper Place and her dad's a . . . a bus

driver,' she had said, wondering if the pleasure of going to tea at Karen's was worth the pain of the lie. That it was a lie that had to be told she was in no doubt whatsoever. Her mum wouldn't let her visit a policeman's house – not when Uncle Albie was into lorry loads again.

'I don't suppose you'd like to take Kelly with you as well, would you?' her mum had asked hopefully. 'I need to go to bingo tonight and she creates ructions when she's left in on her own.'

At the thought of Kelly in a police house Jackie's heart had nearly failed her. 'Can't she sit in with Aunty Flo or Aunty Lil?' she had asked, trying not to sound quite as desperate as she had felt.

Her mum had sniffed and said if that was the way she felt about it she supposed Kelly would have to. She hadn't been pleased, though, and just to make everything worse Jackie hadn't really enjoyed herself at Karen's. Karen's mum had been nice and the tea had been nice but her dad had come home in his uniform and, although he had been nice to her as well, she had felt dreadfully uncomfortable with him. When he had said in a friendly fashion that he understood her dad was in the navy and had asked whereabouts his ship now was, she had stammered out her well-practised lie as scarlet as a beetroot.

'Dad thinks you're shy,' Karen had said to her afterwards when they had gone upstairs to play in her bedroom. 'He thinks it's ever such a shame your gran's so ill. Have we to play Cops and Robbers Halma? What do you want to be? Cop or robber?'

'The cozzers are on Uncle Albie's tail so no talking too freely to anyone,' her mum said to her and Kelly a few days later. 'And you'd best both go and sit in with Johnny and Kevin when you come home from school. Me and your Aunty Lil have a bit of toing and froing to do this evening.'

As Uncle Albie was expecting a visit from the cozzers at any moment Jackie knew very well what the toing and froing would be: the getting rid of whatever remained of the goods he had helped off the back of a lorry.

'Can we sleep at Aunty Lil's?' Kelly asked, knowing that if they did so they would be able to stay up even later than normal, watching late-night films with Kevin and Johnny.

'I s'pose.'

Her mother's voice was so preoccupied, seeds of disquiet began to grow in Jackie's tummy. Was her Uncle Albie really on the verge of being arrested? And with her dad and her Uncle Smiler already locked away what would happen to their little extended family if he were? With a pang of envy she remembered the sense of order and security that had pervaded Karen's home. Karen never had to keep any secrets or tell any lies – or not big, serious ones. She didn't have to be frightened of loud authoritative knocking on her front door, either. Jackie hated police raids. They scared the life out of her. If there were the risk of one tonight, at her Uncle Albie's, she didn't want to be there when it took place.

'I want to sleep at home,' she said, ignoring Kelly's wail of protest. 'Kev and Johnny won't be in tonight, Mum – they never are these days.'

'Hello, gels.' Albie beamed affectionately at his nieces as he stepped over the threshold of number 28, a duffel bag slung over one shoulder. 'I'm kippin' here tonight. Did yer mother tell yer?'

Kelly ran ebulliently towards him so that he could swing her up in his arms. Jackie eyed the duffel bag with a sinking heart. Her uncle had obviously come prepared for a quick getaway. If number 26 were raided he would be out of number 28 and over the back garden fence before they'd got the door open.

'What's it to be then, pigeons?' Albie asked, walking

through into the kitchen and checking that the back door was off the latch. 'Horlicks all round an' a game of Monopoly?'

The raid, when it came, was a dawn one. Even though it was so early Jackie was awake and had been for some time. What she didn't understand about Uncle Albie staying overnight with them was why, if he'd been tipped off the cozzers were very likely on to him, he hadn't scarpered hours ago. Was it because he liked the excitement of evading a raid? Or was it because, like Uncle Smiler, he wasn't too bright in the brain-box department? No matter how she mulled it over she couldn't arrive at a satisfactory answer. Instead she began to think of the day ahead. There was PE in the morning and in the afternoon she and Karen had been paired together for a history project. They were to build a Roman fort and . . .

There came the sound of cars swerving to a halt on Creek Row's cobbles.

'Bye, gels!' Uncle Albie shouted from downstairs, the back door slamming after him.

'*What the bleedin' hell do you think you're doing?*' her mother shouted from her bedroom window a split second later as uniformed officers thunderously hammered on her sister's front door. '*Don't you know decent folk are trying to get a bit of shuteye?*'

Jackie sprang out of bed, snatching hold of her school clothes. She didn't want to be caught in her nightie if the police should turn their attentions to number 28.

Kelly, who had been fast asleep seconds earlier, was scrambling out of the other side of the bed, asking urgently, 'Is it the nasty old filth? Where's Uncle Albie? Has he got away? Has . . .'

Number 26's door crashed back on its hinges and several pairs of booted feet pounded up the stairs.

Jackie could hear her Aunty Lil screaming abuse, and

Kevin and Johnny shouting every swear word they knew – which was a lot. There came the sound of a struggle taking place at the top of the stairs and Jackie knew it was Kevin and Johnny pitching into the police in order to delay a search of the bedrooms. The longer it took for the police to cotton on that their bird had flown, the more time Albie had to do a complete disappearing act.

'He ain't here! He's gorn off with another woman!' she could hear her Aunty Lil storming, all simulated aggrievance. 'He's buggered off to Birmingham with her!'

'He's more likely next door at your sister's.' The clipped, authoritative tones of the responding voice were ones Jackie found oddly familiar. 'Come on,' the speaker continued. 'Let's give number 28 a going-over.'

'*Oh no, you bleedin' well don't*!' Even before her front door was being hammered into the middle of next week Pearl was pressing her full weight as hard as she could against it. 'You'll have to break the door down! I ain't letting you in!'

Jackie sat down on the top stair, her face chalk-white as the police proceeded to take her mother at her word.

'*Bastards*!' her mother sobbed as the lock gave way and burly officers stormed past her to the foot of the stairs.

'This is Jock Sweeting's gaff!' one policeman shouted as, with two others, he sprinted towards the kitchen and three more made a beeline for the stairs. 'There may be hardware about!'

'Don't talk so bleedin' crackers, and get out of my house when you ain't got a warrant!'

Jackie had never heard such naked apprehension in her mother's voice before. As the policemen charged the stairs she scrambled frantically to her feet. All of Creek Row would have been woken by the ruckus and would be hanging out of their windows and standing on their doorsteps for a view of what was happening. Mortified sobs rose in her throat. What if it got talked about at school? What if

Karen got to know that her Uncle Albie was on the run?

'Mind the kiddie!' It was that voice again; the one she was sure she'd heard before.

In another minute realisation would have dawned and she would have made sure he didn't see her face. As it was, in trying to prevent herself being knocked over in the rush for the landing she moved into his way and he practically stepped on top of her.

'Jacqueline?' Amazement at finding one of his daughter's friends in the home of a convicted bank robber stopped Karen's father dead in his tracks.

''Lo, Mr Trotter.' Her voice was barely audible as she plunged into depths of abject misery. There would now be no happy hours spent making a fort with Karen. Karen wouldn't be allowed to play with her or even talk to her ever again.

'*Leave my kid alone, copper!*' Her mother sprinted up the stairs and grabbed hold of Jackie protectively. She didn't want Jackie being led into saying anything she shouldn't. Jackie's ability to lie had never been very good.

'There's no one here, sir,' a policeman said to Karen's father, as he emerged from one of the bedrooms with Kelly clinging to him like a limpet.

Apart from his yell of anguish as Kelly sank her teeth into his leg there was no longer a sense of urgent tension. With no further reason for making out that Albie was hiding in number 28 Kevin and Johnny, standing at the foot of the stall ceased being combative and lit up a couple of cigarettes. Policemen clattered downstairs and emerged desultorily from ground-floor rooms. Pearl's agitated breathing began to return to normal. Only Jackie remained distressed. When the police had driven away, and her mother and Kelly had gone round to her Aunty Lil's for cups of tea, she went into the bathroom and sat on the toilet and covered her face with her hands.

She loved her family but she wanted them to be different.

She didn't want her dad to be locked up with lots of bad men. She didn't want her Uncle Albie to be on the run and for people to be scared of her Uncle Smiler and of Eddie. She didn't want policemen smashing into her home and turning it over. Most of all, she didn't want to have secrets; secrets as to where her Uncle Albie might be; the names of her dad's mates; the knowledge of where the goods came from that her mum and Aunty Lil sold.

And then there were the lies. As the sound of her mum and her Aunty Lil's relieved laughter came, muffled, through the wall from number 26, Jackie began to cry. She hated telling lies to nice people such as the Trotters and the Pulfers. Not that she'd have to lie to Karen ever again. Karen's dad would see to it that Karen knew the truth about her dad and about her uncles and her cousins as well.

She knuckled her tears away. One day it would be different. Fierce determination surged through her veins. One day she would have a home of her own and it would be just like Karen's home or Rosamund Pulfer's home. One day she wouldn't just *pretend* to be called Jacqueline and to be as respectable as Karen and Rosamund. One day she would *be* Jacqueline. She would be Jacqueline no matter what it cost her.

Chapter Four

1978

'Why the bleedin' hell have we been roped in to baby-sit Lavender's dogs?'

Kelly, stomping along at Jackie's side as they crossed Blackheath's postcard-pretty heath, was intensely irritated. It had been bad enough their mum dragging them to Lavender Pulfer's when they had been little kids, without Jackie doing it now they were so much older.

'We're doing it to be company for Rosamund.' Jackie pushed a heavy fall of silk-dark hair away from her face, unhappily aware that, once again, she was telling a lie.

Much as she liked Rosamund it wasn't Rosamund's interests she had at heart. It was her own. It was late July and Raymond was home from university. She knew, from a conversation she had overheard between her mother and Lavender, that he wasn't going to be at home long and that in a couple of days' time he and a college friend would be leaving England on a six-week fruit-picking-cum-cycling tour of France and Spain. If she was to catch a glimpse of him and maybe even pluck up the courage to speak to him – for he wouldn't trouble to speak to either her or Kelly without being spoken to first – she had to do so quickly. Today, with his mother in Brighton at some kind of Women's Institute conference and with Rosamund having been delegated to stay home in order to keep the family's two Dalmatians company, was the ideal opportunity.

Kelly threw her thirteen-year-old sister a look of exasperation. That Rosamund should need company dog-sitting was too utterly pathetic for words. As was the fact that she was dog-sitting at all.

'All she needs do is let Popsie and Posie loose on the heath,' she grumbled as they approached Prince of Wales Road, the narrow street that separated the east side of the heath from the large, very desirable houses that overlooked it.

As Kelly was perfectly aware that the Pulfers' dogs were never let off the lead unless accompanied, and as she had far more important things on her mind, it was a remark Jackie ignored. Instead she continued mentally debating whether or not she should tell her mother that Raymond, when he graduated, intended becoming a policeman.

Perhaps it would be best to say nothing and to let her mother find out for herself. At the thought of what would happen when she *did* find out her tummy muscles tensed in sickening spasms. It had been bad enough, years ago, when Raymond's father's photograph had suddenly appeared on the Pulfers' drawing-room mantelshelf.

'I like to polish this particular photograph frame myself, Mrs Sweeting,' she could remember Lavender saying to her mother in the dim, distant days before the two women were on friendly Christian-name terms with each other. 'It's the last formal photograph taken of my husband. He was a policeman, as you can see.'

There was no mistaking the high-ranking uniform of a deputy commissioner and Jackie had thought her mother was going to choke. She had also thought it would be the last visit they would ever make to the Pulfer home but, to her vast relief, she had been wrong.

'He's dead, Lil,' her mum had said to her aunty. 'So I can't see that his having been a poncing deputy commissioner matters much, do you? It ain't as if I blab to her about Jock and Albie. As far as Lavender is concerned Jock's a seaman and I never mention Albie and neither do the kids. They both know how to keep their traps shut.'

Jackie had been well aware that Aunty Lil had been unimpressed by her mother's easy acceptance of the late Henry Pulfer's profession. Her dad, when he learned of it, had been more than unimpressed. He had hit the roof.

'A rozzer?' he had raged one visiting day when Pearl had drummed up the nerve to put him in the picture. 'A poncing deputy fucking police *commissioner*? Have you gone stark staring bleeding mad, woman? Don't you ken what people will be saying about you, and thinking about you, if they find out?'

'I'm your wife, Smiler Burns's sister and Albie Rice's sister-in-law,' Pearl had responded heatedly. 'No one's goin' to believe I'm a grass and if you even *think* they would you need your bleedin' head seeing to!'

It hadn't been a particularly happy visit to Winson Green. After it, Jackie had been aware of regarding her mother in a different light than before, well aware now of where Kelly's wilful reckless stubbornness came from.

'I ain't staying here all day with you,' Kelly said mutinously, now that they neared the carefully maintained Edwardian splendour of the Pulfer home and garden. 'It's too boring for words.'

Jackie pushed open the elaborate wrought-iron front gate. Kelly had always found snobby Blackheath, the Pulfer home and the Pulfers – Rosamund apart – boring.

'I ain't going!' she had stormed time after time over the years whenever their mum had decided they should accompany her. 'It's a rozzer's house and they're *enemy*!'

'Lavender ain't enemy, you silly little sod,' their mum had always retorted exasperatedly. 'Get your coat on and do as you're told. I want you where I can see you. You get into more trouble on your own than Kevin and Johnny and Eddie put together.'

This grossly untrue remark was one Kelly always took as a compliment. All she ever did was nick a few things occasionally. Marks and Spencer, Woolworth's, British

Home Stores, C&A, Littlewoods; in Deptford, Camberwell and Catford, all had suffered from Kelly's deft shoplifting raids. Kevin and Johnny and Eddie weren't petty shoplifters. They were in another league altogether.

'These were burglaries of gross impudence,' the judge had said when sentencing them to eighteen months' imprisonment for burgling a string of south-east London furniture shops. 'The entire contents of these stores were stolen in a most insolently flagrant manner.'

Even Kelly had agreed with him. It was such a straightforward wheeze. In a hired furniture van and dressed in white boiler suits Kev, Johnny, Eddie and a couple of their mates had pulled up outside their chosen store one evening. Entering the premises with a skeleton key, having immobilised the alarm bell by looping the circuits, they had then proceeded to empty the shop by unhurriedly carrying the contents out of the front door and loading them into the van. If occasional passers-by were suspicious they didn't voice their concerns or interfere. For the most part they assumed, from the boiler-suited team's demeanour, that they were store employees engaged in legal activity.

Such easy success went to the boys' heads and, by the time their run of luck came to an end, they had cleared out so many furniture stores there was barely a stick of furniture for legal sale south of the Thames.

That they'd been done bang to rights for such a tame scam when their bank jobs and security-van robberies hadn't been nailed on them was a source of relief and amusement to all of them. Not that they'd ever made a huge killing on a bank job. Banks weren't the piece of cake they'd been in their dads' heyday. Security screens had inched higher and higher on bank counters so that even Olympic athletes would have been hard put to have vaulted over them.

Eddie, unhappy at not wielding a gun or a cosh as often as he would have liked, began engaging in extracurricular activities elsewhere, running occasionally with one or other of the major organised gangs that dominated Catford, Lewisham, Bermondsey and Deptford. Their interests, for the most part, were protection. And protection suited Eddie's lust for violence perfectly.

'If you don't want to stay, don't.' Jackie had no desire to be saddled with her twelve-year-old sister if she was going to whinge all the time. Besides, Kelly couldn't stand Raymond and, the feeling being mutual, Raymond would very likely leave the house if he thought Kelly was going to be around for long.

'God, that stupid prick Raymond's here,' Kelly said expressively as, with still twenty yards of pathway to walk, Rosamund opened the door to them and the dogs raced out to greet them.

Jackie, too, caught a glimpse of Raymond's tall angular figure in the hallway. He was walking down it, away from the door, as if heading in the direction of the kitchen.

Ever since she had first begun visiting the Pulfer home Jackie had been fixated with Raymond. Seven years her senior, he was so different from Kevin and Johnny and Eddie and the other boys who lived in and around Creek Row as to be from another planet. He spoke the way her teachers at school spoke, never using words such as 'caff' and 'gaff', 'grafter' and 'tasty merchant', 'whack' and 'a monkey'.

And over and above the way he spoke was what he represented: respectability. No one in the Pulfer home had ever had to hide behind the sofa pretending there was no one in because the old Bill were knocking on the door. Nor had they had to leap from their beds, grabbing for clothes because they were being raided and the front door was being stoved in. Raymond and Rosamund could be openly proud of their father in a way Jackie couldn't be, and that was what hurt most of all, for there were so many things about her dad that she *was* proud of – the way he loved and cared for her mum and for her and Kelly, the way he never let a friend down, the way he looked after her Aunty Lil and her Aunty Flo if Uncle Smiler or Uncle Albie were doing a bit of bird, the way he growled deep in his throat when he was pretending to be cross with her and Kelly – for he was never truly cross with either of them.

'Mummy won't be back till seven or eight tonight so we have the whole day to ourselves,' Rosamund carolled chirpily as they walked up to her, the dogs leaping around them in an ecstasy of pleasure.

'That'll be nice.' Jackie meant it. She especially meant it if Raymond were to be home all day as well.

Kelly raised her eyes to heaven. 'Mummy', for Christ's sake. Though over the years she had grudgingly come to like Rosamund, at times like this she despaired of her. It was even worse when Raymond babyishly referred to Lavender as 'Mummy'. Whenever he did so in her hearing she would, unseen by Lavender and Raymond, stick her finger down her throat, pretending to throw up.

Her liking for Rosamund had taken both her mother and Jackie by surprise. It had surprised her, too, and had sprung into life when she had realised that beneath Rosamund's respectable exterior lay a wicked sense of fun and, even more importantly, a streak of wilful recklessness. It was a recklessness no one, apart from herself, seemed aware of. Kelly wasn't even sure if Rosamund was aware of it, for living under Lavender's eagle eye she had precious few opportunities for indulging it. It was there, though, and as a consequence Kelly had warmed towards her and her friendship with Rosamund was now even closer than was Rosamund's friendship with Jackie.

From the direction of the kitchen Jackie could hear the sound of John Travolta and Olivia Newton-John singing 'You're the One That I Want'. Raymond either had the radio on or had taken his cassette player into the kitchen with him. Either way, while the oh-so-apt song was playing she would be able to ask him if he had seen the film it had come from, and the conversation would seem natural and not embarrassingly contrived. Or it would if Rosamund and Kelly weren't also in the kitchen earwigging to what was being said.

'The dogs look desperate for a walk,' she said. It wasn't yet another pork pie. It was true. 'Why don't you and Kelly take them on the heath so they can let off some steam?'

'And what are you going to do?' Kelly's sisterly suspicion was immediate.

Jackie shrugged. 'I came out without having had breakfast so I'm going to make myself a cup of tea and have a slice of toast.'

Neither Rosamund nor Kelly thought her remark odd. Pearl always had a cup of tea in the kitchen before starting work and whenever Kelly or Jackie was with her, Lavender would encourage them to have not only cups of tea, but breakfast as well.

Kelly, who had never been able to work up enthusiasm for scented Lapsang Souchong, shrugged. 'Whatever you want,' she said indifferently. 'Come on, Ros. Let's take these stupid mongrels for a walk.'

The highly bred Dalmatians, sensing a brief period of freedom on the heath, barked even more frenziedly.

Rosamund stepped back into the hall and removed two dog leads from a polished mahogany coat-stand. She liked being out with Kelly on her own. Kelly's conversation, always racy, was even racier when Jackie wasn't with them and it was hard, sometimes, for her to remember that Kelly was two years her junior, not two years her senior.

'I've got an idea, tell me how it grabs you,' Jackie could hear Kelly saying to Rosamund as, with the dogs still clamouring around them, they began walking down the long alchemilla-edged path towards the gate.

Jackie, moving with a fast-beating heart towards the

kitchen and Raymond, didn't wait to overhear what Kelly's idea was. For the rest of her life, she was to wish that she had.

'I ain't hanging round your gaff all day,' Kelly said bluntly as she and Rosamund set off in the direction of the nearby heath. 'It's about as exciting as being in a cemetery. The minute we've done with the dogs I'm off back to Bermondsey. Why don't you come with me? Jackie won't mind looking after Popsie and Posie on her own. She can sunbathe in the garden and pretend the place is hers.'

'Bermondsey?' Rosamund stopped short, her eyebrows flying nearly into her hair. 'You mean you'll take me home with you? To Creek Row?' She made it sound as if Creek Row were Mongolia.

Kelly's throaty chuckle was reminiscent of her mother's. 'Why not? Me and Jackie have been coming to friggin' Blackheath for long enough. It's about time you returned the favour and saw how the other half lives.'

Rosamund could feel excitement pulsing even in her fingertips. For years everything she had heard about Creek Row had fascinated and intrigued her. She hadn't been allowed to go there, though. Although her mother had never made the slightest objection to her being friends with Kelly and Jackie it was a friendship that was strictly on her mother's terms. Jackie and Kelly could cross the class divide and play with her in the garden or on Blackheath's heath but there was never any question of her visiting their home, or of her running wild with them in Creek Row and other Bermondsey streets.

Rosamund hesitated but the hesitation was minimal. Her mother would be furious when she found out. She mentally corrected herself. *If* she found out. Kelly certainly wouldn't tell on her and, though for different reasons, she couldn't imagine Jackie telling on her either.

'You're on,' she said, all interest in walking the dogs

forgotten. 'Will your Rice cousins be home?' Kelly and Jackie's conversations were constantly peppered with mentions of Kevin and Johnny though the remarks, unknown to her, were always heavily censored. 'And will your dad be home?'

Her own father being dead, Rosamund had always been very interested in any details she could glean about her friends' father. Kelly and Jackie obviously worshipped the ground he walked on yet there were times when they seemed reluctant to talk about him.

Kelly wondered if her dad would mind her bringing Rosamund home and decided he wouldn't. 'Most likely,' she said. 'That is, he will be if he ain't round the betting shop or in the pub.'

Rosamund giggled. If any of her schoolfriends' fathers had been in the habit of visiting betting shops or going to the pub mid-week and mid-morning they would have *died* rather than have admitted it to anyone.

'And Kev and Johnny'll probably be round the snooker hall,' Kelly added. 'I don't suppose you've ever played snooker, have you?' It was so safe an assumption she didn't wait for an answer. 'If they're round there, how about us joining them? Then you can give it a try.'

'You're on!' Rosamund was fizzing with excited anticipation. Bermondsey, snooker, and a meeting with Jackie and Kelly's cousins! It all added up to a package of intoxicating forbidden fruit and she couldn't wait to taste it. 'Bugger the dogs,' she said, speaking in the way she always did when alone with Kelly, which would, if her mother had overheard, have given her a cardiac arrest. 'Let's take them back to the house. They can have their walk later. Jackie can take them – or Raymond.'

With one accord they turned round, the dogs kicking up such a fuss of aggrieved disappointment as they were yanked in their wake that Jackie and Raymond heard their approach a good five minutes before their eventual arrival.

'What the hell . . . ?' In annoyance Raymond turned the volume of his portable stereo down so that he could hear the racket even more clearly. He hadn't been mistaken. It was Popsie and Posie. And if the dogs were on their way back so were his sister and Kelly Sweeting.

Raymond had no time for any of the Sweetings. Why his mother should have turned her cleaning lady into a near-friend was beyond him. None of his friends' mothers behaved in such an unconventional way, allowing their cleaning ladies to address them by their Christian names and indulging in long gossipy chats over cups of Lapsang Souchong.

Even worse than his mother's embarrassing familiarity with Pearl Sweeting was the way she had always encouraged her to bring her offensively streetwise brats with her. The elder girl, the one now tediously questioning him as to whether or not he had seen *Saturday-Night Fever* and *Grease*, wasn't so bad. Better spoken than her mother and sister, she had a quiet manner and, being passably pretty in a blue-eyed, dark-haired Celtic kind of way, he found her occasional presence in his home just about tolerable.

Kelly Sweeting, though, was another matter entirely. Kelly Sweeting was a common little bit of work. With her fox-red hair and ebullient self-confidence she was also unnervingly and precociously sexy. Nymphet, Lolita, and jail-bait were all names that seemed to have been especially coined to describe her. Not that she aroused him, or so he lyingly told himself. He'd seen the mocking contempt in her eyes whenever she looked in his direction and it had left him feeling as winded as if he'd been punched in the chest. How dare a twelve-year-old kid from a rough part of London look at him as if she was somehow his superior? The anger he had felt had been white-hot. And now here she was again, walking into his home as if it were her own, and Rosamund, silly cow, was giggling and laughing with her as if she were one of her public-school friends.

'We ain't takin' the dogs for a walk; we're going off on a jaunt by ourselves,' Kelly said to Jackie, ignoring Raymond as she always did. 'See yer.'

Rosamund opened her mouth to tell Jackie where it was they were going, looked across at her brother, and thought better of it. Not only would Raymond make sure their mother learned of her outing, he would create such a stink about it she would probably end up not even going.

'Bye,' she said, spinning round and haring after Kelly in the direction of the front door. There was no point at all in hanging around to be questioned. Easing her conscience was the fact that Raymond and Jackie had looked to be getting on quite well. Perhaps, when it came to taking Posie and Popsie for a walk, they would do so together.

'I don't care what you friggin' think, Kev!' Eddie had his dander up and didn't care who knew it. 'Protection dosh is better'n no dosh at all. We ain't had a decent job for months working just the three of us and I can coin in a monkey a week as a breaker.'

Kevin leaned over the snooker table and shot the yellow neatly into the far pocket. When he was standing straight again he said, 'Five hundred quid a week for smashing some poor bugger to pulp don't sound like a lot of laughs to me, Eddie.' He handed his cue to Johnny. 'Plus when you start running with protection gangs you start having to mind your manners. Step out of line or get lippy and you can end up wrapped in cement and helping support a bridge over the M1.'

Eddie gave a mirthless laugh. 'You talk shit sometimes, Kev. No one messes with me, you know that. I do what I want, when I want, how I want – and I have dosh in me pockets and respect. I like a bit of respect. It makes life very comfy.'

Johnny potted a red and then a blue. They were no longer playing in the High Street snooker hall above

Burton's. Now they played in a privately run snooker hall. The owner paid a 'gift' every week to Eddie in enforced gratitude for Eddie 'looking after' it, and it was where they now spent a large amount of their free time.

Though, like Kevin, Johnny didn't agree with Eddie's method of solving the problem, he sympathised with his frustration at the way things were going for them job-wise. They hadn't had a decent job for yonks. New technology was ensuring that, where banks and security jobs were concerned, the name of the game was fast changing. None of them minded taking risks – getting the old adrenalin going was the best part of any job – but the cake had to be worth the candle and at the moment it wasn't.

'P'raps we need to rethink things a bit,' he said, failing to pot a black and standing back from the table to allow Eddie to approach it. 'P'raps we should be thinking about stealing dosh *before* it's in a security van or a bank.'

'Like the bleedin' Great Train Robbers?' Eddie snorted with derision. 'What a load of wankers they were. Thirty years for nearly all of 'em and their whacks up the spout into the bargain.'

Johnny pushed a fall of barley-gold hair out of his eyes. He had a lot of respect for the train robbers. As far as he was concerned, the planning of the robbery had been perfection; pure poetry. In his dad and his Uncle Jock's style it had been impersonal theft, the money stolen being cash various Scottish banks were sending to the London East Central Post Office for delivery to their respective head offices. No guns had been used. The gang had been armed with coshes and an axe – the axe being necessary in order to break into the mailbag coach. It had been a robbery of awesome effrontery, marred for ever by the brave and unexpected resistance of the train driver. Coshed once, and hitting the back of his head as he fell, he suffered worse injury than anyone had intended.

That apart, the job had been carried out with military

meticulousness and that such detailed planning should have broken down so disastrously in the hours and days immediately after the robbery, resulting in so many of the gang being caught, was a mystery Johnny never ceased marvelling over. Bruce Reynolds, Gordon Goody, Charlie Wilson, Buster Edwards and the ten or so other men who had come in with them on the job had had the world in their pockets and then, because fingerprints had been found at their hideaway, they'd all been nabbed for it.

The failure to ensure that Leatherslade Farm was clean as a whistle was carelessness so monumental, the mere thought of it had him gasping for breath. If he'd been on the job he'd have insisted on the farm being burned to the ground, then there'd have been no evidence found, crooked or legit.

Bruce and Buster had given the police a good run for their money before being caught, and Charlie Wilson, one of the ringleaders, and Ronnie Biggs, a minor member of the gang, had both escaped from prison after sentencing; Charlie for a brief period of freedom, Ronnie to Australia and then to sunny Rio. And there were three, perhaps four, men who had never even been fingered for the robbery and who were, presumably, enjoying their ill-gotten gains to the full.

Remembering this he said mildly, 'Not all of them, Eddie. Three, perhaps four blokes, were never nabbed or named. So for them it was worth it, wasn't it?'

'Doesn't soddin' matter whether it was or not, it ain't a scam that can be pulled again, is it?' Eddie hated the fact that young Johnny always, but *always*, somehow made him out to be a wally. 'Or was you finkin' of hijacking a Boeing full of bullion or raiding the bleedin' gold reserves in Geneva?'

Kevin laughed but Johnny didn't. For one thing Eddie even knowing about Swiss gold reserves was a shock to his system; for another, he didn't find Eddie's remarks laughable. Bullion. It was a wonderful word. He'd stolen a lot in his time but he'd never stolen gold. Perhaps it was time he did. How the devil did it come into the country? By ship? By sea? How was it moved around when in Britain? How did it leave? Used as it was by the government and international banks as international currency it had to leave somehow.

'Come on, Johnny,' Kevin said impatiently. 'Come out of your trance. We've a game to friggin' finish.'

'I was just wondering . . .' Johnny began and then, at the far end of the room, the door to the stairs leading to the street opened and in bounced his youngest cousin followed by a fair-haired, apprehensive-looking girl two or three years her senior.

'I'm glad you're all suited and booted!' Kelly called out cheekily as she headed between empty snooker tables towards them. 'Ros has been wanting to meet all of you for ages and I was hoping we'd find you in your best gear.'

'What did you expect to find us dressed in?' Kevin asked, vastly amused. 'Overalls and balaclavas?'

The reference to their bank- and security-van – raiding gear was lost on Rosamund but Kelly, as Johnny gave her a loving hug, giggled.

'I just wanted the three of you to make a good impression, that's all.' She turned towards Rosamund as Johnny released his hold of her. 'This is my cousin Johnny, Ros. This . . .' she indicated the broad-shouldered hunk standing next to him, '. . . is Kevin.' There was an almost tangible air of toughness about him. His face was hard-boned, handsome, and, in Rosamund's eyes, utterly compelling. 'And this is my cousin Eddie,' Kelly added, indicating a powerfully built young man with a pallid complexion and a wide brutal mouth.

'And as the three of you are no doubt wondering who Ros is,' Kelly continued, her voice thick with an amusement Rosamund didn't understand, 'she's Rosamund Pulfer.'

Kevin, Johnny and Eddie looked at Rosamund with mild interest. They knew all about the family their Aunty Pearl cleaned for – and they knew that Rosamund's late father had been a deputy commissioner in the Met.

Kevin saw a typical middle-class schoolgirl, neatly and conventionally dressed, her fair shoulder-length hair held away from her face by a tortoiseshell Alice band. When she murmured 'hello' to them all, she did so in an accent that could have cut glass.

Aware her surroundings were making her feel like a beached fish he flashed her a reassuring smile. She was only a kid after all and it wasn't her fault her dad had been nearly God as a cozzer and that she spoke as though she had a cucumber up her arse.

'Fancy a game?' he asked, indicating the table behind him. 'There's no point in being in a snooker hall and not playing, is there?'

Both Eddie and Johnny realised that the conversation they'd been having before the Pulfer girl's arrival was one it was impossible to continue. Eddie was miffed, not because he'd particularly wanted to continue the conversation – he knew damn well Johnny would have been scoring points off him left, right and centre if it had gone on for much longer – but because he didn't like spending time with women unless they were flat on their backs.

Johnny wasn't remotely miffed and he certainly wasn't suffering from Eddie's feelings of inadequacy. Inadequacy was a word he wouldn't even have known how to spell. Kelly's impudence in bringing a girl of Rosamund's background and upbringing into a snooker hall patronised by some of the naughtiest villains in south-east London appealed to his sense of humour. The late deputy commissioner would be turning in his grave.

She looked a nice enough kid, he thought, as, blushing furiously, she accepted a snooker cue from Kevin. Aware that Kelly wouldn't have brought her with her – even for devilment – if she had been the usual run of middle-class pain in the neck, he once again began thinking about gold. Gold bullion. A mammoth gold bullion robbery that would make the Great Train Robbery look like child's play . . .

Rosamund was in turmoil. Kevin was showing her how to hold and line up the snooker cue and the dry heat of his hand as it covered hers was burning through her like fire. She'd never before met anyone remotely like him, or like his brother and his cousin. Instead of being casually dressed in jeans and T-shirts, or more stylishly in flares and flamboyantly collared shirts, all three wore sharply tailored dark suits that had an expensive silk-like sheen. Their shirts were a pristine white, their ties knotted hard and high, their black slip-on boots so highly polished they reflected light. The only young men she'd encountered even similarly dressed were Mormon missionaries but Mormon missionaries didn't wear heavy gold-braceleted watches or possess such a dangerous, exciting aura.

That the danger and excitement wasn't a figment of her imagination she knew for a fact, thanks to the amazing incident that had taken place shortly before she and Kelly had arrived at the snooker hall.

They had been walking down Jamaica Road when three girls about Kelly's age, clustered on the platform of a passing bus, had suddenly started shouting jeeringly in their direction.

'We know what your dad is, Kelly Sweeting!' they had chorused as the bus slowed down in the thick traffic. 'Your dad's a villain who's always in the nick!'

Rosamund had been so shocked at the two of them being shouted at in such a way that she'd thought she'd been going to have a heart attack. Kelly hadn't been shocked, though. Kelly hadn't given a tinker's curse.

'I know what my dad is!' she had yelled back at the top

of her lungs as the bus had begun to pick up speed. 'My dad's fuckin' 'andsome!'

When the bus had disappeared amongst a sea of cars, lorries and other buses, Rosamund had said disbelievingly: 'Your dad's not really been to prison, has he, Kel?'

Kelly hadn't hesitated even for a moment. She'd simply turned towards Rosamund, a wide smile splitting her face. 'Course he has. Nearly all thieves end up getting caught for one thing or another. Me dad's pretty clever, though. The only time I've known him do a long stretch was when Uncle Smiler cocked up the job they were on.' She giggled. 'That made things in the family a bit sticky for a while. Aunty Flo was sure Dad was going to do for Uncle Smiler when the two of them got out of the nick, and if it hadn't been for Mum being Smiler's sister, I think he probably would have.'

Rosamund's head had reeled. She'd always known there was something interestingly odd about Jackie and Kelly's home life but she'd never dreamed it was anything *wicked*. 'What about your cousins?' she had asked dazedly. 'What do they think about your dad having being in ... in ...' She couldn't bring herself to say the word 'prison' again and she certainly couldn't say 'nick' as carelessly as Kelly had.

'Being in the nick?' Kelly had finished for her, helpfully. 'They weren't happy about him and Uncle Smiler being nabbed but that's the way things go sometimes, ain't it? What matters is that *they've* never been nabbed for a really long stretch. Leastways Kevin and Johnny haven't.'

Rosamund came to a sudden halt, standing rooted to the pavement. 'You mean your cousins are ... are ...' Once again words failed her. How could she ask Kelly if her cousins were thieves? Or was villain the right word to use? Or should she be asking if they were crooks? Or gangsters?

'Are they at it?' Kelly was enjoying Rosamund's stupefied

state of shock enormously. 'Course they are. The whole bleedin' family is – though not me mum,' she added hastily, remembering that Pearl was trusted with the cleaning of the Pulfer home and not regarding the selling-on of nicked goods as being seriously crooked anyway. 'And not Jackie,' she added fairly. 'Jackie's squeaky clean. Always has been.'

Rosamund's horrified eyes held Kelly's. There was no embarrassment or shame in Kelly's cat-green eyes – only impish amusement. It was an amusement that was contagious. Rosamund began to giggle. It was all so farcically ridiculous. For six years her mother had been employing the wife of a serious villain as her cleaning lady – and for six years she, Rosamund, had been best friends with his daughters.

As she thought of her mother and Raymond's blissful ignorance her giggles turned to helpless laughter. It was all too funny for words. It was also dizzyingly exciting. Here were people who bided by no rules whatsoever; who were utterly and insolently lawless. The knowledge sent tingles down her spine. It was as if she were being given a privileged glimpse of an entirely new and secret world. That she would never break the confidence that had been granted her went without saying, and that Kelly so obviously took this for granted was yet another source of pleasure. It was as if a primitive bond had been forged between them – as if they were no longer merely best friends but sisters.

'You're not bad for a beginner,' Kevin Rice was saying to her now as she successfully potted a ball. 'With a bit of practice you'll soon be a tidy little player.'

Excitement surged through her body. It wasn't childish excitement or innocent adolescent excitement. It was sexual excitement, thrilling and total. If, at fourteen, she was sure of nothing else in life she was sure of one thing. She would lay down and die for Kevin Rice.

Any time.

Anywhere.

Chapter Five

'Detective Inspector Pulfer, the super would like a word with you.'

There was a slight touch of colour in the young policewoman's cheeks. DI Raymond Pulfer was quite a dish in what, with a bit of wishful thinking and a lot imagination, could be called a Robert Redford kind of way. His hair wasn't as strawberry blond as Robert Redford's, of course, and his eyes weren't blue, they were a greenish hazel – or she thought they were a greenish hazel. Raymond Pulfer didn't encourage flirtatious chitchat and she'd never been near enough, long enough, to make absolutely sure.

She knew, though, that she wasn't the only WPC to be frustrated at making no headway with him. Romance, it seemed, was not on his agenda. Having obtained a first-class Honours degree in psychology, with his subsidiary subject local government, ambition, however, very clearly was.

'His old man was a deputy commissioner,' a fellow DI had snidely let slip to their colleagues when Raymond had first joined the squad. 'I reckon our new boy intends following in Daddy's footsteps.' After a few weeks of working alongside Raymond everyone else was of the same opinion.

'I'm pulling you off your present investigation, Pulfer,' the chief superintendent said in a tone far more affable than he was accustomed to using with young DIs. 'I want you to work with DS Humphreys on trying to pin the new protection gang that's raised its head above the parapet in

Lewisham and Deptford. If we don't stamp on it p.d.q. we'll have another Richardson brothers scenario on our hands and we don't want that, do we?'

'No, sir.' Nothing in Raymond's voice betrayed his disappointment that the gang in question wasn't Richardson league. To be in the forefront of a Richardson or a Kray-type investigation was exactly what he was hungering for. He wanted something meaty to get his teeth into; an investigation in which he could really make his mark and which would send his career spinning into the stratosphere.

'The Turks are probably behind it.' The chief superintendent, who had been a stripling detective constable when Raymond's father had been his chief inspector, was almost chummy as he referred to the Turkish Cypriot family known to control most of the crime in the area, 'but the name that keeps cropping up more and more often – and in a decidedly nasty manner – isn't Halide. It's Burns. Eddie Burns.'

The chief superintendent's own son had died of a severe bout of pneumonia at eleven years old. He had been going to be a policeman, of course; following in his father's footsteps just as DI Pulfer was following in the late deputy commissioner's footsteps. Had he lived, Henry Pulfer would have been proud of young Raymond. As it was, the chief superintendent rather regarded him as his own protégé.

Instead of curtly dismissing Raymond, as he would have any other DI, the super said ruminatively, 'Burns's old man is Smiler Burns – an old lag with a record as long as a gorilla's arm. Smiler was always a heavy – but he never ran with a big gang. It was always only him and a couple of other family members. The chip off the old block seems to be casting his net a little wider.'

'Yes, sir.' The tone of the conversation was becoming almost gossipy. Raymond wondered if the super was losing his touch.

The chief superintendent, realising his manner was

verging on the fatherly, thrust memories of his dead son to the back of his mind. 'That's all, then, Pulfer,' he said briskly, bringing the interview to a smart conclusion. 'Let's nip this new protection activity in the bud, shall we?'

'Yes, sir.'

Hoping fervently that there would be a Turkish link, thereby giving the investigation far more clout, Raymond left the super's office in search of Detective Sergeant Humphreys. As he did so a rare thing happened. His mind momentarily wandered on to a personal concern.

Jacqueline Sweeting.

He hadn't seen much of her over the last year or so. Like Rosamund she was at college now – though as Rosamund was a pupil at the Royal Academy of Dramatic Art, referring to her as a college student was, he felt, stretching it a bit. Jacqueline's choice of further education was equally airy-fairy.

She wasn't at university, although according to his mother her A level passes would easily have gained her a place at one. Instead she had chosen to study fashion design at St Martin's College of Art & Design. It meant, of course, that as they were both studying in central London the two girls were able to meet up even more regularly than when Rosamund had been attending a girls' public school in Blackheath and Jacqueline had been a pupil at a large Bermondsey comprehensive.

He'd run into her, quite by accident, two days ago when he'd been having an off-duty drink with another DI in a wine bar in Greenwich. For a second, seeing her so unexpectedly and in an environment so different from the one he normally saw her in, he hadn't been able to place her. By the time the penny had dropped it was too late. He'd already allowed recognition to flare in his eyes and she was smiling in acknowledgement, and his companion was digging him in the ribs, desperate to be introduced to her.

'Hello, Jacqueline,' Raymond had said, sliding off his bar stool as she had come within talking distance. 'Nice to see you. Would you like a drink or have you one waiting?'

She'd shaken her head, jaw-length dark hair swinging sleekly. 'I'm meeting some friends,' she had said, indicating a group of girls seated around a far corner table, 'but they won't have bought me a drink yet.'

Thanking his lucky stars that, unlike her mother and her sister, she was passably well-spoken he had introduced her to his companion, another DI called Richard Ross, and bought her a glass of white wine.

Later, when after a few minutes of small talk she had said goodbye and continued on her way to her friends' table, Richard had given a low appreciative whistle and said: 'That's one hell of a lovely girl, Raymond. Is she one of your sister's friends?'

'Yes,' he'd said noncommittally – and for the rest of the evening had found his eyes straying to the far corner of the room.

It was easy to see why Richard was so smitten. Whilst he, Raymond, hadn't been looking or paying attention, Jacqueline Sweeting had grown into a distinctively beautiful young woman. Even more amazing, considering her background and her leave-nothing-to-the-imagination sister, was that she was beautiful in a quiet classy manner. Being a fashion design student probably had a lot to do with the way she dressed, of course, but, however influenced, the result was memorable – and he was now remembering it yet again.

Not many dark-haired girls of nineteen would have opted on a lovely summer evening for a sleeveless black linen dress and black suede court shoes. The result, however, hadn't been at all dull or sombre. The beautiful cut of the dress emphasised her tall slender figure and she had been carrying a bright red jacket over one arm.

'She's got style,' his public-school-educated companion

had said and, to his vast surprise, Raymond had found himself agreeing with him.

'What did the super want?' the WPC who had summoned Raymond asked, breaking in on his thoughts as she passed him in the corridor. 'You're not in line for a transfer, are you?'

Raymond shook his head, refusing to be drawn. Word would spread soon enough as to why the super had wanted a word with him. He preferred being aloof to being chatty. It reminded people of the rank attained by his father. Once again his thoughts returned to Jacqueline Sweeting. She fancied him, he knew that. Years ago, when she'd been a gawky adolescent, he'd been aware of her clumsily trying to chat him up.

The prospect of being seen out and about with such a striking-looking girl on his arm was exceedingly tempting. The problem was her embarrassingly tarty sister and excruciatingly working-class mother. Her father, too, would very likely be a similar embarrassment, though he seemed to remember being told that Pearl Sweeting's husband was in the navy and so continually away at sea.

He remembered the swell of high, pert breasts and the incredible length of her legs and stifled the beginnings of an erection. A couple of dates in Greenwich or the West End would do no harm. It wouldn't be obvious he was doing a bit of slumming – and the colleague who'd been with him in the wine bar, and who had been so smitten with her, would be envious as hell.

When Raymond phoned the Sweetings' number and, on hearing Kelly reply, had abruptly replaced the receiver without speaking, Jackie was with Johnny aboard a Southend-bound ferry.

'Eddie's getting really out of order, Johnny,' she said unhappily as they sat at the front on the otherwise empty top deck, the Thames breeze tugging at their hair. 'Even my dad is getting jumpy about him. Word is that when the new bloke at Catford's Celestial refused to cough up Eddie put a gun in his mouth and threatened to blow his head off.'

Johnny suppressed a groan. He knew all about Eddie's little habits with guns and had been hoping Jackie would remain in happy ignorance of them.

'Who told you?' he asked, unable to keep the exasperation from his voice. 'Kevin?'

She shook her head, her wide-spaced thick-lashed eyes deeply troubled. 'I just heard, that's all. Everyone's talking about him, Johnny. It's getting so that people are thinking you and Kevin are like him. If you're not careful, you won't be known for doing bank and security jobs, you'll be known as a couple of nasty heavies.'

Despite the pulse now throbbing at the corner of his jaw Johnny grinned. 'I doubt it, sweetheart. Me and Kev are top of the range and everyone knows it.'

Jackie felt the nerves in her stomach tighten in a mixture of pleasure and despair. Sweetheart. The endearment hadn't been thoughtlessly used and she knew it. For as long as she could remember she and Johnny had sought out each other's company in a way he had never done with Kelly and she had never done with Kevin or, heaven forbid, Eddie.

It was a closeness that had come near to grief when she had been nine years old. Longing for respectability with all her heart, she had tried to persuade Johnny to long for it, too. She had met with utter and abject failure. Johnny, at fifteen, was a law-breaking tearaway and he had told her, in no uncertain terms, that he had every intention of remaining one.

'All straight-goers are mugs, Jax,' he had said categorically. 'And working-class mugs are the dumbest of all 'cos they're shit poor.' His eyes had taken on the colour of flint. 'If that's what you want, Jax, you'ave it, but don't

74

ask me to 'ave it with yer, 'cos I won't. Not now. Not ever.'

His utter refusal to see things from her point of view had been a blow from which she had never really recovered.

'A penny for them,' he said now as the boat began to round the Isle of Dogs. 'Or a penny for them as long as you're not still brooding about Eddie.'

Despite her anxieties, at the teasing note in his voice, a smile touched the corners of her mouth. It was almost impossible to remain anxious or depressed when in Johnny's company and she was certainly not going to do so today. It was his birthday and, continuing a tradition that was now many years old, they were spending it together on the river. She wondered if she should tell him about her meeting with Raymond Pulfer – and of her fierce hope that he would soon be contacting her to ask her for a date.

Taking a criminal like Johnny into her confidence where Raymond, a policeman, was concerned, was, she knew, an odd thing to do but she had never had any secrets from Johnny and, considering how fiercely she disapproved of his way of life, he kept surprisingly few of his activities secret from her.

'I saw Raymond Pulfer in the Bar du Musée at Greenwich on Tuesday night,' she said, carefully avoiding eye contact with him and looking across to the far side of the river where the masts of the moored Cutty Sark speared a gloriously blue sky.

'And how is your favourite cozzer?'

Johnny's voice was light and easy but the pulse on his jawbone had begun to beat visibly again and a new expression had entered his eyes.

'He looked . . . well.' She had no intention of allowing him to goad her. 'It was rather strange seeing him suddenly and casually in a wine bar. He was . . . chattier than usual.'

Johnny tossed a cigarette stub over the side of the boat.

Jackie was floundering; wanting to say something and not quite being able to put it into words. He bent his knee slightly, wedging a silk-socked, snakeskin-shoed foot against the back of the empty bench seat in front of them. 'By chattier I presume you mean friendlier?' The sun glinted on the gold of his wristwatch. It was only eleven o'clock. He had six or seven hours, maybe even longer, to try to get to the bottom of her bizarre amorous preoccupation with Raymond Pulfer – and to replace it with an amorous preoccupation with himself. 'You mean he tried to pull you?'

Jackie turned her head abruptly, her eyes flashing fire as they met his. 'Raymond Pulfer isn't one of your lager-lout mates, Johnny! He's refined!'

Despite the fierceness of his anxiety where she and Raymond Pulfer were concerned, Johnny threw back his head, roaring with laughter. 'Christ Almighty! He'd better hightail it double-quick out of the Met if he is!' he said when he could finally trust himself to speak. 'Cozzers may be a lot of things, sweetheart, but refined they most certainly ain't.'

'He's polite and well-mannered.' Jackie spoke through gritted teeth. 'You and Kevin could learn a lot from Raymond.'

Johnny gave another short laugh but this time there was no amusement in it. 'I dare say we could. We could learn how to fit someone up for a job they've never pulled. We could try a bit of intimidation in the cells – a bit of old sleep deprivation to get statements that are sweet. We could stop and search black kids whenever we were a bit bored and wanted to pass the time of day. We could pocket backhanders for turning a blind eye. I 'spect you're right, Jax. I 'spect there's a lot we could learn from Raymond – only we don't want to. And I don't want you learning anything from the poncing bastard either.'

There were white lines around his mouth and his grey

eyes were so dark with the heat of his anger she could barely tell iris from pupil.

Her own eyes were wide with shock and her heart was beating high somewhere in her throat. She and Johnny often differed passionately but real anger between them was something so rare as to be nearly nonexistent. Now it had erupted, seemingly out of nowhere, shattering the pleasure of their day together.

'Not all policemen are bent.' She wanted so passionately to convince him of something she believed utterly to be true that her voice was unsteady, her nails digging so deep into her palms that her knuckles were drained of blood. 'I don't believe in a million years that when Raymond's father was a deputy commissioner he was taking backhanders and bribes and putting people away he knew were innocent – and I'd stake my life on the fact that Raymond would never do so!'

Johnny moved so suddenly and sharply that for a disbelieving second she thought he was going to hit her. Instead, springing to his feet, he stood with his back to the deck-rail, looking down at her with blazing eyes.

'Sweet Christ, Jackie! Have you heard yourself? Since when have the filth been "policemen"? You're talking like fuckin' Rosamund – and she only talks like that 'cos she don't know any better! For you and me, darlin', and for everyone like us, the filth are enemy!'

'Not to me they're not!'

A dozen yards or so away a middle-aged man, binoculars slung around his neck, emerged from the companionway and, unpleasantly startled at finding himself the only spectator to what was obviously an escalating and very private row, beat a hasty retreat.

Johnny and Jackie were oblivious.

'You may be a villain, Johnny, and the rest of our family may be, too, but I'm not and I never will be!' The passion of years was in her voice. 'I couldn't choose who I wanted

77

to mix with when I was a kid but I can now – and I want to mix with people like Raymond – people who I can respect and admire!'

'And does "mix with" mean "sleep with"?'

His sneer was a whiplash full of barely suppressed violence. Dear God in heaven, how long had he been in love with her? Since she'd been fourteen years old? Twelve? Longer? He didn't know. He only knew that ever since he could remember – ever since as a snotty-nosed kid he'd pushed her round the park in her pram – she had always been special to him. Now here she was, wearing an ice-blue dress she'd made herself and which looked as if it had cost a fortune, standing provocatively only inches away from him and near as dammit admitting she had the serious hots for Detective Inspector Raymond Pulfer.

'Because if it does,' he continued harshly as she sucked in her breath, 'I might just have something to say about it.'

'How ... dare you speak like that?' Her voice was a croak and her cheeks were flying scarlet banners. Her feelings for Raymond were secret; private. How had Johnny guessed her unspoken hopes with such unerring accuracy? She flushed an even deeper colour. If her feelings were so mortifyingly transparent had Raymond, too, guessed at them?

Wildly she looked towards the river bank, wanting to get off the boat, wanting to put an end to a row that was getting worse by the minute. There were no piers in sight. Greenwich was behind them. Southend was an hour and a half away.

'I dare,' he was shouting back at her, 'because you matter to me more than anyone else in our entire bleedin' family!'

He wanted her so much his teeth ached. He wanted her so much he was beyond being fearful of her reaction as he at last put into words the true nature of his feelings for her. Distractedly he ran a hand through his hair. 'Christ,

Jackie! I'm in love with you! You can't be so dim you don't know that!'

The blood was pounding in her ears and her heart felt so tight within her chest she thought it was going to explode. With all the strength she possessed she kept her eyes fixed on the shimmering north bank of the Thames. She couldn't look at him; *dared* not look at him. If she looked at him now – if their eyes met – she would be utterly lost.

Of course she knew he was in love with her. How could she not know when her feelings for him had always been so special? But she'd long ago determined never to acknowledge the nature of those feelings. He was her cousin, for one thing, and cousins didn't fall in love. And despite all his charisma and chutzpah he was an out-and-out villain – a thief who robbed banks and security vans and who often did so armed.

As a child, bent on becoming 'respectable', she had longed for him to feel the same; for them to be allies. If he had done so she would, she knew, be responding to him now very, very differently. At the thought of just how differently her throat felt crackly dry and the blood drummed along her veins.

For a heartbeat of time temptation almost overwhelmed her. Almost, but not quite. She wouldn't – she *couldn't* – live life with a man who was a professional thief. She remembered the terror and shame of waking as a child to the sound of policemen battering on the front door and, seconds later, of them invading the house in search of her dad, or her uncles, or stolen goods. The pounding of their feet as they charged past her up the stairs, the shouting and the screams of abuse – for both her mother and her Aunty Lil were screamers of epic proportions – were sounds she had long ago vowed would never be part and parcel of any home of her own.

When she fell in love – when she married – it was going

to be to someone like Raymond Pulfer. She wanted a home like the Pulfer home. A quiet home where nothing heart-stoppingly unexpected ever happened. A home that felt safe. A home that was orderly and respectable. A home where criminality was as alien as the moon.

'I'm not in love with you.' As she said the words, her face still resolutely averted from his, she experienced a sickeningly familiar sensation. It was the sensation she always experienced when telling a lie.

He seized hold of her shoulders, swinging her round to face him, knowing that he had to make her face the truth or risk losing her for ever. 'You're the worst bloody liar in the world, Jax!' His voice was raw, savage with certainty. Then, before she could draw breath to respond, he took the only action left to him. He pulled her against him in a grip from which she could not possibly free herself, his mouth coming down on hers hot and hard, in swift unfumbled contact.

'I don't know where Johnny is but as it's his birthday I suppose he's having himself a good time somewhere.' Kelly was perched on the boot of Kevin's souped-up Cortina as, the bonnet open, Kevin and Eddie cast critical eyes over the engine. 'And I don't know why you're both still so edgy about the carburettor. I did a perfectly good job on it yesterday.'

Eddie grunted noncommittally. Kelly's amazing aptitude as a mechanic was something that deeply narked him and he'd no intention of falling over with admiration just because she'd done something magical with a spanner.

'It doesn't friggin' matter whether the motor goes like a bomb or not seein' as John-boy ain't around to friggin' drive it,' he said, his voice heavy with frustration. 'He knew me and Kev wanted to do a bit of work today.'

He made it sound as if he and Kevin had intended doing a bit of carpentry or a bit of painting and decorating.

Kelly, knowing differently, cocked her head to one side, all interest. 'What kind of work? Something off the cuff? Something I could help out with?'

Kevin grinned. Kelly's cheeky impudence always amused him. 'I don't think so, chicken. Eddie wants to swipe a sub-post office.'

'So?' Kelly recrossed her legs. She was wearing high-heeled, mid-calf-length, black suede, lace-up boots, a pair of gold-on-black stretch bellbottoms, and a white bikini top.

Kevin's grin deepened. Ever since she'd been fourteen Kelly's dress style had bordered on the skimpy, leaning heavily towards displaying the goods. His Uncle Jock was always complaining that his younger daughter looked like a tart out for a bit of trade and his Aunty Pearl, whose own idea of fashion was as brazenly eye-catching as she could get away with, was always leaping to her defence.

'So that means no: you can't help,' he said, closing the bonnet and pressing down hard on it in order to ensure it didn't spring open again. 'Why don't you give Ros a bell and we'll meet the two of you later for a drink?'

'Stop soddin' speaking fer me. I ain't helping you pour drinks down your girlfriend's throat.' Eddie looked as unhappy as he felt. He didn't like it when things didn't go as he'd planned. It upset him. He was short of the readies and he'd wanted to do a sub-post office. Any sub-post office. Now that such an afternoon's graft was off the agenda he certainly wasn't going to settle for spending time with Ros friggin' Pulfer. Kev might think she was the greatest thing since sliced bread but he didn't. As far as he was concerned she was a pain in the arse.

Kevin shrugged. Eddie's moodiness never got to him. He was too used to it.

Kelly uncrossed her legs and slid off the Cortina's boot so that she was standing facing him. 'I may only just have got a licence,' she said fiercely, 'but I'm just as ace a driver as I am a mechanic. You taught me, Kev. You know how good I am. I could act as your stoppo this afternoon as easy as falling off a log.'

Kevin hesitated for a second and then gave another shrug, this time of dismissal. 'You're seventeen, Kel. Uncle Jock would have our guts for garters if we took you on a job.'

'No, he wouldn't.' She stood with one hand on her hip, sparks flashing in her eyes, the sun glinting on her fox-gold hair. 'I've already acted as a stoppo for him and your dad and Uncle Smiler. You didn't know that, did you?'

'No, I bloody did not!'

It was hard for anyone to take Kevin by surprise and, having so spectacularly done so, Kelly's sense of triumph was euphoric. 'Dad says I'm the bee's knees because I draw no attention – well, not of the wrong sort. I mean, whose going to suss me for a getaway driver?'

'Christ, Kev, she ain't wrong.' Eddie didn't go a bundle on his Aunty Pearl's husband but there were times when he had to admire the old git.

Kevin's first reaction was to wonder what Johnny would say when he was told; his second was to marvel at his uncle's effrontery and total amorality. He wondered if his Aunty Pearl knew that Kelly was a fully active member of the family business, and doubted it. Jock was, of course, spot-on in that as a stoppo, parked outside a post office or a bank, Kelly would attract no unwanted attention. Who in their right minds would suspect a seventeen-year-old girl of being part of a hit-and-run robbery team? Not that Kelly looked seventeen. She looked, instead, to be a very streetwise eighteen- or nineteen-year-old. And her driving ability was, as she had claimed, absolutely ace.

'Blimey,' he said, hardly able to Adam and Eve it, 'do you know the risks you'll be taking, sweetheart?'

Kelly's full-throated giggle was so infectious even Eddie gave a wolfish grin.

'Course I do,' she said, incandescent at being accepted as one of the boys; part of the team. 'It's the risks that make it so much fun.'

It was at that moment that alarm bells began to ring in Kevin's head. Kelly was too young; too blazingly confident; too dangerously reckless. It was only one job, though. One job couldn't hurt. Suppressing his misgivings he got down to business.

'We drop Eddie off round the corner from the post office minutes before the DSS and pension cash is taken in, right? Eddie will be in his road-sweeping gear. You then park right on top of the post office and I go in and begin filling out a TV licence form. As I'm doing so and the cash delivery van arrives, Eddie will troll up, doing his stuff in the gutter with his brush.'

Even just talking about the job gave him a sense of heightened awareness sending adrenalin racing along his veins. They'd be unarmed, relying solely on surprise and physical strength. This always spoiled the fun for Eddie, but even if Eddie was dead-brain enough to risk an armed robbery sentence for sub-post office pickings, he and Johnny weren't.

'What if I borrow a carry-cot?' The interruption was from Kelly. 'When the cash van pulls up next to me they'll be even less suspicious about the Cortina if they think there's a baby in the car – and one of my old dolls wrapped in a shawl will look just like a baby.'

Eddie gave a whistle of approval. Kelly was good. She was very, very good.

Kevin was equally impressed. A young woman in a car with a young baby. They could use the same wheeze on bigger jobs; bank jobs. That, however, would mean the job they were now about to go on would not be a one-off for Kelly.

'There'll be two postmen. One will get out of the van first, check the street, pop his head into the post office and check all looks OK. This is the guy who'll have the screamer box attached to his wrist.'

'Screamer box?' Kelly had her head tilted slightly to one side. A screamer box sounded like something out of a Hammer horror film.

'An alarm box. It'll be handcuffed to him so there's no way of dealing with it. When it goes into action, which it will the minute *we* go into action, you just mustn't let the sound of it panic you. Now, as I was saying, when the first postie has popped his head into the post office and seen nothing abnormal – I'll be on my tod filling out a form, remember? – he gives his mate with the cash-box the nod that the coast is clear. Matey gets out of the van and dashes into the post office while screamer box man remains on the pavement.

'When Mr Money-bags is in the post office I wait till he's right behind me, then, like any good citizen on lawful business I slip the TV licence form in my pocket – and turn and smash him on the chin. Eddie will sandwich him from the rear. We grab the money, send him flying, sprint for the car, dealing with the second postie in the same way we've dealt with his mate . . .'

'And ignoring the bleedin' wailing that'll be coming from his screamer box,' Eddie finished for him. 'And then it's up to you, Kel. No bleedin' cock-ups no matter what, understand?'

Kelly pushed her Afro mass of fiery waves and curls away from a face rosy with daring. 'You know your trouble, Eddie? You worry too much.' Giggles bubbled up from her throat. 'You boys had better fasten your seat-belts when you jump in the car. You'll be away so fast you'll think you're flying!'

Chapter Six

For Jackie, imprisoned in the circle of Johnny's arms, there was a brief second of stupefied disbelief and then his hair was coarse beneath her fingers, her tongue sliding past his; her certainty as to the utter rightness of what was happening, total.

Later – much later – he said unsteadily, 'I love you, Jax.' His voice against her ear was hoarse, raw with feeling; his arms still so tight around her she could feel the slamming of his heart. She could feel his erection, too, and her response was as unequivocal as her response to his kiss had been.

'I love you, too, Johnny.' Her words were breathless as, fitting her body as close against his as was humanly possible, she moved her head ever so slightly so that, once again, his mouth could passionately cover hers.

Later still, walking along Southend's crowded front, their arms around each other's waist, he said wryly, 'I used to think I was bleedin' peculiar, Jax, feeling the way I did about you, us being cousins and everything.'

She giggled, her head against his silk-shirted shoulder. She, too, had once thought that, though cousins could quite obviously love one another, they couldn't be *in* love with each other. Now she knew differently. She wondered what on earth Kelly was going to say when they told her. Even more importantly – what were her mum and dad and Aunty Lil and Uncle Albie going to say?

'They'll be tickled pink,' Johnny said when she voiced her thoughts. He flashed her a smile that sent her tummy tumbling into somersaults. 'How d'you think Pearl's goin' to take to me calling her Mum instead of Aunty?'

She gasped, losing her footing, almost falling.

'Hey, steady on love.' He was laughing as he helped her regain her balance, so happy his ticker was singing like a skylark. 'I didn't ask how she'd feel when our kids start calling her Grandma!'

She tried to speak and failed. Things were going so fast that her head was spinning. Marriage to Johnny? Marriage to a man half the women of south-east London would happily suicide themselves for? She was conscious of the pressure of his hand at her waist. No one, ever before, had held her in quite such a way. There was ownership in his fingers. Utter assurance.

He was looking down at her quizzically, his blond hair falling low over his forehead as it always did, his grey eyes very clear and light and violently alive.

Answering laughter bubbled up in her throat. Of course she was going to marry him. How could she *not* marry him? Johnny, living life straight, was all she'd ever wanted for as far back as she could remember. He *knew* her. She never had to pretend when she was with Johnny as she had to pretend when, first at school and now at college, she was not Jackie but Jacqueline. Even though the way he had lived his life, till now, was so very different from how she had lived hers, on a deep primitive level that was beyond her understanding she knew they were soul mates and that they were meant to be together. As for her other daydream, the one which centred on Raymond Pulfer, that was now merely dust in the wind. Reality was Johnny with his laughing eyes and sexy self-assurance. Johnny, who loved her so much he was prepared to change his way of life and marry her.

'And are there going to be many children?' she asked sunnily, knowing that, despite the crowds of people milling around them in front of the endless amusement arcades, he was going to kiss her again.

'As many as you want,' he said, and this time when he kissed her he held her in one arm, his free hand on the high full curve of her breast, his thumb caressing her nipple through the thin cotton of her ice-blue dress.

Dimly she heard an elderly female voice saying indignantly to a companion, 'What a disgraceful public exhibition!' and was uncaring.

She was happier than she'd ever been in her life before; so confounded by desire she could barely stand; so certain of her future happiness she would have staked her life on it.

'Get that woman out of the way! Go! Go! Go!'

The weary young woman in question, her Family Allowance book in her hand, had been too busy mulling over who she was going to pay with the inadequate amount of cash she was about to receive to take much notice of the only other customer in the post office, a young man filling out a form, or of the arrival, behind her, of a cash delivery man.

The milkman, knowing her old man had done a bunk, was dunning her for money and she was wondering whether to pay him up to date, fobbing off the television rent man and the Littlewoods agent. The kids could, after all, live without a telly – though she'd have a bleedin' hard time convincing them of it. As for the pain-in-the-neck Littlewoods agent, Marlon and Tracey had their school clothes on their backs now, so there was no sense in worrying about the fact she was already six weeks behind in her payments. There'd be Christmas in another few months, of course, and . . .

Kevin's terrifyingly swift movement as he spun around, shouting, frightened her so much she nearly lost control of her bladder.

'What's 'appening?' she shrieked as a vicious shove sent her reeling out of the way and Eddie and Kevin simultaneously attacked the cash delivery man, making it all too obvious what was happening. '*My kids are outside*! *Don't you 'urt my kids*!'.

Alarm bells were screeching, the half-concussed delivery man was sent sprawling into a display stand of UB40 leaflets, the postmaster – from behind the safety of his security-glass shielded counter – was shouting blue murder.

'*Go*!' Kevin was yelling again at Eddie, the cash-box in his grasp. '*Go*! *Go*! *Go*!'

The woman knew enough about bureaucracy to know that once the police arrived it'd be a case of 'no further business for the rest of the day'. Despite being winded by the force with which she'd been sent flying against the nearest wall she charged after Eddie and Kevin as they sprinted for the street, '*Not with my bleedin' Family Allowance, you don't*!' she yelled gamely. '*'Ow will I pay my milkie, you bastards*?'

'That fuckin' cow'll be able to pick us out blindfold in a line-up!' As Eddie hurtled into the waiting car he was wishing to God he'd had a gun on him so he could have shot the stupid bitch.

'But she won't.'

Even as he'd been racing for the car, with his free hand Kevin had been pulling three crumpled twenty-pound notes from his jeans pocket. Now, as Kelly screeched away from the kerb and Eddie fell back against the rear seat, Kevin leaned out of the front passenger window, tossing the notes in the Cortina's wake. 'Give the kids a good time on this, darlin'!' he shouted cheekily. 'Tell 'em it's Christmas!'

Through the driving mirror Kelly saw the running woman frantically grabbing at the fluttering notes.

'She's well happy,' she said with a grin, slicing across the road as they approached a main T-junction and swooping down it to the left.

'We've got trouble.' Eddie was far from happy. It got on his tits when Kev played at being bleedin' Robin Hood and now, just to put the gilt on the gingerbread, far behind them a bleedin' police car had sprung into view.

'Christ!' Kevin's good humour vanished. He didn't mind risking his neck for real gain but not for a piddling few thousand quid. Frantically he tried mentally recreating a map of the streets they were travelling. Johnny would have known them like the back of his hand – he always did. If he didn't, whatever the job, he didn't pull it. It was as simple as that.

'Left and left again, Kel,' he instructed tautly, wishing to God he'd never let Eddie talk him into such an unplanned job; wishing to God he'd never let Kelly talk her way in on it; above all, wishing Johnny, not Kelly, was at the wheel. 'We've got to lose them or gain enough distance to be able to dump the car!'

Kelly's eyes flicked to her driving mirror. Though the police car was still a hefty distance away and the traffic was heavy she, like Kevin and Eddie, was in no doubt at all that they were its quarry. Its blue light was flashing, its siren screaming, and it was slicing its way down the busy road behind them like a knife through butter.

'*For Christ's fuckin' sake move the fuckin' car*!' Eddie yelled at her, spittle forming at the corners of his mouth. '*You said you could drive the bleedin' thing, so bleedin' drive it*!'

Kelly *was* driving it. The needle on the speedometer flicked to seventy-five, to eighty, as the Cortina careened in and out of traffic, swinging across a petrol-tanker's path in a manner that had Eddie and Kevin pop-eyed and dry-mouthed.

'*For Christ's fuckin' sake . . .*' Eddie gasped as she screamed into a small left-hand turning and then left again.

Kevin was beyond speech. It was just possible . . . just . . . that Kelly was going to get them out of the trouble they were in. Then he heard the change of tone in the distant, screaming police siren. The police car had followed them left. They weren't going to make it – not unless they made a run for it.

'We're going to have to dump and leg it!' He already had his hand on the door handle. To stand any chance on foot with the cozzers so hard on their heels they'd have to leave the cash-box behind but it'd be better than going down for a stretch.

Instead of slamming on the brakes, Kelly burst out of the side road onto a dual carriageway, rubber squealing.

'For fuck's sake, Kel!' Eddie yelled, fast losing his edge. 'We need out of this car! We need out of it, *now*!'

'Sit tight.' There wasn't the slightest panic in Kelly's voice. 'I said I'd get us away and I'm going to get us away.'

The police car veered out of the side road behind them. It was gaining on them fast. So fast that even if they'd been in a street where they could have made a run for it, it would have been a nonoption.

'She's bleedin' barmy!' Eddie was hugging her headrest, so agitated he was nearly in the seat with her. 'She's taking us straight into Orpington High Street, Kev! There'll be another panda blasting up to the far end of it, closing us in, and even if we leg it they'll have us cornered within minutes!'

'Eddie's right, Kel . . .' Kevin began urgently, and then he saw what she had seen – the open gates of a pub yard and a Bass-Charrington delivery lorry lining up, about to back into it.

Pub yards nearly always had two entrances and the pub in question was bang close to the corner with the High Street. It was a safe bet that the second entrance would cut off the corner, leading not into the High Street but a back street and, if Kelly could nip into the pub yard before the delivery lorry backed into it, the lorry would then bar the way to the police car. The police car's driver would either have to wait for the Bass-Charrington lorry to re-emerge into the road, leaving the gateway again clear, or he would have to make a screaming detour into the High Street and out of it again. Either way, in the precious few minutes lost, Kelly would have them clear away to somewhere they could dump the car, separate, and leg it. The cash-box wouldn't be a glaring giveaway for it was already disguised by a launderette bag Kelly had filched from her mother. There was only one gigantic God Almighty snag. The pub was on the opposite side of the road and the traffic lanes were separated by a grassy central reservation.

'Hold tight.' Kelly knew that Eddie didn't have the advantage of a seat-belt and didn't care. He'd been pissing her off ever since the chase had begun. Kevin hadn't been yelling abuse at her so why should he? With a bit of luck he'd be right through the windscreen and on the bonnet before she brought the Cortina to a smoking standstill. Then, perhaps, he'd mind his manners a bit more when she next acted as his and Kevin's stoppo.

'*Kel, for Christ's sake!*' There was naked disbelief in Kevin's voice.

'I told you you'd think you were flying.' As cool as lake water Kelly was wheeling the car round, sending the Volkswagen that had been hard behind them, slewing to the left. Tyres screeched as other cars took evading action. Horns blared. Drivers shouted. The Cortina took the central reservation like a stallion at a gate; rocked across it; bounced down again on to tarmac. The cars that had been slowing down to veer around the nose of the Bass-Charrington lorry as it positioned itself to back into the delivery yard, accelerated like maniacs to get out of the way.

The lorry was about to reverse through the gates from the left; Kelly was approaching them from the right.

'*He's goin' to beat you to it! You can't make it, Kel!*'

The police car was still embroiled in the mayhem they'd occasioned on the other side of the central reservation. The Bass-Charrington driver, looking left in order to assess the amount of room he was going to have between his lorry and the gatepost, was still unaware of them – and of their near-suicidal intention.

'*You're goin' to kill us, you stupid bitch*!'

This time it was Eddie shouting at her. Kelly gritted her teeth as she braked to a screaming near-stop, slewing the Cortina round between the tail end of the still slowly reversing lorry, and the right-hand gatepost.

On the left-hand side of them wood scraped metal; on the right-hand side, metal scraped metal. There was the sound of breaking glass as both driving mirrors were simultaneously sent flying.

'*We're goin' to be bleedin' crushed to bleedin' death*!' Eddie was near-demented. The police car was no longer at a safe remove on the far side of the central reservation. Like the Cortina it, too, had rocked across it and, from the sound of its siren, was nearly on top of them. They certainly couldn't now escape its occupants by making a last-ditch run for it for they couldn't even open the car doors, not with the Cortina sandwiched between the six-foot-high gatepost and the rear right-hand corner of the delivery lorry.

Kelly swore, her knuckles white on the steering wheel, her foot hard on the accelerator. There was the sound of grinding metal, of a cacophony of shouting from both inside the car and outside of it and then the Cortina was free, shooting across the cobbled yard towards the mercifully open gates at its far side.

In a movement Kevin later recalled as being one of pure poetry, the Bass-Charrington lorry lurched backwards into the space they'd left and stalled, blocking the gateway completely. He, Eddie and Kelly couldn't see the panda scream to a halt, nor hear the police yelling at the lorry driver to move the hell out of it, but they knew exactly what was taking place behind them as Kelly torpedoed out of the pub yard into a maze of narrow back streets.

'Dump the car, Kel!' Kevin was euphoric. 'We're goin'

to have enough time to scatter and leg it. I'm going to head back to the High Street so I can hop a bus. Eddie, get out of that street-cleaning gear and quit the area without being too hasty about it. Mooch, don't run. Kelly –'

'Save your breath, Kev.' Kelly slewed the Cortina to a halt inside a church car park heavily screened by trees. 'We passed an old lady a second or so ago and I'm going to give her a bit of company. No matter how many police cars shoot past they won't be suspicious of a girl with her granny.'

As she was talking she was slamming her scraped and buckled car door behind her. The car was a wreck but it didn't matter. It was a ringer that couldn't possibly be traced to them and it had served its purpose.

From somewhere not too distant came the sound of police sirens. The hunt was still on and they weren't clear away yet.

'I'm off,' Eddie said tersely, dumping his street-cleaning gear on the Cortina's back seat and swinging a leather jacket over his shoulder, holding it by the thumb. 'See yer.'

Kelly crammed a disguising green velvet Baker's Boy beret over her flaming red hair. 'Where do we meet up, Kev?' she asked as Eddie began legging it down the street in the direction they had been going.

'The snooker hall.' He was hauling the heavy cash-box, in its laundry bag disguise, out of the car. Kelly had been amazing, absolutely ace, but precious seconds couldn't be wasted telling her so. 'Scoot,' he said, kicking the car door closed with his foot.

As the sound of the nearby police sirens intensified Kelly scooted. Not until she had caught up with the old lady did she look behind her. Considering the mammoth weight of his 'laundry', Kevin was making brisk progress towards the High Street and, hopefully, a Bermondsey-bound bus. She grinned. Never again would she assume that a man carrying laundry was a wimp.

* * *

93

'So I'm walking along with this oh-so-respectable old girl,' Kelly said in the snooker hall an hour and a half later, her voice filled with bubbling laughter, 'blue-rinsed hair and very lah-di-dah. There are police cars screaming everywhere. I'm shitting bricks in case Kev isn't clear away and what does the old love say?' She struck a suitably affronted pose, mimicking the old lady's refined accent to a T. "What an insufferable noise! The police should turn their sirens off when they're in a built-up area. Not to do so is really very inconsiderate, don't you agree, dear? Very inconsiderate indeed."'

Kevin and Johnny roared with laughter. Rosamund giggled. Even Eddie chuckled. The only person not vastly amused was Jackie. Johnny had his arm lover-like around her shoulders and so far, because all attention had been focused on the contents of the laundry bag and of how Kevin, Eddie and Kelly had made it back to base, no one had noticed the oddity of it.

Appalled as she was at Kevin and Eddie having taken Kelly on a raid with them she didn't intend making an issue of it. Not now. Now all she wanted was to revel in the knowledge of her new-found relationship with Johnny. There would be time enough later for rows with Eddie and Kevin – and with Kelly. She wondered when Johnny would break the news that they were going to be married. Their mutual happiness was so blazingly obvious it seemed incredible that no one had yet noticed it.

As if reading her thoughts Johnny squeezed her shoulder. She leaned even closer against him, smelling the light tangy fragrance of Eau Sauvage. Though Eddie and Kevin couldn't possibly be aware of it, finding a substitute for Johnny on the job they had just pulled had been spot-on, for they were soon going to have to find a permanent substitute for him. It wasn't going to be Kelly, though. Jackie didn't think even their dad would stand for that – and she was certain their Uncle Albie wouldn't.

'What are you having, Ros?' Kevin took out of his back pocket a roll of notes that would have choked a horse. 'The usual?'

Rosamund nodded. She was as much at home in the snooker club as Jackie and Kelly. Once, the conservative, middle-class way she dressed would have set her apart. Those days, however, had ended the morning she was accepted at RADA. Now, to her mother's despair and Raymond's scorn, her clothes were as outlandish as Kelly's – though not so flagrantly provocative. Only her perversity in wearing her fair hair as she had always done, shoulder-length and held away from her face with an Alice band, singled her out as being different – or did until she spoke. Despite her RADA training in class accents the instant she opened her mouth there was no mistaking her middle-class upbringing and public-school education.

'So when are we goin' to stop poncin' about on piddlin' raids and join a firm?' Eddie asked, as the youth who was always on hand to provide them with whatever tipple took their fancy, handed Rosamund the gin and bitter lemon Johnny had shouted for.

'Neither Johnny or me want to join a firm.' Kevin's voice was as unperturbed as his manner. 'We've got our own firm – or hadn't you noticed, Ed?'

'You call me, you, Johnny and three old lags a firm?' Eddie's contempt was blatant. 'I've bin acting as a breaker for a *real* firm – and they're interested in you and Johnny as well.' He didn't add that the mob he was running with wouldn't treat him with real prestige unless he brought some talent in with him – and Johnny and Kevin were certainly that.

It was a scenario Rosamund had listened to many times before and she closed her ears to it, concentrating instead solely on Kevin. He really was the most *masculine* – looking man imaginable. She'd been fifteen – just – when they'd first slept together. She'd never been his girlfriend, of course. His girlfriends were always sick-makingly glamorous and impossibly sexy. He'd kept coming back to her, though, a night here and a night there. And though weeks and months would go by when he barely seemed aware of her existence he never forgot about her completely. And he was never a bastard to her – not in the way he often was to his girlfriends.

'The best thing in life ain't women, it's money.'

It was Eddie, again. The conversation had obviously changed tack and lightened up.

'And the second best is spending it.' This time the speaker was Johnny.

There were gales of near-drunken laughter. It was always the same after a successful job; nervous tension released in frenetically high spirits.

The humour became more ribald and Rosamund ignored it, thinking again of Kevin – of Kevin naked and in bed with her. Never in her bed at home, of course – and never in his bed at number 26. He and Johnny had a spacious flat in a converted warehouse near Tower Hill. Neither of them lived in it, both preferring the tribal atmosphere of Creek Row, but it was where they stashed loot – and where they entertained a seemingly endless succession of very willing women.

She took a sip of her gin and bitter lemon, too deep in thought to taste it. That other women – uninhibited and experienced – so eagerly scrambled into the bed she scrambled into, turned her stomach. She wanted to be made love to on a bed that was exclusively theirs – a bed that held no other memories for him but those of her.

'I met him down a pub in the Old Kent,' Kevin was saying now, the conversation having obviously taken yet another turn.

She didn't know who he was talking about and wasn't curious. Curiosity was something a Creek Row woman, even an honorary one, never indulged in.

She thought about bed again. Christ, but she wanted to

be there! Not with just anyone, though. She'd tried that, with fellow students and even, once, a tutor, and it hadn't worked. The trouble with actors – even aspiring ones – was that they were too self-absorbed, too worried about their own performance and how *they* were doing, for them to be any real good in bed. If they were considerate, they were too considerate.

She didn't want to be treated like a lady in bed – not after the way she was used to being treated by Kevin. Any hint of polite uncertainty about what she might like, or not like, to do had her screaming up the wall. She wanted to be *taken*, thank you very much. It excited her to feel powerless and subjugated. When she had found someone who was suitably dominant with her – a Bruce Willis looka-like playing the part to the hilt – he had been utterly devoid of tenderness. And it was Kevin's ability to be both master-ful *and* unexpectedly tender that left her weak at the knees and begging for more.

'Are you having another whisky mac or a lemonade? Make up your friggin' mind, gel!' It was Johnny talking to Jackie, his voice thick with affection.

Rosamund liked Johnny. It was impossible not to. She sometimes thought that if Raymond knew Johnny even he would like him. She didn't like Eddie, though. Whereas Kevin's toughness excited her, Eddie's aura of sinister and barely suppressed brutality scared the living daylights out of her. Some women, however, were mesmerised by him.

She took another sip of her gin and bitter lemon, reflecting that those who were, never talked too much about what went on when they went to bed with him. Rumour had it, though, that they were always physically hurt – and in very nasty ways.

'And to provide her with everythin' a baby could want he even robbed Mothercare,' Kevin was saying, still talking about the bloke he had met in a pub down the Old Kent Road.

Everyone laughed, even Jackie. It was such a rare event for Jackie to be at the club – and for her to be seemingly uncaring whilst villainy was being discussed – that Rosamund tried to share the camaraderie of the moment by catching her eye.

She failed to do so because Jackie was looking radiantly up into Johnny's face as, her arm around his waist, his arm around her shoulders, he flashed her an intimate downslanting smile.

Rosamund's mouth rounded in a gasp of incredulity. She couldn't be seeing what she *was* seeing! It was Raymond Jackie had the hots for – it always had been, even though Raymond was too much of a snob for Jackie to have a hope in hell of ever landing him.

'Anyway, the job's up for grabs and I think we should do it,' Kevin was saying, the edge in his voice indicating he was now talking serious business. 'What do you reckon, Johnny? It'll mean being armed.'

There was a sudden tension that was palpable. Eddie was chewing the corner of his lip. Kelly was listening as intently as a cat, her head tilted slightly to one side. Johnny was now looking at Kevin, and Jackie had a totally new expression in her eyes as, sucking her breath in sharply, she urgently tried to regain eye contact with him.

'The rewards should be worth the risk – or they will be if you're utterly certain about the info.' Johnny's manner was easy and casual but everyone knew that the decision as to whether the job was on or off was down to him.

'I'm certain. What'll be needed is for you to –'

'You're wasting your time talking to Johnny, Kev.' Jackie's voice was oddly tight and high. Nervously she pushed a long smooth wave of shoulder-length hair away from her face. 'He won't be doing this job with you. You're going to have to find someone else.'

If she'd said Johnny was an alien about to fly back to Mars she couldn't have met with more incredulity.

For a stunned moment – a moment that seemed to last an eternity – no one spoke. No one was capable of speech. For a female to have made *any* interruption when a job was under discussion was unthinkable. That Jackie was the person doing the interrupting made the unthinkable completely unbelievable.

'I'm sorry, Jackie. I'm not with you.' Kevin had a hand raised silencingly towards Eddie, who was, he knew, about to explode. 'We're talking jobs, Jackie. If you don't like it, you'd better make yourself scarce.' He looked queryingly from her to Johnny, waiting for some kind of an explanation, realising for the first time how peculiarly close to each other they were standing.

Jackie slipped her hand into Johnny's, her pearl varnished nails digging deep into his sun-tanned flesh.

'Johnny won't be doing any more jobs with you, Kev.' Her voice was unsteady, fraught with nervousness. 'He's packing it in.'

Apart from Kelly's quick intake of breath there was a silence that could have been cut with a knife.

Kevin's eyes held Johnny's. He didn't know what the bleedin' hell was going on but he soon would – and he'd soon sort it. Eddie's eyes had a gleam in them that meant he was beginning to enjoy himself. Kelly was frowning. Rosamund was goggle-eyed.

Still Kevin waited for Johnny to put them all in the picture; still he didn't do so.

Jackie's nails dug even deeper into Johnny's flesh. 'You tell them, Johnny.'

To Rosamund, Jackie's voice sounded terrified. She looked terrified, too, as though she were on the verge of a precipice and might, at any moment, tumble into an unimaginable abyss.

Kevin, too, was aware that for a reason he couldn't fathom Jackie was on a knife-edge. He was also aware of what a stunning-looking couple they made. Johnny's hair

Nordically gold, Jackie's so black it had a blue sheen. Both were taller than average, Johnny broad-shouldered and lean-hipped, Jackie wand-slender. Their clothes, too, marked them out. Johnny had always been a posy dresser, shirts with his initials emblazoned on them, everything to match: socks, ties, shoes. Even now in casual gear his mauve silk shirt was unmistakably Italian; his white trousers French; his shoes genuine snakeskin. As for Jackie, he'd never known her not to look a million dollars – and she did so now in a pale blue dress that skimmed her body like a sheet of ice.

'Johnny?' Her eyes were fixed on his face, desperate with need.

'Well, Johnny?' Kevin asked as Johnny still didn't respond to her; didn't even meet her eyes but maintained eye contact with him. 'What gives, mate? Does Jackie know something we don't?'

Johnny lifted a shoulder in a barely perceptible shrug. 'She seems to know something *I* don't,' he said, his voice hard and queerly abrupt. 'As for whether we take hardwear on the job in question, Kev, the answer is yes. We need to be tooled up – otherwise we'll be sitting ducks.'

Jackie gave a strangled cry and for a moment Rosamund thought she was going to fall. Instead, breaking her hand-hold with Johnny, she stepped away from him and he turned his head towards her swiftly, a pulse throbbing at the corner of his jaw.

'You can't mean what you're saying!' To everyone present it was obvious that Jackie was over the edge of the abyss now, and falling. Her voice was strangled in her throat, raw with pain. 'Not after this afternoon! Not after everything you said!'

'I never said anything about packing up the business, love.' At last his eyes were holding hers. 'You forgot the old golden rule, Jax.' He paused and then said with gentleness so unexpected it sent shivers down Rosamund's spine.

'Never assume, Jax. It's always a mistake. It's always bloody fatal.'

'Oh God!' Jackie pressed a hand against her mouth, unable to tear her eyes from his. 'Oh Christ!'

He reached out to take hold of her again, saying, 'It doesn't have to be the end of everything, love.' There was such barely reined-in passion in his voice and such urgency Rosamund found herself wildly thinking about bed again.

'No.' Jackie moved abruptly backwards, freeing herself from his hand. 'No,' she said again and then, blinded by the tears she could no longer control she spun round and made a beeline for the door.

Johnny made no move to go after her. Instead he turned back towards Kevin as if nothing of much importance had happened, only the pulse throbbing at the corner of his jaw indicating the depth of his inner turmoil.

'I'm going after Jackie,' Rosamund said to Kevin, putting her empty glass down on the corner of the nearest snooker table.

'I'll get you another drink in for when you get back.'

As she hurried for the door leading to the stairs and the street, Rosamund knew that Kevin would be buying a stiff drink for himself as well – and that he badly needed it.

By the time she reached the crowded pavement Jackie was already a good distance away, her dress a distinctive flash of blue as she dodged between women laden with shopping, running like a hurt child in the direction of home.

Rosamund, too, broke into a run. How long had Johnny and Jackie been lovers? For that they were lovers she didn't have a second's doubt. She sprinted down the busy street only to find the gap between herself and Jackie widening as traffic lights, at a road Jackie had already crossed, changed infuriatingly to green.

Did Kelly know about Jackie and Johnny? She remembered Kelly's stunned intake of breath and doubted it. Not waiting any longer for the lights to turn to red she hared across the road, dodging an irate cyclist. Kevin hadn't known, that had been obvious. Panting for breath she rounded the corner into Creek Row just as a distraught Jackie raced into number 28.

Seconds later, aware that somewhere in the house a telephone was ringing she hurtled over the doorstep just in time to see Jackie pick up the phone, her face tear-ravaged, and to hear her say disorientatedly: 'Raymond? Sorry . . . what did you say? Yes . . . yes, I will, Raymond.' Painfully she gulped for breath. 'Yes, I'd love to. Eight o'clock in the Bar du Musée.'

Chapter Seven

'Tell me again about the info man,' Johnny said to Kevin. 'How can you be sure he'll keep shtumm?'

They were having their first real meet about the job and, as it was brass tacks time, there were no women present, not even Kelly.

Kevin, immaculately suited as always, was perched on the corner of their mother's kitchen table, one Gucci-booted foot on the linoleum-tiled floor, the other lightly swinging.

'He's Freddie Jessup's brother-in-law and he wants to play.'

Johnny grunted. Freddie Jessup was a small-time crim. It meant their informant had references – of a sort.

'Don't be a bleedin' old woman, Johnny.' Eddie was irritated, as usual. 'If we've got an armoured-van security guard who wants to play why bleedin' pussyfoot around wondering if he'll keep shtumm? He'll lose his whack if he doesn't. And what are the whacks going to work out at? What sort of money will it be carrying?'

Kevin pulled a saucer towards him and stubbed a cigarette out in it. 'A hundred to a hundred and fifty grand.'

Eddie's irritation vanished. He gave a wolfish grin. 'Sounds good to me, Kev-boy. How much opposition are we likely to get?'

'Not much this week or next. That's the beaut of it. It's holiday time and they're operating one man short. Usually it's two of them up front and one in the van. During the holiday period they're down to being two-handed – and both of them will be sitting up front.'

Johnny grunted again. Kevin was right. The job was too

good to turn down. 'We'd better have a meet with the guard, then,' he said, wondering where Jackie was; who she was with. 'If he comes across sensible, no nonsense, I'll recce it out, watch the van leave the depot, check the route. It might be a good idea to bring Uncle Jock in on it. He and Dad have been kicking their heels for weeks now and though Dad's too lazy these days to give a toss, Jock's restless.'

'I ain't working with Jock.' Eddie's good humour had vanished. 'He always behaves as if he's "the man", and he ain't. Not no more, he ain't. If there's three of us, and only two guards, what's the problem? 'Specially as one of the guards is in on a whack.'

'Because we're a family.' Johnny's voice was raw-edged and Kevin's eyebrows rose slightly. It wasn't like Johnny to lose his rag – especially over something and nothing. 'One for all and all for one. That's how it's always been, Ed. That's how it's always going to be.'

'You're fucking soft in the head!' Eddie had had it up to the eyeballs with Johnny. He was years younger than him and Kevin and yet he always came on like he was a 'face', just like Jock did. Trouble was, in their setup there wasn't an undisputed leader, and there should have been. He knew who it should be, as well, and it wasn't Kevin or Johnny, and it certainly wasn't Jock.

'And you're a fucking bozo, Eddie.' Johnny was pissed off with Eddie's mood-swings and unpredictability. Why the hell shouldn't they bring Jock in on jobs? Even though he was now getting on a bit he was still ace. Even he and Kevin weren't as nimble on their pins as Jock.

Usually when he had a go at Eddie he did so in tolerant laid-back amusement. This time, stung raw by his show-down with Jackie, it was different. He meant it and Eddie knew he meant it.

'I'm goin' to bleedin' do for you, Johnny-boy!' As he sprang for him a kitchen chair clattered over on its side and a milk bottle toppled.

Johnny had a whole lot of inner torment to give vent to – and he did so by going for Eddie no holds barred.

'Pack it in, you two!' Fists and feet were flying and as neither of them took a blind bit of notice of him Kevin found himself hoping to God Eddie hadn't a knife on him. It wasn't the first time, of course, that Johnny and Eddie had brawled. They'd all brawled with each other at one time or another. When they'd been kids it had been one of their favourite ways of passing time. This time, though, there'd been genuine goading in Johnny's voice and deep-seated fury in Eddie's response.

'For Christ's sake!' he shouted, trying to separate them as Johnny gave Eddie a whack that had him reeling, nose bleeding, against the sink. 'Give it a rest!'

Eddie had no intention of giving it a rest. Lunging forward he fisted Johnny hard and low in the groin. Johnny doubled up, rolling across the floor in agony. Eddie dived on top of him, blood from his nose spraying his clothes, Johnny's clothes, Kevin's clothes. An overfull swing-bin went flying, empty food tins rolling, potato peelings spilling.

It was Lily who put a stop to it all. '*Oi, you lot!*' she yelled, kicking open the kitchen door and walking in on the mayhem with a heavy bag of groceries in either hand. '*Fuckin' well turn it in!*'

Though Eddie had no time for his Uncle Jock who had, after all, merely married into the family, his respect for his dad's sisters was ingrained. Reluctantly he took his hands away from Johnny's throat. Johnny, much as he wanted to continue the fight, had no intention of doing so in front of his mother. Panting heavily, smeared with blood, the two six-footers hauled themselves to their feet.

'Just a friendly fight, Ma,' Kevin said, grateful it had come to an end without real damage having been done.

'Sorry, Aunty Lil.' Eddie, still short of breath, towered over her like a giant. 'Do yer want an 'and with yer shopping?'

'What? And get blood all over it?' Lily dumped her bags

down on the table. 'No I do not, Eddie Burns. Clear off so I can put my kitchen back to rights.'

Eddie threw Johnny a look that said they still had a score to settle and headed for the door.

An hour later, cleaned up and wearing a fresh change of clothes he was in an afternoon drinking club in Catford, being treated with suitable respect.

'It's goin' to be quite a big number, Eddie,' the heavily built man, sinister behind a pair of dark glasses, said wheezily. 'Some friends of ours, Sussex way, have just pulled off an extremely lucrative tickle. So lucrative we thought we'd muscle in on the action. They're a small firm – no heavies – but that's their mistake, ain't it?' There were sniggers of laughter from others in the room. 'The boys'll be with you, but it's goin' to be your show, Eddie. You can be trusted, know what I mean?'

Eddie knew perfectly. The firm in question were old hands – nearly as old as his dad and Albie and Jock. They were thieves, not heavy villains. In the old days no fellow crim would have parted them from their takings – 'Never steal from your own', that was the golden rule. But it wasn't the old days and rules were made to be broken.

After downing another couple of pints followed by brandy chasers, Eddie gave the nod that he was ready to hit the road. He was in fine form again, far happier amongst his present companions than when down at the snooker hall with Kevin and Johnny. Family. It got on his bleedin' wick. They thought they were so bleedin' clever, just because they were into safe-blowing and bank jobs and security-van raids. Yet how often did such jobs come up? And even if they did come up how many of them came to fruition? Bleedin' few, was the answer. Which was only to be expected the pernickety way Johnny-boy recced them out. It would be the same with the job now under discussion.

Within minutes of leaving the club, Eddie was leaning back comfortably against the leather rear seat of the Jag laid on for him as the driver – a *real* driver, not a crazed lunatic like Kel – sped the fully loaded car around the South Circular heading towards Croydon. Even though they'd been promised no real opposition, the security guard who'd brought them the job having guaranteed it, Johnny-boy would be sure to find a hiccup somewhere and then the job would be called off as so many others were.

The Jag plunged down an underpass in the centre of Croydon, emerged and surged onto the Brighton road. Despite the banter going on around him Eddie's thoughts were still full of Kevin and Johnny. They might get on his tits but they were family and no one ever heard him rubbish them. Why the hell couldn't they see the light and come in with the Catford mob? Heavy villainy was a piece of cake compared to the endless waiting and tedious planning that a bank job or security-van raid entailed. There was no busting a gut to find an insider willing to play. There was certainly no mind-bending long-term strategy, such as Kev and Johnny were into, placing people in likely companies and paying them a retainer until the time came when information they'd gleaned could be put to use.

For some reason he couldn't fathom it was the planning of jobs, more than the execution of them, that gave Johnny a buzz. He was like a friggin' wartime army major, plotting everything to the smallest detail, leaving nothing to chance. The commandos – that was the outfit that would have suited Johnny. As he thought of how Johnny would have looked in uniform he gave a mirthless chuckle. Christ. Johnny would be as happy as a pig in muck in a commando officer's uniform. It wouldn't surprise him if Johnny didn't already have one stowed away to dress up in on rainy days.

'It may take us a few days to get what we want,' one of his companions said, breaking in on his thoughts and tossing a cigarette butt out of the half-open front passenger window. 'The money'll be stashed. They won't be sitting right on top of it.'

'They'll put their hands on it quick enough.' There was hard certainty in Eddie's voice. He'd never failed to get what he wanted out of anyone yet. The trouble with most heavies was that there was always a point beyond which they were reluctant to go. He'd always been divvy in that respect – and why not? It was the fact he was prepared to go the limit that had given him his reputation. Only if someone was scared shitless did they give you whatever it was you wanted. If his dad had taught him nothing else in life, he'd taught him that.

He looked unseeingly out of the window at fields and small woods. Why it was so traditional to be either a thief or a gangster, but never both, was something he'd never been able to fathom. Surely his dad had been a bit of both? He certainly didn't remember Albie or Jock objecting too much when his dad had minded their backs for them. They'd been too bloody grateful! On the other hand, his dad had never gone in for extortion, or not that he knew of. The Krays and Richardsons had been the kings in his dad's heyday, yet his dad hadn't ventured north of the river to run with the Twins and to the best of his knowledge he hadn't run with Charlie and Eddie Richardson, either.

Surrounded by thugs that were *his* thugs, for 'the man' had made it crystal clear that this show was *his* show, Eddie grinned. If he'd been up and running when the Krays had been swindling, extorting, terrorising and murdering, *he'd* have been in with them. The Krays had been the business. He cracked his knuckles. He, too, was the business – as certain Brighton-based crims were about to find out.

'That's odd.' It was the next morning and Lily had just brought Kevin an early morning mug of tea. She was standing near the window, looking down through the nets to the street.

'What's odd?' Blearily Kevin pushed himself up against the pillows. He'd asked to be woken early because he'd arranged an early meet with Freddie Jessup's brother-in-law but it wasn't an experience he was enjoying.

'There are two men sitting outside in a taxi. The milkman seems to have changed and there are two dustmen sweeping the road . . .'

Wide-awake in an instant Kevin threw the bedclothes aside. As he did so there came the sound of the front door being stove in and before he had even grabbed hold of his trousers the bedroom door was rocking back on its hinges and ten policemen were crashing into the room.

'What the bleedin' hell . . . ?' he yelled in protest as he was leaped on from all sides and pinned back down on the bed.

'Don't move your arms, Rice, otherwise we'll blow your fuckin' head off!'

Lily was screaming and for once in her life it was in genuine terror. There was the sound of police cars screeching into the Row, sirens at full belt. More feet pounded the stairs. From the kitchen Albie could be heard shouting in useless protest. Flo and Pearl were in the street. 'If I had a pisspot I'd pour it over yer heads, yer cunts!'

That was his Aunty Flo. She'd always had a mouth on her like a navvy. Where the Christ was Johnny? As Kevin felt himself being cuffed and, still flat on his back, manhandled into his pants, he tried desperately to remember if Johnny had slept at home the previous night.

'You're heading for a line-up,' the officer in charge snapped with satisfaction as innumerable pairs of hands hauled Kevin from the bed and to his feet.

'Christ! What for? International terrorism? Assassinating the Queen Mum? Buggering the Pope?'

'Less of the bleedin' sarcasm, Rice.' The speaker emphasised his words with a kick to the back of Kevin's legs as, determined not to let go of him, fellow officers jostled Kevin down the stairs.

As Kevin made their task as difficult as possible his mind

was racing. He was being taken in for a line-up for the sub-post office job. It couldn't be anything else. Which meant Johnny was off the hook, but what about Eddie and Kelly?

'*Scum*! *Bastards*! *Filth*!'

This time it was his Aunty Pearl doing the shouting. As he was bundled into the police car he was grinning. The women in his family could certainly give the verbal. All except Jackie, of course. And Ros. At the thought of Ros his grin vanished. He didn't want Ros being told he'd been collared. After all, with a bit of luck he'd be home by the time the pubs opened. He ducked his head down, trying to see through a window half hidden by bulky coppers 'Pearl!' he bellowed, 'Don't –' and was hit so hard on the back of his neck he nearly choked.

'Don't know what I don't know,' Pearl said fraughtly to Rosamund the instant Rosamund, in response to a phone call from Kelly, walked over the threshold of number 28. 'Johnny's God knows where and Kelly's gone off trying to track him down. The filth were like bleedin' lunatics. You'd 'ave thought Kev was Frank Mitchell the way they went for 'im.'

Rosamund was trying to regulate her breathing but it wasn't easy. She knew very well who Frank Mitchell was or, more correctly, who he'd been. Nicknamed the 'Mad Axeman', way back in the sixties he'd escaped from Dartmoor and every police force in the country had been on his heels. They never found him because it was rumoured that the Krays, who had sprung him, murdered him when minding him became a nuisance.

The thought of Kevin being mentioned in the same breath as Mitchell and of his being man-handled as Mitchell might have been had her wanting to vomit.

Pearl, fretting over the utter certainty with which Kevin had been taken down for a line-up, was unaware of the unnecessary additional distress she was causing. 'Eddie ain't around either,' she said, wishing to God Johnny would show so that he could put her, Jock, Albie and Lil, in the picture. What the hell had Kevin done that had necessitated such a show of force by the rozzers? And he hadn't been charged. It hadn't been an arrest. Technically all Kevin was now doing was helping the police with their inquiries. 'Jackie's in the kitchen, all frigid disapproval. I could murder her. She's not a bleedin' bit of help at times like this. Never has been.'

Jackie. Rosamund's heart felt as if it was failing her. What would Pearl say if she knew Jackie had gone out on a date with Raymond last night? Even more to the point, what were Kevin and Kelly going to say? And Johnny?

'Are you 'aving a cup of tea or are you off to your acting doodah?'

RADA. She never broke time from classes. She loved being there far too much. She couldn't go in this morning, though. Not with Kevin facing a line-up at London Bridge nick.

'I'll have a cup of tea, Pearl.'

As she followed Pearl through into the kitchen she was well aware of the bizarre position she was in. Over the years her friendships with Kelly, Jackie, Johnny and Kevin had resulted in her being totally accepted by the Sweeting family. They trusted her. Even Jock had come to look on her as a near daughter, accepting that she'd keep her mouth shut and that she wasn't a danger. Yet she *wasn't* family – and it wasn't as if her actual family were merely what Jock called 'straight mugs'. With her long-dead father having been a deputy commissioner in the Met and her brother now a detective inspector her family was, in Creek Row eyes, most definitely 'enemy'. Would this incident with Kevin remind them that she wasn't really one of them? Would they suddenly start clamming up in front of her?

She clenched her hands fearfully, her nails digging into her palms. 'When are we likely to hear anything?' she asked as Pearl barged the kitchen door open. 'Will he be allowed to phone home after the line-up?'

Pearl gave a mirthless laugh. 'He will if nothing's bin pinned on him. Get your arse off that chair and make a cup of tea, Jackie, for the Lord's sake.'

Jackie's eyes met Rosamund's, so near to being expressionless that Rosamund felt a fresh stab of shock. It was as if something catastrophically profound had happened to Jackie; as if she were no longer quite the same person she'd been a couple of days ago.

As she sat down at the kitchen table Rosamund mentally corrected herself. It wasn't a couple of days ago that Jackie had undergone a deep inner change. The change had come about yesterday after the emotionally charged scene she'd had with Johnny in the snooker hall.

She still hadn't had a chance to talk to Kelly about the incident in the snooker hall – or about what had happened afterwards when she had run in on Jackie's phone conversation with Raymond.

'I'm off to college, Mum.' Jackie's voice was rinsed of all emotion as, having plugged the kettle in for the tea, she picked up her art portfolio. 'I'm going to be late but it's better than not going at all.'

'Well, with a bit of luck when you get in for your tea Kevin'll be back. Or he will if he ain't been charged with blowing up a jumbo jet or stealing the Crown Jewels.'

Jackie ignored her mother's bitter assumption that the police were going to fit Kevin up for something, no matter how ridiculous.

'I shan't be in for tea, Mum. I'm meeting a friend from college. We're going to the pictures.' There was tension in every line of her body. For one brief second her eyes again met Rosamund's and then the kitchen door was banging behind her and, seconds later, the front door.

'She's an unemotional little madam.' Not understanding her eldest daughter one little bit, Pearl heaved herself to her feet and opened the fridge, reaching for a bottle of milk. 'The least she could do is stay home till we hear whether Kevin's picked out or not. Poor Lil's in a right state. The filth were armed to the bleedin' teeth. She says if Kev had moved so much as a muscle they'd have had his bleedin' head off.'

With her elbows on the table Rosamund pressed her fingers to her mouth. Whether it was the thought of the police being armed or the certainty that Raymond was the 'friend' Jackie was meeting that evening that was making her feel so ill she didn't know. She only knew she felt so nervously frazzled it was all she could do to stop from shaking.

When had Raymond's attitude towards Jackie changed so drastically? He'd always been snobbishly contemptuous of the Sweetings. Not that he knew much about them. He certainly didn't know that Jock Sweeting was an old con – and neither, of course, did their mother. That Jock was an old navy man was a pretence Pearl had kept up all through the years she had 'done' for Lavender. If he and Jackie became an item he'd be bound to discover that the male members of her family were major criminals and *then* the fat would be in the fire. Raymond would take the attitude he'd been made a fool of and would make nailing the Sweeting clan a personal vendetta. She certainly wouldn't be able to continue her sexual relationship with Kevin – no matter how sporadically – not and remain living at home.

'It ain't like Johnny not to be around, either,' Pearl was saying as she plonked two mugs of steaming tea down on the table. 'Not when he's needed.'

Rosamund was barely listening to her. Not for the first time she was toiling with the problem of how long she could continue straddling two very different worlds. At home in Blackheath with her Blackheath friends and at RADA with her fellow students, she was Rosamund Pulfer;

middle-class, respectable, a law-abiding member of law-abiding society. In Creek Row she was Ros, the trusted friend of robbers and thieves; part and parcel of an anarchic, lawless world, uncaring of authority of any kind.

Her lawless world knew about her respectable world and, having decided long ago that she would always keep her mouth shut, was indifferent to it. Her respectable world, however, most certainly didn't know of her alternative lifestyle in Creek Row and, if it had known, would have been appalled.

She caught sight of her reflection in the mirror that hung above the table and corrected herself. Her straight friends wouldn't merely be appalled. They would cut her dead. It wouldn't matter that she, herself, wasn't a thief. By consorting with thieves she was condoning theft. It was enough to ensure complete and utter ostracism.

'Of course Kevin's a stupid prick for not staying at that flat of his if he knew the cozzers were on to him,' Pearl was saying confidingly, her hands around her mug of tea. 'I suppose that's where Johnny is at the moment. He'll have a new girlfriend, I expect.'

Rosamund made a noncommittal sound that could have meant anything. If Johnny did have a new girlfriend she was exceedingly new for she was absolutely sure that, until yesterday, Jackie had been the love interest in Johnny's life. It was interesting that neither Pearl nor Lily had cottoned on to the nature of the relationship that existed between their children but then, until the moment it had come to an end, she and Kelly hadn't tumbled to it either.

And now Jackie was seeking consolation with Raymond. Tingles prickled Rosamund's scalp as her thoughts came full circle. An affair between Raymond and Jackie would put an end to her own high-wire balancing act. She would have to decide once and for all which way she was going to fall – the straight world or the criminal world.

Her reflection stared back at her; hair just fair enough

not to be mousy, shiningly held away from her face with a plaited head-band. She wore a black miniskirt, a little tartan jacket and tartan tights. She looked every inch a normal nineteen-year old with normal middle-class values. Yet if she was ever pushed into making a choice she knew she would find it easier to live without respectability and the mausoleum-like tedium that, in her experience, went with it – than without the drama and excitement and adrenalin-charged highs that were part and parcel of life in Creek Row.

'And if Johnny's not with a girlfriend he's probably with Eddie,' Pearl continued, chewing the corner of her lip, 'which might mean that Eddie's laying low, keeping out of trouble.'

Eddie was far from keeping out of trouble. He'd gone down to Brighton, intent on establishing a reputation for being trouble – heavy-weather, nasty, vicious trouble – and was succeeding spectacularly.

'Quit trying to bluff it out, Lonnie,' he said in an almost bored voice. 'Your partner did that and he won't be working with you again – not for a long time – probably never.'

Seated in an armchair, in the living room of his council flat, sixty-five-year-old Lonnie Dyson was experiencing an urgent desire to evacuate his bowels. Twenty-four hours ago he and his long-term partner, Jimbo Porritt, had been sitting very happily on a couple of hundred thou in used notes, the ill-gotten gains of a very nice bit of peterman work.

Now, according to the graphic description given him by the gorilla seated opposite him, Jimbo was without a pot to piss in again – and as he'd been slow off the mark saying where his stash was hidden his backside was razored to ribbons. Of course, as he hadn't been with Jimbo when Burns and his henchmen had caught up with him he had no proof Jimbo had been striped but the sopping bloody rags Burns had dropped on the carpet a few moments ago were certainly proof that something nasty had been done to him.

'There ain't no dosh 'ere. I never keep nuffink 'ere.' His mouth was dry and he didn't like the way his chest was hurting him. A heart attack at his age could be curtains. He'd been a crim all his life and had never run into this sort of trouble before. Sure, there were always the chancers who, if word spread he'd had a successful tickle, would crawl out of the woodwork, spinning him a line about how some of the deed boxes he'd nicked had been their grandpa's or of how the money he'd lifted was their brother-in-law's stash. He'd always known they were liars, of course, and the liars had always known he'd known they were lying. A token amount handed over had kept them sweet. It was all part of the game. A skim here, a skim there, everyone happy.

What he was facing now was very different. What he was facing now wasn't an acceptable part of the game at all.

'Then tell us where you do keep it. You and me can have a nice little drink together while the boys go fetch it. Got some brandy in, have you? A nice drop of Rémy?'

Lonnie swallowed hard. The gorilla from the smoke had the most chilling eyes he'd ever seen. They were the palest blue imaginable; rinsed-out, washed-out, cold-as-ice blue. He thought of poor old Jimbo's striped arse and fought another urge to shit himself. How the hell had the south Londoners heard about his and Jimbo's lucky break? For the last ten years the two of them had hardly scooped anything over ten thou. This time it had been two hundred thou and they'd both seen it as pension money. He couldn't give up a pension just because of a threat of violence. If he stalled them he might be able to drum up some support from somewhere. Have a reception committee waiting for them when they made their return visit.

'There's no dosh 'ere,' he said again, blinking rapidly. 'But if it means so bleedin' much to you I could put my hands on it, given a day or two. I'm too old to tangle over this. I'll do you a seventy-thirty split. Seventy my way, thirty yours. What d'yer say?'

'I'd say you're a right little comedian, wouldn't you, boys?'

Eddie's audience, knowing what was coming, made amused noises of agreement.

'You're a right liberty-taker, do you know that, Lonnie?' Eddie was enjoying himself. He liked stringing things out a bit. 'And I don't like liberty-takers. I don't like them one little bit. So, for the last time, where can my pals put their hands on this little stash of yours? Five hundred thou you and Jimbo got away with, didn't you? Or was it six hundred?'

'Christ All-bleedin'-Mighty! It weren't nuffink like that!' Lonnie could feel himself beginning to shake. What if he handed over his complete take and the bastard now tormenting him insisted he was being short-changed?

'Will a little bit of electricity loosen your tongue, Lonnie?' Eddie's voice was all sweet reason. 'It usually does, know what I mean? Those sort of burn marks on your prick make a lasting impression.'

'You're bleedin' mental!' Lonnie's bitten-down nails dug deep into the moquette-covered arms of his easy chair. 'Who d'yer think you bleedin' are? Ronnie bleedin' Kray?'

Eddie grinned. It was the first intelligent assumption old Lonnie had made. He turned his head slightly, looking towards the sidekick who had held a screaming Jimbo Porritt down for Eddie as he'd razored him. 'I think it's time we plugged the little old magic box in, don't you? We can't waste all day waiting for Granddad to see sense, can we?'

As the heavy in question unzipped the sports bag at his feet, removing a small black box spiked with electrical leads and with an ominous-looking handle, Lonnie lost the battle he'd been waging for well over twelve minutes. He shat himself.

'Phaugh! Yer dirty old bleeder!' Eddie's companion could stand a lot of things, blood and sick and even piss, but he couldn't stand the smell of shit – not when it was locked soft and steaming in someone's pants.

'I'll tell you where the dosh is! I'll tell you where it is!' As he was dragged from the easy chair and roped to a dining-chair Lonnie couldn't get the words out fast enough. What was the point of a pension if he wasn't alive to enjoy it? His heart was hammering so hard he was sure it was on the verge of packing up altogether – and what was that pain shooting down his left arm? Christ Almighty, but he had to put an end to this scene before it put an end to him. 'It's at my sister's!' Eddie's friends were tugging his shit-soiled pants down around his knees; were clamping steel electrodes onto the shrivelled worm that was his prick. 'She's landlady of the Duke of Edinburgh! I swear to God! On my mother's life! On –'

'Telephone her.' Eddie was thrusting a telephone towards him. 'Tell her you have a mate who's on his way to collect it. We don't want to have to go through this kind of hanky-panky with your sister, do we? How old is she? Fifty? Sixty?'

Lonnie was gasping for breath, his fingers scrabbling for the right numbers on the telephone. Vi would know the situation stank. What if she refused to play ball? What if . . . ? 'It's Lonnie! A mate's coming round for my dosh, Vi! Give it him, OK? *Don't fuckin' argue with me, Vi!* GIVE IT HIM!'

Confident that the money was as good as handed over Lonnie's last three words were echoed by Eddie. He had, after all, waited a long time to play with his new little toy, though Lonnie had been wrong in thinking he'd stolen the idea from Kray folklore. He hadn't. It had come from Eddie Richardson folklore. As he at last gave the word to give

Lonnie's prick the works, his own prick hardened like an iron bar. Lonnie's scream of agony went on for a very pleasing length of time. He wondered if the length of time would be shorter with some people, longer with others.

'Get round to the Duke of Edinburgh,' he said to his audience as the blubbering stinking mess that was Lonnie Dyson slumped against the ropes binding him.

'Is he done for?' There was an edge of apprehension in the enquirer's voice. No one wanted to be facing a murder charge – not just for acting as errand boys. 'I thought you said the electricity wasn't enough to kill anyone?'

'It ain't.' Eddie nudged Lonnie's lifeless form with his foot, taking care not to get shit on the toe of his shoe. 'He must have had a heart attack. It happens when geezers get to his age. He's probably not bin takin' enough exercise.'

Even though he knew he now had a major problem on his hands Eddie couldn't help feeling pleased. He'd been hurting people for years but he'd never killed anyone before. Lonnie was a first.

'Roll up a carpet from somewhere and stuff him in it,' he said, aware that plans were going to have to be drastically changed. 'And get round the Duke of Edinburgh double-quick. We'll call on old Jimbo again on our way out of Brighton and we'll tell him his mate's slipped through our fingers – that his stash was collected for him and that he's done a bunk with it – and we'll make sure he's too scared to utter a peep of doubt. Then we'll steam back to the smoke and deliver our little carpet-wrapped parcel to a swimming baths I know of.'

'A swimming baths?' The stench in the small living room was becoming unbearable and everyone wanted out – and in more ways than one. What had been a straightforward skimming job had turned into what was potentially a very dangerous situation. Everyone had their hands stuffed very firmly in their pockets. Their clothes and shoes they could dump. The car was a ringer and would go straight to a breakers' yard. 'A *swimming bath*?' someone said again, certain now that Eddie really was a basket-case. 'We don't need to bleedin' drown him! The poor sod's dead already.'

'Swimming baths,' Eddie said, covering his mouth and nose with his handkerchief, 'have massive furnaces to heat the boilers. At least the old types do. Now are you going to stand gagging in this stink-hole all day or are you going to put some gloves on and do the necessary?'

There was something in Eddie's manner and in his tone of voice that brooked no argument. Besides, if he really did know of a swimming baths that had a crematorium-like furnace . . .

'Whatever you say, Eddie.' Like the old pros they were they began hunting for something waterproof to wrap Lonnie in, prior to rolling him in the carpet. A raincoat would be a help; a plastic coated wipe-down tablecloth would be even better; a shower curtain, or protective decorating-sheeting, would be even better still.

Eddie grinned. The trip hadn't gone to plan, but it hadn't been a failure, either. He hadn't lost his bottle over Lonnie's little accident. Word of it would spread and his reputation for being someone to seriously fear would be enhanced. Kevin and Johnny would have to start treating him with a lot more respect – and so would Jock.

At the thought of his uncle his prick began to harden again. Unless Jock Sweeting started giving him the necessary respect he'd find himself wrapped in carpet Lonnie Dyson style. He wondered if the smoke from the swimming baths' furnace would be visible from Creek Row. He hoped so. It would add a nice touch to what he was beginning to think was a very good idea indeed.

Chapter Eight

It was crowded in the small wine bar but even so, to Raymond's intense satisfaction Jackie was turning all heads. Her dress was a narrow sheaf of black crepe with long arms and high neck, stopping just short of black suede shoes, her back revealed from neck to waist. Unlike the last time he had seen her, her shining black hair wasn't swept into a high knot, but was skimming her shoulders, held away from her face by two heavy ivory combs.

She looked a million dollars and he was fast realising she always did. He thought of the envious looks that would be cast his way if he were to escort her to the annual Met Police Ball or to any other police thrash where wives or girlfriends were standard requirement.

'You look more West End than Greenwich tonight, Jacqueline,' he said, handing her a glass of white wine, the expression in his eyes openly admiring. 'Shall we eat up town? Bertorelli's, perhaps? Or Kettners?'

'Bertorelli's would be nice.' Jackie had never heard of Bertorelli's before and was counting on the fact that no one she knew from Creek Row would have either and that they certainly wouldn't be likely to be dining there. Kettners, in Soho, she knew well. It was a large restaurant complete with a champagne bar and ever since Kevin had been in his late teens he had taken the entire family there every New Year's Day, his treat. Whether he went there at other times of the year she didn't know and neither, on this particular evening with Raymond as her escort, did she want to find out.

'Excuse me a moment while I give them a bell to see if

they have a table,' Raymond said, sliding off his barstool and to his feet. 'I'll ring for a cab as well. No sense in driving up town and then not being able to drink.'

Jackie smiled agreement, hoping her momentary surprise hadn't shown. Kevin and Johnny would never have made such a remark and neither would any of their friends. They cabbed it around town a lot, of course, when blind drunk, and they also cabbed it when they didn't want to give the rozzers the opportunity of pulling them in on the excuse of their having committed a minor motoring offence. To admit to taking a cab so as not to run the risk of driving when above the drink-driving limit was, however, something she'd never heard anyone do before.

As Raymond began pushing his way through the crush towards the public telephone located at the rear of the wine bar she was aware of a most peculiar sensation. In the 'them-and-us' situation with which she'd grown up she had yearned, for as long she could remember, to be one of 'them'; to be part of respectable society. Now, in Raymond's company, she felt for the first time that she was finally making that transition.

For the last twenty-four hours, ever since the agonised moment in the snooker hall when she had realised that Johnny was never going to go straight, not even for her, she had been locked into a world of almost unbearable emotional pain. Now a shaft of comfort was piercing that pain. She had been true to herself; true to her principles; and now in a totally unlooked-for way it was as if she was somehow being rewarded.

Raymond Pulfer was seeing her in a completely new light. He didn't merely fancy her. If the expression in his eyes a moment or so ago had been anything to go by he was falling for her in a big way. If he truly began to love her . . . wanted to marry her . . .

Her fingers were so tight around the stem of her wineglass it was a miracle it didn't snap in half. She didn't feel for him what she felt for Johnny – but then she didn't want to. She didn't want the pain that came with such emotion. Her feelings for Johnny weren't logical or sensible and, most of all, they weren't safe – and it was safety she craved.

Respectability and safety. The words were, surely, synonymous? In a safe secure world she would be able to love properly. Raymond, with his middle-class upbringing, public-school education and his career within the Metropolitan Police Force, was respectability personified. With Raymond she would be safe and, owing him everything, she knew that if she were given the chance she would love him with total commitment.

She'd been so deep in thought she'd barely been aware of the noise level in the narrow, crowded wine bar. Packed to capacity, people were still trying to squeeze in, even though it was now standing room only.

'Shoulder your way through,' a vaguely familiar voice said tersely to his companion. 'Christ knows why there's such a crush when all they serve is bleedin' vino.'

Jackie turned her head sharply, her hair swinging. The heavily built speaker and his burly companion were mates of Johnny and Kevin's. Every so often, when a job needed it, they would supply Johnny and Kevin with extra muscle.

'Where are the birds, then?' Her cousins' companion-in-crime was now saying. 'Ain't they soddin' well here yet?'

Jackie was no longer looking towards them. The instant she had recognised them, knowing that they would almost certainly recognise her, she had swivelled round on her barstool so that her back was towards them.

'Please don't let them see me!' she prayed in silent fervour. 'Please don't let them squeeze in at the bar next to me. Please don't . . .'

'Sorry I took so long.' Raymond, having pushed his way back through the crush, was at her elbow. 'We've a table booked for eight. Do you want another drink here or shall we get a cab and have the next drink up town?'

Jackie could sense Johnny and Kevin's mates behind her only feet away. If she were to step down from her barstool now and turn ... The thought of the kind of greeting she might meet with made her feel physically sick. Raymond was a rozzer and he wasn't a fool. He would recognise the two young men for what they were, local criminals, and once he knew she was even on nodding terms with them that would be the end of their budding romance. No more respectability. No more safety. No more anything.

'I ...'

'We'll go. It's so crowded in here you can hardly breathe.'

Decisively he put a hand beneath her elbow. Without looking foolish there was nothing she could do but slide off the barstool and stand beside him. He was very tall. She hadn't realised before just how tall. He didn't have the blatant muscularity of Johnny or Kevin, though, or of Johnny and Kevin's friends, now only inches away. What he had instead was an air of unmistakable authority.

'Excuse me,' she heard him say as, still holding her protectively by the elbow, he began to forge a way through towards the door.

Her head was down as if she was trying to see the floor, her hair curtaining her face.

'Well, bleedin' 'ell, if it ain't one of our favourite rozzers!' the hatefully familiar voice now said sarcastically. 'Evenin', Detective Inspector Pulfer. Havin' a nice night out, are yer?'

Raymond had no intention of getting into an undignified verbal exchange. He'd got the scumbag's number and he'd do for him one day. The knowledge enabled him to grit his teeth and, saying nothing, to continue making for the door.

Jackie, her head still down, her face shielded by her hair, was aware of derisive laughter following them and then, seconds later, of a merciful breeze of fresh air as they stepped out of the wine bar door and onto the pavement.

'Sorry about that,' he said sincerely, tucking her hand

in the crook of his arm. 'If I'd known types like that frequented the Bar du Musée I'd never have taken you in
there.'

'It's all right.' Her relief was so vast her legs felt wobbly.

He shot her a wry smile as they began walking in the
direction of the nearest taxi rank. 'They were villains,' he
said, aware that she hadn't asked but putting her in the
picture anyway. 'Nasty ones. It isn't an expression I use
lightly but that kind of human garbage is the scum of the
earth.'

She stumbled slightly and his arm shot around her shoulders as he steadied her.

'Careful. I don't want to have to carry you into
Bertorelli's.'

His voice was lightly joking but there was a very different
expression in his eyes as, looking down at her and coming
to a standstill, his arm remained around her shoulders.

The breath was tight in Jackie's chest. He was going to
kiss her. She just knew he was going to kiss her. It was a
situation she had daydreamed about when she had been a
schoolgirl. Now, however, coming so soon after the earth-
rocking experience of being kissed by Johnny, she felt only
panic. It was too soon. They were in a public street and it
wasn't even dark.

'I think perhaps . . .' she began hesitantly, her panic
growing.

He wasn't listening to her. He had turned fully towards
her, looking down at her. The satin-dark fall of her hair
was brushing his wrist and an impulse of sensuality was
going up like a flare inside him. There was a restraint about
Jacqueline Sweeting that he found profoundly erotic. Like
her namesake, Jacqueline Kennedy Onassis, there was an
intriguingly cool quality to her dark beauty and, also like
Jacqueline Kennedy Onassis, she possessed a sense of style
that was uniquely and very, very elegantly, her own. No
one, in a million years, would ever guess how nauseatingly

common her mother and sister were or that she'd been born and brought up in the back streets of Bermondsey.

'I think you're incredible,' he said truthfully, his words cutting across hers and then, uncaring of pedestrians and traffic he drew her even closer towards him and, bending his head to hers, kissed her deeply in the mouth.

Jackie's first reaction was one of resistance. It was a reaction she quickly stifled. There was nothing fumbling or inept about Raymond's kiss. His mouth was warm and dry and as his tongue slipped past hers she responded instinctively to his self-assurance, the words 'respectability' and 'safety' beating in her ears like waves on a beach.

Even as her arms slid up and round his neck, and as she shut her eyes, she knew that there would have to be a day of confession. She couldn't marry Raymond – and with all the intuition of a full-blown psychic she was certain she would one day marry him – without putting him in the picture about her father's her uncles' and her cousins' criminal records. But that wasn't something she had to think about now; not when they were going up town on their first proper date; not when she was feeling so very, very respectable and so very, very safe.

'God, but I'd loved to have seen the rozzers' faces when their prime witness walked down the line-up straight past Kevin and picked out one of their own!'

Kelly was perched on the end of Jackie's bed, a towel wrapped turban-style around her freshly shampooed hair, an old T-shirt serving for a nightdress.

'Kev says it was all the woman could do not to give him a wink. I bet she had a right old shopping spree with the notes he dropped her.'

'What notes?' Jackie was sitting up in bed, her hair brushed sleekly away from her face and held in the nape of her neck by a narrow ribbon; her pyjamas Marks and Spencer ivory polyester. 'How could Kev possibly have nobbled a line-up witness?' It wasn't a conversation she particularly wanted to pursue but late-night gossip between herself and Kelly was an ingrained habit. 'He didn't even know a line-up was on the cards, did he?'

Kelly hugged her knees and gurgled with laughter. 'No, but he'd taken precautions. When we zipped away from the PO she ran out into the street after us and he threw her three twenties.'

'She was bloody lucky no one saw.' There was no amusement in Jackie's voice and there was certainly no admiration. It wasn't that she would have wanted the woman to have picked Kevin out – not in a million years. She wasn't going to applaud Kevin's action, though. It would be tantamount to being approving not only of the bribe but of the robbery as well.

Kelly was used to Jackie's frozen-faced disapproval when funny stories about jobs were being told and it didn't detract from her own amusement one little bit.

'The station sergeant was spitting bullets at having to release Kev. He told him he knew he was as guilty as a fox caught in a chicken run with feathers up his arse.' She was giggling so much she could hardly speak. 'Poor sods,' she managed at last. 'You have to feel sorry for the rozzers sometimes, don't you? Kev sprang so suddenly on the bloke he chinned that the geezer never got a good look at him and apparently the sub-postmaster is so short-sighted he wouldn't be able to recognise his mother unless she had an identity card. The woman collecting her Family Allowance was their only hope.'

'What has Dad said about you acting as Kevin and Smiler's wheelman? Has he given you a bollocking over it?'

Jackie was hoping desperately that the answer was going to be yes. Her shock when she had learned of Kelly's involvement in the post office robbery had been profound and it had only been because her showdown with Johnny had come so hard on its heels that she hadn't, as yet, had a blazing scene with Kelly over it herself.

Kelly tilted her towel-turbanned head slightly, looking at Jackie with an expression in her eyes Jackie couldn't for the life of her make out. 'You really don't know an awful lot about Dad, Jackie, do you?' she said at last. 'It's as if you're always hoping that one day he's going to go straight; that he really isn't so very crooked after all; that he only thieves because his childhood in the Gorbals was so bloody awful that if he hadn't he'd never have had a rag to his back.'

'Dad's childhood *was* bloody awful.' Jackie pushed herself up against the pillows, the book she had been reading when Kelly had waltzed in from the bathroom and disturbed her, slipping off the bed on to the floor. 'His dad was an alcoholic, his mother was a prostitute –'

'Which is something to remember when you're swanning round St Martin's being called Jacqueline,' Kelly interrupted drily. 'The point is, Jackie, none of that really matters, not to Dad. He thieves because he likes easy money and thrives on excitement. He likes to feel the old adrenalin surging through his veins. It makes him feel alive. He's an anarchic- whatever you call it. An anarchist. He doesn't like law and order. He finds it boring. He likes outwitting people, especially pompous prats in authority, like rozzers. He likes the sensation of being a member of something totally way-out; a closed society; an exclusive club with its own rules and own traditions. No chickens. Above all, no grasses.'

She paused for a moment, knowing she was truly shocking her sister and knowing she was going to shock her even further. 'Telling him I was with Kevin and Smiler on the post office job was no big deal at all, Jackie. If I'm an ace wheelman it's because Dad taught me to be one. And he did it on live jobs, too.'

Jackie sucked in her breath, tried to speak and failed.

'Sorry, Jackie.' Kelly pulled the towel from her hair. 'But you asked for it, you really did.'

She stood up and crossed to her own bed. Her hair was so dry it didn't need blow-drying. All it needed was combing through.

'And while we're having such a brutal heart-to-heart – what's been going on between you and Johnny?' She climbed into bed and picked up a comb from her bedside table. 'It was quite some scene in the snooker hall. Real Scarlett and Rhett stuff.'

'Nothing's going on between me and Johnny.' It was a struggle for Jackie to speak and she only just managed it. Kelly was only seventeen and yet their father had allowed her to act as his wheelman. Worse. He had *taught* her to be his wheelman. Did their mother know? Kevin must have known or it wouldn't have occurred to him to take her on the post office job. Perhaps the whole family knew and she was the only one who had been in happy ignorance.

Kelly tapped her comb against her teeth. She loved Jackie to bits and she hadn't enjoyed the last few minutes, knowing she was shocking the socks off her. What she had said had, however, needed saying. Jackie playing at being 'Jacqueline' when they'd been kids had been one thing. Her doing it now, and her being ashamed of the family when she was in 'Jacqueline' mode, was quite another. She wondered if she should tell her of the rumours that were flying around concerning Eddie and decided against it. Jackie facing up to a little reality was one thing. Her being forced to face up to the fact that their cousin was divvy enough to electrocute people for fun was quite another.

She put her comb back on her bedside table, shaking her hair into its habitual Afro frizz. Something was going to have to be done about Eddie – the problem was, what? Kevin and Johnny were already beginning to distance themselves from him. She would have liked to have had a chat to both of them about it but Johnny had been keeping himself very much to himself ever since the snooker hall incident and Kevin, immediately on his release after the line-up, had buggered off to Devon with Ros.

She turned her bedside light off, settled her head against her satisfactorily pummelled pillows and closed her eyes.

'Kelly?'

Her eyes flew open against the darkness of the bedroom. She'd been so deep in thought about the problem that was Eddie that she'd almost forgotten about Jackie.

'Kelly. There's something I think you need to know.'

'If it's about you and Johnny tell me in the morning.' Now that she had begun thinking about Eddie and the rumours of what had happened at Brighton she couldn't get them out of her mind. Her dad had served time, years ago, for armed robbery but he'd never shot anyone. He and her Uncle Albie had carried shooters on bank jobs in order to instil fear and to make sure that no one was fool enough to try it on with them. He hadn't carried a gun with the intention of killing or maiming. He wasn't a man who indulged in violence for pleasure. What Eddie had done to the poor bleeder in Brighton would turn Jock's stomach – as it did hers.

'It isn't about me and Johnny.'

Kelly sighed. She wanted to get her head down and to get some sleep but it was obvious that until she'd humoured Jackie she wasn't going to be able to do so.

'Then what is it about?' Once again she was thinking of Eddie. Perhaps he wasn't just divvy. Perhaps he was a serious basket-case. A full-blown psycho.

'It's about me and Raymond.'

Kelly froze. If Jackie had failed to engage her attention before she had every particle of it now.

'I think he's in love with me – and if he is I'm going to go all the way with it.'

'You can't!' Kelly had shot into a sitting position. 'Christ Almighty, Jackie! He's a *copper*! Hell, he isn't even a *bent* copper! How can you shack up with a copper and still be in and out of this house? You can't. It isn't possible. You're either one of us or you're one of them. You can't be both.'

'Ros is.'

Though it was too dark for Kelly to see, Jackie's hands on top of her duvet were clenched tight, her nails digging deep into her palms.

Kelly felt such a surge of exasperation it was all she could do to prevent herself marching across to Jackie's bed and shaking the life out of her.

'It might have seemed like she was for a little while but it was only when she was a kid,' she said, wondering which scenario was worse: Eddie, crossing from thievery to the worst kind of gangsterism or Jackie marrying a copper and cutting herself off from them all. 'And even Ros has realised she has to come off the fence one way or another.'

Jackie turned her head against her pillow, looking towards the dark outline of Kelly's bed. 'What do you mean? Is she going to stop coming down to Creek Row? Is –'

'She's throwing her lot in with Kev.' It was no real surprise. Until now Kelly hadn't even thought it worth mentioning. 'Kev's finally begun treating her as a proper girlfriend. They're in Devon together. If you're still so brain-dead as to want your relationship with Raymond to continue you'd better have an urgent word with her. Once Lavender knows about Ros and Kevin, and just who and what Kevin is, she'll never speak to any of us ever again. As for Raymond . . .' She gave a mirthless laugh. 'Once DI Raymond Pulfer realises you're Jock Sweeting's daughter, and just who your uncles and your cousins are, you'll never see him for dust.'

She slid back down her pillows, pulling her duvet up to her chin.

''Night, Jackie,' she said, knowing she was being unkind and too vomit-makingly disgusted by the idea of Jackie in a close embrace with Raymond Pulfer to care. 'Pleasant dreams.'

Moonlight streamed through the half-open windows of the opulent hotel bedroom. The curtains were pulled back, and from a nearby bay there came the rhythmic muffled roar of waves chasing up a beach.

Rosamund lay within the circle of Kevin's arms, her cheek resting against his naked shoulder. She was euphoric; happier than she'd even been before in her life. From the moment Kevin had walked into number 28, after his release, something had changed between them. It was as if, seeing the anxiety etched on her face and the agonised concern in her eyes, he had realised how very deep her feelings for him were; had realised that, unlike the gangster groupies always so eager to share his bed and to be seen hanging on his arm, she loved him with total unselfishness and would always be there for him through the bad times as well as the good.

'I love you,' she said softly, her lips brushing his sun-tanned flesh.

In the moonlit darkness she saw a corner of his mouth crook into a smile.

'I know,' he said, feeling his sex stir even though it was barely an hour since they had last made love. His arms tightened around her. 'You're going to be spending more time with me from now on, Ros. If it causes problems for you at home you can always move in to number 26. Mum won't mind.'

The blood surged through her body like a hot tide. He was near as dammit asking her to move in with him. Not quite, though. He'd said number 26, not the Tower Bridge flat. Kevin, as always, was hedging his bets. She fought the disappointment. What he was offering was more than enough and was certainly more than he'd ever offered any-one else.

She slid her hand between his legs, savouring the hot heavy weight of him in her palm. For her, too, his being taken down for the line-up and subsequently being released had been a turning point. Seated with Pearl at the Sweetings' kitchen table, terrified he was going to be picked out and charged, she had realised once and for all where her loyalties lay. Criminal and womaniser though he was, she was unconditionally in love with Kevin. If he ever gave her the nod she would go to him no matter what the cost in heartache and sacrifice – and that there would be heartache and sacrifice she hadn't a minute's doubt.

In condoning Kevin's criminal way of life – in sharing it with him and living with him off the proceeds of it – she would make it impossible for her family to have any further contact with her.

Where Raymond was concerned the sacrifice would not be so very great for, unlike Kevin and Johnny, and Jackie and Kelly, she and Raymond had never been very close. As children they had attended boarding schools situated in different parts of the country and so had never seen much of one another and, when they had been together in vacation time, Raymond's innate superciliousness had always got up her nose.

Her mother, though, was a very different matter. Cutting herself off from her mother, especially now that her mother was suffering from disabling arthritis, was going to cause her a great deal of anguish – and it was anguish she wanted to postpone for as long as possible.

'I don't think there'll be any great problem at home, not for a while, anyway,' she said, feeling herself deliciously dampening again as he hardened in her hand. 'Ever since going to RADA I've occasionally stayed overnight with friends.'

She didn't add that the 'friends' had often been male. What Kevin didn't know couldn't hurt him and besides, those days were done with. She'd only experimented sexually elsewhere because it had seemed as if she was going to have to learn to live without him and she'd been desperate to find someone who would take her mind off him. She'd never succeeded, of course, and now there was no longer any need for her to try.

He rolled across her, pinioning her beneath him. 'You're a greedy little baggage, sweetheart, do you know that?' he said, his teasing voice thick with reawakened desire. 'You're like that little kid in Dickens. No matter how much you get you always want more.'

She giggled, or tried to. With his fingers touching the soft warm flesh of her breasts, the fever he always aroused in her rising higher and hotter, giggling didn't come easily. She wanted to moan; to cry out with primeval female longing. Instead, fighting to maintain control for just a few seconds longer, she managed a giggle. 'It wasn't sex Oliver Twist wanted more of, Kevin. It was porridge.'

Even though he had parted her legs and entered her, he cracked with laughter. 'Blimey, gel,' he said, resting his weight on one elbow and looking down at her with laughter-filled eyes. 'We don't want any of that, do we?'

'It wasn't porridge . . . as in serving a prison sentence.' Laughter and desire fought for supremacy. Her breath was coming in short gasps; her knees were high, the yearning to have him as deep inside her as possible, desperate. 'It was . . . the kind of porridge . . . you eat.'

Desire overrode amusement. He was moving within her, his hands on her breasts, his thumbs brushing her erect nipples. As his mouth burned hers, hot and hard, she was almost insensible with pleasure. For this man, she would do anything.

'Oh God, I love you,' she gasped hoarsely, only seconds away from a climax of cataclysmic intensity. 'Only you, for ever!'

His response was a deep groan of pleasure. With one hand wrapped tightly in her hair, the other kneading her breast, he slewed her across the bed in a tangle of sheets. Always a noisy lover, his groans were turning into shouts as, his face contorted with passion, he forged single-mindedly towards his third mind-blowing conclusion of the night. In perfect timing Rosamund gave a cry of ultimate female satisfaction, her nails raking his back, her legs wrapped around his waist.

The indignant hammering on the wall from the adjoining room was almost enough to bring the pictures down. Neither of them paid it the slightest attention. Sweaty and sticky and panting like beached fish they were vaguely surprised to find that they were no longer on the bed but the thickly carpeted floor.

'Champagne.' As Kevin eased his weight from off the top of her, Rosamund's voice was a croak. 'Is there any left?'

They'd drunk a bottle of Bolly earlier on in the evening and she doubted there would have been two bottles in the room's refrigerated drinks cabinet.

'I'll ring down for some. What's the point of paying these prices if we can't get twenty-four-hour room service?'

He stood up, wonderfully well-muscled, looking around in the moonlit darkness for the phone.

She heaved herself back onto the bed and reached for the bedside light. She was no longer just a major criminal's girlfriend. She was a fully fledged moll. A smile curved her mouth as the room was plunged into muted rose-tinted light. For her fellow students at RADA a moll was a dramatic part in a play by Damon Runyon. For her it was real life.

From out of nowhere came the thought that perhaps she should call it a day at RADA. Kevin obviously wanted her to spend a lot of time with him and, not being a man who kept regular working hours, that meant he wanted her with him at all hours of the day, especially when he was in one of the many afternoon drinking clubs he frequented. If she couldn't fit her present lifestyle conveniently around his he might start looking around for someone who could.

Kevin, too, was deep in thought as he rang room service. He'd always found Rosamund's fair-haired, middle-class and refined kind of beauty, sexually disturbing. When he'd first made love to her as far as he'd been concerned it had been no very big deal but her friendship with Kelly and Jackie meant that she was always around and, over the years, not only had he intermittently kept going back for more but the two of them had become friends.

It was the friendship bit that had always made his relationship with her different to his other sexual relationships – that and the fact that she came from a police background.

Although he liked Ros a lot, Johnny had warned him not to get seriously involved with her many times, as had his dad and Jock.

'Nice kid though she is, when it comes down tae it, she belongs tae the other side,' Jock had said grimly. 'She might hae proved herself capable of keeping her trap shut but she dinna' know the real rules – how can she? Women only really understand 'em if somewhere along the line a family member, dad or granddad or an uncle or a brother, has been in the nick. Then they know about the waiting and they accept it when it's their turn tae to be doing it. Not only hasna' Ros a clue about the nick – her family are dyed-in-the-wool filth. I canna' exactly see you rubbing shoulders with DI Pulfer at family thrashes, can you?'

The answer had been, of course, that he couldn't.

He'd realised, though, when he'd walked into his Aunty Pearl's kitchen after being released from London Bridge nick, that it wasn't a problem he would ever have. Ros wouldn't try and split herself down the middle. She wouldn't continue trying to keep a foot in both camps. If he wanted her – really wanted her – then she'd be his and she'd be loyal to him one hundred per cent.

'Come *on*,' he said irritably into the telephone receiver as it continued to ring at the other end. 'Answer the bleedin' phone, for Christ's sake.'

Lying on the bed, still naked, Ros giggled. Kevin was always so in command of every situation that seeing him rattled by his inability to get hold of a bottle of champers as quickly as he would like amused her no end.

He had the grace to grin. Despite his knock-this-chip-off-my-shoulder-if-you-can attitude, he was generally very even-tempered – especially so with women and most especially with Ros. He remembered the sensation when they had been making love and his spunk had shot out of him. It had felt like hot gold. His grin deepened. It was a metaphor he liked, for gold was very much on his mind – and not just any gold.

After months and months of making the right sort of contacts he was privy to a major heist that was just the kind of heist he and Johnny hoped to put together for themselves one day. He wasn't one of the main team. Even with his reputation the crowd he had gained contact with regarded him as little more than a labourer. Being a labourer would, however, serve his purpose. If he and Johnny were ever to pull a mammoth bullion job they had to have all the necessary contacts when it came to melting the gold down and disposing of it. The team he was proving himself useful to at the moment were just such men.

'A bottle of Veuve Clicquot in room 12, please,' he said tersely when someone finally answered the phone.

The heist was so major, security about it so tight, he hadn't even breathed a word to Johnny. Even just thinking about it sent shivers down his spine.

'Make that two bottles of Veuve Clicquot,' he said, rolling the name of the company to be heisted around in his brain.

Brinks-Mat. He couldn't wait.

Chapter Nine

Kelly surveyed the Harley Davidson with pride. It was a late seventeenth birthday present to herself, paid for out of her whack from the sub-post office job. What she loved most about the bike, apart from its speed, was the gear needed in order to ride it: tight-fitting black leather trousers, black leather bomber jacket and spaceman-like crash helmet complete with smoke-tinted visor.

The visor, especially, appealed to her. In the right sort of circumstances it would be just as disguising as a stocking mask or a balaclava – and far less attention arousing.

'I'll be able to act as a lookout and be totally unrecognisable,' she had said gleefully to her dad. 'I'll simply be taken as being a motorbike messenger – especially if I lean against the bike and pretend to be studying a clipboard. No one will give me a second glance – and if they do they'll certainly never be able to recognise me.'

Jock nodded. He liked the way his younger daughter's brain worked. No matter what the circumstances she always had an eye for the main chance – and she was ballsy with it. She'd proved that when she'd got Eddie and Kevin out of trouble during the sub-post office raid.

'It'll be guid cover for a lookout,' he agreed, nursing a pint-sized mug of steaming tea heavily laced with condensed milk. 'You could use the visor to signal with. Up for a problem. Down for all clear. The only thing is, you canna' be both lookout and wheelman, which means that unless Johnny is going to grace us with a bit of his time we'll have tae bring someone else in.'

Kelly, who had been perched on the arm of an easy

chair, slid down sideways and backwards into it, the abrupt movement sending her dozen or so Indian-style bangles rattling and jangling.

Johnny and Kevin. For the first time ever both of them were being uncooperative about pulling a big family job. Kevin had other irons in the fire – though just what, no one, not even Johnny, seemed to know.

As for Johnny . . . Kelly sent her bangles skittering again as with her trousered legs hooked over the arm of the chair she tugged a glitzy black string vest down over her black half-cup bra. Johnny seemed intent on nothing else but laying as many women a day as there were hours in it. If the last couple of girls she'd seen him with were anything to go by he was definitely becoming a quantity, not quality, man.

What Jackie thought about this new phase in Johnny's sex life no one knew. No one, not her mother, not Rosamund, not Kelly, could get her to talk about him. Equally aggravating was Johnny's utter refusal to cast any light on what had been going on between them, either.

'It's none of your business Kel,' he had said in a hard, abrupt voice when she'd asked.

She had known better than to persist – which meant she was still wondering. Whatever had gone on between Johnny and Jackie, and then gone wrong, it had obviously cut Johnny very deep. For the first time ever he wasn't interested in organising a job, which meant if there was to be a decent job, she and her dad were going to have to organise it.

She ran a hand through her spicy-red Afro frizz. The sub-post office job had been a near-unorganised, spur-of-the-moment heist that hadn't been worthy of them. Certainly Johnny, if he had been around that day, wouldn't have sanctioned it. It had been far too careless, involving too much risk for too small a reward. If she and her dad were going to organise a job for themselves and Albie and

Smiler to pull, then it needed to be a decent job. Something worth the risk involved. Something that would give her dad increased respect amongst fellow crims.

'Is there anything worth following up on the fifth-column grapevine?' she asked, chewing the corner of her lip.

The fifth-column grapevine was the intelligence service provided by dishonest men in responsible employment without whom not many heists, of real value, would ever be carried out. The cultivation of this grapevine was something Jock always put immense time and effort into, as did Kevin and Johnny. Some jobs brought to their notice were too risky even to try; others were clocked as 'possibilities' and put in the diary for consideration.

'The Isle of Wight-tae-Portsmouth caper is still on the back burner,' Jock said musingly, 'but it's a biggie. We'd probably need outside help even if Kevin and Johnny were in on it wi' us.'

Kelly noticed her dad didn't include Eddie as being a possible member of the team.

'All the collective money from post offices on the Isle of Wight is shipped over tae Portsmouth every Saturday for delivery tae the main sorting office. The ferry terminal platform and the train station platform run into one another and my info is that the waiting delivery van is always parked in one of the train station's loading bays. The money parcels will be neat and tidy and, if we make the hit at a holiday time when the platforms will be packed with people off tae the Isle of Wight, there's a very guid chance of us diverting it. The way I've always seen it is tae have a van reversing up next to the PO van and, despite the screamer boxers, tae simply go for it mob-handed.'

Kelly giggled. Her dad always made everything sound so simple which, because he had so much bottle and never panicked, no matter how perilous the situation, things often were.

'There's another tip-off I've always meant to follow up,'

Jock continued, warming to his theme. 'A postal worker at Mount Pleasant swears blind that one of his regular trips as a van driver is a five a.m. run tae pick up old mailbags which are always on the station platform cheek by jowl with Midland Bank pouches. He says it'd be easy-peasy, if we commandeered his van, for us tae collect the Midland stuff instead. Not being on a money run the Post Office van wouldna' be armoured or laden with alarms and so wouldna' be hard to hijack. The Midland security wouldna' be put on the alert by the sight of the PO van – not when it's at the station the same time they are, regular. All it needs tae carry it out is a lot of front – providing the snout's information still holds guid, of course.'

'Let's set up a meet with him and recheck it all out.' Kelly was itching for some action and was beginning to realise why Eddie got so impatient with jobs that necessitated a lot of painstaking preplanning. 'And in the meantime why don't we do something that's quick to set up? A small wages snatch or lifting takings about to be banked? Betting shops must bank loads of cash at a time and they don't have the benefit of armoured vans or lots of security backup. Why don't I recce one out north of the river? I can go over there on the bike. It shouldn't take more than a few trips to get to know how often and when and where they bank.'

Jock gave a cracked-tooth grin. He and Albie hadn't pulled such a stunt in years. There was no need for Smiler to come in on it with them, though he'd see to it Smiler got a percentage of whatever they got away with. Within the family that was the system. Smiler did the same with them if he did a job without them. Overall, things worked out pretty evenly.

'You may find they don't bank everything,' he said musingly. 'Pools money, for instance. If they handle pools money they'll only be acting as the middleman. They willna' be banking it themselves.'

Kelly sprang from the easy chair, eager to change into her biking gear and to be on the move. 'Whatever they do with it there'll be a weak link in the chain somewhere. You don't fancy coming with me, Dad, do you? I've never had anyone riding pillion.'

Jock's grin nearly split his leathery face. 'And you're no starting wi' me. Be on your way, but be careful, mind. Dinna' come tae anyone's attention.'

She came to Dexter Howe's attention almost immediately. A woman who had worked in the High Street betting shop as a cleaner, and who had been fired for bad timekeeping, had tipped him that it was an easy touch. She didn't want a percentage of anything that came of her tip-off because she was, she had explained, 'as honest as the day was long'. All she wanted was a little sweet revenge.

Parked up in a ringer, twenty yards or so further down the road from the shop, Dexter grinned. The little old 'honest' dear had told him that her boss delivered to the bank at 10.30 a.m. every Monday, regular as clockwork. 'Stupid old sod just parks the cash bag on the floor beneath the front passenger seat,' she had said contemptuously. 'It's only a quarter of a mile down the road to the bank so I s'pose he thinks he's safely there before he even sets off.'

After staking out the shop for two Monday mornings running Dexter had come to the conclusion that the disgruntled cleaning lady was right. The betting shop manager was a stupid old sod and his takings were begging to be lifted. The road on which both the shop and the bank were situated was a busy one. As far as Dexter was concerned that was all to the good. There were three sets of traffic lights. To Dexter each set represented an opportunity for a lift. The only bit of vital preparatory work necessary was the sabotaging of the front passenger door lock and that little bit of mechanical handiwork he'd carry out in the early hours of next Monday morning.

His eyes narrowed as he continued to watch the motorcycle messenger. Had his little old dear been spilling her info into other ears besides his? To his practised eyes it certainly looked as if the motorcycle messenger was doing a bit of what he was doing himself – checking up on the timing and regularity of the betting shop manager's trips to the bank. His suspicion was edged with doubt, though, for the messenger's slim suppleness and feminine way of moving indicated he was gay – and gays didn't generally go in for jobs where a bit of hard aggro might be called for.

Ten thirty. As precisely on time as if on an army manoeuvre, the betting shop manager strode out of his doorway and across the pavement to his car, a Mk II Cortina. Walking round to the driver's door he opened it, lobbed the modest-sized bag he was carrying into the well of the front passenger seat, and turned his key in the ignition, gunning the engine into life.

Dexter grinned with satisfaction. He had no need to tail the Cortina. He knew the quarter-of-a-mile route to the bank like the back of his hand. Traffic was always heavy and slow-moving. The chances of a red light slowing things to a temporary halt were high. Not that he intended leaving an important detail like that to chance. Next Friday he'd have his walkie-talkie with him and he'd be in contact with his kid brother, who would be at the third set of lights. It was a pelican crossing and he had the timing, from the button being pressed in order to change the lights to red to the lights actually changing, off pat.

He'd box the Cortina in from behind, be out of his own car like a flash and have the sabotaged front passenger door of the Cortina open before the Cortina's driver had had time to blink. Then, leaving the ringer to obstruct the traffic and as a present for the police, he'd be off on the motorbike his kid brother would have conveniently left parked just beyond the lights, weaving in and out of cars that wouldn't stand a cat in hell's chance of following him, let alone of catching him.

His leather-gloved hands tightened on the steering wheel. The motorcycle messenger had put away his clipboard and was pootling nonchalantly – far too nonchalantly – in the Cortina's wake. Dexter's handsome black face hardened. The messenger was definitely doing a size-up – and he'd be damned before he allowed a poofter to muscle in on a job he'd marked as his own.

'I like it that you and Jacqueline have begun seeing much more of each other,' Lavender Pulfer said a little tentatively to Raymond as she set a fresh jug of coffee on the breakfast table. 'There was a time when I thought you had a rather snobbish attitude towards the Sweetings, but –'

'Jacqueline is nothing like the rest of the Sweeting tribe.' Raymond's voice was crushing. He hated personal conversations of any sort with his mother; they always made him feel deeply uncomfortable and, anyway, his personal life was no affair of hers.

'Jacqueline *is* different, I quite agree.' Though she never ate breakfast and had already had her first coffee of the day, she seated herself at the small round table, opposite him. 'I've always had an exceedingly soft spot for her,' she continued, trying to sound nonchalantly musing, as if nothing very much was on her mind. 'Over the years she and Rosamund have grown as close as sisters.'

She paused, hopeful that the word 'sisters' would sink into Raymond's subconscious. When she had said that she had always had a soft spot for Jacqueline she hadn't been exaggerating. Jacqueline Sweeting was a lovely girl – stylish, good-humoured, intelligent and, above all, affectionate. She had been stunned to discover that Raymond had begun dating Jacqueline but she had also been deeply pleased. The Sweeting family wasn't on a par with their own family socially, of course, but she had never been a snob and wasn't about to start becoming one. If Raymond's romantic liaison with Jacqueline endured and if he married her . . .

Her hand was a little unsteady as she lifted her cup of coffee to her mouth. For a woman in her perilous state of health a daughter-in-law with Jacqueline's loving, caring nature, would be a blessing from heaven.

Raymond's response to her remark was to make a noise in his throat that could have meant anything. His thoughts, if Lavender could have read them, were that she was talking tosh. Though Jacqueline and Rosamund were the best of friends it was Kelly Rosamund was truly the closest to.

Lavender set her cup back down on its saucer. It would have surprised Raymond to know it but she was perfectly aware of how he disliked chatting to her. Once upon a time, when she had first become aware of his antipathy, it had wounded her deeply. Now, though it still hurt, it was a fact of life she stoically accepted. From what she could glean from other women who had adult sons, they never took their mothers into their confidence in the chummy way daughters tended to do.

'This last few months I've kept thinking about the advantages of a smaller house,' she said, rather as if she were discussing the weather or the price of carrots. 'In fact to be absolutely accurate, Raymond, I've kept thinking of how much easier a garden flat would be for me to run, especially now that you and Rosamund are so seldom at home.'

Though she hadn't a malicious bone in her body she would have been inhuman not to feel a stab of satisfaction at the way his almost rude indifference had snapped into instant alarmed attention.

'I wouldn't sell this house, of course,' she said, not indulging in the temptation to prolong his alarm. Despite his patronising attitude towards her he was, after all, her only son – her dearly beloved only son. 'Not until I knew for sure that you wouldn't want to continue living here once you married.'

Raymond's eyes held hers steadily. The family home was set in the most exclusive part of Blackheath Village and at present prices was easily worth a quarter of a million pounds. He had always assumed that on her death the house would be sold as part of her estate, the money resulting from its sale being divided between himself and Rosamund. Was she now suggesting that if he wanted to raise his own family in it she would arrange for the house to come directly to him? At the thought of the way it would increase in value over the years he could practically feel himself salivating. The transfer would have to be carried out before her death, of course, and Rosamund would have to be sweetened.

There was other money, in safe investments, which could go to Rosamund. If the house could be his, without having to be sold as part of his mother's estate, it would be far preferable to inheriting the money from its sale. It was the kind of house only a very, very successful man would own. The kind of house that, on police pay, he would never be able to consider buying for himself for very many years, no matter how accelerated his future promotions might be.

'And if I did?' he said warily, wondering what the catch was, sure that there must be one.

'I would like to think of your father's grandchildren growing up in this house. It would be what your father would have wanted and I couldn't, of course, think of making such an offer to Rosamund. Some fly-by-night might end up marrying her merely for the pleasure of moving in.'

It was as if she were thinking haphazardly out loud and for the first time Raymond wondered if perhaps his mother was on the verge of early Alzheimer's. Panic seized hold of him. A disease like that and anything could happen. She might, on a whim, leave her entire estate to Battersea Dogs' Home.

He pushed his cup of now cold coffee away from him and folded his arms on the table, leaning towards her slightly. 'Are you saying that if I married within the foreseeable future you'd sign the house over to me, moving out of it and into a garden flat and making other financial arrangements for Rosamund?'

Lavender smiled. 'I'm saying that if you married the right girl I would be very tempted to make such an arrangement. But it would have to be the right girl, Raymond.'

She rose to her feet. 'It would have to be someone I could truly regard as a daughter . . . one on whose loving affection I would be able to count as my arthritis becomes even more disabling.'

Raymond sucked in his breath. She couldn't possibly mean what he thought she was meaning . . . could she? He'd only dated Jacqueline Sweeting a mere half-dozen times.

His thoughts were in ferment as he watched her walk from the kitchen her beige-tinted hair as beautifully coiffured as always, her classically cut skirt and oatmeal-coloured cashmere twinset replicas of the skirts and twinsets that she had worn when he was a child. Only her arthritic hips and the walking stick that now went everywhere with her indicated her increasing age and growing frailty.

Underneath the seemingly off-hand conversation what his mother had really been saying was: 'Marry the girl I want you to marry and the house is yours. Continue living as a bachelor or marry someone who may not look after me very well when I'm completely crippled and you will merely come in for half its selling price.'

He felt a fresh surge of panic. If instead of living in it until she died, which is always what he had assumed would happen, she sold it, God only knew what would happen to the money. She could end up going completely dotty and swanning around the world on luxury liners. Even worse, she might be taken advantage of by an unscrupulous old boy on the make, marry him and leave him the lot!

Never before had it occurred to him that his inheritance might in any way be at risk – but then, never before had it occurred to him that his mother might try to blackmail him.

'It doesna' sound too likely, hen,' Jock said, rubbing his stubbled chin thoughtfully and not seeing the situation in the same light Dexter had seen it. 'A quarter-of-a-mile run down a busy road dinna' leave much chance of a hijack.'

'Couldn't we do a grab before he gets in his car?'

Jock shook his head. 'With traffic so busy we wouldna' be able to make a quick enough getaway.'

Kelly, perched as usual on the arm of his easy chair, cocked her head to one side. 'The bike would be able to nip through the traffic and away.'

Jock rumbled with laughter. 'Aye, hen. The motorbike could certainly do that but what about me and Albie? We couldna' exactly run along behind. And you couldna' pull the job single-handed. A grab is never as easy as it might look. Some hits put up quite a fight and it needs a lot of physical strength tae wrestle the goods from them – and sometimes it needs quite a fight to get away at all, especially if do-gooders pitch in on the side of law and order.'

Kelly ran her fingers through her hair so that it haloed her head like a lion's mane. 'I 'spect you're right, Dad,' she said reluctantly. 'I'm going to have another look at it, though. If the geezer in question always travels by himself, he's got to be worth a second glance. Shall we go down the Connoisseur for a drink? Johnny might be in there and even if he isn't, there'll be some "faces" and we might pick up a bit of likely gossip.'

'If you like, hen.' Jock never needed his arm twisting when it came to going somewhere for a drink, especially when the watering hole in question was a favourite haunt for fellow crims. 'Kel and me are awa' down the Elephant and Castle,' he yelled in the direction of the kitchen and his dearly beloved. 'If Kev calls in, pass the message on. He'll know where we are.'

'A family friend, Deputy Commissioner Laing, is speaking to the Crime Writers' Association Thursday evening, at the Press Club,' Raymond said to Jacqueline as he drove her to what he fondly believed was her home, after a night out at the cinema. 'He was one of my dad's protégés in the dim and distant past – and he's asked me if I fancy going along. He says they're an interesting bunch – always some famous names there. Dick Francis, P. D. James, Bertie Denham. Bertie Denham is Lord Denham, by the way. Ruth Rendell, Desmond Bagley, Lady Antonia Fraser, people like that. Would you like to come with me? We could have dinner afterwards. From what I've heard, the whole caboodle is usually over by eight or eight thirty.'

Jackie felt a mixture of pleasure and panic prickle the nape of her neck. As Raymond's companion she would, in effect, be the guest of a deputy commissioner of the Metropolitan Police! What on earth would her dad say if he knew? And would she really be rubbing shoulders with people as famous as Dick Francis and as socially high-flying as the aristocratic and glamorous Lady Antonia Fraser?

'I'd love to come.' As usual her low voice, with its beguiling hint of huskiness, betrayed no hint of her inner turmoil. 'What should I wear? Something cocktail-ish or something more casual?'

'I suspect either would be OK.' Raymond pulled up outside a large block of council flats just off Jamaica Road. 'I reckon quite a few people there will be going on to other functions and so you won't be overdressed in a cocktail dress. On the other hand, writers definitely have a bit of the hippie in them, don't they? Which means you can be as casual as you want.'

Though Raymond hadn't been the remotest bit of help Jackie had no intention of pursuing the subject. She didn't want to come across as unsophisticated and clueless. She would wear black – it was impossible to go wrong in black – and she'd keep everything very simple. The dress she'd worn on their first date, with its starkly high neck and dramatically revealing nape-of-neck-to-waist slit, would be a good choice.

Raymond switched off the engine and turned towards her, sliding an arm around her shoulders to draw her closer.

'You're driving me nuts, Jacqueline,' he said throatily, sliding his free hand up beneath her skirt.

It was true. When he had first begun dating her, taking into account the kind of background she came from, he had expected to find her easy meat. To his stunned surprise his expectations of easy sex had been brutally disappointed. There were lots of perks to dating Jacqueline: the head-turning attention she aroused; the envious looks that came his way; but when it came to carnal satisfaction he hadn't received even so much as a cursory blow job.

Not that he was in the market for a blow job parked up in a car off Jamaica Road. With a career like his he needed apprehending for indecent behaviour like he needed a hole in his head. There'd been other times and places though, and the result of his efforts when in those other places had always been the same. Zilch.

An intelligent man – at least about most things – he didn't get the feeling that her cock-teasing was a feminine wile, part of a deliberate strategy to reel him in and land herself an engagement ring. He knew her well enough by now to know that that kind of devious behaviour just wasn't in her nature – which left only one explanation. Jacqueline Sweeting, hard though it was to believe when her mother was so common and her sister was such a tart, was a young woman of high moral standards.

As she gently stalled his roving hand with her own an

incredible thought occurred to him. Was she still a virgin? She was nineteen. He dismissed the idea as ridiculous. She was simply taking things slowly in their relationship, that was all. No girl of her age was a virgin – not unless she was as ugly as sin and couldn't find a taker. All the same . . .

He had been kissing her and now he drew his head away from hers, looking down at her speculatively. Her hair, worn down the way he liked it, spilled softly over his wrist as he continued to keep one arm around her shoulders.

'Jacqueline . . .' with the rising in his crotch nearly crippling him his forefinger traced the outline of her generously full mouth. 'You're not by any chance still a virgin, are you?'

In the dark interior of his Toyota Cressida her eyes, luminous and thick-lashed, held his.

'Yes,' she said simply after a fractional pause that wasn't remotely calculated. Then, not waiting for his reaction, she moved away from him, opened the car door and got out.

'Jacqueline . . .' Not attempting to get out of the car himself he leaned across to her still open door. 'Thursday. I'll pick you up at five thirty. Crime Writers' meetings are very early evening affairs. The time won't be a problem for you, will it?'

She shook her head, the night breeze blowing strands of hair across her face. 'No.' She smiled. She was looking forward to the Crime Writers' meeting enormously. His question about her virginity and her answer had, however, embarrassed him just as much as it had her, of that she was sure, and she'd known no other way of dealing with it other than to get out of the car. 'Thanks for a lovely evening, Raymond. Good night.'

''Night, darling.'

He remained in the car watching her as she crossed the pavement and walked over the small paved area fronting the dilapidated tower block. Right from their first date she'd been adamant that he didn't walk her up to the entrance and, imagining that she was embarrassed at living at such a slummy address, he hadn't pushed it. The kerb opposite the tower block's entrance was where he dropped her off and where, when necessary, he picked her up.

She turned at the double doors, blowing a last good-night kiss. Seconds later, as she disappeared into the tower block's maw, he eased the Toyota away from the kerb, driving off towards the salubrious exclusiveness of Blackheath.

A minute or so after he had done so Jackie emerged from the tower block's rear entrance her jacket collar high around her throat. It was barely a five-minute walk to Creek Row. She'd be home before Raymond was as far as New Cross.

'You should have brought Dad down with you.' Kevin was propped comfortably at the bar in the Connoisseur, a pint glass in one hand the other draped proprietorially around Rosamund's shoulders.

He looked quite the business, his suit Italian, his shoes handmade from MacLarens in Albemarle Street. The top button of his shirt was undone, his silk tie slightly to one side, as if he had forgotten that he was about to take it off. The effect was one of sexy careless nonchalance.

'Albie's got his feet up in front of the telly. It would've been easier tae move a mountain than tae get him tae come wi' us.' Jock's cracked-tooth grin nearly split his face. He was feeling good. He had one of his drop-dead gorgeous daughters on his arm – a daughter who was accepted by all his mates as being one of the boys and who was as much a member of the family firm as Kevin and Johnny – and he had a good gut feeling about the Isle of Wight-Portsmouth post office cash job. Over the weekend he and Albie were going to trundle down to Portsmouth to have a meet with their informant and take a close look at the ferry terminal and the way the money bags were off-loaded and then loaded on to the waiting postal van. It would probably all be done by a one-manned electric trolley and there'd be two men to do the loading into the van, possibly three, plus the van driver, of course . . .

'What's it to be?' Kevin was asking him, breaking in on his thoughts. 'A whisky mac?'

It was early and the club, which was often packed to the gunwales, was only sparsely populated. 'Aye, a double.' Jock cast his eye over the early-evening drinkers. There was no one there of special interest to him though there were a couple of heavies from the mob Eddie was running with. He returned his attention to his family, finding Kevin and Rosamund's body language of far more interest than anything else that was going on.

Kevin had always treated Rosamund rather as if she were a glorified gangster-groupie – paying her attention one minute, ignoring her the next. Much as they liked Rosamund Jock and Albie had warned Kevin off from the beginning. Though Rosamund was regarded as being almost family, she wasn't family – and considering the kind of family she came from, she never could be family.

He'd long ago made it his business to know all there was to know about the late Henry Pulfer. His police career had been long and illustrious and, apparently, free from even the slightest hint of corruption. Thanks to a first-class Oxbridge degree and his enviable family contacts, Raymond Pulfer was fast following in his father's footsteps – though word was that as regarded incorruptibility Detective Inspector Raymond Pulfer wasn't quite the shining example his father had been.

Of course when it came to marriage there were crossovers from pukka respectable families into professionally criminal ones; sometimes, especially when it was a girl doing the crossing over, they even worked. It was harder for boys. A boy had to prove himself by engaging in a whole series of criminal activities. All a girl had to do was to be utterly loyal to her man.

Rosamund was laughing at something Kevin had said, the expression in her eyes as she looked across at him one of blatant adoration and total commitment.

Jock rubbed his chin with his hand. He didn't have a second's doubt that Rosamund would always be utterly loyal to Kevin; that she was crazy in love with him had been obvious ever since she'd been fourteen or fifteen; that was on the credit side. On the debit side she was the daughter of a high-ranking copper and her brother was a Metropolitan police detective inspector. A marriage between her and Kevin would mean Trouble with a capital T. It would be far, far better if Kevin followed age-old practice and, as a young criminal, married the daughter of an old criminal, thereby keeping everything 'in the family'.

'What ho, Jock, my old mate,' a slurred voice said, a hand clapping him on the shoulder with easy familiarity. 'How's business in your neck of the woods, then? Booming?'

It was one of the Catford heavies. He was an evil-looking git but then they all were.

Jock shrugged, knowing it was a question to which no answer was expected.

The heavy grinned and pulled up a barstool. It took a little manoeuvring before his bulky weight was perched comfortably but he eventually achieved success.

'Your Eddie-boy is making quite a name for himself but then I 'spect you've heard.'

Jock had. He hadn't liked what he'd heard and he didn't like what he was hearing now. No one should have been talking about what had happened in Brighton, not even to him. That people were talking meant that Eddie was utterly sure no one was going to grass on him – and that meant he was utterly confident of his ability to terrorise absolutely.

'Have you heard the one about the Rottweiler and the

nig-nog?' his unwelcome companion asked. 'There was this nig-nog and he . . .'

Jock tuned out, though not because he found racial jokes offensive; he'd lived in Creek Row far too long for that. Bermondsey was, after all, the one part of south-east London that Oswald Mosley and his Blackshirts had been popular in, way back in the thirties. Jock wasn't one hundred per cent sure but he thought Kelly and Jackie's Rice grandfather had been an active Mosley supporter.

When, finally, the comedian in their midst decided he'd graced them with his company for long enough, he eased himself to his feet, saying as a parting shot to Kevin: 'Still favouring The Fox in Hackney, Kev?'

Kevin's slight smile didn't reach his eyes; they were granite-hard as he tapped the side of his nose. 'Keep it out, sunshine.'

Jock kept his face impassive but only with effort. Rumour was that the biggest robbery of the decade, the raid on the Security Express headquarters in Shoreditch a little over a year ago, had been planned in detail at The Fox. A daylight raid, it had netted a minimum of six million pounds, probably more and, as yet, there'd been no arrests. If the card Kevin had been keeping to himself this last few months was some kind of involvement with the Security Express mob . . .

'I can practically hear your brain cells working overtime,' Kevin said to him drily. 'Just trust me when I say I know what I'm doing and it'll be to our long-term advantage, OK?'

'OK.' Jock wasn't going to argue with him but he wasn't convinced and he wasn't a happy bunny. Not by a long chalk.

Four days later Kelly sat astride her parked Harley thirty yards or so further up the High Street from the betting shop. She was partially concealed by a van as its driver ferried trays of bread into a mini supermarket. Though her viewpoint was partly obscured she could see the betting shop doorway and the left-hand side of the manager's parked Cortina.

As the manager strode out of the shop and across the pavement she flipped down her spaceman-like visor and kick-started her bike. It was obviously going to be a duplicate run of last Monday's journey and she didn't know quite what she expected to gain from it. As her dad had said, there was no point on the journey where a hijack could take place. It was activity, though, and with Kevin still spending time on business of his own and Johnny on a binge of booze and women she needed something to do – and it had to be something she could do on her own.

As she eased the Harley out into the traffic her eyes sharpened. A Vauxhall that had been parked up on the far side of the road had made a slick U-turn and had tucked itself neatly in the Cortina's wake. The driver was young, black, and she was almost certain his hands were gloved.

She dropped back swiftly behind a furniture removal van, her heart beginning to race. Was someone else doing what she was doing? Was the young black guy even, perhaps, about to make a hit?

The first set of traffic lights were at green. In a line of fairly heavy traffic the Cortina and the Vauxhall cruised through them. Kelly, still using the removal van as a shield, followed.

By the time they had negotiated the second set of traffic lights Kelly was convinced the Vauxhall's driver was up to no good. A regular black dude would have been itching to break out of the slow-moving traffic but the Vauxhall's driver was showing no signs of impatience. His attention, as hers had been the previous week, was centred on the Cortina.

The third set of traffic lights was manually operated. A

black kid, aged about twelve or thirteen, had pressed the button to change the signals to red. A woman driving a Peugeot estate car came to a halt at the crossing. Behind her, and immediately in front of the Vauxhall, the Cortina halted. Even before the boy had begun to cross the road the driver's door of the Vauxhall had burst open and the black dude was out of the car, sprinting towards the Cortina.

'Go for it!' Kelly yelled, completely on his side as, before anyone else had cottoned on to what was happening, the black dude had wrenched open the Cortina's passenger door.

She saw the Cortina's driver make a desperate lunge towards his passenger-side footwell; saw the black dude's teeth flash in a wide, triumphant grin as he beat him to it. Then, as the kid continued to cross the road with an insolently slow swagger, the raider, grasping a bank cash bag by its neck, began sprinting – not back towards his car, but away from the scene towards a nearby intersection where a powerful-looking motorbike was very conveniently parked.

Kelly didn't think twice. She opened the throttle and, as the Cortina's driver stumbled out of his car shouting dementedly for someone to call the police, she blasted past him, sending the boy still stalling traffic on the crossing jumping nearly out of his skin.

She had seconds, that was all. Car horns were blaring. Car doors were being opened. The robbed manager was running vainly in the black dude's wake. The black dude was a mere five foot away from his motorbike ... four foot ...

With reckless daring Kelly bore down on him and, leaning dangerously far over, yanked the cash bag from his grasp. It was the speed at which she was travelling that gave her the necessary momentum for success – that, and the element of total unexpectedness.

For a split second, the sheer bloody impudence of the grab was more than Dexter could believe. He was aware that a motley selection of do-gooders were now out of their cars and, though he'd no intention of glancing behind him to make sure, he sensed that at least a couple of them had joined ranks with the betting shop manager. If they caught up with him and, by sheer force of numbers, held on to him until the cozzers arrived it would be assumed that the poofter now zooming off with the stolen cash bag was his accomplice.

Realising he could find himself going down for a job done for someone else's benefit, he raced the last few feet to his bike and sprang astride it, rage and indignation roaring through his veins. No wanking white poofter was going to laugh all the way to the bank at his expense! No way, man! He was going to catch up with the white fucker if it was the last thing he ever did – and when he did catch up with him he was going to give him the going-over of a lifetime!

It was still only a mere two and a half minutes since he had wrenched open the Cortina's sabotaged door and, despite the mayhem in the busy main road caused by so many drivers either hopping out of their cars to join in the vain dash to apprehend him or slowing down to see what all the fuss was about, no police cars were as yet screaming to the scene. Taking full advantage of their tardiness he roared away from his ineffectual band of pursuers, hard on the Harley's tail.

His quarry was almost at the end of the short minor road in which his bike had been parked. A T-junction, the left-hand turn led into a large council estate, the other did a dogleg up and over a railway bridge and then, on a long continuous curve, followed the boundary of a cemetery.

To his intense satisfaction the Harley turned right.

Seconds later he followed at suicidal speed.

*   *   *

Kelly was on a mind-blowing high. It was the first time she'd been chased on the Harley and, confident of getting away, she was loving every minute of it. Unlike the time when she had acted as wheelman for Kevin and Eddie she'd done her homework with an A to Z and knew there was a small access road immediately after the railway bridge and prior to the cemetery. If she could veer down it before her pursuer made the bridge, there was every chance he'd belt straight on down the curving road, assuming her to be just far enough ahead of him to be out of his sights.

The cash bag was wedged precariously in front of her. At the thought of her dad's face when she waltzed in home with it laughter fizzed in her throat. What she had done had been absolutely bloody brilliant. Even Johnny couldn't have bettered the impudence of it.

She was approaching the short steep rise of the bridge. Was up and over it. The unmade access road abutted it so sharply she almost missed it. Nearly out of control she slewed into it, bucketing over potholes. Almost immediately she was aware of the enormity of her mistake. Though in her A to Z the access road had been shown to lead into a minor road, it was now a dead end, its previous exit blocked by a newly built six-foot-high wall.

Once again she slewed the Harley round, gouging clouds of dirt from the rutted track. It was too late to evade her pursuer by racing back over the bridge as he roared on down the road flanking the cemetery. Her little wheeze hadn't worked. Her fellow robber had already rocketed into the dead end and was bearing down on her at what seemed a passable imitation of the speed of light.

There was no sense in hanging around. She wasn't going to be able to barge past him and even attempting to do so, on a machine weighing nearly half a ton, was likely to result in serious injury.

Twisting the neck of the cash bag around her wrist, she was off the Harley and sprinting for the fence that separated the dead end from the cemetery's southern boundary. Someone would retrieve the bike for her. With a bit of luck her pursuer wouldn't be able to vault the fence with the ease she knew she could.

Luck was definitely not on her side. Safely over the fence and racing across uneven ground in an uncared for part of the cemetery she heard the unmistakable thud of his feet as he vaulted the fence after her.

He was going to catch her up. Unless he tripped over one of the half-buried headstones there was no way she was going to outrun him.

He didn't trip. Instead, with a flying rugby tackle, he brought her to the ground.

Hampering though her helmet had been while she had been running, it came into its own now, saving her from being concussed on the broken-off foot of a stone cherub.

'You bleedin' fuckin' joker!' His entire weight was on top of her as, seizing her wrists, he pinioned them above her head, forcing her to release her hold on the cash bag. 'I'm going to give you a doing-over you're never going to forget!'

Eyes the colour of burned toffee blazed in his black face. His eyebrows were winged, his cheekbones high, and his hair was twisted into short funky dreads. He was, without doubt, the tastiest hunk she'd seen in a long time, if not ever.

The giggles that had been fizzing earlier in her throat now erupted.

'Oh yes, please,' she said through them, wriggling seductively beneath him and hooking one of her legs over the top of his. 'That would be so . . . o . . . o nice.'

For one split second he froze and then his hands were on her helmet, dragging it off. Even though her hands were now free and she could, in theory, have made an attempt to regrab the cash bag, she didn't even attempt it. In enjoying the look of shocked disbelief on his face she had forgotten all about the money.

'Well,' she said, green cat eyes dancing, spicy-red hair springing around her head like a dandelion clock, 'for a really good doing-over I think you'll have to unzip my bomber jacket, don't you?'

Even though they were both wearing leather pants she could feel his instant response. His teeth flashed in a dazzling grin.

'Thank Christ you didn't turn left on to the housing estate,' he said devoutly.

As a battered stone cherub stood guard over them he pulled her bomber jacket zip down to the waist and sucked in his breath.

She was topless and bra-less beneath it, her breasts full and high, her nipples a silky rose red.

It wasn't his birthday but it felt like it – and Christmas. Every Christmas he'd ever had all rolled into one.

Chapter Ten

Raymond was on a high. Things were going well. He'd been given the nod that his accelerated promotion curve was about to climb even more steeply. At this rate, if he continued playing his cards right, he'd be a detective chief inspector by the time he was thirty.

He fingered his black bow tie, making sure it was absolutely straight and, waiting for Jacqueline to return from the ladies' room, resumed his scrutiny of Beoty's extremely comprehensive wine list.

The Lewisham/Catford protection assignment had proved to be a gift from heaven. He'd come to a very advantageous understanding with the newest – and most ambitious – member of the Halide empire. It had resulted in his being able to tip off the Customs investigation boys as to a Dover–Catford-bound lorry that would, when tracked, prove extremely fruitful.

If Halide ever suspected which of his soldiers had set him up, giving the police the excuse they had been looking for, for so long, to pin something, *anything*, on him, he didn't shout the name loud and clear. He was charged with importing cannabis and, hours earlier, Raymond had had the pleasure of hearing him receive a nine-year sentence.

By rights, of course, Halide should have been arrested and charged with any one of a number of major crimes, ranging from murder to massive-scale drug-dealing, and then the nine-year sentence would have been a far more satisfactory twenty-five or thirty years.

Raymond made his choice of wine and set the wine list to the side of his plate. The cannabis fit-up had served its purpose, however. His superiors were extremely pleased with his performance in the affair. His squad's surveillance had been a matter of weeks, not expensive months, and very little had been paid out to informants.

A smile touched his mouth as he waited impatiently for Jacqueline's return. The reason he had been able to run the operation with such a minimum of expense was because there had been no informants. There had only been his liaison with Eddie Burns and no one knew, or ever would know, about that.

Through mammoth gilt-framed wall mirrors he saw Jacqueline emerge from the doorway leading to the loos. She looked stunning, her shiny dark hair swept high in an elegant chignon, her dress of white crepe-de-chine spectacularly beautiful.

He felt a sense of satisfaction so intense he was close to purring. His liaison with Eddie Burns would yield great rewards. Halide's nine-year sentence had left a vacuum of power in the Lewisham/Catford setup – a vacuum Eddie was about to fill. With the understanding he and Eddie now had that could only be to his good. His private life, too, was in high gear. As a girlfriend Jacqueline was a sensational success. At the Crime Writers' bash his father's one-time protégé, Deputy Commissioner Laing, had been bowled over by her. She had been in the front row when he had given his talk, her long legs neatly crossed at the ankle. All the time Laing had been doing his stuff he'd hardly been able to take his eyes off them.

The Chairman of the Crime Writers, Madelaine Duke, a birdlike woman with a ferociously strong personality and obviously fierce intellect, had been delighted to discover that Jacqueline was familiar with her work. Any nervousness he had had that Jacqueline would be out of her depth in such cerebral company had been dispelled almost immediately, as it became obvious she was an avid reader. When she began asking Madelaine Duke if *Top Secret*

Mission really had been based on her own activities in 1945 and '46 and Madelaine had assured it had been, referring off-handedly to both 'the Allied Commission' and 'the British Intelligence Organisation', he had been the one out of his depth.

It wasn't that Jacqueline tried to make an impact – far from it. Her entire manner was one of quiet composure. She was a listener, far more than she was a talker, and as an attentive and beautiful listener in a roomful of egocentric writers she couldn't go wrong.

After Laing's talk, when wineglasses had been refilled and socialising had begun with a vengeance, they had become separated. He had been cornered by a severe-looking woman who was eager for tips on the relationship between squads such as his own and the Customs investigation branch.

Jacqueline, on the other hand, had been introduced by the Association's Vice-Chairman, Peter Chambers, to the breathtakingly beautiful Lady Antonia. Intensely frustrated at not being included in the invitation he had seen Laing join the trio and, moments later, had heard him guffaw with laughter.

Later on in the evening when Jacqueline was on the far side of the room, listening with a pucker of concentration to something Peter Chambers was explaining to her, Laing had taken him to one side.

'Wonderful girl, your fiancée,' he had said emphatically. 'She'll make a marvellous police wife. Like your mother – a lady I admire greatly – she has all the right qualities.'

Raymond had opened his mouth to correct Laing's mistake and then, thinking better of it, had quickly closed it again. If the belief that Jacqueline was his fiancée was earning him brownie points with a man who would be one of the deciding voices when it came to his promotion, there was no sense in scuppering them.

Now Jacqueline was finally approaching their table and

he rose to his feet, saying truthfully, 'You're turning heads as usual, darling.'

Her mouth curved in the smile he found so enigmatic and when they were again seated he reached across the table, taking her hand in his. Her fingers were long and slender, the nails almond-shaped and palely polished.

Though he hadn't yet ordered any wine and had only had one large gin and tonic as an aperitif he was still slightly intoxicated from the champagne he had drunk earlier in the day to celebrate Halide's conviction.

'You're a jewel of a girl, Jacqueline,' he said a trifle woozily, meaning every word. She was. Apart from the sex, of course. The fact that she would only go so far in the sexual stakes, and no further, was driving him demented. In all other ways, though, she was peerless.

His mother adored her so much she was prepared to settle the house on him if he married her. Deputy Commissioner Laing, who would no doubt be sitting on every selection panel he ever came in front of, had made it known to him how highly *he* thought of her. Despite her regrettable background and upbringing she was more than capable of holding her own in whatever strata of society she found herself. She was as beautiful as a dark-haired Madonna by Raphael and, designing and making everything herself, dressed as if she had millions of pounds at her disposal. He was the envy of all his colleagues. Tonight, he was, he knew, the envy of every man in Beoty's.

His thoughts continued to centre on Jacqueline as the generous gin and tonic he had just finished drinking began reacting on the large amounts of champagne he had already consumed.

Though he was certain Jacqueline wasn't holding back sexually for any reason other than high moral standards she most certainly *was* holding back. An engagement ring on her finger would, however, put an end to that little flaw in their relationship. The prospect gave him an erection so swift and violent he half expected the table to move. An engagement ring – and eventual marriage – would also mean his mother handing over the house to him. A house worth, at the very minimum, a quarter of a million pounds – and not only would she transfer possession of it to him she would also move out of it.

He thought of the influential dinner parties he would be able to give in it – of the way Jacqueline would so stylishly preside over everything, knocking everyone for six. Marrying Jacqueline wouldn't only put him out of sexual torment, it would be a good career move, too.

'Jacqueline . . .'

The elderly Greek waiter who had been on the verge of approaching and taking their order sensed the moment was a private one and paused.

'Jacqueline . . .' He hesitated, but only for a moment. He'd never made a bad decision in his life and this decision had so much going for it, it couldn't possibly be the exception to the rule. Jacqueline would secure him the family home; would be an asset to him socially and professionally; would ensure he remained the focus of male envy. The only conclusion possible, considering all these advantages, was that he should marry her.

The surroundings were perfect for a proposal. Beoty's was one of London's most elegant and prestigious restaurants; white napery gleamed, elegant wineglasses glittered, candles glowed. His hands tightened on hers. 'I'm in love with you, Jacqueline,' he said, taking the fatal, fatal plunge. 'Will you marry me, darling?'

The elderly waiter, reading Raymond's lips, went in search of the wine waiter. The champagne, when it was called for, would be nestling in table 3's ice-bucket within seconds.

'You needn't fret about my mother's reaction,' Raymond was saying, aware he had rendered Jacqueline speechless and assuming it was because she couldn't imagine making such an unexpected leap in social class. 'She's already told me how happy it will make her if we marry.'

'But ... but ...' Jackie felt as if her breathing had been suspended. His proposal had been so out of the blue ... so totally unexpected. It was, of course, what she had always daydreamed about. Marriage to a man respectable beyond reproach and a Blackheath middle-class lifestyle. Daydreams were one thing, however, and reality another. How could Raymond, a detective inspector, all set to rise to goodness only knew what rank, marry into a family of known criminals? Her father's prison record, combined with her Uncle Albie's and her Uncle Smiler's, was longer than the proverbial arm. 'But my family ... you don't know, Raymond. You can't possibly imagine –'

'I do and I can and you needn't torment yourself making explanations.' The last thing he wanted to do was to discuss her family. 'I know everything I need to know about them,' he said firmly, suppressing the thought of her mother and her sister with an inward shudder.

There wouldn't, thank God, be any need for he and Jacqueline ever to have anything to do with them. If they married on one of the new-style wedding and honeymoon package holidays, on a beach in the Seychelles or Mauritius, the Sweetings wouldn't even be guests at the ceremony.

'Everything?' Jacqueline felt as if her entire life was on the line. Somewhere on the periphery of her vision she was aware of a waiter hovering with a champagne-laden tray and of other couples on nearby tables and banquettes laughing and talking.

Raymond thought of the crummy block of flats in Jamaica Road. 'Everything,' he said with finality, wondering what his chances now were, that night, of getting inside her knickers. 'And there's no need for us to talk about it, understand?'

Jacqueline let out a long, long sigh of blessed relief. She

should have known that Raymond, being a DI, would know all there was to know about her family. Sweeting was, after all, an uncommon name. When it came to old-fashioned safe-blowing methods there was only one Sweeting: her dad. Raymond knew. Of course he knew. And he didn't care. She felt such a rush of warmth towards him she wanted to kiss him on the mouth there and then. She was going to be the best wife possible to him. She was going to be loyal and supportive and . . .

Johnny. His image was so burningly vivid it was as if he were in the restaurant with them. She fought to suppress it. She wouldn't think about Johnny. She *couldn't* think about Johnny. There were more ways than one of being in love and this, the emotion she shared with Raymond, was the right way; the enduring way.

She could admire Raymond in a way she could never admire Johnny. She was proud of Raymond, too; proud of the rank he had achieved in such a short space of time; proud that he was the best sort of policeman: fair, compassionate, incorruptible. How could she ever be proud of Johnny when he was, and always would be, a major-league rogue?

'Oh, yes!' she said, twisting her fingers through his, driving thoughts of Johnny out of her head with super-human effort. 'Yes, I'll marry you, Raymond. I'll be *honoured* to marry you.'

Raymond's hands tightened on hers. Jacqueline was expressing exactly what he felt ought to be expressed. Her family, too, would no doubt feel similarly honoured. If they thought they were going to come the old pals act with him, though, they were going to be disappointed. No way was he going to socialise with them and, when they were married, he'd see to it Jacqueline didn't socialise with them either.

Pearl screamed. She was a good screamer and often relieved her feelings in such a way. This time, however, her screams were occasioned by far more than the need to let off steam.

'I thought you, of all people, might have been pleased for me, Mum,' Jacqueline said, white-faced. 'You've always got on like a house on fire with Lavender. You love Rosamund to bits. You –'

'*Lavender and Ros ain't detective inspectors, you stupid cow!*'

Pearl felt as if she were having a heart attack. Jock was going to go ape-shit – and then he'd kill someone. And it wouldn't be Jackie he'd kill – at least not first. It'd be her. He'd always said, right from the start, that no good would come of her charring for Lavender. 'Her auld man might be dead, but once a police family, always a police family!' he had ranted in the early days when he'd still been in Winson Green. 'Nae guid will ever come o' it – so gie it the elbow, hen. Sharpish.'

She hadn't given it the elbow. He'd been behind bars and she'd been so angry with him for being there that she'd kept on charring for Lavender just to spite him. Later, of course, she'd kept on because she and Lavender had become friendly and Kelly and Jackie had become friends with Rosamund. Despite his perpetual simmering annoyance at her contact with the Pulfers Jock, too, had come to be very fond of Rosamund.

Raymond, however, was another matter entirely. Raymond was the proverbial fly in the ointment and always had been.

'So what's laughing-boy goin' to do with this fancy first-class degree or whatever it is he's got?' she had asked Jackie when Jackie had told her Raymond was coming down from Oxford. 'Be a bleedin' politician?'

'He's going to join the Met,' Jackie had said, as cool as you like, and it had been then that Pearl had known she had made a very big mistake in not having heeded Jock's warning.

As a graduate entrant to the force Raymond had quickly

become a sergeant and undergone fast-stream training. Now, five years after joining, he was a detective inspector and already on the verge of promotion to detective chief inspector – which all came to show how a first-class degree, impeccable family connections and Masonic lodge membership could fast-track a police career.

'You've got to break it off.' Pearl's voice was raw with urgency. 'You've got to break it off before Ros gets wind of it and spreads the word, because if your dad so much as hears a whisper all hell'll be let loose!'

Jackie could feel her heart slamming somewhere up in her throat. She'd known this wouldn't be easy but somehow she'd imagined that at least her mother would understand – that she might even be supportive. Without her mother's support the whole scenario was going to be a living nightmare. Her dad's reaction was going to be everything her mum was predicting – and probably a lot worse.

What she needed was an intermediary, someone who would be able to make her dad see that she wasn't marrying Raymond in order to hurt Jock deliberately and be flagrantly disloyal to him.

If her mother wouldn't take on that role, who else would? She thought of Kelly and jettisoned the idea the same second it came into her mind. Kelly's reaction, when she was told, was going to be nearly as bad as their dad's. Rosamund, then? Her dad was very fond of Rosamund. Perhaps Rosamund would be able to make him see that having a daughter married to a policeman didn't have to mean his disowning her. Some sort of an understanding could surely be reached, especially as Raymond was being so magnificent about riding the knowledge of her family's criminality.

'I need to see Ros,' she said abruptly, snatching up her shoulder bag and swinging it over her shoulder.

'You need to 'ave your bleedin' head seen to!' Pearl yelled after her as she made a beeline for the front door.

'That bleedin' boyfriend of yours'll do for your dad and your uncles and your cousins sooner than it takes to spit!'

The whole bleedin' family will go crackers when they find out,' Kelly said to Ros, not sounding overly bothered. 'Mum's goin' to throw a right wobbly.'

'Because he's West Indian?' Ros was bemused. Much as she loved them all, it hadn't occurred to her that the Sweetings could afford to be snobby about anyone.

'Because he's black,' Kelly said succinctly, and giggled. 'Black and big and beautiful.'

Ros giggled with her, knowing Kelly wasn't talking about the size of Dexter's shoulders. 'And at it,' she added, aware of how Dexter and Kelly had met. 'At least *that* won't cause any problems in your family. He's never done time, though, has he? He's never been nicked?'

Kelly shook her head. They were strolling through Battersea Park, one of Kevin's two Rottweilers at their heels, and the late summer sun glinted gold on Kelly's fox-red hair. 'No,' she said with pride. 'He's too smart. It's only stupid crims who've got form. Or crims who've been grassed on or dropped in it,' she added, remembering her dad's long stretch in Winson Green.

'Kevin won't object to him.' Rosamund loved peppering her conversation with references to Kevin, especially now it was generally acknowledged that he and she were an item. 'Not when you tell him Dexter's a pro boxer. As Dexter trains at the Thomas à Becket, Kev may know him already.'

'Yeah.' Kelly pushed her heavy Afro fringe away from her eyes, Indian rings on every finger. 'Kev and Johnny'll come round quickly enough.' Her eyes narrowed. 'Eddie won't, though. Eddie, as usual, is going to be a problem.'

Rosamund picked up a stick and threw it for the dog. She didn't like talking about Eddie. Eddie, with his lightning-quick moods and strange pale eyes, still scared her to death.

'When are you going to take him home?' she asked practically. 'Or will you simply take him down to the snooker club?'

Kelly shook her head again, her Afro taking on even more body and bounce. 'Nah. The snooker club would have all the wrong vibes. Dexter was once knifed in a snooker hall. It's why he took up boxing.'

'Why not ask Kevin if he fancies going for a drink at the Thomas à Becket on a night when Dexter's training? No matter what Kev's first reaction when you tell him Dexter is your bloke he won't make a big deal out of it in the Becket, plus if he's aware right from the beginning that Dexter is a pro light-heavyweight, he's going to have a lot of respect for him.'

Kelly gurgled with delighted laughter. 'That's a wicked idea! We could go on to the Connoisseur afterwards in a foursome. Eddie's bound to be there and if it's Kev who introduces Dexter to him Eddie will be sweeter about it than if it was me who broke the news.'

As far as Rosamund was concerned Eddie being sweet about anything would be one of life's major miracles. Despite the warmth of the sun she shivered. She had bad vibes, as Kelly would say, about Eddie Burns – very bad vibes indeed.

'So is this job on, Jock?' Albie stuffed his hands deep into the pockets of his ex-army jacket. The breeze blowing off the Solent held a very definite autumn chill. 'And if it is, will we be able to pull it off without bringing any outsiders in?'

Jock dropped a glowing cigarette butt and ground it out beneath his heel. 'You, me, Smiler, Johnny, Kev and Eddie. It should be enough.'

'And Kel,' Smiler said gloomily, putting in a rare twopennyworth. 'She'll want to be in on it, I 'spect, and we'll need a second wheelman. We can't all travel back together, can we? It'd be inviting a pull.'

Jock nodded noncommittally. He'd certainly be bringing Kelly in on the planning side of things but he didn't think he wanted Kelly in on the action. It was too big a job. If things went boss-eyed they'd be going down for a long time. Where Kelly was concerned it was all too much of a risk.

'We've seen all we need,' he said, turning his back on the ferry terminal. 'The parcels come out of the ship's hold in a threepenny-bit-shaped trailer – a safe on wheels. The trailer is hoisted by a derrick on to an electric trolley and then it's trolled down tae a loading bay at the left-hand side of the main entrance tae the station. There's no sense in us going for it then, nae matter how crowded the platform. We need tae wait till it's being loaded onto the post van and we have our own transport right along side o' it. There's going tae be three posties to deal wi' in all, two o' them on the platform and the driver.'

'And we're goin' to go for it when they begin slinging the parcels into the van?' Smiler asked.

Jock, accustomed to Smiler never cottoning on to anything fast, nodded. 'We keep our heads down right tae the last minute as recognition is going tae be a problem – we canna' Balaclava up on a job like this. If they have even a few seconds warning as tae what we're about it'll be a balls-up. I'm going to go in unarmed but wi' gloves on. When I chin the unsuspecting chappie wi' the screamer box the rest of you will go for it.'

'With the usual tools?' Albie asked. 'Smiler with a shotgun and Johnny with a handgun?'

Jock nodded. It would be enough. Smiler's shotgun was bulky but he'd keep it in two pieces beneath his coat right till the last minute.

'That's it then,' he said, pleased with their morning's

work. They'd watched at least twenty sacks being slung into the back of the waiting post van and he reckoned each sack would be worth at least twenty thousand pounds. 'Let's get a cup o' tea and be awa' home.'

Smiler ran a hand as big as a spade over his thinning hair. 'I heard a bit of news the other day, Jock,' he said as they began to walk off in the direction of the railway station buffet. 'Course, the geezer who told me could 'ave made a mistake but Pulfer ain't a common monicker, is it? And if 'e is right, and if our Jackie is sweet on 'im – well, it'll need sortin', won't it?'

'What'll need sorting?' Jock dug in his pocket for money for the teas.

'If this 'ere DI my mate was tellin' me about is Kev's posh bint's bruvver.'

Jock stood still, his hand still in his pocket. 'Ros?' There was a hard, sharp quality to his voice. 'We talking about Ros?'

Smiler nodded and pulled his jacket collar up against the increasingly cold breeze. 'Course I am. Kev ain't pullin' any other posh bint, is 'e?'

Jock rocked back on his heels, breathing in hard. 'And you've been told Jackie is sweet on her brother? Her brother being DI Raymond Pulfer?'

Smiler nodded. He was beginning to feel very uncomfortable. Perhaps he should have let someone else break the news to Jock. Albie perhaps . . .

'Christ All-bleedin'-fuckin'-Mighty!' Jock spat the words through his teeth, knowing he'd been an A-one prize prat. Why had he ever allowed the contact between his family and the Pulfers to continue? Why hadn't he realised long ago that Jackie might find Raymond Pulfer just as attractive as Rosamund obviously found Kevin? Crossovers were a two-way street and Jackie always had been little Miss Squeaky Clean.

His nostrils were pinched white. Whatever was now happening between DI Raymond Pulfer and his Jackie it was all down to Pearl. If she hadn't gone charring for the Pulfers in the first place ... if she'd jacked the job in when he'd told her to ... but she hadn't and this was the result.

'Are you all right, Jock?' Albie was asking, concerned. 'Yer don't look too good.'

Still he didn't speak. Couldn't speak. Hard man though he was he'd never used his fists on Pearl. He'd slapped her around occasionally when they'd both been in drink and she'd been out of order but it had never been anything approaching a major number. As for his girls – he'd never laid a finger on them. Any physical chastisement, when they were small, had always been Pearl's department.

His breath hissed between his teeth as he sucked it in, thinking of all the possible repercussions if Jackie really was screwing around with a DI. By God, she was going to feel the edge of his temper! And so was Pearl. He was going to teach the two of them a lesson they'd never, ever, forget.

The gymnasium, upstairs at the Becket, was busy. There were sweat-soaked bodies working out on heavy bags and speed balls. Dexter and his sparring partner were in the ring, both wearing head guards and going three-minute rounds with a minute break in between. Elsewhere there were cliques of men in deep conversation. Some of them, if they were promoters or managers, were transacting business. Others were simply keeping themselves up to date with fight gossip.

As Kevin entered the gym, suited and booted and with a camel cashmere coat slung nonchalantly around his shoulders, and Rosamund and Kelly on either side of him, there were several pauses in conversation and, where the heavy bags and speed balls were concerned, a hiccup in the rhythmic sound of gloves drumming leather.

'Wotcha, Kev mate,' a well-known agent, who was on friendly terms with him, called out.

From many other people it was a respectful, ''Lo there, Mr Rice.' Though Kevin wasn't a heavy in the sense that Eddie was, he was known to be a big-league player. There were rumours he was one of the six men who, earlier in the year, had raided the Security Express to the tune of five or six mil. The rumours were well known to Kevin and, though he'd had nothing to do with the raid, he had enjoyed them and certainly had not scotched them.

'Blimey, who's the skirt?' could be heard clearly whispered.

Though Ros knew she was a great looker, she didn't imagine she was the 'skirt' being referred to. Not when Kelly was wearing outrageous Vivienne Westwood underwear as outerwear.

'Jock Sweeting's daughter,' was the general response with 'Sweetie-pie's youngest,' and, 'Keep your pecker in your pants, she's his cousin,' being amongst the others.

'So, who have you dragged me in here to admire?' Kevin asked Kelly, grateful that, unlike Kel, Ros didn't dress like a stripper enjoying a ten-minute teabreak. 'And if he let you get the better of him on a job what makes you think he'd be so blindingly useful to me and J.?'

'I only got the better of him temporarily,' Kelly responded, hugging his arm. She'd told Kev enough about the grab to make him laugh and to ensure his interest but she hadn't told him how it had concluded, or Dexter's name, or that he was black.

'The dude in the ring is Dexter Howe,' she said now as, aware of her presence and the identity of her companions, Dexter slammed a punch that sent his partner reeling. 'Word is, he's in line for the light-heavyweight title. He's pretty impressive, isn't he?'

Dexter's partner, an Irishman, had recovered from the shock of having a friendly spar suddenly turn into a serious number and was doing his best to respond in kind.

'Who? The Lucozade with the scar?'

Kelly nodded. Rosamund looked blank.

Seeing her bewilderment Kevin translated. It was a task he'd grown accustomed to over the years. 'The black, the spade, the Lucozade. Get it?'

Rosamund nodded. The Lucozade in question looked absolutely wonderful in the ring, his gleaming arm muscles bunched, his back muscles rippling. She wasn't remotely surprised that Kelly had fallen so heavily for him.

'Yeah. He's pretty fit,' Kevin said as Dexter's trainer strolled over to have a word. 'I wouldn't mind having a couple of hundred on him next time he fights pro.'

'He's extremely likely champ material,' Dexter's trainer said, giving Kevin a matey pat on the back. ''Lo, Kev. Long time no see.'

His eyes rested speculatively for a moment on Rosamund and then shifted to Kelly. And stayed there.

'My lady,' Kevin said by way of introduction as he slid an arm proprietorially round Rosamund's shoulder, 'and my cousin, Kelly Sweeting.'

'Happy to meet you, ladies.' Dexter's trainer continued to feast his eyes on Kelly. 'Your dad used to pop in here quite reg'lar at one time. Ain't seen him around lately, though.'

'Oh, he's around and about,' Kelly said, pleased as punch that Kev was on matey terms with someone who was, quite literally, in Dexter's corner. 'Have you known Dexter long?' she asked, hoping to lead him into saying more complimentary things about Dexter.

'For as long as he's been coming here training.' He dragged his eyes away from her cleavage, returning his attention, fleetingly, to the ring 'Oy! That's enough aggro in there, you two! Come on out and meet Mr Rice.'

'Is this the bloke?' Kevin asked Kelly as the big Irishman ducked under the ropes and Dexter's trainer moved towards him to unlace his gloves.

'Nope.' Kelly was fizzing with anticipation. Ros's idea to have Kevin meet Dexter in the Becket's gym had been absolutely brilliant. The atmosphere was one hundred per cent right, giving Dexter all the cred he could possibly need. She wrinkled her nose at a strong whiff of wintergreen. Already, even before they'd been introduced, Kevin was aware that Dexter was a dude with reputation.

Dexter had his head guard off now and she darted to his side, hugging his sweat sheened arm. 'This is,' she said in reply to Kevin's question. With her free hand she blotted a bead of perspiration from Dexter's magnificently muscled chest and then, her eyes holding Kevin's, licked it from her finger in a gesture so flagrantly sensual it left no doubt at all as to the nature of their relationship.

Kevin's eyes narrowed. Kelly was habitually outrageous but bringing a Lucozade into the family circle – which is what he immediately sensed she was about – was going it a bit, even for her.

'I think we'd better all have a drink and a chinwag when you've showered, don't you?' he said to Dexter, clearly excluding Dexter's trainer and his sparring partner from the invite. 'Downstairs in the bar in twenty minutes suit?'

'The Connoisseur would be better,' Kelly said swiftly, eager that the evening should continue as she had planned and also wanting Kevin to know that the Connoisseur, which was owned by one of London's biggest 'faces', was somewhere Dexter was known. 'It's Dexter's usual watering-hole,' she added, knowing exactly what Kevin would deduce from such information.

'OK, then.' Kevin shrugged. He didn't care where the chinwag took place; he was too busy trying to remember why Dexter Howe's confident, self-assured, handsome black face was so familiar. He'd seen it before. He knew he'd seen it before. He just couldn't, for the life of him, remember when or where.

*   *   *

The second Jock entered the house, flinging the door back so violently a hinge broke, Pearl knew he'd been told about Jackie's affair with Raymond Pulfer.

For twenty years she'd known she'd been married to a man who, though he never used unnecessary violence on a job, was more than capable of violence. The respect given him by fellow crims, especially fellow crims who had served time with him, was evidence enough of that. It was a side of his personality he never gave vent to at home. Neither she, nor their girls, had ever had reason to be scared of his temper. Looking at him now, though, as he stormed into the house, his granite-grey eyes glittering, his fists bunched, his jaw so tight with tension the veins in his neck stood out like cords, Pearl wasn't merely scared. She was petrified.

'She ain't here!' she yelled, springing to bar his way, praying to God that Jackie, who was upstairs, would hear and have the sense to do a disappearing act, even if that disappearing act meant shinning down a drainpipe.

Jock's only reply was a blow that sent her reeling out of his way and into the television set. The television crashed from its stand to the floor, a silver-framed photograph of Kelly and Jackie, taken when Kelly was a baby, falling with it.

A near-hysterical Pearl scrambled to her knees amid shards of splintered glass. 'It ain't as bad as you think, Jock!' she shouted as he slammed into the kitchen and then, finding it empty, retraced his steps at lightning speed, making for the foot of the stairs. 'She ain't really goin' to marry him! Her sayin' she was was just a bit of silliness!'

'Mum?' Disturbed by the shouting and the sound of crashing furniture, Jacqueline stepped anxiously out of her bedroom onto the landing. 'Are you all right, Mum?' she called, crossing to the banisters so that she could lean over them and see down into the hallway. 'What on earth is . . . ?'

It was a sentence she never finished. From the foot of the stairs, as his eyes locked with hers, her father gave a roar, his face so contorted with rage it was barely recognisable. '*Sleep wi' the enemy, would ye? Have a copper fur a boyfriend, would ye?*'

Even as he was hurling the words at her he was charging up the stairs, taking them two at a time.

Jackie spun round, looking for refuge. Her bedroom door had no lock on it. The only room in the house with a lock on the door was a small bedroom set half under the roof which her dad sometimes used as a temporary stash.

She sprinted for the narrow flight of stairs leading up to it. As she did so she was aware that her mother's hysterical voice was now coming from the street. 'Albie! Smiler! Don't stand there like two bleedin' sacks of spuds! Stop him from killin' her, for Christ's sake!'

Her mother was wasting her time, and Jackie knew it. Much as her Uncle Albie doted on her, and formidable as her Uncle Smiler was when it came to physical strength, neither of them would interfere in a domestic between father and daughter – not when the domestic was within their own family.

'I should hae taken my belt to you an' your mother years ago, when I came out and found ye poncin' up to Blackheath!' her dad was bellowing as he rounded the top of the first flight of stairs and sprinted along the landing towards the foot of the second flight. 'This family's never been guid enough fur you since then, has it?'

Jackie flew up the curving flight of stairs as if she had wings on her heels. If she could only make it into the spare bedroom and lock the door on him . . .

'Nae daughter o' mine shags filth!' Jock rasped, closing the stairs between them. Five stairs, four stairs, three.

Jackie was sobbing, hardly able to believe that her lovely loving dad was chasing her with murder in his eyes.

One more step and she would be on the landing. A yard and she'd be inside the bedroom, slamming the door shut and turning the key . . .

'*Naw way*!' His arm hooked round her legs, bringing her crashing down on the top step. She kicked out wildly, losing her shoe. 'How long hae ye been seein' coppers behind ma back?'

As she twisted round, trying to gain leverage to free herself he wound a hand in her thick mane of hair, slamming her head against the hard edge of the stair. 'Ye dinna' think you could get awa' with it, did ye?' In his blind fury his Scots accent was raw and thick. 'Ye dinna' think it would pass unnoticed that a lassie o' mine was gi'ing it awa' to a scumbag copper, did ye?'

'Stop it, Dad! Stop it! Stop it Stop it!'

He slammed her head hard against the step edge again and she drew a knee up, ramming him hard in the groin. The pain inflicted and the sheer unexpectedness of it threw him off balance and as he let go of her hair she twisted like a fish, slithering down a couple of steps.

'*Ye'll never see the cunt again*!'

As she struggled to get to her feet he had hold of her once more, this time by the shoulders.

'*As fur marrying the cunt* . . .!' Feeling as if he was about to vomit, Jock shook her so violently he missed his footing on the step they were toe to toe on.

As, together, they half fell down the next two steps, Jackie continued to fight him, pummelling his chest with her fists, half-blinded by tears and the hair falling wildly over her face. 'I will marry him! I will! I'll do what I want . . .'

He slapped her across the mouth with so much force she saw stars. She tasted blood, too. Incoherent with shock and pain and, for the first time in her life, fear of him, she began to scream.

The screams were loud and clear as Kevin, Rosamund, Kelly and Dexter rounded the corner into Creek Row, intent on seeing if Johnny was home and if he wanted to go to the Connoisseur with them.

'What the bleedin' hell . . . ?' For one brief second Kevin stood in total shock and then, as he saw his dad and Smiler standing ineffectually on the pavement outside number 28; saw that the door was half-hanging off its hinges; saw an hysterical Pearl dash out of his own house, dragging his mother in her wake, he began to run.

Kelly was hard on his heels. Rosamund tried to follow but her legs were trembling so much she couldn't keep up with her. Dexter hesitated, fairly sure the trouble was family trouble and uncertain as to whether his assistance would be welcomed or resented.

'It's Jock, Kev!' one of the middle-aged women, her hair an unlikely shade of platinum blonde, shouted to Kevin as he raced past her. 'Jackie says she's going to marry Ros's brother and Jock's trying to kill 'er!'

As Dexter saw Kelly hare after Kevin into the house the disturbance was coming from he gave up trying to work out the pros and cons of what he should do and sprinted after her. If someone was in a murderous mood he needed to be on the scene to make sure Kelly didn't get hurt. He was seriously confused, though. Kelly had told him enough about her family for him to know that Jackie was her sister and that Jock was their dad.

He'd already had the benefit of chatting to Ros and, as she was Kevin's lady and quite obviously regarded as being part and parcel of the Sweeting/Rice family, he couldn't for the life of him imagine why Jock Sweeting had lost his marbles over the fact that Jackie wanted to marry Ros's brother.

'For Christ's sake!' It was Kevin who was doing the blaspheming, and as Dexter bounded up the Sweetings' stairs like an Olympic hurdler, he could well understand why.

The bathroom door at the top of the stairs was wide open and even though Kevin had already charged into the bathroom, Kelly at his side, Dexter could see enough to know that Jock Sweeting was forcing Jackie's head down the toilet bowl with the apparent intention of drowning her.

In the couple of seconds it took for him, too, to charge into the bathroom Kevin had got an arm around Jock's throat, half strangling him as he yanked him backwards, trying to make him break his hold on the desperately flailing Jackie.

Kelly was shrieking like a banshee, kicking at Jock and biting his arms as, despite his near strangulation, his grip on Jackie's head remained fast.

With five of them in the bathroom there was barely room to manoeuvre but Dexter knew that unless Jock Sweeting was put out of commission completely he would, the instant his hold on Jackie was broken, turn on Kevin in a full-scale, no-holds-barred fight.

As he hauled Kelly protestingly out of the way, doing so with so much force she fell backwards against the bath edge, he saw that Kevin had succeeded in breaking Jock's hold on Jackie. Gasping and choking, her hair and face drenched, she pushed herself away from the toilet bowl and as she did so Jock, still held by Kevin in an armlock, drove his elbow hard into Kevin's solar plexus.

The moment was now Dexter's and he took full advantage of it. Before Kevin could double up in pain from the blow and before Jock could spin round to face him, continuing the fight in earnest, Dexter slammed a right hook straight at Jock's exposed jaw.

It was an expert, devastating blow, delivered with the wrist turned inwards at the point of impact and despite Jock's toughness his legs buckled, only Kevin's close proximity preventing him from crumpling to the floor. Semiconscious, he slumped against Kevin's chest and as Kelly dragged a sobbing Jackie out of the bathroom, Kevin continued to take his weight, saying dazedly: 'Christ All-bleedin'-mighty . . . what set this little lot off, then?'

'Whoever it was who told him our Jackie was knockin' around with a copper.'

The helpful informant was his mother. The tiny landing outside the bathroom and the stairs leading down from it were crammed. Jackie was sobbing uncontrollably, her soaked hair plastered to her skull, her eye make-up running in rivulets down her face. Kelly was holding on to her, saying in a cracked, near-hysterical voice. 'I *told* you no good would come of you seeing that tailor's dummy ponce! Look at the state Dad's in! How do you think he's goin' to feel, losing his temper at you like that?'

'For the love of God let me get to 'im.' Pearl was squeezed on the landing next to Lily, Albie and Smiler and half a dozen nosy neighbours crowding the stairs behind them. 'That blackie bloke's near done fer 'im.'

She shoved her way into the bathroom, terrified that Jock had been seriously hurt. 'Who the bleedin' hell is he, anyway?' she asked Kevin abrasively as she shouldered her way past Dexter to get to Jock's side. 'Coming in here, hitting my old man, throwing his weight around . . .'

'Christ Almighty, Aunt Pearl, have a bit of sense, will you?' Jackie was still sobbing as if she was never going to stop; Kelly was still ranting on about how bad Jock was going to feel; his Uncle Smiler was on the stairs, making unhelpful cracks about nig-nogs, a particularly stupid neighbour was suggesting that someone call the police and Kevin's patience was nearly exhausted. 'If Dexter hadn't floored him, me and Jock would've been hammering it out in the street by now – and you wouldn't have wanted that, would you?'

By now he'd eased Jock's slumped form into a sitting position on the cork-tiled floor. 'And get everyone out of the house, will you? He's going to be up and on his feet in another min and when he is, he ain't going to want an audience.'

'No one need go to any effort to get me out of the house!'

Jackie's breath came in harsh gasps, tears still raining down her face. 'I'm leaving it and I'm never coming back! I'm going to marry Raymond and I'm going to live *decently* and *respectably*, not like . . . not like . . .'

Her arms flailed as she sought for a word that would do justice to her anguish.

'Not like us. Is that what you're trying to say, Jackie?' Kevin left the now groaning Jock to Pearl's care and walked out of the bathroom towards her, his eyes narrowed. 'Not like your family? You know what the score is if you marry Pulfer, don't you? You can't sit on both sides of the fence. It's him or us. If I were you, it's a choice I'd think pretty hard about.'

Rosamund, standing at the bottom of the stairs, felt the nape of her neck prickle. She had faced the same kind of choice and, though she hadn't yet had a showdown with her mother and Raymond over it, she had made her decision. She loved Kevin and, if being with Kevin meant abandoning the way of life and the values she'd been brought up with, then she was going to abandon them. If Jackie made a similar choice, opting for a life with Raymond, the rift between her and the rest of the Sweeting/Rice tribe would be almost unbridgeable. In marrying Raymond, Jackie wouldn't merely be marrying an outsider. She would be moving irrevocably into the enemy camp.

'Don't tell me what I can or can't do!' Jackie's breathing was still coming in harsh painful gasps and her split lip, still trickling blood, was beginning to swell. 'My dad does *this* to me and you give *me* ultimatums! I'm leaving. I'm leaving now. Right this very minute.'

She turned on the small landing, pushing her way past Kelly and her Aunty Lily, stumbling down the stairs past Albie and Smiler.

'Jackie! *Jackie!*' Jock was groggily on his feet, trying to follow her, his hard-boned face contorted with savage remorse.

Jackie heard him but she didn't turn her head; didn't pause. She shouldered her way past a couple of nosy neighbours who had congregated in the hall; past Rosamund; out of the house and, uncaring that she hadn't even a handbag with her, out of Creek Row.

Back in number 28 Jock sat down on the stairs, holding his grizzled head in his hands, his shoulders shaking.

Jock crying was a sight Pearl and Lily, trudging into the kitchen to make a restorative pot of tea, were spared. Kelly didn't see, either. Leaning against the wall, her head back, her eyes closed, she was crying silent tears of her own. Smiler saw and his eyes nearly popped out of his head. Albie saw, too, and looked away, deeply embarrassed. Kevin remained standing, staring down the stairs towards the broken front door, thinking about the consequences of Jackie shacking up with DI Raymond Pulfer, and it was left to Dexter to sit down beside Jock and put a hand comfortingly on his shoulder.

The movement attracted Kevin's attention and his eyebrows pulled together, his brow furrowing. Trouble wasn't over by a long chalk – not when Kelly still had to explain to Pearl and Jock that the 'blackie bloke', as Pearl had called him, was her new boyfriend.

Chapter Eleven

Jackie never remembered how she got from Creek Row to Blackheath. All she knew as she walked off the grassy heath and into the private road that led to the Pulfers' house was that passers-by were looking at her with either alarm and concern or with blatant curiosity.

She opened the Pulfers' gate, noticing for the first time that the back of her hand was smeared with blood. Had the blood come from her split lip or from somewhere else? She began to shake. Her dad hadn't punched her with his fist but he'd done near everything else. There was blood in her hair from where he had slammed her head on the edge of the stair step. Her knees and shins were bruised and grazed, her tights torn from where she had repeatedly fallen as they had fought and struggled their way down the stairs and along the landing into the bathroom.

At the thought of the bathroom and her dad forcing her head down the toilet bowl, she retched, wanting to be sick. How could he have done that to her? How could he have done *any* of it to her? His anger had been so monumental she had truly thought he was going to kill her. Perhaps, if Kevin and his West Indian mate hadn't arrived when they had, he would have killed her.

She pushed her way through the open gate, too unsteady on her legs even to begin to wonder at the oddity of Kevin bringing someone black into Creek Row. Though she'd always wished her dad wasn't a crim, and though, ever since she could remember she'd always been deeply ashamed that he was, she'd never been ashamed of *him*. It was as if what he was to her and Kelly and their mum, and what he did, were two very different things. Now, having seen the dark side of him, a side she'd never even suspected existed, she didn't know what her feelings were.

She did know, though, that she wasn't going to go back home. Lots of students at St Martin's shared houses and flats together. She'd put an ad on the college noticeboard saying she was looking for a room.

'Jacqueline?' Lavender's voice, as she stepped out of the house with the aid of a walking stick, was uncertain. She'd caught sight of Jacqueline from the drawing-room window and, incredibly, Jacqueline had looked *drunk*.

Jackie lifted her head and as Lavender saw her face, the reason for her dishevelment and disorientation was hideously obvious.

'Oh dear God! Raymond! *Raymond!*' Knowing that Raymond was somewhere in the house, and moving as fast as her arthritis allowed, she hurried towards Jackie. 'My dear child – what happened to you? Where is your handbag? Have you been mugged? Have you been hit by a bicycle? A car?'

Jackie shook her head, her hair, usually so smooth and sleek, a tangled mess. 'No, Lavender.' Her voice was hoarse and exhausted, raw from sobbing. 'It's nothing like that. It's . . . it's . . .' She was unable to continue, not knowing how she could possibly explain to Lavender the reason for the appalling scene between herself and her father. Lavender still didn't know that Jock was a criminal – breaking the news to her was something she and Raymond had yet to do – and so Lavender wouldn't have a clue as to why her father had reacted as he had to the news that she was going to marry Raymond.

Raymond, of course, would understand. Raymond, well aware of the depth of the tribal taboo she was breaking, had probably been anticipating her father's reaction and had no doubt intended that, when she told him, he would be with her.

'What the devil . . . ?' he exclaimed now, his tall lean figure bursting out of the house and running towards her, concern and bewilderment on his face.

'It's nothing,' she said again, this time very quickly, flashing him a look which would, she hoped, indicate that what had happened couldn't be discussed in front of Lavender.

'Someone's hit you,' he said flatly, his nostrils pinched white with anger. His arm was around her shoulders. 'And you're in shock.'

It was true. She was trembling as violently as if she had flu.

'I'll go and put the kettle on.' Lavender's reaction was identical to what Pearl's would have been. 'A cup of hot tea is what is needed – a cup of tea laced with brandy.'

As Lavender, leaning heavily on her stick, hurried off to be of practical use, Raymond turned Jackie towards him.

'What happened?' he asked in a manner that brooked no argument.

Jackie had never grassed on anyone in her life and under other circumstances would have gone to the stake rather than reveal that her dad had been violent towards her. The present circumstances were, however, special. She and Raymond were going to be married and there was no place in their relationship for secrets from each other.

'Dad knows about us,' she said reluctantly. 'When I told him we were going to get married he went crackers. He came out with everything we thought he'd come out with. How we'd only marry over his dead body. How he'd see me in hell before he'd see me married to you.' She gave a small, despairing shrug of her shoulders. 'You can imagine the kind of thing.'

Raymond couldn't. He stared down at her, goggle-eyed. What the devil was she talking about? Her father couldn't object to her marrying him – they'd never even met! Even if they had met, how could a man of Jacqueline's father's class possibly object to her marrying him – Raymond Pulfer? He was an upper-middle-class high-flyer, for Christ's sake! If anything, Jacqueline's father should have been on his knees, thanking God that his daughter had landed such a catch.

'He did *that* to you?' He was looking with disbelief at her split and swollen lip. 'He did that because you told him you were going to marry me?'

Jackie nodded, not wanting to talk about it any more and knowing there was no need to do so. Raymond knew, now, why she looked as she did and, when she told him that she had left home and would be looking for a flat to share with fellow students, he would understand why.

Try as he might Raymond still couldn't quite take in what she was telling him. What kind of a man was her father, for Christ's sake? A certifiable lunatic? A hard-line Marxist with a crackpot hatred for the bourgeoisie? It just didn't make sense. It just didn't make any sense at all.

She leaned her head against his shoulder. 'I could do with that cup of tea your mother promised,' she said, weary with emotional exhaustion. 'And then I think I'd better go to college. I want to put a note on the noticeboard saying that I'm looking for accommodation.'

'You're not going anywhere looking like that!' His alarm was instant. If anyone who knew she was his girlfriend saw her, gossip would be rife. His arm tightened around her shoulders. 'You need antiseptic on that lip. You may even need stitches.'

As he began walking her into the house seething anger was taking the place of stunned disbelief. So Jacqueline's father would see her in hell before he'd see her married to him, would he? They'd only marry over his dead body, would they? Well, he'd see about that. If he, Raymond, wanted to marry Jacqueline, no brain-dead Bermondsey bully was going to stop him.

There was no sense in Jacqueline moving in with fellow

students, either. When his mother learned that it was Jacqueline's father who had slapped her around in such a monstrous fashion she would be more than willing for her to move into a guest room, especially when he told her how imminent the wedding was going to be. The house transfer could be put in hand immediately, before she had the chance to change her mind about it.

He deposited Jackie in the drawing room – even in a crisis he wasn't about to start drinking cups of tea in the kitchen – and went in search of his mother, becoming more pleased about Jackie's father's thuggish behaviour by the minute.

It would, for one thing, put an end to his mother's romanticised perception of the Sweeting family as being storybook Cockneys with hearts of gold. Perhaps now, at long last, she would end her inappropriate friendship with Jacqueline's mother. Though he hadn't the remotest intention of ever entering into a classic son-in-law/mother-in-law relationship with her, he certainly didn't want it coming to anyone's attention that his mother-in-law had once been his mother's charlady.

Buoyantly he pushed open the kitchen door. At one fell swoop he'd not only been given an excuse to prompt his mother to set the house transfer in motion immediately, but had also been given the best reason in the world for not having social contact with Jacqueline's family. It was all very satisfactory – almost as satisfactory as the news of his promotion to chief inspector.

As he remembered the news that had been given him only twelve hours earlier he felt euphoric. A DCI at twenty-six! Everything, but everything, was going his way. Careful not to let his glee show on his face or in his voice he said to Lavender: 'You'll be interested to know, Mother, that Jacqueline wasn't mugged.' He wanted his next words to hit her like a thunderbolt and paused, playing for maximum effect.

She had been setting a tea tray, her back towards him. As

she turned awkwardly to face him, moving her stick from her left arthritically swollen hand to her right, he said in a self-satisfied, I-told-you-so manner: 'The person who assaulted her was her father. He did it because for some inexplicable reason he objects to her marrying me and was, presumably, hoping to change her mind about her doing so.'

Lavender gasped, the blood draining from her face.

'I don't know why you should be so shocked,' he continued maliciously. 'I've been telling you for years what kind of a family they are – the exception being Jacqueline, of course. Jacqueline has no intention of returning home and I would like to invite her to stay here. I think, under the circumstances, the sooner the wedding takes place the better, don't you?'

'Oh dear me . . .' Lavender was so distressed that without the aid of her walking stick she would have fallen. 'Oh dear, dear me . . .' Blindly she groped for the nearest chair. 'Why on earth would Mr Sweeting react in such a way, Raymond? And to be so violent! Pearl has never indicated that he is violent. In all the years I have known her I have never seen her bruised or marked. Was Mr Sweeting drunk, do you know? Was –'

'Would it make any difference if he had been?' Raymond's voice was sharp with impatience. Dear God in heaven! His mother wasn't going to try and make excuses for Sweeting, was she? If he had his way the old bastard would be facing a charge of grievous assault. 'The man is obviously a lout of the first order,' he said, his tone of voice leaving her in no doubt that his opinion of Jacqueline's father was a great deal worse than that. 'From now on Jacqueline will be having nothing to do with him. Her home will be here. We are agreed on that, Mother, aren't we?'

'Oh yes.' Dazed, Lavender tried to collect her thoughts. How could she have remained in ignorance, all these years, of Mr Sweeting's brutish nature? Kelly and Jacqueline had always seemed so devoted to him that it had never occurred to her that he could be anything other than kindly and decent. As a seaman he was, of course, away from home a good deal and so the girls would not have spent long periods of time in his company . . .

Raymond broke in on her thoughts. 'Under the circumstances I think a small wedding would be best.' He set the teapot she had filled a minute or so ago on to the tea tray. 'I'll have a word with the vicar at St Michael's and All Saints about a date.'

He picked up the tray. 'And we'd better start looking for a suitable garden flat for you, hadn't we? There's no sense in letting the grass grow under our feet now that we've decided what's to be done. You'll want to be near us, of course,' he added magnaminously as she held the door open for him. 'Round the corner in Manor Park might be the best place to start looking.'

Lavender sucked in her breath, about to protest at the speed with which things were going, and then thought better of it. Jacqueline as a daughter-in-law was, after all, what she had always wanted. Jacqueline's father's bizarre and extreme antipathy to the marriage was unfortunate but it was an antipathy that would, no doubt, be overcome, in time.

'Yes,' she said to her intimidatingly highly organised son, 'I'll telephone a few local estate agents and I'll make an appointment with Mr Darby.'

With his back safely towards her as he carried the tray out of the kitchen Raymond permitted himself a self-satisfied smile. Mr Darby was the family solicitor. The house transfer proceedings were well and truly underway.

Lavender followed in his wake, not knowing whether to admire or be disturbed by his ability to make swift far-reaching decisions without first conferring with the person those decisions would concern most. In this particular circumstance the decision he had come to had, of course, been admirable but there were times when his manner could only be described as high-handed. It was an aspect of his character Jacqueline was obviously familiar with and with which, fortunately, she appeared to have no problems.

Lavender's mouth twitched in a slight smile. That was one of the advantages of Jacqueline and Raymond having known each other for so long. They knew all they needed to about each other and, when they married, there would be no nasty surprises lying in wait for either of them.

'Dexter coming in on this job wi' us is going tae come as a nasty shock tae Eddie,' Jock said as he, Albie, Kevin and Johnny held a meet in the Manley Arms.

'Why? 'Cos he ain't family or 'cos he's black?'

Jock knew Albie was perplexed at the way Dexter had become almost overnight a part of the team and, to tell the truth, he was more than a little bemused by it himself. It was because of the way Dexter had handled things during the ruckus in the bathroom, of course, for if Dexter hadn't slugged him he and Kevin would have knocked each other senseless and the consequences, where family was concerned, could well have been catastrophic.

There were other reasons as well, reasons which he didn't intend sharing, even with Albie. One was the sympathetic way Dexter had put a hand on his shoulder in the dreadful few minutes when, Jackie having walked out of the house, he had come to a realisation of just where his rage had led him.

The other reason was, quite simply, because of Kelly. He had lost one daughter over her choice of boyfriend and was damned if he was going to lose another – and, where Dexter was concerned, there was no need. Dexter wasn't the Bill. He was a crim. He was also an ace boxer. Taken all in all his being black was neither here nor there – at least not to him. It wasn't to Albie, either. Albie's concern was Smiler and, even more than Smiler, Eddie.

'Both,' Jock now said, answering Albie's question. 'What matters, though, is that he soon will be family – or he will be if Kelly has anything tae do wi' it – an' he's a tasty merchant wi' a lot of ability.'

'Where is he now?' Kevin tossed a whisky chaser down his throat and then shot the cuff of his jacket, looking down at his Rolex Oyster. 'I need to be on my way.'

Jock flashed him a sharp look from under grizzled brows. Kevin was spending very little time in Creek Row these days and had already indicated that he couldn't be counted on, one hundred per cent, for the job now under discussion: the Portsmouth job.

'It's just poss I might have to scarper the country for a bit when the number I'm working on over the river comes off,' he'd said in private to Jock earlier in the day. 'It might be as well to fill Dexter in on the Portsmouth job, then if push comes to shove he can take my place.'

Bullion. Jock knew the job Kevin was referring to involved gold bullion but he was still in the dark about how much was involved, where it was going to be lifted, and how. It was quite possible that Kevin himself didn't have any of this information. It was a mammoth job and he wasn't one of the major players. He was in on it as a labourer – his prime motivation being to see how the melting down of the gold and the handling was carried out. Once he was fully genned up and with contacts made they would then be able to think about a bullion haul of their own.

'Dexter's down the Becket,' he said, aware that Kevin was about to shoot over to The Fox, in East London. 'He'll be here any mo, though. Why dinna' you hang on fur a bit?'

'Nah.' Kevin pushed his chair away from the corner table they were seated around, and stood up. 'I've things to do, plus I think you should count me out of this one. Dexter can stand in for me. That way you'll still have two drivers, one minder and three goers. It's pretty minimal but it should be enough.'

'Who's the second driver?' Albie's creased and crumpled face was a study in concentration.

'Kelly.' Jock spoke off-handedly, as if it was no big deal, and as if it wasn't a contradiction of what he'd said earlier about the job being too big for her to be in on. 'If Dexter's a player then she's a player,' he said as Albie opened his mouth to protest. 'That's the way the two of them want it an' if it's okey-dokey wi' me, it shouldna' gie anyone else any problems.'

'It'll give Aunty Pearl problems if she gets to hear about it,' Johnny said drily. 'And it'll give Smiler problems.' He ran a hand over his blond hair, smoothing it flat, knowing that his Uncle Smiler wasn't a serious problem. Smiler would do as he always did. He'd do exactly what Jock wanted and if that meant him accepting Dexter as part of the firm, then that is what he'd do, no matter how reluctantly. Eddie, however, was another matter entirely.

As Kevin left the pub, and as his dad and Jock began poring over a large-scale map of the Portsmouth area in order to work out where the second getaway van should be waiting, Johnny pondered the problem of Eddie.

It wasn't a new problem. Eddie had always been a headache, even when they'd been youngsters. His being family meant it was something that had had to be put up with. His present behaviour, however, was so way out of order that even tribal considerations could no longer be allowed to count. Knowing that Eddie was their cousin and part of the family firm, people who were scared of him were becoming scared of them. As his dad had said when Jock had been getting their first round in, 'It ain't much fun being treated as if I was a Kray – not at my age. I went in the White Horse in Lewisham last night and it was like the stand-off at the OK Corral. No bugger'd come near me.'

What was true for Albie was more than true for him and Kevin. Being treated with respect was one thing. Being treated as if they were torturers and murderers was quite another.

Johnny chewed the corner of his lip, wondering if Jock had had an ulterior motive when he had invited Dexter to join the family firm. He still hadn't told Eddie of his decision and everyone knew that, when he did, Eddie would go ape-shit. Jock wasn't going to back down, though, that was obvious. And if Jock didn't back down and he, Kevin and their dad didn't take Eddie's side, Eddie was going to be left with only one option – and that was to give the family firm the old heave-ho. Which would suit Jock, and them, very nicely.

'We could have Kelly waiting in a second van just before Cosham, at the junction with the A3,' Jock was saying musingly, ringing the spot on the map with red Biro. 'She could then get us all the way to Croydon on minor roads – or she could if we managed to evade police roadblocks. The alternative would be tae go tae ground in Portsmouth. We could rent a lock-up garage nice and handy to the station. Everything would hinge, though, on not being cornered in it.'

Johnny gave him credit for being a cunning old devil where the Eddie situation was concerned but still didn't give the Portsmouth plans his attention. Eddie was one reason his thoughts were elsewhere. Jackie was the other.

He felt a rising in his crotch just thinking about her – and he felt rage: rage so all-consuming there were times when he thought it was going to destroy him. Her marrying someone other than him was bad enough but that the bloke in question was a copper was a monstrosity he could no way come to terms with.

He clenched his jaw, a pulse spot pounding. In marrying

Pulfer, Jackie wasn't only turning her back on him; she was turning her back on her entire family. How could any of them continue having anything to do with her? When news got out about it Jock would be a laughing stock and, even worse, he might find himself not completely trusted any more. To maintain any kind of credibility the family would have to be seen to have cut off all contact with her.

There was a pain in his chest defying all description. If he'd been fanciful he'd have said his heart was, quite literally, breaking. He grimaced, cracking his knuckles as he did so. No one could say he hadn't tried to get her out of his mind. He'd had it off with so many different women over the last few weeks that even he hadn't been able to keep count of them. Not one of them had made any kind of an impression. Jackie had been part of his life ever since, as a five-year-old kid, he'd gone with his mum to see her only hours after she'd been born. There was a bond between them so deep he couldn't remotely imagine having a similar one with anyone else.

He was just about to begin brooding on how much of his childhood had been spent pushing her up and down Creek Row in her pram, when Eddie slammed the pub door open.

The handful of regulars enjoying a drink turned to see who was making such a dramatic entrance and, in double-quick time, swung their heads away again. Though many of them had known Eddie since he'd been a rag-arsed young hooligan, none of them wanted to attract his attention.

Johnny's eyes narrowed. There was now going to be a very nasty scene and he found himself wishing that Kevin hadn't been in quite such a hurry to zip off.

In a single-breasted mohair suit tailored to emphasise the intimidating width of his shoulders, and wearing a brilliant white shirt and thin black tie, Eddie swaggered over to their corner table. 'You wanted a word?' he said in a disinterested voice to Jock.

Jock nodded, not showing by so much as a twitch of an eyelid that beneath his laid-back manner he was as taut as a tightly coiled spring. 'Aye,' he said, one arm casually resting on the back of the chair Kevin had been seated on. 'Though it'll wait till you've got a drink in hand. What's it tae be? A pint and a chaser?'

Eddie nodded. 'A pint of Worthington and a Rémy,' he said, still not sitting down. There was a map on the table. Were his two uncles and Johnny having a meet? And if they were, why wasn't his dad there? Why, for that matter, wasn't Kev there?

As Albie scooted off to the bar to order a fresh round of drinks Eddie kicked a chair out from under the table and sat down on it. 'What's this then?' he said, with a nod towards the map. 'Got a job lined up at last, have you?' There was jeering contempt in his voice.

'We may have, but that's no' why I want a word.'

Eddie's chipped-ice eyes narrowed. There was something very odd going on. Something that stank to high heaven. 'What is it?' His eyes flicked to Johnny's. 'Has Kev been collared for a job?'

Johnny shook his head. Whatever the outcome of the present meeting there was one thing to be grateful for. Eddie hadn't a clue about the imminent bullion heist.

'It's a family matter,' Jock said as Albie set two brimming pints of Worthington on the table and a glass of bitter, with a bottle of light to liven it, and then trotted back to the bar for the fourth pint and the chasers. 'Kelly's got herself a boyfriend an' as it seems he's going tae be a permanent fixture an' as he's a pretty tasty merchant wi' a lot of ability – Ah've decided he should come in wi' us.'

'Come in with us? What the bleedin' hell are you rabbiting about?' Eddie was certain he hadn't heard right. He couldn't have heard right.

'As he's going tae be family he's going tae join the family firm.' Jock's cracked-tooth grin reached nowhere near his eyes. 'His name's Dexter Howe. He's a pro boxer. You've likely met him down the Becket.'

'I've never heard of the little pile of dog's business!' Eddie pushed his chair violently backwards. 'How the fuck can you bring someone in the family firm that I've never even fucking met?' Another thought struck him. 'What d'you say his fucking name is? Dexter? It's a fucking nig-nog name!'

'Aye.' Jock's arm didn't move from where it was so carelessly resting on the back of the empty chair but there was a tenseness about him now that was unmistakable. 'He is on the dark side of dusky now you come tae mention it.'

Eddie's eyes bulged. 'A Lucozade? And you think you can bring him into the family firm? You're bleedin' cracked!'

'Naw I ain't.' Jock shifted his arm slightly. 'Kevin's easy about it and so are Johnny and Albie.'

Eddie sucked his breath in and swivelled to face Johnny. 'Is this ton of shit for real?'

Johnny gave a careless shrug of his shoulders and poured his light ale into his beer. 'Jock's the boss, Eddie. You know that.'

He couldn't have said anything more provocative to Eddie and he knew it. He also knew that Eddie would be tooled up and he himself wasn't. Jock had set up the confrontation and had presumably come prepared for its consequences, but Albie wouldn't have. It had been years since Albie had carried so much as a handkerchief on him. It meant that even though it was three to one, he and Jock and Albie were going to be on rocky ground when Eddie's brain cells finally registered the position he'd been cornered into, and he went loco.

Eddie's eyes, usually so rinsed of all emotion, were popping with agonised frustration. The bastards wanted rid of him! It was the only possible reason they'd be bringing a blackie into the firm. Because he'd become the business – and everyone in south-east London *knew* he was the business – they were so bleedin' jealous they wanted him out! His own family, his own flesh and blood, and they didn't want to work with him any more!

Knowing exactly who was responsible for the treachery he lunged across the table towards Jock.

Glasses toppled; beer cascaded. The barman, who had been so unnerved by the way the Burns/Sweeting confrontation was going that he'd already phoned for police assistance once, now did so again, this time in frantic haste. The regulars scattered, either taking cover or making hasty exits. Jock, who'd been waiting for Eddie's attack ever since Eddie had walked in the pub, sprang upwards like a bullet from a gun to meet it. If the table hadn't been between them the advantage his small height gave him – the ability to leap up and nut an opponent on the bridge of the nose with so much force the bone crumbled – would have stood him in good stead. As it was the vital contact was never made. Eddie had him pinned down, a knife to his throat.

'*I'm goin' to fuckin' do for you, you half-baked fuckin' ponce!*' he roared, out of his head with hatred and rage. All his life, all he'd ever wanted was to be the big man where his uncles and cousins were concerned. Now, even though the hardest of hard villains regarded him as being well the business, he was still being given no respect from where he most wanted it. Jock Sweeting was, as always, besting him and this time he was going to kill the Scots bastard.

It was Johnny who foiled him. Seizing hold of the empty bottle of light ale, he sprang on top of him, ramming the bottle neck hard into Eddie's groin.

'*Drop the blade or I'll shoot your balls off!*'

Blood was seeping from Jock's neck and, with his jugular vein on the point of being severed, was about to become a torrent. The bluff, wild as it was, worked for just long enough. Eddie froze; police sirens screamed; and the pub door swung open and Dexter strolled in.

If it wasn't that one wrong move would have left Jock bleeding to death on the pub floor, Johnny would have cracked with laughter. If timing was one of a boxer's most essential qualities, it was no wonder Dexter was ace.

Eddie, aware that someone had made an entrance and assuming, from the racket the police cars were making, that it was an advance party of cozzers, swung round, releasing Jock and hurling Johnny from off his back in the same swift, violent movement.

Dexter had already sent his jacket skimming out of the way and, pecs and biceps bulging, had his hands balled into lethal fists.

Eddie, aware instantly of who he was facing, forgot all about Jock, who was hauling himself to his knees and, quite literally, spitting blood.

'So you're the black bastard in question?' he snarled, stowing the knife as, from the pub's car park, there came the sound of police car doors slamming.

Dexter was as aware as everyone else that the filth were about to storm in and that the present party was over, but that wasn't why he checked so suddenly.

'*You!*' His tawny eyes were blazing in recognition, his ebony skin suddenly tight over his cheekbones. '*You're the bastard who nearly knifed me to death in the billiard hall!*'

Eddie's snarl turned into a bared-teeth grin. 'And next time I'll fucking succeed,' he promised as the police burst in. Before all five of them had to go through the usual 'there's no trouble, officers, our mate ain't really bleedin' to death, he's had a little accident, that's all,' routine, he wheeled back round to face Johnny, Jock and Albie. 'And I'll do for you three! And for Kev! You ain't my family any more! You're fuckin' enemy!'

Chapter Twelve

'You want me to be your bridesmaid?' Ros stared at Jackie in dumbstruck amazement. 'Only me? Not Kelly as well?'

'Be realistic, Ros!' It was rare for Jackie to lose her temper but she was under severe stress. Raymond had obtained a special licence and the wedding was taking place on Saturday. Under the circumstances it was hardly something she could object to. That he still wanted to marry her at all was miracle enough. It gave no time, however, for bridges to be built with her family and the thought of being married without a single one of them present was a prospect she could hardly bear.

'Kelly wouldn't act as a bridesmaid at a police wedding to save her life,' she said bitterly. 'Not even for me. You heard the line she took when dad laid into me. She was more concerned he was going to feel bad about it afterwards than she was about the fact he was half killing me.'

Ros blanched. Totally unused to violence of any kind she'd found the scene that had taken place between Jackie and Jock truly horrific and didn't want to be reminded of it. Kevin had tried to put it into perspective for her, pointing out how utterly impossible it was for a family such as his to have any kind of police connection, but his total acceptance of what had happened only made her feel more uneasy, not less.

What was Kevin's attitude going to be now, for instance, if she agreed to be Jackie's bridesmaid? He would very likely go completely up the wall. Yet if she wasn't Jackie's bridesmaid her mother would have to be given an explanation and, as Jackie and Raymond still hadn't told

Lavender the reason Jackie's family so objected to the marriage, what explanation could she possibly give?

She kept her eyes fixed on the wedding dress that Jackie had hung on the wardrobe door. They were in a room that had been her mother's best guest room and was now Jackie's bedroom. 'I'd love to be your bridesmaid Jackie,' she said truthfully, seated on the bed whilst Jackie remained standing near the window. 'But I'm going to have to clear it with Kevin first.'

Jackie's Celtic-blue eyes flashed fire. 'If you're going to do that, Ros, you may just as well say no now!'

Jackie had a point and Ros knew it. 'I'm sorry, Jackie,' she said inadequately. 'I always thought I'd be bridesmaid to you and Kelly, and that you and Kel would be my bridesmaids, but it's just not going to work out like that, is it? Raymond is being absolutely ace about everything – I can hardly believe just how ace – but no one else is taking the same live-and-let-live line and I don't want to rock the boat between me and Kevin. Not when everything is going so well.'

She nearly said more and stopped herself just in time. The news about the baby could wait until after the wedding. Jackie had enough on her plate at the moment without wondering what the hell was going to happen when Lavender learned she was going to be a grandma – and that the father was a crim who hadn't done an honest day's work in his life.

'And just how well is everything going between you and Kevin?' There was an uncharacteristic hard edge to Jackie's voice. The Kevin/Ros situation was crazy and someone had to point out to Ros that the mistake she was on the verge of making was one that would ruin her entire life.

Rosamund's eyes flicked back to the wedding dress. As Jackie had been given no time in which to make a dress the dress had come from Pronuptia in Hanover Street. In white velvet, long and narrow and with a deeply sculpted sweetheart neckline, it was both elegant and strikingly unusual. 'It's going very well,' she said, still not meeting Jackie's eyes. 'In fact I think ... I'm almost sure ... that we'll be getting married soon.'

'But you *can't* marry Kevin!' Jackie was so appalled she forgot all about the anguish of being married without having any of her family present. 'You have no idea of the kind of lifestyle you're letting yourself in for! You'll never know where he is or what he's up to ... except that it'll be to no good. He'll be nicked for something eventually and, when he is, it'll be for a big number. What are you going to do then? Have you any idea how lonely life is for women whose husbands are doing time? It's something you have to be brought up to, Ros, and you haven't. Playing at being a moll is one thing, *being* one is something else entirely.'

The minute Jackie had begun speaking so out of turn Rosamund's eyes had flashed to hers. 'I'm here to give you a bit of moral support, Jackie. Not to be lectured,' she flared back, real warning in her voice. 'I'm in love with Kev, *truly* in love, and considering the ruckus there's going to be when my mother and Raymond find out who – and what – he is, I don't need hassle from anyone else.'

At the mention of Raymond Jackie sucked in her breath. He'd been absolutely wonderful about the fact that her dad was an old crim. Not once had he given her a hard time about it. Always coolly controlled, his way of handling it had been not to speak about it, an attitude for which she'd been profoundly grateful. That their marriage was going to be far from an asset to him professionally was, of course, obvious – and equally obvious was that Raymond believed it was a difficulty he could overcome. How, though, would he overcome having not only a professional criminal as his father-in-law but one as a brother-in-law as well? It would probably be totally impossible.

Her nails dug deep into her palms. 'You *can't* marry

Kevin,' she said fiercely, fighting down hysteria 'It would destroy your mother. It would probably mean an end to Raymond's career. It would –'

'God, you're being short-sighted and selfish!' Rosamund sprang to her feet, her eyes blazing. 'How do you think my mother's going to feel when she realises how Raymond is compromising his career by marrying you? And what about the fact that neither you nor Raymond has told her yet? That wouldn't be anything to do with the fact that Raymond wants the house transfer safely taken care of first, would it?'

'The house transfer?' Jackie blinked, not having a clue what Rosamund was talking about.

'And I've been damned decent about that,' Rosamund continued, now on a roll and not about to stop. 'Some people would have created a stink about it. After all, Raymond's going to get the benefit from the arrangement immediately, isn't he? I'm not going to be receiving anything substantial until after Lavender dies.'

'I don't know what private family affair you're talking about, Ros, but it's not what I want to talk to you about.' Jackie pushed a heavy fall of hair away from her face. 'What I want to talk about is Kevin. You're being totally blind about him. Yes, he's drop-dead gorgeous. Yes, he lives a reckless dangerous lifestyle – one that you find exciting. Yes, he's generous with money – once he has it. But he's a *criminal*, Ros. I hate saying this just as much as you're going to hate hearing it but beneath all the charm Kevin is one very dangerous man.'

'So?' Rosamund was white with defiance. 'I *like* dangerous men. They make me feel protected. They make me feel they'll never let anything happen to me.'

'God, but you're being stupid!' Jackie hadn't intended letting their heated exchange develop into a full-scale row but she couldn't help herself. 'Have you taken a close look at the way my mum and aunties live? Is that the kind of a life you want for yourself? Having the police sledge-hammer their way into your home at five o'clock in the morning? Having your husband on the run? Lying to people about what he does and where he is? Excitement is only a small part of living with a man like Kevin. The rest is all heartache and sacrifice – especially when, as in Kevin's case, he's a womaniser who is hardly going to let a wedding ring put a stop to his fun. Your education hasn't remotely prepared you for life with such a man, Ros. You quite literally don't have a clue as to the realities of it.'

'Perhaps not, but I'll take my chance!' Rosamund was at the door. 'And while all this unasked for advice is being dished out – have you thought of the difficulties you're going to have fitting into Raymond's lifestyle? Being wife to a high-flying copper isn't all moonlight and roses – and if you're in any doubt, ask my mother.'

She yanked the door open, saying as a parting shot: 'And whatever happens to Kevin I won't be lonely, not when his family – *your* family – will be my family. What company will *you* have when Raymond is working all hours God sends? You won't have Kel because Kel won't come within a mile of this house, and you won't have me, because once Raymond knows about Kevin I won't be *allowed* to come within a mile of it.'

Slamming the door behind her she made for the stairs, Jackie's jibe about Kevin's infidelity ringing in her ears. Jackie had been outrageously out of order saying such a thing. People changed. The way Raymond had changed was proof of that. The old Raymond wouldn't have put his career at risk for anyone or anything but the new Ray-mond, loving Jackie and wanting to marry her, was doing exactly that.

She ran down the stairs and as she did so Lavender opened the drawing-room door and stepped out into the hallway, moving with difficulty but as well groomed as always. 'You haven't left a radio or a television on somewhere, dear, have you?' she asked with a slight frown of concern. 'I thought I heard shouting a few moments ago.'

'It would be the television in Jackie's room.' Rosamund wasn't in the habit of lying but had discovered that, when necessary, she could do so with disturbing ease. 'She's watching one of those hideous Australian soaps.'

Lavender's carefully pencilled eyebrows arched in surprise and Rosamund felt a flash of guilt. No matter how out of order Jackie had been she didn't deserve to be labelled an Australian soap addict. 'I'm going to meet Kelly,' she added, not wanting to risk another run-in with Jackie by staying at home. 'Bye.'

She rushed out of the house, feeling yet another shaft of guilt, for she hadn't the slightest intention of meeting up with Kelly. She was going to go over to the Tower Hill flat in the hope of finding Kevin there – and if he was, she was going to tell him about the baby.

'Come on, love. Time you were on your way.' Kevin patted Shirelle Dobson's peach-like naked rump affectionately. 'I've to be up and off and I ain't leaving you here. You know the rules.'

Shirelle did and she didn't like them. A hostess in one of the Soho clubs Kevin frequented, she'd been an on-off girlfriend of his for years. Over the last few months their relationship had, much to her regret, been most definitely off, on account of the wishy-washy-looking posh bint he had begun giving near undivided attention to.

She rolled away from him on the king-size bed, not bothering to pull a sheet with her. 'Why don't we take the day off together, Kevvie?' she asked seductively, reaching across to an onyx bedside table for a packet of cigarettes. 'We could zip down to Brighton. That Lancia of yours'll have us there in half an hour. Or we could go out Windsor way. Perhaps have lunch at The Bell.'

Kevin swung his legs from the bed and stood up, his

lean, splendidly muscled body in top condition. 'Nah,' he said easily, already regretting the previous night's drunken impulsiveness that had led to her being in the flat. 'I've a lot on today, babe. People to see, places to go.'

Shirelle pouted sulkily but knew better than to push it. Despite his laid-back manner, when Kevvie said a thing, he meant it.

'What about tonight then, lover?' she asked, rolling off the bed and to her feet. 'I should be working but I can square it.' She slipped her feet into her high-heeled shoes so that, sashaying naked across the room to where she'd left her clothes, she'd look to best advantage.

Kevin was indifferent to the efforts being made to regain his attention. The bullion heist was imminent and there was an important meet at lunchtime. He strode into the en-suite bathroom and opened the frosted-glass door of the power-shower cubicle. Later on he'd be seeing Ros. Later still he intended having a word with Johnny about the Eddie problem.

'*Ple-ease*, lover,' Shirelle persisted. Nakedness and high-heels having failed to gain her what she craved she had pulled the dressing-table stool to where, arching her back and straddling it in pin-up pose, Kevin could see her from the bathroom.

Kevin saw and his only reaction was a stab of annoyance. She had the thickest auburn bush he'd ever seen and looked every inch a tart. He gave a wry grin as he stepped into the shower. Shirelle looked a tart because she *was* a tart. He turned the shower knob to hot, luxuriating in the impact of the powerful needles of water. His Ros couldn't look a tart if her life depended on it. He soaped himself down, stifling the beginnings of an erection. It was Ros's classiness that made her so special, that and the knowledge only he was privy to – that beneath her cool English Rose looks she was a red-hot volcano.

He rinsed himself down, grinning broadly as he did so.

The girls who worked Soho knew all the tricks all right but for sheer sexiness his public-school-educated, well-bred Ros was the bee's knees.

When he first heard the doorbell, as he was stepping out of the shower hoping he was going to find Shirelle fully dressed and ready to leave, it didn't occur to him to panic. He simply assumed Johnny wanted to talk to him about Eddie and had mislaid his key.

'I'll get it,' he shouted, wrapping an aquamarine towel around his waist and draping another around his neck.

Shirelle, who didn't care who she opened the door to as long as, in doing so, she gave the impression she was Kevin's lady, behaved as if she hadn't heard. Still naked apart from her high-heeled shoes she pirouetted out into the hallway, opening the door wide.

For a second it was doubtful whose shock was the greatest; Rosamund's, Shirelle's, or Kevin's.

'Well, if it isn't Miss Prim and Proper,' Shirelle said sarcastically, recovering first and folding her arms beneath her melon-sized breasts. 'If you wanted to make it a threesome, honey, you're a little late.'

'Shut it, Shirelle, and get the hell out,' Kevin said tautly, striding towards the door, his hair sleekly wet, his skin glistening with water droplets.

What happened next was something neither Shirelle, by now enjoying herself hugely, nor Kevin, who was expecting Ros to break down hysterically, even remotely expected. Ros, who had never in her life been on the receiving end of violence and had certainly never dished any out – who hadn't even scrapped in her privileged school playground – gave a howl that would have done credit to a banshee and sprang for Shirelle's face, her nails clawed.

'For Christ's sake!' Kevin sprinted towards them certain that Shirelle would have Ros a hospital case within minutes.

'*You stay out of it*!' The shouted sob came from Ros as

she raked both sides of Shirelle's face, gouging blood.

Shirelle gave a scream of disbelief and pain and then went for Ros like a wildcat, grabbing at her silky-straight shoulder-length hair, yanking it with such ferocity Ros's blue velvet head-band went flying and her head nearly came off her shoulders.

'*Cunt*!'

'*Whore*!'

'*Fucking bitch*!'

'*Tart*!'

As they rolled and fought and kicked the only difference in the insults they were hurling at each other was that Ros was the one not being foul-mouthed.

Aware that unless he got some trousers on he was going to look a right pillock trying to separate them, Kevin leaped for the far side of the rumpled bed where, the previous night, he had dropped his designer label chinos.

Shirelle, streetwise to her magenta-lacquered fingertips, was spitting kicking and biting, no holds barred. Her rage at what was happening was, however, nothing compared to Rosamund's.

At a deep primitive level Rosamund was fighting for her entire future – and not just her future but her baby's future. Unless she kicked the whore who'd been sleeping in Kevin's bed out of the flat – the flat she had begun to regard as theirs – she and Kevin had no future. She had to show him that she, and she alone, was the woman in his life and that she could not and would not tolerate other women sleeping in the bed that had become hers.

'*Jesus Christ*!' Kevin was fighting his way into his pants. A mirror had been toppled; a Lalique vase was laying in smithereens on the floor; a whisky decanter had been smashed and the place was beginning to stink to high heaven. If he didn't sort things double quick his entire flat was going to be wrecked.

'*Get out of here, you tramp*!' A panting Rosamund

grabbed a champagne bottle that had been standing empty by the bed and, holding it by the neck, slammed it violently against the edge of the dressing-table so that she held a jagged lethal weapon in her hands. The word 'glassed' was one she wasn't even familiar with but Shirelle was. Her face had already been clawed to ruination. She wasn't going to have it permanently mutilated.

'I hope you know your girlfriend's sick in the head!' she sobbed to Kevin in fury, scooping up her clothes. 'She's a schizo! A fuckin' psycho!'

'Get *out*!' Rosamund stepped towards her, her teeth bared, the broken bottle raised.

Shirelle spat at her one last time and, still naked, her clothes clutched to her chest, backed out of the flat.

Rosamund slammed the door on her and then, reaction to the unbelievable way she had behaved kicking in, began trembling so violently her teeth chattered.

'Jesus . . .' Kevin said again, taking the bottle from her and tossing it onto the bed. 'When you lose your rag you don't mess about, love, do you?'

She leaned against his bare chest, beginning to sob, all fight gone.

He hugged her close, his mouth against her hair, a chuckle beginning to rise in his throat. The sight of Ros going for Shirelle with a broken champagne bottle in her hand was one he wouldn't forget in a hurry. How many more surprises was this lady of his going to give him?

'Promise me . . . please promise me . . . she's going to be the last,' Ros was saying through her tears.

He hugged her tight. Not only was it a promise easy to give; it was a promise he might even keep. 'I promise, sweetheart. Truly.'

The chuckle he had been fighting down refused to be suppressed any longer.

Rosamund pushed herself sharply away from him, her eyes, red-rimmed from crying, meeting his. 'This isn't something to laugh at, Kevin! I have to *know* you won't be unfaithful to me again because . . . because . . .'

She couldn't finish her sentence. Her heartbeats were slamming like hammer blows. This wasn't the way she had intended telling him her news and she was terrified as to what his reaction was going to be. 'Because I'm having a baby,' she finished, adding quite unnecessarily, '*your* baby.'

To Kevin's credit he barely blinked. Getting married hadn't been on his agenda but there was no real reason it shouldn't be, especially if the lady in question was Ros. He grinned. At least now he'd be able to make amends for giving her grief and he rather liked the idea of becoming a dad. Family had always been important to him and, as he was going on for twenty-eight, it was high time he had a nipper of his own.

'Then we'd better have a ring on your finger before you're too fat to fit into a wedding dress,' he said, answering all the prayers she'd ever prayed.

'Oh, Kevin!' Her fine-boned face was radiant. 'Oh, Kevin, do you really mean it?'

He cracked with laughter, his wet hair tumbling sleekly over his brows. 'Course I mean it, darlin'. We'll go out tonight and celebrate – dinner by candlelight, champagne, red roses, the lot.'

She threw her arms around his neck, ecstatic with joy. 'I love you, Kevin Rice! I love you with my whole life!'

'That's all right then,' he said, still laughing, aware of the meet he had to make and knowing there wasn't time for lovemaking. 'Look, love,' with genuine regret he unwound her arms from his neck, 'I have to be across the river in half an hour. I've something big on the cards – mammoth big. It's going to mean that after tonight I won't be around for a few days. Afterwards . . .' He paused, excitement blazing in his eyes and pulsing along every nerve-end in his body. Afterwards the world would be their oyster, but he couldn't tell her that; not yet.

'Afterwards . . .' he said again, wrapping his arms around her waist and whirling her around so that her feet left the floor, '. . . afterwards I'm going to buy you an engagement ring with diamonds so big they'll make the diamonds in the Crown Jewels look like ice chippings!'

'I still fink we should be going fer the mail van when its left the station and is on the road,' Smiler was saying in a troubled voice as he sat in the back of the Transit van that was taking him, Jock, Albie, Johnny and Dexter down to Portsmouth.

'Why go through all the aggro of a hijack when we don't need to?' As both Jock and Johnny raised their eyes to heaven Albie was, as usual, amiability personified. 'This way the van's stationary. It couldn't be easier.'

Smiler picked up his sawn-off shotgun and began polishing it. 'I still don't like it,' he persisted stubbornly. 'It's all right fer you and Jock and the blackie, you ain't armed. Hiding a tool as big as this under my coat ain't comfortable.'

'Then give it me, man. I'll carry it.' This was the first big job Dexter had done with Kelly's family and his patience, where her Uncle Smiler was concerned, was fast running out. 'And I ain't "the blackie". The name is Dexter and you'd better start remembering it.'

'Cool it, you two.' There was definite warning in Jock's voice. Tension always ran high before a job and it was vital to keep it properly focused. 'We're just coming up to Petersfield. Another fifteen minutes and we'll be on top of Portsmouth. How's Kelly doing, Johnny? Is she still tucked in behind us?'

Johnny glanced in his driving mirror and nodded. 'Yeah. She's sweet as a nut.'

Everyone fell back into tense silence. Jock's thoughts were centred entirely on the job in hand. Had they covered every eventuality in their planning of it? Had he and Albie and Smiler's four visits to the ferry and train terminal been sufficient for them to be quite sure of the routine where the unloading and loading up of the registered mail parcels were concerned? Had Johnny and Kelly gone over the escape route from the station to the lock-up sufficient times? Had it been sense opting for the quick sprint to the lock-up, where they had a second getaway car stashed but where there was the chance they would be cornered, or should they have hared immediately back to London, risking roadblocks? Would it have been wiser waiting till it was the Christmas holiday period?

The best time to have done it, of course, would have been in August, at the height of the holiday season. The ferry and station platforms would have been crowded and they would have been unnoticeable until the very second they went into the attack. They'd missed that deadline, though, and there was no sense putting the job on a back burner until next August. Another nine months and the job might not be there to do. Some other tossers would very likely have done it for them. He gnawed his knuckle, his eyes narrowed. He, Smiler, Albie and Johnny always worked like clockwork together and Dexter and Kelly were a hundred per cent sound. It was going to be all right. It was going to be a doddle.

Albie's thoughts were, as usual, unanxious. He would rather have had Kevin with them than Dexter who was, as far as he was concerned, an unknown quantity, but if Jock had confidence in him then there couldn't be anything to worry about. Kelly's nig-nog boyfriend was certainly a likeable bloke. He'd never seen anyone with such an infectious grin. It went right from one ear to the other.

Dexter wasn't grinning at that particular moment. He was looking out of the van's rear window, keeping a close eye on the metallic blue Volkswagen a car or so behind them. The final plan decided on left an awful lot of responsibility to Kelly for she was the one who would have to impede any police cars too close behind them as they made for the lock-up. At the present moment she was over-taking one of the cars in front of her and he gave her a wink, flexed his biceps and began counting down the minutes to Portsmouth.

Johnny glanced down at his watch, thinking not about the job he was about to carry out, but about the job Kevin had set out on four hours earlier. He'd been keeping his eyes peeled all the way through Guildford and other built-up areas for the latest headlines on news placards but so far all that was being displayed was yesterday's headlines *re* the gunmen in Northern Ireland who had burst into a Protestant chapel, killing three people and wounding seven.

The nerves in his belly coiled into a tight knot. The Portsmouth job was a biggie and would pull them all at least eight years if they were caught but the Brinks-Mat was major. If anything went wrong Kevin could easily be looking a twenty-year stretch in the face.

'Another ten minutes and we'll be in Portsmouth,' Jock said to him, breaking in on his thoughts and pulling a pair of gloves from his back trouser pocket. Smiler began climbing into the overcoat with the two special inside pockets that would conceal his shotgun. Dexter stayed relaxed, knowing what it was he had to do; knowing that he'd have no trouble doing it.

Despite their lack of Balaclavas, which would have been too instant a giveaway of their intentions, none of them was going to be easily recognisable. 'Always 'guise up', was Jock's motto and he was wearing plain-lensed horn-rimmed glasses and over the last couple of weeks had grown a grizzled beard. Johnny's distinctive straw-coloured hair had been darkened to brown and, though he hadn't grown a full beard like Jock, he was sporting a moustache which, for some reason Dexter couldn't quite work out, aged him by about ten years.

Albie's disguise was the beret he was pulling on. It turned

him instantaneously into a Frenchman. No such subtlety would have been adequate for Smiler. He had a grotesque grandad mask pulled down around his neck. For the moment it was hidden by a Millwall scarf but the minute they went into action he would yank the mask up and on. For himself Dexter had a woolly hat which, when pulled down over his face, had eyeholes cut into it and was as good as any Balaclava.

'It's nicely busy,' Johnny said ten minutes later, edging to a halt at the far side of the bridge that led across to the station.

Behind them Kelly flashed her lights and continued on, past them, heading towards the street immediately prior to the lock-up they'd rented.

'Right?' Jock asked everyone tersely. 'Everyone straight about what they've to do?'

Four brief nods were his reply.

'Then let's get busy looking inconspicuous.'

He, Smiler, Albie and Dexter all alighted from the van and then, without another word to each other, began to stroll off towards the station entrance.

Johnny slid the Transit once more into gear and drove it at a decorous pace across the bridge, parking it up within sight of the station's loading bay. The Royal Mail van wasn't yet parked up but he wasn't worried. It soon would be.

Switching off the Transit's engine he checked that his handgun was tucked snugly into his belt, adjusted his jacket, and stepped out of the van.

Casually, as if he hadn't a care in the world, he walked into the station. Smiler was slouched against a public telephone apparently studying a railway timetable. Albie was at the station buffet, enjoying a cup of tea. There was no sign of Jock and Dexter and he didn't look for them. Instead, mingling with passengers who had just alighted from a London train, he strolled in the direction of the ferry terminal, pleased to see that their timing had been spot on and that the ferry was just docking.

With growing tension he positioned himself so that he had a good view of the hold. As passengers began disembarking the unloading procedures began. A derrick was swung into position. Cargo began to be hoisted up and out of the hold. As the threepenny-bit-shaped container holding the money parcels was winched into view he felt a surge of elation. The job was on. In another five minutes or so they would have liftoff.

An electric trolley with driver, a screamer box attached to his wrist, was waiting on the dockside to receive the container.

Johnny had seen all he needed to see. Abruptly he turned, striding back down the platform with all the scores of people who had just disembarked and were about to board the London train. As he passed the left-hand-side entrance to the loading bay he ran a hand over his hair. It was an innocuous enough gesture but both Jock and Dexter, whom he still couldn't see, would be watching and registering his signal that the trolley was on its way.

He crossed the concourse to the parked Transit, checked that the rear doors were open and then swung himself up behind the wheel and gunned the engine into life. Smiler, he knew, would be strolling towards the loading bay's station entrance where the Royal Mail van was now clearly in evidence. Albie would be slipping off his buffet stool and also moving into position. Jock would be striding down the platform mere yards in front of the electric trolley, his closeness to it no more noticeable than that of dozens of oblivious travellers making for the front No Smoking section of the train.

From where he was seated in the still stationary Transit van he could see that the Royal Mail van's driver's mate had jumped out of the van in readiness to help the trolley driver off-load the mailbags from the trolley.

Smiler and Albie were now unobtrusively in position, as

was Dexter. The electric trolley slid through the station's entrance to the loading bay and the excitement in Johnny's belly reached exploding point. This was it! *Ten seconds ... nine seconds ...*

There was some banter going on between the van driver and the guy driving the trolley. *Eight seconds ... seven seconds ...*

The first mailbag was heaved out of the container and, together, the van driver's mate and the trolley driver slung it into the van. *Six seconds ... Five seconds ...*

The trolley driver, the screamer box conspicuously attached to his wrist, turned slightly, facing towards the station platform. *Four seconds. Three seconds.* Jock, obviously unarmed and still looking completely innocuous walked briskly towards him. *Two seconds ... one second ...*

The geezer with the screamer box smiled towards Jock. Whether Jock smiled back or not Johnny never knew. The seconds were out and he was reversing the Transit at top speed into the loading bay on the blind side of the PO van. As he did so everything was screaming bloody mayhem.

Jock slammed straight into the van driver's mate, chinning him semi-conscious and sending him flying. Smiler, hideous in his grandad mask, his shotgun in his hands, was yelling '*Down! Down! Down!*' as the van driver prepared to launch himself from the PO van. Dexter and Albie were already hurling mailsacks into the back of the Transit. The screamer box was shrieking at full belt; all hell was being let loose on the station platform; somewhere another siren was wailing. '*They'll have my job for this, you bleedin' bastard!*' the trolley driver was shouting, so overcome with rage and frustration he was almost sobbing.

Ten mailbags. Eleven. Twelve.

Jock was now at it with Albie and Dexter, lifting and hurling in demented frenzy. There was still no sound of a police siren but time was fast running out.

Thirteen. Fourteen. Fifteen.

There were another five mailbags to go but not another precious second could be wasted.

'*Go! Go! Go!*' Jock yelled, hurling himself into the back of the Transit. Albie and Smiler and Dexter hurtled in after him and Johnny let out the clutch, slewing the van out of the loading bay and across the concourse.

There were police car sirens now – what sounded to be dozens of them – as Johnny sliced the van through the traffic on the bridge and rounded a corner on what felt to be two wheels. He knew the route to the lock-up like the back of his hand. If he could make it without being in the sights of a police car all well and good. If he couldn't . . . He screeched round another corner and crashed a red light. If he couldn't it was all down to Kelly.

'*Get those fucking doors shut!*' Jock was yelling to Smiler who, being the last one to topple in on top of the mailbags, was the nearest to the van's crazily swinging doors. Risking life and limb Smiler leaned out, grabbing at them, pulling them shut as Johnny screeched round yet another corner and he fell backwards.

The police sirens sounded to be zeroing in on them from all directions.

'Are they in your mirror yet?' Jock shouted to Johnny, scrambling over the mailbags to take up a position immediately behind Johnny's driving seat.

'Nah.' Johnny veered onto the wrong side of the road to overtake a line of slow-moving traffic, rocked back in the teeth of an oncoming lorry and, ignoring the smell of burning rubber, swooped down a left-hand turn.

'They bleedin' will be in a minute,' Smiler said, struggling back into a sitting position and ripping his granddad mask from his face. 'What 'appens if they cut in up ahead of us, between us and Kel?'

'They won't.' Johnny was always ice cool in such situations and though no one was a hundred per cent convinced they all kept their traps shut. The last thing a driver in Johnny's position needed was back-seat aggro.

Johnny swerved from the side road he was in to an even smaller side road and, though the police sirens were now deafening, began to drive at something near to normal speed. The lock-up and their second get away van were only two streets away. He couldn't approach them like a maniac for everything depended on his being able to stash the Transit in the garage without attracting undue attention.

'*They're on to us*!' As Johnny exited the end of the street Smiler caught a glimpse of a police car bursting in on it behind them.

Johnny swore. They were too near for him to ignore the lock-up and try to out run them. They were also too near, unless Kelly did her stuff, for him to be able to swing into the lock-up unseen and for the rozzers to be under the impression that they were still fleeing, though now so far ahead as to be out of sight.

Increasing everyone's tension, even Jock's, to near screaming point, he took the next corner at almost decorous speed. Kelly was in position, her car engine running. It was a quiet suburban street. There were cars parked at either side of the road but no other traffic. There was a woman a little distance away, her back towards him, pushing a pram. He flashed his lights, prayed to God, and as Kelly slewed her car broadside on across the middle of the road, exited from it neatly just as the police car burst around the corner behind him.

Jock's jaw was clamped tight. The risk Kelly was running was enormous. What if she hadn't judged her distance from the corner correctly? What if the police car slammed straight in on her? What if she was seriously hurt? What if . . . ?

The lock-up was placed between a short row of terrace houses and a builders' yard. As the sound of screeching tyres ripped the air and there came the sound of shattering glass, Johnny swung the Transit neatly off the road between gates that, thanks to Kelly, were wide open.

Smiler and Dexter leaped out of the back of the Transit, slamming the gates shut. Johnny snapped the engine off. Everything hinged on the next few minutes. The rozzers would either be fooled by Kelly's tactic and delayed by it long enough for them to assume that the Transit was now streets and streets ahead of them and making for the nearest turn-off to the A3 and London, or they wouldn't. If they weren't, then a search of every garage in the street, the builders' yard and their lock-up would be carried out pronto and they'd be caught like rats in a trap.

'Come on, Kelly-girl,' Johnny said beneath his breath, stowing his gun in the glove compartment so that there'd be no truthful accusation of him having tried to evade arrest by using it. 'Give it all you've got, for Christ's sake.'

Kelly's heartbeats were slamming like pistons. The second Johnny had swung past her, lights flashing, she had hurled the estate car broadside on across the road, thanking God for the lack of witnesses. It was an exercise carried out with only a split second to spare. She was still in the act of throwing herself from the car, bursting a bag of judiciously prepared pig's blood against her chest, as the police car squealed round the corner.

Screaming hysterically she staggered a few yards away from the Volkswagen towards the far side of the road where, if it had chosen to, there was enough room for the police car to have squeezed through, continuing its chase. As it was, slewing to an emergency stop in order not to smash head-on into the Volkswagen, and faced with what appeared to be a critically injured woman, the driver of the car radioed in his situation while his companion ran to Kelly's aid.

Kelly, knowing everything depended on enough time

lapsing for it to be assumed the Transit was happily haring towards the A3, bit hard on the plastic bag stowed hamster-like in her cheek and, as the officer reached her side, gushed up blood all over him from what appeared to be a dire injury.

Only as, in the ambulance, Kelly heard the policeman accompanying her radio in that the Transit he and his colleague had been pursuing was now heading through side streets in the direction of the A3, did she breathe a sigh of relief.

Admitted into Casualty under the same false name she had used when hiring the Volkswagen, and knowing the policeman assigned to her would soon be questioning her as to the circumstances of her accident, she asked to use the ladies' room. Ten minutes later, her blood-stained clothes covered by a coat she had lifted, she was in a mini-cab heading, as had been pre-arranged, to the train station and a London-bound train.

Back in the lock-up the mailbags had all been opened, registered money parcels being separated from parcels that were of no consequence.

'How much do you reckon it'll come to?' Dexter asked Johnny as Johnny shaved his moustache off with an electric razor, and Jock and Albie stashed the money parcels into three large suitcases that had been brought down days previously in the boot of their second get away, a big roomy Merc.

'Enough,' Johnny said easily, confident by now that no search of the street's garages was, as yet, taking place, and happy to be dealing with three large respectable-looking suitcases and not cumbersome mailbags. He clicked his electric razor off, wiped his upper lip over with his hand and said, 'Why don't you watch the news tonight when you're back in the smoke? That way, if they announce the amount stolen, it'll save counting it.'

'When will you get back?' It was the only thing that

hadn't been spelled out to him and Dexter was curious. 'Tonight? Tomorrow?'

Johnny lifted his shoulders slightly. 'I'll be back as soon as the heat is off and the roadblocks are lifted. Until then I'll be a guest at a quiet little hotel and the dosh will stay locked where it is.' Albie and Jock had finished their task and he slammed the boot lid down on the suitcases. 'If it still seems dodgy in a few days' time Kel's mum will round up a few kids and bring them down here on the train. I'll pile them all in the car with ice-creams to take them back to London and I can practically guarantee we'll have a trouble-free run.'

'Ready, Dex?' It was Jock. Smiler had gone over the Transit to ensure nothing, apart from the dross mail and mailbags, had been left in it. The van itself was a ringer and, like Kelly's Volkswagen, could not be traced back to them. There was nothing left now but for them to split.

Dexter nodded. Smiler opened the lock-up's gates and looked cautiously out into the street. It was as clean as a whistle.

Johnny slid behind the Merc's wheel. In another ten minutes he'd be in his pre-booked hotel enjoying a large gin and tonic.

'See you,' he said casually as he drove the Merc out into the street, its boot stuffed with their ill-gotten gains. 'Have a nice choo-choo ride home.'

'Bugger off,' Smiler said sourly. He hated traipsing home on the train and resented the fact that Johnny always fell for a cushy number where transport was concerned.

Albie grinned. Jock gave Johnny the thumbs-up. Dexter began closing and locking the lock-up doors. He rather liked Johnny's crack that if they listened to the news they wouldn't have to bother counting their loot for themselves. Three hours later, when he, Jock, Smiler and Albie emerged from the Portsmouth–London train at Waterloo Station and he saw the headline on a news placard, 'Brinks-Mat robbers get away with £26 million in gold bars', he was reminded yet again.

'Will you take a look at that?' he said disbelievingly to the others, hardly able to credit the figure he was reading and aware it made their own haul look like chicken-feed. 'The bastards that lifted that little lot will be glad not to have to count it!'

Jock looked towards the news placard. Dexter expected him either to whistle through his teeth with the same disbelief he felt, or to curse roundly in sheer envy. Instead Jock staggered, his knees seeming temporarily to give way beneath him and then, with a great war-whoop of elation he began to run across the crowded concourse, jumping up every few yards, kicking his heels and punching the air triumphantly with his fist, shouting, '*Yes! Oh yes! YES! YES! YES!*'

Chapter Thirteen

Fifteen-year-old Sharon Doughty dug shocking-pink-painted nails into the pillow she was kneeling face down over, and choked on a scream. Eddie thrust with more force than ever, not because he particularly liked fucking birds up their arseholes but because he liked hurting them and he'd long ago discovered that, carried out with a few of his own creative refinements, this was one of the most satisfactory ways of doing it.

This time Sharon's scream was loud and high. She felt as if her back passage was being raked by razor blades and wasn't far wrong. Eddie screwed his eyes shut, seizing hold of the brass bed-head to give himself more purchase. She was bleeding. He could feel the blood dribbling out of her and onto his bollocks. But she wasn't bleeding enough. Not yet.

Women. He'd never understood why Kev and Johnny-boy were so hung up on them. Even as a spotty teenager, slipping a sweaty hand up fat sausage thighs into sticky knickers had never been his idea of pleasure. He'd never let on that it wasn't, of course. No one would have thought him the business if they knew he wasn't red-hot about shagging.

'Please stop . . . Oh please, please stop!' Sharon wanted her mum. Her mum had told her not to hang around with the new friends she'd made down at the Roxy, friends who were all a good five or six years older than she. She hadn't taken any notice. Her new mates went into clubs she'd never have got into with her schoolmates – clubs where they met exciting people. *Famous* people.

When her mum had blown her top about her going out of the house looking like a tart she'd stuffed her going-out gear into a carrier bag and left it behind the dustbin in the back garden.

An hour later, dressed in her school uniform, she'd said she was going round to do some homework with Susie Leach and could she stay the night as Susie's mum was in hospital and her dad was working nights and Susie didn't like being in the house alone.

The bit about Susie's mum being in hospital hadn't been a lie and as her mum had known it wasn't, there'd been no hassle. Sharon had simply walked out of the front door, nipped round the back to retrieve the carrier bag and then waltzed down to McDonald's in Catford, changing her clothes and putting on her make-up in the ladies' loo.

It had been a wicked night out. One of the blokes in the club they'd gone to had been in *EastEnders* and another geezer had said he was an international businessman and had been so loaded with cash it had practically been coming out of his ears. He'd said she looked just like a model, and in her black leather miniskirt and black lacy stockings she'd felt like a model. She'd felt sexy and sophisticated and when she thought of Susie, staying in like a kid and doing homework, she'd nearly bust a gut she'd laughed so much.

Then Eddie Burns and his entourage – that was the word the *EastEnders* bloke had used about the geezers in Eddie Burns's wake – had strolled in and the evening had taken on a very special kind of buzz. It had been 'Yes, Mr Burns', 'No, Mr Burns', and people had scurried round him like he was some kind of film star. He'd been wearing dark glasses so that he looked like a film star, too. She'd thought herself so lucky when he'd singled her out.

She didn't think herself lucky now, though. She hurt so much she could barely think at all.

'Please!' she begged through snot and tears. 'Oh please stop, mister!'

Eddie, reaching what for him passed for a climax, decided he'd had enough. He had other things on his mind – namely the Brinks-Mat heist and who had pulled it. Merciful minutes later, zipping up his pants, he walked out of the room, leaving her sprawled, bleeding and moaning, on the bed.

'Dog's breath,' he said when he interrupted the card game his waiting henchmen were playing. 'Ain't you noticed no matter what a tart looks like the night before, in the morning she'll always have dog's breath. It makes you want to puke.'

'D'you want me to shove her in a mini-cab?' one of the men who had helped dispose of Lonnie Dyson asked, laying down his cards and blowing a ring of smoke into the air.

'Do what you bleedin' well like with her,' Eddie said indifferently, and then gave a wolfish grin. 'You can give her one up the jacksie if you want. She loves it. Can't get enough of it.'

The man in question, a mountain of flesh, gave an answering grin and pushed himself away from the card table, lumbering in the direction of the stairs.

By the time he'd heaved himself up them Sharon had crawled from the bed and, ignoring all her other clothes, was struggling to ease her pain-wracked body into her coat. With her coat on she could sneak down the stairs and into the street and somehow – some way – reach the sanctuary of home.

The man mountain lumbered into the room and kicked the door shut behind him.

Helplessly, hopelessly, Sharon began to whimper.

Eddie slumped down into a black leather executive office chair, tilting it backwards. Brinks-Mat. It was the heist of the decade – probably the heist of the century. It was also exactly the kind of heist Kevin and Johnny had always dreamed of pulling. They couldn't have been in on this one though – it was simply too mammoth. Immediate news reports said that the take had been something in the region of twenty-six million. He cracked his knuckles. The rumour in the crim world was that even the raiders were stupefied by the size of their take. *Could* Kevin have been in on it? He'd certainly had something on his mind these last few weeks and whatever it was he sure as shit hadn't been talking about it – at least not to him.

As he thought of the way his cousins and uncles had manoeuvred him out of the family firm he sank into an even deeper pit of hate. It wasn't that he'd wanted to remain in their poxy little firm – he'd already shown he was far too big a number for it – but they should have *wanted* him. They should have wanted him to take control: to be the boss. Instead they'd taken on Kelly's nig-nog boyfriend. He felt his gorge rise. They were going to regret what they'd done. He was going to do for Jock short-arse Sweeting and his nigger friend. He was going to croak them and dump them where he'd dumped Lonnie Dyson.

As for Kevin and Johnny . . . his eyes glittered. He had the perfect solution for them. He was going to tip Ray Pulfer off that they were in on the Brinks-Mat. Even if they were as clean as whistles it would seriously inconvenience them and they'd have to put whatever else it was they were planning on ice, putting them out of circulation for a bit – and if they weren't clean as whistles? He clenched his knuckles until the bones shone white. If either one of them had been in on the Brinks-Mat, excluding him from it, he'd see to it that they were collared for it – and he'd get his paws on their stash.

He grinned to himself, his black mood beginning to lighten. With Raymond Pulfer's help he was becoming extremely skilful at fitting up people he could do without – it was the main source of his secret power base. Thanks to the two of them working so well together heads in the heavy game were rolling left and right. Each time one did he moved smoothly into the vacancy left, accruing even more 'soldiers', and Pulfer gained the kind of kudos that would soon see him before yet another promotion board. Kevin and Johnny hadn't cottoned on to it yet but they had no chance against him, none at all.

It was a beautiful day for an early December wedding. St Michael and All Saints' spire pierced a crisp blue sky and the heath the church backed on to glittered with a light covering of frost.

'Nervous?' Rosamund asked Jackie as she and Deputy Commissioner Laing, who was to give Jackie away, waited inside the church porch for the change in music that would indicate it was time for Deputy Commissioner Laing to escort Jackie down the aisle.

'No.' The emotion Jackie was feeling was so chaotic and confused that mere nervousness simply didn't seem to apply. There was gratitude. At least she wasn't completely bereft of family. Kevin could easily have given Rosamund the hard word where being a bridesmaid was concerned and he hadn't done so.

Other emotions, such as how she felt being given away by Deputy Commissioner Laing and not her father, were less easy to define. Hurt shot through her and she snapped down on it fast. Even when, as a child, she'd daydreamed of marrying someone respectable and straight she'd surely never imagined her father giving her his blessing for such a marriage – had she?

She moved her delicate bouquet of stephanotis and yellow bud roses from her right hand to her left and tentatively adjusted the circlet of matching flowers crowning her upswept hair.

One thing was certain: she'd never envisaged marrying without being surrounded by friends and family. Considering the speed with which the wedding had been arranged

Raymond had performed miracles where invitations had been concerned and the church was full, but with his relations and friends, not hers.

On his father's side of the family there was a near regiment of aunts, uncles, cousins, nephews, nieces. On his mother's side Lavender's sister was there even though she, like Lavender, suffered with disabling arthritis. Raymond's immediate superiors were there, as were a clutch of detective sergeants, detective inspectors and detective chief inspectors.

DI Richard Ross, who had been with Raymond in the wine bar the night she had met him with such momentous results, was acting as best man. The church was full of flowers. A photographer had been hired and had already taken photographs of her and Deputy Commissioner Laing and Rosamund entering the church. The reception was to be held at the Clarendon Hotel, which faced the heath, only a stone's throw from the church.

What story Raymond had spun their guests in order to account for their being invited a mere couple of weeks before the ceremony Jackie didn't know. Whatever his explanation it had obviously been credible for there was no shotgun atmosphere. It was the sort of wedding she'd dreamed about having as a child. It was orderly and traditional and dignified. The gentle organ music being played came to a close. There was a slight pause and then Handel's *Wedding March* began to resonate majestically throughout the church.

'Ready, my dear?' Commissioner Laing asked her in a fatherly manner.

She nodded, exchanged an emotion-filled look with Rosamund and then, her arm resting lightly in the crook of the deputy commissioner's, stepped with him into the nave and began the momentous walk down the flower-decked aisle to where Raymond was waiting for her.

*   *   *

'Numbers 1, 3, and 5 have been arrested! The inside man has grassed on every name he knew and it's fucking curtains!'

Kevin was in a public telephone box in Streatham.

'*What*? *When*? *How*?' he shouted into the telephone receiver, hardly able to take in the mind-boggling enormity of what he was being told.

'The only ones not fingered are those the twat didn't know about,' his informant said savagely, 'so it's go-to-ground time – no meeting up. It's too much of a risk.'

The line went dead and Kevin slumped against the wall of the booth, nearly insensible with shock. Numbers 1 and 3, 'The Bully' and 'The Colonel', arrested. Of the small number of men who had carried out the actual raid, 1 and 3 were the prime movers and shakers. Number 3, especially, had been the organisational mind behind everything. What the fuck was now going to happen to 1 and 3's mammoth take? More to the point, how was he going to safeguard his own take? Bullion wasn't paper money. It couldn't be stuffed into a suitcase.

He reeled outside the booth and leaned heavily against it. He was in nightmare-land – the country every robber feared. No matter how meticulously planned a robbery, no matter the trust between those carrying it out, no matter how successful the raid itself, whenever a job hinged on inside information – and big jobs nearly always did – there was always a colossal weak link. Inside-information men weren't professional criminals. They weren't steeped in the code of never grassing – and they sure as hell weren't experienced in standing up to relentless police questioning.

He groaned. He and everyone else involved with the Brinks-Mat had known that their inside-man would be rigorously questioned in the immediate aftermath of the raid, as would every other Brinks-Mat employee. That was the way it always was. A company's employees were always the first suspects.

In this instance, though, the inside man hadn't been an unknown quantity. A security guard whose information and help had been crucial, his sister was number 3's girlfriend and, though he hadn't a prison record, was as near to being one of their own as made no difference. It hadn't occurred to any of them that the police would break his indignant claims that he'd known nothing about the raid, knew none of the men involved in it and was as innocent of having anything to do with it as a new-born babe.

Instead, within crucial days he'd broken down under questioning, admitted involvement and, far worse, committed the heinous sin of naming names. Kevin passed a hand across his eyes. What the bleeding fuck was he to do? He couldn't be seen in any of his old haunts, and going back to Creek Row was out of the question, yet somehow he had to get in touch with Johnny and Jock. And Ros. Christ Almighty. He couldn't be away on his toes without first seeing and explaining things to Ros.

He looked around him, half expecting to find himself already under surveillance. The street was congested with traffic, the pavement busy, but not sinisterly so. He chewed the corner of his lip. He could ring the snooker club or the Connoisseur in an effort to make contact with Johnny or Jock but as they were his known hang-outs it was just possible the phone lines were being tapped. The Becket and Dexter would be much safer. Dexter wasn't known as being one of his associates. If they met up he wouldn't have rozzers on his heels.

With a last quick scan of the street he turned his back on it, entered the phone booth once more and dialled the Becket's number.

'Let me introduce you to Aunt Elspeth and Uncle Willie, darling.'

Jackie had shaken hands with all their guests when she and Raymond had received them at the entrance of the

Clarendon's dining room but there were so many new faces and names it was impossible to remember them all.

'You and Jacqueline must visit us soon,' Elspeth Pulfer, his father's youngest sister, now aged seventy-five, was saying to Raymond. 'Little Coombe is lovely even in winter.'

Jackie smiled politely and allowed her attention to wander. On the far side of the dining room Rosamund was naughtily sharing her glass of champagne with a young niece barely school age. Still seated at the top table Lavender was deep in conversation with Deputy Commissioner Laing. The wedding cake had been cut and in just over an hour Jackie and Raymond would be leaving for Heathrow and a flight to Paris.

'If I could just have another couple of photographs taken outside on the heath . . .' Micky Duggan, their eager-beaver photographer, was saying hopefully to Raymond.

'Darling?' Raymond looked questioningly at Jackie. God, but she looked wonderful. She looked amazing. A word in Laing's ear and their wedding photograph would be on the next cover of the *Police Gazette*.

'I don't have time,' she said truthfully. 'We're due to leave in an hour and I still have to change . . .'

It wasn't that changing out of her wedding dress and into her going-away outfit would take long, but if the length of time Micky had taken when photographing them earlier was anything to go by, the couple of extra photographs could well take up the complete hour.

'Perhaps another one of you and your best man, sir?' Micky persisted.

Raymond gave a shrug of assent. A few minutes out on the heath would be a welcome break from Elspeth and Willie and other aged relatives.

Micky Duggan's eyes gleamed. He'd been wanting to get the groom on his own ever since he'd arrived. He wasn't a full-time wedding photographer – weddings were, for him, merely pin money. His weekday job was as a staff photographer for a local paper and if the name Sweeting hadn't rung alarm bells for Detective Chief Inspector Raymond Pulfer, it had certainly rung bells for Micky, who was something of an expert where south-east London crime and criminals were concerned.

'A DCI getting hitched to a Sweeting?' he'd said to his girlfriend when he'd taken the brief for the wedding, and he'd cracked with laughter. 'That can't be right, surely to God.'

Despite his disbelief, in best photojournalism style he'd been diligent enough to make a few inquiries and what he came up with had made his day.

Jacqueline Sweeting, DCI Raymond Pulfer's bride, was Jock Sweetie-pie Sweeting's daughter. With a police commander acting in Sweeting's stead and giving the bride away it was a story to salivate for. All he needed was to get Pulfer to talk about it.

Tense with anticipation he walked out of the hotel and across the road to the heath, Raymond at his side, the slightly tipsy Richard Ross a yard or so behind them.

'Here, sir?' he suggested, as they stepped onto coarse grass. 'One of you on your own, perhaps?'

Raymond obligingly took up a suitably relaxed stance.

Micky began fiddling with his Nikon light meter. 'It's been a wonderful wedding, if you don't mind my saying, sir,' he said, aware there was no time for pussy-footing about. 'In fact, under the circumstances, it's been quite unforgettable.'

'Circumstances?' Raymond's voice had a sudden edge to it. What the devil was being insinuated? Did Duggan know how hurriedly the wedding had been arranged and if he did, *how* did he know? When he'd engaged him, he'd told him a previously hired photographer had let him down so that it wouldn't seem odd his being booked at such short notice.

'Your being a detective chief inspector and the bride's

father being . . .' Micky broke off with a conspiratorial smile and a slight shrug of his shoulders. 'Well, you know, sir. The bride's father being Sweetie-pie Sweeting. He served eight years for the Midland Bank job in Redhill, didn't he?' Micky knew damn well he had. The *Mercury* had a file on Jock Sweeting, as it did on every local criminal who'd ever been convicted. 'And it's pretty well accepted he was in on the Kensington Barclays job in the seventies, isn't it?'

Raymond gawped at him goggle-eyed and Micky felt a surge of emotion almost orgasmic in intensity. Pulfer hadn't known! The story was getting better and better by the minute.

'Have you taken complete leave of your senses?' Raymond's words were choked as his brain raced pell-mell. Jock Sweeting. A gelly man of notoriety. Known associates, Smiler Burns and Albie Rice. Both related to him by marriage. Both from Bermondsey. Both with a list of offences a mile long. What Duggan was telling him couldn't possibly be true. The name was a coincidence, that was all. Duggan was having a joke at his expense.

'I looked him up in the *Mercury's* research file,' Micky said, watching in fascination as the blood drained from Raymond's face. 'He's a Jockney, isn't he? Born in Scotland, lives in Bermondsey. Two daughters, Jacqueline and Raquel. The Rice brothers are his nephews. Nothing major's ever been pinned on those two, has it? Rumour is, though, that . . .'

Raymond didn't need telling what the rumours were. Realisation after realisation was slamming into him with such force he felt as if he was being run over by a train. If the Rice brothers were related to Jock Sweeting they were related to Jacqueline – and if they were related to Jacqueline they were now, by marriage, related to him.

He squeezed his eyes shut tight and clenched his fists, feeling like a vertigo sufferer who could only stop the ground from shelving away beneath him by hanging on to it with both hands. Kevin and Johnny Rice didn't have convictions for armed robbery but they sure as hell *were* armed robbers.

Another realisation came to him, one so terrible he thought his heart was going to stop. Eddie Burns was related to the Rice brothers. He, Raymond, was now related to his informant; an informant who was the biggest psychopath in south-east London.

He tried to breathe and couldn't. He tried to speak but no words would come. He was no longer on the edge of a bottomless abyss; he was plunging into its depths like a falling stone.

'Raymond? You all right, mate?' Richard Ross was asking in growing concern. He'd been standing a few yards away in a happy champagne haze, admiring the view across the heath towards Greenwich Park, and hadn't overheard a word. It was the gagging sound Raymond had begun making that had made him aware something was amiss.

Raymond was far from being all right. He was looking into the future and instead of it being rosy and full of bright promise – Detective Superintendent in five years with forty or so officers in his team – it was a bleak dead end. A black void. Maybe even expulsion from the force.

What was Laing going to say when he found out he'd just given Jock Sweeting's daughter away in marriage? What were the powers that be going to say, period? Would he be stripped of his recent promotion? Would they transfer him to somewhere he couldn't be an embarrassment? The Outer Hebrides, for instance? For the first time since he'd been in short pants he wanted to weep.

He made a gesture like that of a blind man in Richard Ross's direction, saying fiercely to Micky Duggan, 'Not one word, understand? I'll speak to you later but for now, not one bloody word!'

In rapt fascination Micky watched him as, with uneven

movements, Pulfer began to make his way back across the heath towards the hotel, Richard Ross staring bewilderedly after him.

'If you're in that kind of a hole, man, Johnny and Jock may already be being tailed,' Dexter said flatly, speaking on the telephone to Kevin. 'Kelly'd be a better choice. Where shall we meet? The Spaniards? Hampstead's just about as far from home turf as it's possible to get.'

'Get her to have a word with Johnny and Jock,' Kevin said tersely. 'They'll know what I need and where it all is.'

'Will do, man.' Dexter was succinct. All that needed to be said had been said and he knew Kevin wouldn't want to be hanging around in a phone box for any longer than was absolutely necessary.

With the connection severed Kevin ran a hand through his tousled hair. He'd had twenty minutes or so in which to come to terms with the blow that had been dealt him and he now had a fair idea of how he was going to play things.

He'd sell his share of the gold on – Johnny would deal with that for him. He wouldn't come out of it with what he would have done if he'd stayed around while it was melted down and recast, but what the hell, he'd still have more cash than any of the Great Train robbers ever had.

The message he'd asked Dexter to pass on to Jock and Johnny would ensure that when Kelly met him at The Spaniards she'd have two false passports and two false driving licences with her.

He'd take the ferry to Calais with one of the passports – though it was extremely doubtful that, as a foot passenger, it would be needed. Then he'd take a train up to Amsterdam and fly out of there to somewhere that didn't have an extradition treaty with Britain. If he made sure there was no metal on him for any detectors to pick up he could pack himself up with body packs and take at least three hundred thousand dollars out with him that way.

The rest he'd carry in his luggage. It was a risk, of course, but then what wasn't? There'd be no real reason for him to be stopped; not when he was 'guised up and travelling as an innocuous businessman.

The more he thought about the present scenario the less of a nightmare it began to seem. Let other buggers sweat it out during the weeks and month it would take to melt down the ingots and recast them – and until they were recast they couldn't possibly be disposed of, not when every one of them carried an identifying assay mark. Melted down, though, and mixed with copper and silver, the recast ingots could be made to look like scrap.

Number 3's masterplan had been that then, via a snide bullion company, the ingots could be forwarded to the official government Assay Office in Sheffield where each bar would be weighed, taxed and legitimized. The bullion company would then be free to sell it to licensed bullion dealers who would, as middlemen, melt the impurities out and market it to the jewellery trade. It would then be virtually impossible to link any of the gold showing up in London's Hatton Garden jewellery district with gold bars stolen from the Brinks-Mat warehouse. With such an effective laundering scenario in place he wouldn't have the slightest trouble in off-loading his share.

He grinned to himself as, ignoring his car in case it came to police attention, he hopped on a bus in the direction of Hampstead. He hadn't been going to skip the country but now he'd been left with no option he didn't mind the idea at all. Ros could join him in a month or two as long as she did so by a circuitous route. Hell, he'd been part of the biggest robbery of the decade. Three of the team might have been collared but he was still free and intended remaining free. He even knew where he was going to go. He was going to emulate Ronnie Biggs and go to sunny Rio and when he got there, boy, was he going to party!

*　　　*　　　*

The bedroom door opened suddenly and was slammed shut.

'Is that you, darling?' Jackie called out from the en suite bathroom where, dressed only in a bra and underslip she was brushing confetti out of her unpinned hair.

Raymond didn't answer her. He simply stood in the centre of the hotel bedroom, engaged for the afternoon so that they would be able to change from their wedding clothes in comfort, his fists clenched as tight as a man in rigor mortis.

She hadn't deliberately deceived him, of course. In the short walk across the heath and into the hotel he'd had time to recall with professional clarity scenario after scenario that had taken place between them, conversation after conversation.

She thought he'd known. Criminally stupid though he'd been he wasn't so stupid as to believe she'd deliberately deceived him. Jacqueline wasn't a liar. Lying wasn't in her nature. What she was, though, was supremely and monstrously naïve. How in a million years could she have remotely imagined he would have embarked on a relationship with her if he'd known who her father, uncles and brothers were?

'Raymond?' Still uncertain whether it was Raymond who had come into the room, or Rosamund or Lavender, she walked out of the bathroom into the bedroom.

As soon as she saw him – saw the expression on his face and his coiled tautness – alarm flooded through her. 'What is it?' she asked urgently. 'What's wrong?' Swiftly she crossed the room towards him. 'Has there been an accident? Has –'

'*I know who you are*!' He spat the words through gritted teeth, making no move towards her.

She stopped short, totally bewildered. Was he drunk? There had been a generous amount of champagne at their reception and drunkenness took different people different ways. She'd never yet seen Raymond drunk and this peculiar attitude might be Raymond's way of being drunk.

'But of course you know who I am,' she said tolerantly, and with a wide loving smile she slid her arms up and around his neck.

He wrenched them away in a savage movement that couldn't remotely be mistaken for silly tipsiness.

She stepped away from him so quickly she almost fell. 'Raymond! For God's sake! What is it? Why are you looking at me like that? Raymond, please ... *What's happened?*'

She looked wonderful, her dark hair tumbling to her shoulders, her skin creamy pale against her oyster-silk lingerie. He stared at her with loathing. She'd ruined him. Ruined his future. Ruined his life. Ruined every bleeding, bloody thing possible.

'*I know who you are,*' he said again savagely. 'I know who your uncles are, who your cousins are. You've ruined me. You know that, don't you? As soon as word of who you are gets out ... as soon as Laing knows ...'

He shuddered. Somehow, some way, he had to try to regain control of things. Perhaps with luck on his side the nightmare could be contained. At the moment only Micky Duggan had cottoned on to the fact that Jacqueline was related to one of south-east London's most notorious criminal families. Perhaps if he drummed up a big enough payment he'd be able to square him. Perhaps the whole thing was survivable – just. Their marriage wasn't survivable, though. Their marriage was a fiasco he wanted out of at the earliest possible moment.

Even if he'd had the slightest of doubts as to her essential innocence the look now on her face would have dispelled them.

'But ... but ... you've known ever since you asked me to marry you!' She stumbled backwards, hit the wall next to the window and grabbed at the floor-length curtain to steady herself. 'You're a policeman . . . you have access to files . . . records . . .' Her voice was thick with barely reined in hysteria. 'When you asked me to marry you I told you how impossible it would be and you said you knew all about my family . . . you said that what they were didn't matter!'

'I said their being rough as hell and social nightmares didn't matter!' He was shouting now, knowing he'd said no such thing explicitly and not caring. She should have *known* the sense in which he'd said her family and background didn't matter. No one could be so stupid they'd imagine a man of his position would marry so far beneath him without it at least being worthy of comment.

'Christ Almighty, Jacqueline! If I'd had one glimmer of a realisation . . . If I'd thought for one single second . . .' Words failed him. He wanted to weep and, though he'd never hit a woman in his life, he wanted to hit her. What right had she to be staring at him in such agonised disbelief and horror? It was *his* life that had been screwed up irreparably – not hers. It was *his* career that was about to take a nose dive into oblivion.

He sucked in great lungfuls of air. He had to stop shouting. He had to stop shouting *now*. The hotel was thick with their guests and he didn't want anyone overhearing him. He'd divorce her, of course. As things stood at the moment he could get a divorce on the grounds of nonconsummation.

He thought of the comments that would be made when news of his divorce on such grounds became common knowledge amongst his colleagues. The entire Metropolitan Police Force would believe he couldn't get it up. He shuddered. Disgraced or not he wasn't going to be a figure of fun as well. No. The best route would be to try to square Micky Duggan first. If he could make sure Duggan kept his knowledge to himself he would have a breathing space in which he could file for divorce on the grounds of mutual incompatibility. It would take time but the wait would be worth it – especially if he managed to prevent Jacqueline's father's identity from becoming common knowledge.

'What . . . what are we going to do?'

Her eyes were dark with apprehension and such deep distress that, incredibly, he felt almost sorry for her. 'What are we going to do?' he repeated tightly. 'We're going to . . .' He was about to say 'get the quickest divorce on record' and stopped himself just in time.

If he was going to survive the next few months with his reputation and career intact he was going to have to tread carefully. To face her with grim reality now, when his guv'nor and colleagues were still milling in the hotel dining room, would be an act of gross stupidity. She would in all likelihood start screaming and shouting at him and, even if she didn't, she would most certainly become hysterical.

'We're going to survive it,' he snapped, being deliberately ambiguous. *He* was going to survive it, what she was going to do he neither knew nor cared, though with sixty or so of their wedding guests still here celebrating, it wasn't the time or the place to say so.

'Get dressed,' he said tersely, his prime concern now being that noone would suspect, as they left the hotel for their honeymoon in Paris, that their marriage was already on the rocks. 'And smile, for Christ's sake. This is the happiest day of your life, remember?'

Chapter Fourteen

Twice in the hours after Jackie and Raymond had departed for their honeymoon Rosamund tried to pluck up the courage to tell her mother that she was pregnant and who the baby's father was, and twice she couldn't bring herself to do so. It wasn't so much that her courage failed her as that her mother looked so happy she just didn't have the heart to spoil what was, after all, a very special day for her.

'I don't suppose it matters too much,' Kelly had said when she told her she'd duffed the scene with Lavender. 'You won't show for ages.'

'Lord, I hope not! I want to walk down the aisle, not waddle down it!' Rosamund had responded with feeling.

'An aisle?' Kelly's cat-green eyes had opened wide. 'I can't quite see Kevin doing his stuff in church, Ros. I think Bermondsey Register Office might be the best you can hope for.'

Rosamund had been secretly appalled but had had the sense not to show it. Thinking about it afterwards she, too, couldn't quite imagine Kevin in church and, after all, what really mattered was that she and Kevin were married. Compared to that fact, where they married, and how, was not really that important.

'I need to see you urgently,' Kelly was now saying to her on the telephone. 'Can you get over here double quick?'

Even though the telephone line to Lavender Pulfer's speedily acquired garden flat was as safe as any telephone line possibly could be, Kelly, as usual, took no chances. Not naming names or places on the telephone was the ingrained habit of a lifetime.

'Yes. Sure.' Knots of excited anticipation began tightening in Rosamund's tummy. She hadn't seen Kevin for days – not since he'd gone on the job he'd described as being 'a big number'. Kelly's phone call surely meant he was back in circulation again and that it was celebration time. Putting off her plan to try to meet up with Jackie – ever since her return from honeymoon Jackie had been almost impossible to contact – she crammed a jaunty red Baker's Boy beret on her fair hair and, grabbing an Alaïa sheepskin jacket from the hall coat-stand, hurried off joyously in the direction of Bermondsey.

'Kev's going to have to scarper,' Kelly said, coming to the point immediately as she walked with Rosamund out of number 28 and towards the Jaguar XJS that was her present to herself out of the Portsmouth haul. 'He wants to see you to say goodbye to you before he goes.' She slid into the driving seat, leaving Ros to open the passenger door. 'It's a bugger, but at least the chances of him getting away are good.'

'What on *earth* do you mean?' Rosamund was so stunned with shock that her cut-glass accent was back in full force.

'Three of the team have definitely been grassed up,' Kelly said, the engine roaring into life as Rosamund scrambled, alarmed and bewildered, into the seat beside her. 'Whether Kev has or not he doesn't know.' She slid the Jaguar into gear, an awful lot of shiny stockinged leg showing between the top of her snakeskin boots and her black leather mini-skirt. 'Either way he can't afford to take any chances. Did you see the papers this morning?' She pulled away over Creek Row's cobbles at speed. 'It's on every page.'

'I don't know what you're talking about, Kel.' There was more than an edge of panic in Rosamund's voice. 'The only thing in today's papers is the Brinks-Mat raid. Which job have Kevin's mates been grassed on? Is it the one he kept saying was such a big number? Why do you say he's got to leave the country? He *can't* leave the country. I'm having a baby. We're going to get married.'

Kelly surged out into Jamaica Road. 'Kev's big number job was the Brinks-Mat,' she said, knowing that Ros had finally to be put into the picture. 'Now do you understand? Kev can't hang about to get married. He's leaving the country today.' She glanced at the clock on the dashboard. 'Within the next couple of hours, maybe a tad less.'

Rosamund screamed. She couldn't help it. Nothing she had ever experienced had prepared her for the kind of bombshell Kelly was so calmly hurling at her. How could Kevin have been in on the Brinks-Mat? The Brinks-Mat was the biggest robbery in British history! It was *millions*!

'They didn't know the haul was going to be so big,' Kelly said, reading her thoughts. 'The security guard who was their inside man – the man who's grassed – thought the take would be one or two mill. What happened was that there was an unexpected delivery to the warehouse of three tons of gold only hours before the raid. Pretty creamy, eh?' She flashed Rosamund a dazzling smile. 'Another couple of hours and it would have been in an armoured van and on its way from the Heathrow warehouse across to Gatwick. As it was . . .' she giggled. 'As it was, Kev and his mates saved the van driver a trip.'

'But . . . but what is Kevin going to *do*?' As Kelly careened around the Elephant & Castle roundabout with scant regard for other road-users, Rosamund felt as if she was about to have a heart attack. 'If other people have been grassed up, surely he will have been grassed up as well? How can he hope to leave the country? All the airports and ferry ports will be being watched, won't they? How come number 26 hasn't been raided? Or has it been raided and you haven't told me?'

With each question her voice rose, edging nearer and nearer to full-blown hysteria.

'What about the gold? He isn't still in possession of it, is he? If he's still in possession of it and he gets caught he'll be facing ten years, twelve years, maybe even fifteen years or longer!'

'He ain't goin' to get caught.' Kelly glanced in her mirror, making a diving left turn into Waterloo Road. 'This time tomorrow he'll be flying out of Amsterdam on his way to sunny Rio.'

'He can't!' The panic Rosamund had been fighting to control finally slipped its leash. 'He can't leave the country without me, Kelly! What about the baby? I can't have a baby if I'm not married!'

'God, Ros. You are *so* middle class! 'Course you can have a baby without being married. People have babies without being married every day of the week.'

'Not people like me!' Rosamund was just about to retort hysterically, and changed her mind about doing so fast. The situation she was now in was the kind of situation Jackie had been referring to when she had said there was a world of difference between acting the part of a gangster's moll and being one. The horrendous goodbye now facing her – the not knowing when she and Kevin would see each other again – was all part of what she had to take on board if she was going to spend the rest of her life with Kevin. And she *was* going to spend the rest of her life with him. All right, so he was on the run at the moment, but he wouldn't always be on the run.

'We will be able to be together on our own for a little while before he leaves for Amsterdam, won't we?' she asked, zeroing in on the thing of most immediate importance.

Kelly kept her eyes on the road ahead. They were across the river now, heading out of Holborn towards Blooms-bury. 'Course,' she said, suddenly aware she hadn't explained to Ros that Kevin wasn't waiting for her on his own but that her dad and Johnny and Dexter were with him. Perhaps she'd be able to chivvy them into making an early departure, though knowing how important the meeting they were having was and how insensitive her dad was about such things, she rather doubted it. There were a lot of things Ros still had to learn about the realities of being a gangster's lady and one was that when push came to shove, wives and girlfriends and children came second in importance on their agenda.

'So you reckon your name wasna' one the twat handed over tae the old Bill?' Jock was asking Kevin.

Despite it being December and chill enough to freeze the proverbial balls off a brass monkey they were sitting, for privacy, in the beer garden at the back of The Spaniards. Kevin was immaculately dressed and, apparently, a good two stone over his normal weight. Ready to leave for the train down to Dover en route for Amsterdam, the excess weight he was carrying wasn't fat, but money body packs.

A cashmere coat was slung casually over the back of his wrought-iron garden chair. A banker's pigskin expandable attaché case was at his feet. His hair was several shades darker than normal and had been cropped into a severe, businesslike style. His glasses were Christian Dior and gold-rimmed. He looked nothing like Kevin Rice and from now on, even in his own head, he *wasn't* Kevin Rice. He was Robert Wilkinson, businessman. His photograph on the passport he was carrying had been taken of him in full Robert Wilkinson rig. He had an international driving licence, major credit cards and a fistful of receipts all in the same name and he knew Robert Wilkinson's fictitious past life almost as well as he knew his own.

He shook his head now in answer to Jock's question. 'My drum hasn't been turned over, has it?' he asked reasonably. 'Though you might warn Ma it's on the cards. You know how she likes a bit of warning if the house is going to be raided.'

'In that case, if you haven't been grassed, why risk a pull at Amsterdam airport?' Johnny didn't like the thought of Kevin chancing everything on the gamble he wouldn't be taken aside for a random body search. 'Why not lay low in Glasgow or Edinburgh for a bit?'

'Because with three of the team down it's only a matter of time before me and the rest get our collars felt.'

Dexter hunched a little deeper into his bomber jacket and then blew on his hands, rubbing them together to warm them. 'If I was going to hole up anywhere I'd hole up in Jamaica, not Brazil,' he said, wondering how much longer it was going to be before Kelly arrived with Ros and he and Kelly could split and find somewhere warm to sit. 'At least they speak English in Jamaica. You'll have to learn Spanish if you stay long in Rio.'

'Portuguese,' Kevin corrected, well aware of Brazil's drawback where language was concerned.

'Portuguese then. It's the same difference. A pain in the arse. Why don't you opt for Jamaica? My family would give you a great welcome. I'll give you their address. You never know when it'll come in handy.'

'Ta, mate,' Kevin said, aware he was going to need all the trustworthy contacts possible. He pocketed the scrap of paper Dexter gave him. 'I don't know why you're all looking so bleedin' down in the mouth – everything's in hand. I've done a tasty deal where my whack's concerned and I'm goin' to be takin' so much out on me that even if the rest comes to grief it ain't goin' to matter too much.

It wasn't completely true that absolutely everything was in hand. There was the little matter of the attaché case still in his possession – not the one now at his feet but the one in his wardrobe at the Tower Hill flat. In it were six gold bars, all with identifiable serial numbers stamped on them, their net worth being something in the region of £50,000.

He hadn't sold them on for far less than their actual worth as he had the other ingots he'd had in his possession.

Irrational though it was, he'd wanted to hang on to at least one caseful of the gold and, now he had done, he had to make a quick decision as to what to do with it. It would be tempting trouble down on Johnny and Jock's heads to ask them to stow it for him. With their records, if either of them was caught in possession of it, they'd be charged with having being in on the job and would be slammed away for twenty or twenty-five years. The only member of the family who ran no risk of ever having her property searched was Jackie. Jackie wouldn't knowingly take possession of Brinks-Mat gold, of course, but if Kelly handled things right Jackie might find herself doing so in happy innocent ignorance.

'The girls are here,' Johnny said, almost as relieved to see them as Dexter. If Kevin was going to leave the country then, in his book, the sooner he did so the better. This hanging around Kevin was doing, all for no other reason than that he wanted to see Ros before leaving, was getting on Johnny's wick. From out of nowhere came the thought that if the boot were on the other foot and the girl in question had been Jackie, he, too, would be refusing to budge until he had seen her and said a proper goodbye to her.

The knifing pain he always felt when thinking of Jackie seared through him. Jackie had said she was going to live a straight life and, married to a DCI, she sure as hell was doing so. Though it was rarely spoken about he knew no one in the family, not even Pearl, had adjusted to it or ever would adjust to it.

Kelly and Ros were fast crossing the gravel towards them and he clamped down on his thoughts of Jackie, knowing that indulging in them did him no good at all.

Kevin had sprung to his feet but instead of running headlong into his arms Ros had come to a sudden stop. Not until Kevin said with a laugh, 'Come on, love. I know I look a bit of a fat sod at the moment and the haircut leaves a lot to be desired but I thought you loved me for my beautiful soul, not my looks,' did she realise who he was.

'*Kevin*!' Her voice was a choked sob as she hurtled over the last few yards and threw herself into his arms.

'Steady on, love.' The usual note of laughter was in his voice as he hugged her close, rocking her against him. 'There's no need for tears. I'm buggering off to the sun not the nick.'

'Let me come with you! I'll come just as I am. I won't go home to pack anything. Please, darling. Please!'

Jock cleared his throat, embarrassed and irritated by Ros's inability to understand what was required of her in the present situation. A dyed-in-the-wool moll would have understood instinctively the impossibility of accompanying her man when he was on the run. 'See you later, hen,' he always said to Pearl whenever he left the house, and it was understood between them that the 'later' could be hours, days, or even weeks.

'I can't, love,' Kevin was saying gently, his mouth close to her ear. 'I'm going to be ducking and diving. You know how it is.'

Ros fought back a sob. She'd thought she'd known how it was but was fast realising that the difference between knowing something in theory and knowing it in practice was enormous.

'But the baby . . . the wedding . . .'

Dexter pretended not to hear. Jock chewed the corner of his lip. One of Johnny's eyebrows rose slightly. It was the first any of them had heard about a baby.

'When I'm sorted and the heat is off I'll send for you. I'm sorry, love, but it can't be any other way. If continuing to live with your mum becomes impossible when the baby begins to show move into number 26 or 28 or, better still, move in to one of the houses on Sheppey. Ma and Flo spend nearly all their time down there and they'll be grateful for the company.'

Defeat was staring her straight in the face and Rosamund knew it. Wishing with all her heart that Dexter, Jock and Johnny were a million miles away she accepted it as best she could, saying urgently, 'When are you going to leave? We'll be able to have some time together first, won't we?'

He shook his head, knowing very well that the time together she wanted was time in bed. After the effort he and Johnny had spent expertly stowing money packs on his person he wasn't about to strip them all off – not even for a bit of blissful nookie with Ros.

'I'm going now, love,' he said regretfully. 'Johnny was going to drive me down to Waterloo but we can go there together, without him, if you're easy about driving the car back.'

'Of course I'm easy about driving the car back!' She'd have driven a team of wild horses if necessary. 'Are you going to be safe leaving the country looking as you now do? Where will you go? How long will it be before you contact me?'

Kevin breathed a sigh of relief, knowing her present line of anxious questioning meant she had accepted the situation and wasn't going to give him any more aggro about it.

'Yes. I'm not sure. I don't know,' he said, answering all three of her questions in turn as Jock, Dexter and Johnny rose to their feet.

Aware it was now time to go, he picked up his navy cashmere coat and slid carefully into it, then he picked up his heavy attaché case and slipped his free arm around her waist.

'Come on, love. We'll be getting married on a beach in Brazil or in Jamaica in a few months' time and I'll have so much bullion dosh you won't be able to spend up no matter how hard you try.'

Ros tried to respond with a smile but it wasn't easy. She didn't care about the bullion dosh and hadn't even thought to ask him how much his cut had been or how it had been – or was going to be – laundered or where it all now was. All she cared about was his safety and their being together.

'Good luck, mate,' Dexter was saying to him as he slapped him on the shoulder. 'Don't be on *News at Ten* tonight. It'd give me bad dreams.'

'Dinna' use any of the domestic phone lines when you make contact,' Jock was saying unnecessarily. 'Ring Jackie – being a police phone the line will be safe as houses – and just say she's tae let us know you're fine and dandy and that you're in Bridlington or Jarrow.'

'Bridlington or Jarrow?' Ros looked bewilderedly into Kevin's face – a face so altered by the loss of his crisply curling hair, and the glasses he was wearing that it was almost like looking into the face of a stranger.

'Brazil or Jamaica,' Kevin translated for her, amused, as always, by the naïvety she never quite managed to lose.

It was then Johnny and Kelly's time to say goodbye to him, and Rosamund removed her arm from around his waist, standing a little to one side so that tight hugs and heartfelt words of good luck could be exchanged. He said something to Kelly that, for one split second, quite obviously shook her rigid and then had her cracking with laughter.

By the time the goodbyes were over and they were in the car, on their own, Rosamund felt as if her control was going to slip again. How long would it take Kevin to drive to Waterloo? Twenty minutes? Half an hour? And then he'd be gone. She wouldn't see him for weeks, perhaps even months. The worst possibility – that they might not be reunited in time for the baby's birth – was such a horror that tears of panic burned her eyes.

She clenched her hands tightly together in her lap. She had to think positively, not negatively. Kevin was going to leave the country and, by doing so, remain a free man. She didn't want him to remain in Britain and be arrested for the Brinks-Mat, did she? If he were, there would be no reunion to look forward to. Their baby would be an over-the-age-of-consent adult by the time they would be together again.

They were approaching the Embankment, drawing closer and closer to the station. Acutely conscious of her own nervous tension she was aware that Kevin was almost indecently relaxed. She looked across at him sharply as they surged on to Waterloo Bridge and began to drive across it to Waterloo Station, her eyes widening. The bastard wasn't merely relaxed. He was enjoying himself! She knew that, whenever he was on a job, he got the most enormous buzz, because he had told her so – and he was on a buzz now. Danger and tension were meat and drink to him. She felt an almost overpowering urge to shout angrily at him that they weren't meat and drink to her but it was too late for such histrionics. They were at the station. He was parking the car. Getting out of it. With legs that felt as if they were made of cottonwool, she stepped out, too.

'This is it, darlin'. Are you coming with me to the ticket office?'

'Yes.' How could he even ask of it of her? She would go with him to the ends of the earth – if he'd let her.

He bought a return to Dover, even though he would only be using one half of the ticket, and clutching hold of his free arm she walked with him towards the platform barrier.

He came to a halt then, putting his attaché case down close to his feet, taking her in his arms.

'I love you, sweetheart,' he said huskily. 'We're going to have an ace life together.'

'And we'll be married?'

'We'll be married,' he said, and kissed her long and deeply in a way that made it impossible for her to doubt his sincerity.

She clung to him as if he was a life raft and she was drowning in a stormy sea. 'Keep safe! Stay free!' she said fervently as, gently and reluctantly, he lifted her arms from around his neck.

He pressed two fingers to his lips and then pressed them to hers. 'Always,' he said and then, with a jauntiness she knew she would never forgive him for, he picked up his attaché case and strode away from her down the platform, turning only to give her one last wave before boarding the train.

She was blinded by tears. Choked by them. If only she'd had a little warning she would have handled things so much better but there hadn't been any warning. A couple of hours ago she'd been happily looking forward to marrying Kevin and moving in with him, the only unpleasant scenario on her horizon being the necessity of telling her mother about him, and now he was a wanted man fleeing the country.

There was a newsstand near the exit of the station and on a placard was emblazoned 'Brinks-Mat guards doused with petrol!'

Rosamund felt as she'd walked into a brick wall. Her Kevin wouldn't have poured petrol over anyone to make them co-operate – would he? Violence of that kind simply wasn't his, or Johnny's, style. Her hand was trembling violently as she opened the door of the parked car. The Brinks-Mat hadn't been a family job, though, had it? Who was to say how the robbers had behaved? She turned the key in the ignition, tears still rolling down her face and dripping on to her skirt. Kevin could quite well have been one of the team without having been one of the men who actually broke into the warehouse. Why hadn't she asked him what his role had been? Why hadn't he told her without being asked?

She lurched into gear, swinging the car – a Ford Capri – out into the stream of traffic heading towards the

Elephant & Castle roundabout. She would take the car back to Creek Row and speak to Kelly. Kelly would most likely know what part Kevin had played in the raid.

Dimly she became aware that a police car was flagging her down. With an entire upbringing steeped in the acceptance of never having anything to fear in such situations she hurriedly pulled over.

Seconds later, after hastily wiping the tears from her face, she was winding her window down and saying in her best public-schoolgirl accent, 'Yes, officer. Can I help you?'

'Would you turn your engine off please, madam?'

Obediently she did so, wondering why on earth he had stopped her. Had she been driving erratically? She was very distressed, of course, and probably had been.

'Are you the owner of this car, madam?'

'Yes, of co –' she began automatically. Her sentence remained unfinished as realisation slammed in. She wasn't driving her own car. She wasn't driving Kevin's legally owned car. Kevin's legally owned car was a high-powered Jaguar. The car she was now in possession of was a Ford Capri. Was it a ringer and would there be back-up documentation in the glove compartment? Or was the car simply one that had been stolen for convenience that morning? Stolen so that if the police were on the lookout for Kevin his distinctive Jag wouldn't come immediately to their attention?

'I . . . it's a friend's car . . .' Frantically she opened the glove compartment, praying there would be some documentation that would back up her statement. Even if there was, he would still be able to book her for driving without proper insurance but she was white, middle-class and pretty. If she spun him a story of how the situation was a one-off emergency he'd surely let her off with a cautionary word of warning.

'If you'd just give me a minute, officer. I'm sure I can explain . . .'

There was nothing in the glove compartment but a tube of Polo mints.

No wonder Kevin had asked her if she was easy about driving the car back to Creek Row! No doubt if Johnny had driven it down to Waterloo as planned, the car would have been dumped by now.

'Would you step outside the vehicle, madam?'

'I think you are being unnecessarily officious, officer. The car isn't mine, that's true. It belongs to a friend – a fellow RADA student...'

'Out of the car, please.'

There was nothing remotely friendly or conciliatory in his manner. His radio was crackling and as she stepped out of the Capri he was detailing the car's description over it.

'I'm not sure of her name ... I don't know her that well ... but we were having breakfast together near the Academy and she was suddenly taken ill...' Rosamund was gabbling, clutching at straws, and she knew it. 'She felt totally unfit to drive and asked me if I'd drop her car back home for her...' She tried an apologetic, silly-little-me smile, but it fell on stony ground.

'Could I have your full name, address and date of birth, madam?'

'But why on earth ...? This is an imposition, officer ... This is –'

'This car is stolen, madam,' he said, switching off his radio.

'*Stolen?*' Her voice rose to a squeak of simulated disbelief. 'But how terrible ... I wonder how on earth ...'

. The policeman wasn't wondering anything. 'Your name, address and date of birth,' he said again.

Wildly Rosamund wondered if she should give a false name and address. It would be checked, though, and not only would doing so be a criminal offence, it would also make her look stupid. 'Rosamund Pulfer,' she said through dry lips. 'Cedar Lodge, Blackheath Park, Blackheath. Date of birth fourth of June 1964.'

The policeman switched his radio back on, reporting her details. 'And now, madam,' he said when he had finished, 'I must ask you to accompany me to the police station to help with inquiries.'

'I don't want to! I refuse to be treated like a ... like a ...' She tried to say the word 'criminal' but she thought of Kevin and the word stuck in her throat.

'Then I have no option but to inform you, Rosamund Pulfer, that you are under arrest.'

'*Arrest*?' This time there was nothing simulated about Rosamund's near-hysterical response. Wildly she looked around for help but there was no help to be had. 'You can't arrest me! My father was a deputy commissioner in the Met! I'm –'

'I don't care if your father was Dick Whittington,' he interrupted tersely, unclipping the handcuffs hanging from his belt.

Cars exiting off Waterloo Bridge were slowing down to catch a clearer view of what was going on. Little knots of pedestrians were gathering.

'I don't believe you're doing this!' She had never felt so humiliated, so shamed in all her life. She was being handcuffed. In full view of dozens of prurient eyes she was being frog-marched across to the police car. 'This is gross heavy-handedness, officer! This is ...'

She was being hustled into the rear of the police car.

'*A drunk driver, is she*?' a woman Rosamund hated with all her heart shouted out from the pavement. '*They're a bleedin' disgrace*!'

A second police officer, seated in the driving seat, was radioing in details of her arrest.

Rosamund wasn't listening to him. She was agonisingly aware of her handcuffed wrists and thinking about Kevin. Her handcuffs would soon be removed and, even if she were charged with being in possession of a stolen car, she would hardly be likely to receive a prison sentence. If Kevin were caught and handcuffed it would be the end of the line; the prelude to years and years of imprisonment. She squeezed her eyes tight shut, willing him with all the mental strength she possessed, to stay free.

Raymond was not having a good day. Micky Duggan had him by the short and curlies. Instead of being satisfied with the obscenely large amount of money already paid to him he was threatening that, unless similar payments were made on a regular basis, he was going to go public with his story of Raymond's connection by marriage to the high-profile Sweeting/Rice clan.

As if that nightmare wasn't bad enough his life at home had become a living hell. Jacqueline just couldn't get it into her head that their marriage was over. She was distraught to the point of emotional breakdown about the fact that he hadn't known before their marriage who her father was but felt it was a misunderstanding they were both to blame for. 'All that matters is that we love each other,' she had said repeatedly, white-faced. 'And if the worst comes to the worst and you have to leave the force you could get highly paid work with a private security company.'

How he had refrained from hitting her he still didn't know. His major mistake, of course, had been in sleeping with her. She just couldn't grasp that he couldn't resist going to bed with her even though he no longer loved her. Not, in retrospect, that he now believed he ever had been in love with her. If it hadn't been for his mother's not so subtle bribery where the house was concerned, he would probably never have proposed to her. The house, at least, was now securely his. If only he could come to a reasonable understanding with Micky Duggan . . .

'Excuse me, sir.' The young detective sergeant now facing him across his desk looked oddly uncomfortable. 'It'll

be of no consequence, sir . . . no connection to yourself . . .
but I thought . . . just to be on the safe side . . .'

'Yes?' Raymond snapped through gritted teeth.

'A report from London Bridge nick. A young woman
found in possession of a stolen car. I just happened to note
the name, sir. It was Pulfer, sir. Rosamund Pulfer.'

Raymond's eyes glazed. What the sweet fuck was happening to his life? A few weeks ago it had been orderly,
organised and enviable. Now it was careering into farce at
every given opportunity. What the devil was Rosamund
doing in possession of a stolen car? Almost as soon as he'd
asked himself the question he knew the answer. It would
be something to do with Kelly Sweeting. Christ Almighty,
she'd probably been out with Kelly on a job of some sort!
His family had been infiltrated by the canker of the Sweeting family to such an extent it was going to take the inter-
vention of the Virgin Mary to free them of it.

'Right,' he said crisply to the uneasily hovering DS. 'As
you say, it's of no consequence but drop the report in my
tray and I'll look it over.'

The DS escaped from the room with relief and the
minute he had done so, Raymond snatched the report from
his in-tray. The Rosamund Pulfer in question was his sister
all right. The stupid cow had even given her correct
address.

He ran a hand over his short, smoothly slicked hair,
feeling as if he were on the edge of a nervous breakdown.
If this little incident came to Duggan's attention he'd milk
it for all it was worth. Even if Duggan didn't seize on the
name Pulfer when it came up in the local court, he would
be going public sooner or later about the fact that a high-
profile bank robber was DCI Raymond Pulfer's father-in-
law and that the Rice brothers, whose names figured
prominently on the CRO list, were his cousins by marriage.

A bead of sweat glistened on his upper lip. He hadn't a
shadow of doubt that when that happened his career would

be over. He remembered Jacqueline's remark about his perhaps finding work with a private security company, and fought down nausea. He could never lower himself to that level. Never. No way. No how. Not in a million years. There was a solution, of course, and it was one he'd been toying with for quite some time. If Duggan wouldn't be reasonable about the situation – if he wouldn't be satisfied with a one-off large payment of money – then he'd have to be frightened off. Seriously frightened off.

He wiped the sweat away from his upper lip with his thumb and forefinger. He'd phone Eddie. Decisively he pushed his leather swivel chair away from his desk and rose to his feet. Eddie owed him. It wouldn't be a problem.

It was a bitterly cold day and he scooped his Burberry from his coat-stand, striding out of his office and out of Tintagel House, a man intent on fast-tracking his life back into normality by the simple expedient of making a telephone call from a public telephone.

Chapter Fifteen

Jackie was seated at the breakfast table, her hands wrapped around a mug of coffee that was fast growing cold. Through the patio windows she had a clear view down the long rear garden. Christmas was only days away and orange-berried firethorn was in its full winter glory. She tried to take some pleasure from them but her despair and unhappiness were too deep.

How could everything have gone so very, very wrong between Raymond and herself?

The kitchen wall clock ticked away the minutes. A robin flew into the garden and perched on the birdtable where, earlier, she had put a sprinkling of birdseed.

Receiving no answer to her question she pushed her chair away from the table and rose to her feet. It was obvious, of course, that their farcical misunderstanding – she believing he knew all about her family's criminality and he not having a clue about it – was a major disaster, but it was a disaster they should have been overcoming together. They weren't overcoming it together, though. How could they when they barely communicated with each other any more?

Bleakly she began making a fresh pot of coffee. The only thing they now did together was make love or, to be more accurate, have sex. It was an exercise that, on Raymond's part, was conducted without loving words or tenderness. Consequently, instead of drawing them closer, it only emphasised the growing sterility of their relationship.

She had tried to bridge the chasm now yawning between them. Even though his attitude in the bedroom made her feel like an object, not a person, she had always been generously responsive to him. It had gained her nothing. He had merely taken her response as being his due right and she had felt awkward and uncomfortable – as though she had indulged in sex with a stranger.

The coffee began to perk and, looking through the window above the sink, she noticed that the winter jasmine was in tiny bud. Perhaps, if she cut a branch for the house, it would flower in time for Christmas.

At the thought of Christmas she felt such a depth of despair she didn't know how she was going to contain it. What sort of Christmas were they going to have when Raymond could hardly bring himself to speak to her? It wasn't as if they would have Lavender and Rosamund for company. Ever since Lavender had learned of Rosamund's pregnancy and that the father was Jacqueline's cousin – and that for some reason he was in Jarrow with no apparent profession and no evident intention of returning in order to marry Rosamund – she had been as glacially remote as the moon.

Raymond, of course, had been so cataclysmically horrified by Rosamund's news that she'd thought he'd have a stroke.

'An armed robber, Sweet Christ! My *sister* is carrying an *armed robber's* bastard!' he had raged. 'All because your mother came here as a charlady! All because you and your tart of a sister had the temerity to think you were Rosamund's social equals and could be her friends!'

'Kevin has never served time for armed robbery,' she had found herself saying stiffly through frozen lips. 'And Kelly isn't a tart.'

'Kevin Rice is down on my parade room's Target Criminal Board as being an armed robber!' he had shouted, spittle at the corners of his mouth. 'As are his brother, his father and both his uncles!'

He had slammed out of the house and she had known

that no amount of bridge-building would now make things right between them. Before Rosamund had dropped her bombshell there had been a slight chance. Now there was none.

The worst part of the whole affair had been Raymond's refusal ever again to allow Rosamund over their doorstep. Without Rosamund as an occasional visitor Jackie's loneliness was total.

She carried her freshly made cup of coffee back to the breakfast table and stared down at the newspaper lying on it. The headline emblazoned on its front page hadn't miraculously changed since when, an hour or so ago, she had first seen it. 'Local Press Photographer Brutally Murdered', it read. The accompanying columns told how Micky Duggan, aged twenty-seven, had been found dead in his Forest Hill flat – the cause of death severe head injuries. Robbery was being ruled out as a motive, for expensive photographic equipment in the flat had not been taken.

Despite the warmth of the central heating system she shivered. She had liked Micky Duggan. She had been fraught with nerves when he had arrived at the house on her wedding day to take photographs of her and Rosamund and Deputy Commissioner Laing, prior to their departure for the church, but he had made her laugh and forget her tension. Her heart hurt at the memory. There had been no laughter since then. She didn't know who it was who had told Raymond she was Sweetie-pie Sweeting's daughter, but whoever it was, they had ensured that her honeymoon was a monumental disaster.

She drank her coffee, wondering if Raymond knew of Micky Duggan's murder. It would be very odd if, as a DCI, he didn't know about it but he certainly hadn't mentioned it to her. She decided to leave the newspaper on the table so that he would be able to read about it when he came home.

The wall clock clicked past the hour. It was ten o'clock and she'd done nothing but sit and stare into the garden and drink coffee. She ached for the frenetic structure in her day that college gave her but St Martin's had broken up for Christmas and, when the new term commenced in the second week of January, she wouldn't be among the returning students.

When, a couple of weeks before their wedding, Raymond had said he didn't see how she could continue as a fashion design student and be the kind of wife he wanted her to be, she had decided to put her career on hold for a little while. He, after all, was risking so much for her where his career was concerned that it had seemed the very least she could do. Now, of course, she knew that he hadn't been risking anything at all – at least not knowingly – and the intensive programme of entertaining he had been so eager for them to undertake he now never mentioned.

She moved away from the table yet again and carried her cup across to the sink. For years and years, as a little girl, she'd dreamed of living in this house and, her dream having come to fruition, she hated it. Without Lavender's tranquil presence the house seemed more a mausoleum than a home. She'd tried, of course, just as she had tried with their personal relationship in the bedroom. Even though it was winter there were potplants and flowers in the rooms. A crimson-bracted euphorbia stood on the hall table. A shell-pink cyclamen graced the low marble-topped coffee table in the drawing room. There were African violets in the bathrooms and an Indian azalea on the kitchen window sill.

Originally she had intended scattering about lots of her possessions from Creek Row in order to put her own stamp on the house until such time as she and Raymond were able to shop for things that would transform it from having been his parents' house to being their own. That idea, however, had quickly died when they had returned from their honeymoon. Her loneliness in the house had become so intense, her distress so deep, that she'd only been able to survive it by keeping everything as it had been when it had been a happy house and she'd been an eager visitor to it.

It certainly wasn't a happy house now. The row she and Raymond had had that morning had been their worst so far. He had accused her of deliberately deceiving him into marriage. He had said that her refusal to indulge in pre-marital sex had been nothing to do with high moral standards but had merely been yet another of her tricks to entice him to the altar. He had been insistent that she hadn't been a virgin when they had married, as he had believed, and he had called her a slag and a whore and other filthy names. Then, when she had begun shouting back at him, he had hit her.

It had been a hard, open-handed slap across her face and it had sent her reeling against the banisters at the top of the stairs. Even if she had fallen down them she doubted if he would have cared. With what was becoming a habit, he had slammed out of the house and silence had reverberated around her.

It still did so. Unable to bear it a moment longer she turned abruptly away from the sink and walked swiftly out of the kitchen and into the hallway. She was going to go for a walk across the heath. She tugged a pair of knee-high black suede boots from their shoe-box and began hauling them on and zipping them up. She was going to go for a long, long walk.

She threw on a maxi-length, cream-coloured, wrap-around, wool coat and yanked its tie-belt into a knot. Somehow, some way, she had to clear her head so that she could think clearly. Somehow, some way, she and Raymond had to escape from the hell they'd been plunged into and find a way of rebuilding their relationship.

*　　*　　*

He saw her the instant she emerged from the private street and into Prince of Wales Road. The road crossed the east side of the heath and at its Blackheath Village end there was a pub called the Princess of Wales and opposite the pub, on the heath proper, there was a tree-shaded pond.

The pub wasn't yet open and he was standing near the pond watching a small boy sailing a boat made out of a piece of wood in which had been embedded, hedgehog-like, a score or so of long nails.

It wasn't the first time he had waited for her and it wasn't the first time that, though she had not seen him, he had seen her. It was, however, the first time he had seen her since her marriage and had been determined to speak to her.

Instead of heading towards Blackheath Village and the shops, she crossed the road on to the heath, beginning to stride out across it, her collar pulled high against the cold wind.

He tossed the stub of the cigarette he had been smoking on to the rough grass and, hands buried deep in the pockets of his fleece-lined forties RAF bomber jacket, strode after her.

Her hands, too, were deep in her pockets and her shoulders were hunched, her head down. She was walking fast, as if she had large dogs with her, desperate for exercise. Her shoulder-length hair was streaming in the wind and, even from a distance, he could see that there was tension in every line of her body.

There was tension in his body, too; a crippling sexual tension he couldn't alleviate no matter how many women he slept with. When, yesterday, he had waited in Prince of Wales Road in the hope of meeting her accidentally on purpose, he had told himself he was doing so because no one in the family, not even Ros, had seen her for weeks and because it was about time someone did. The minute he had seen her, though, he had known he had been lying to himself. He wasn't trying to see her merely to maintain family contact. He was trying to see her because he *had* to see her. Because he was as crazy about her as he'd always been. Because she was the only woman he'd ever been in love with; the only woman he could ever even *imagine* being in love with.

'Jax! *Jax!*'

She spun round so suddenly she almost lost her balance.

Always wand-slender, she'd lost weight – a lot of weight he now saw. Her beautifully boned face looked almost gaunt and there were dark shadows beneath her eyes.

Her shock at seeing him so unexpectedly was obvious and there was another expression, too, in her eyes; an expression she clamped down on so swiftly he wondered if he had, perhaps, mistaken it. It couldn't, surely, have been *relief*? Of all the emotions she might just possibly have felt at seeing him, relief was surely the least likely?

'Johnny?' Her voice was huskier than usual, as if she had been crying. 'Why are you here?' Bewilderment gave way to anxiety. 'There's nothing wrong at home, is there? It isn't Dad . . . or Ros?'

'No.' He shook his head, puzzled as to why Ros had sprung so swiftly to her mind, even more puzzled by her tense, overwrought appearance.

'I had a telephone call a couple of weeks ago from Kevin,' she said, once again the coolly composed Jackie of old, though he suspected the effort it was costing her was enormous. 'He said would I let Ros know that he was in Jarrow. I said I would and that . . . and that I'd appreciate it if he didn't make a habit of using me as a telephone messenger. He was obviously laying low after a job and if Raymond should have intercepted the call . . .'

'Quite.'

He remained a couple of feet away from her, his eyes holding hers. Raymond Pulfer knew about him and Kevin then. Until now he hadn't been quite sure whether Pulfer knew just who his cousins by marriage were. Whatever he knew about them or, more precisely, suspected about them – for they hadn't been successfully collared for a job for years – he certainly hadn't a glimmer that it was Jackie's family who had pulled the Portsmouth job and that Kevin had been in on the Brinks-Mat. Jackie, he knew, would never grass about any jobs the family did, but sharing that kind of information with her could serve no good purpose and so was pointless.

He said, instead: 'You know Ros is having a baby?'

She nodded and he could well imagine that Rosamund's announcement about the baby to Lavender Pulfer had been an experience no one in the Pulfer household was ever likely to forget.

He continued to hold her eyes. 'Ros is living at number 26. She has the place more or less to herself as Mum and Dad are down at Sheppey, I'm usually at the Tower Bridge flat, and Kev is, as you know, away for a while. Kelly and her bloke are round there with her most of the time.'

Once again she nodded. It was as if she found it difficult to speak; as if the slightest information about life in Creek Row was almost too much for her to bear. The wind was ruffling Johnny's thatch of straw-coloured hair and he raised a hand, smoothing it down. It would have hurt like hell if she had looked every inch a radiantly happy new wife, but the bleakness of spirit he sensed in her was far worse.

With every fibre of his being he wanted to pull her into his arms but instinct told him that if he did so she would try to struggle free and run. Her running in flight from him was a scenario he couldn't easily contemplate.

He was just about to continue with the small talk, avoiding the dynamite-loaded topics of the Portsmouth raid, the Brinks-Mat raid and Kevin's disappearance from the scene, when the sun inched from behind a bank of cloud and he saw something on her face he hadn't seen before. He saw the faint imprint of marks. Fingermarks.

'Christ Almighty, Jax!' He knew now why she looked as she did. He knew and found it totally incomprehensible. 'What the bleedin' fuck's going on?' Rage so terrible he could barely control it roared through him. Pulfer and Jackie hadn't yet been married a month! No matter what the consequences he was going to kill the fucker – and he was going to do it with his bare hands.

Her hand had flown instantly to her cheek, her eyes so dark he could barely tell iris from pupil.

'I . . . it's nothing!' There was naked alarm in her voice. 'My face must be chapped with the cold . . . it's so windy . . .'

'Windy my arse!' He seized hold of her, no longer caring what her reaction might be. 'You've been hit open-handed! I ain't so bleedin' blind I can't recognise fingermarks, Jax.'

'It was nothing . . . a little row that got out of hand. It isn't something that will happen again.'

'Too fuckin' right it won't happen again!' He had her arm in a vicelike grip. 'We're going back to that monstrous pile of bricks you call a home and I'm going to sort the fucker! And if he ain't there I'm goin' to wait for him!'

'No!' She was stumbling over the rough grass as he dragged her along at his side. 'No, Johnny! Please! Raymond isn't just some bloke in a pub. He'll have you for GBH!'

'He won't be alive to have me for anything!'

It wasn't loose talk. He meant every word. It had been bad enough losing her to a copper but at least he'd believed she was going to be happy with him. Pulfer was, after all, offering her everything it seemed she wanted: financial security, stability, respectability. If he was displaying signs of being a wife-beater within weeks of their honeymoon, what was Jackie's future going to be like? Men who laid into women didn't, as time went on, do so less often. One thing was for sure: in hitting Jackie, Pulfer had come well and truly unstuck. He wasn't going to get away with using

Jackie as a punch-bag – and that was where forceful open-handed slaps nearly always led.

'Johnny, please stop! You can't go to the house! It will make things a hundred times worse!'

He came to an abrupt halt, swinging round to face her. 'No way is he going to get away with this, Jax.' His teeth were gritted and there was a pulse pounding at the corner of his jawline. 'The man is an educated professional, for Christ's sake. If you'd married a lout I could understand it, but a detective chief inspector laying into his wife – it's carrying police brutality a bit far.'

'He isn't brutal.'

She was struggling for breath, partly because of the pace he had been marching her along at, partly because of the panic she was feeling. If Raymond came home to find Johnny in the house . . . Beads of sweat broke out on her forehead at the very thought. There would be a fight, of that she hadn't a second's doubt, and neither man would fight by the other's rules.

In Johnny's world fights, no matter how savage, never became police matters. A man had to be bleeding to death before he'd allow himself to be off-loaded at a hospital casualty department and then, after treatment, he'd haul himself out before the police arrived to question him as to how he had received his injuries. When it came to the little matter of removing stitches he'd do the job himself or get an obliging mate to do it for him. What he would not do was to give the name of his attacker, or attackers, to the police. Depending on the circumstances retribution might be sought but, when it was, it wouldn't be sought via the law.

It wasn't the way Raymond would function. If Johnny slammed so much as even one punch at him Raymond would have him charged with assault, or perhaps even grievous bodily harm, and there was no telling what other charges would then be drummed up against him. There were other considerations as well. It would make her and Raymond's horrendous situation even more horrendous. He would believe she had invited Johnny – a known criminal – into their home and it was an action he would never forgive.

'He isn't brutal,' she said again, not able to bear the thought of Johnny believing such a thing about him. She began to shiver violently, though not from the cold. 'You have to understand things from Raymond's point of view, Johnny. It's all been such a shock to him and he's trying so hard to come to terms with everything and for a man in his position it's very, very difficult.'

'What's been a shock to him?' His brows had flown together in a deep frown. He hadn't intended wasting time on finding out why Pulfer had hit her for, as far as he was concerned, the whys and wherefores were immaterial. If, however, her talking about it to him would help build bridges between them he was more than prepared to listen.

She pulled her coat collar close against her throat as the wind whipped her hair around her face. 'He . . . I . . .' She'd confided in no one and now the moment to do so had arrived she didn't know where to start or how to trust her voice from breaking.

'Yes, love?' he prompted gently.

Suddenly he was no longer the man who had hurt her so deeply when he had refused to change his way of life for her. He was her friend. He was, as he had always been, her very best friend.

She made a small despairing gesture with her free hand. 'I thought Raymond was marrying me knowing all about Dad's criminal record . . . all about Uncle Albie and Smiler and you and Kevin.'

His face was almost as masklike as hers. He, too, had been under the impression that if Pulfer hadn't known about him and Kevin he had, at the very least, been aware of Jock's identity. Certainly that was the impression he had gained from Ros. 'And he didn't?' It was taking all his self-control not to reveal the emotion he felt at the thought of Pulfer's rude awakening.

She shook her head. 'It was a . . . a shock to him,' she said, aware she was uttering the understatement of the year. 'If word gets out about it, it may well cost him his job and it will certainly cost him future promotion.'

'Does that matter now?' There was genuine incredulity in his voice. 'A public-school-educated high-flyer like Pulfer is never going to come to terms with having your dad as his father-in-law – surely that's obvious to you by now? You made a mistake, Jax. As did Pulfer. Accept it and call it quits . . .'

'I don't *want* to call it quits!' Tears stained her cheeks. 'I married Raymond because I admire and respect him, and this awful, awful start to our marriage is something I'm going to make up to him!'

He could hardly believe his ears. He knew some women were masochists who couldn't get enough of being treated badly but he'd never had Jackie marked down as one.

Suddenly he had had enough. When he had set out to meet and talk to her he'd had no clear idea of what he was going to achieve but the minute he had seen Pulfer's fingermarks on her face he had come to an assumption. He was going to beat Pulfer to within an inch of his life and Jackie and he were, once again, going to be an item. Now, incredibly, not only had she no intention of returning to him but she was talking about Pulfer as if he was Mr Blameless and Perfect – and he wasn't. Not if the rumours Johnny had heard were true.

'You're piling mistake on mistake, Jax!' he said savagely. 'Pulfer isn't at all the kind of copper you believe him to be. From what I've heard he's as bent as they come. A mate of Kevin's says that –'

'*Liar!*' Her accusation was impassioned, holding no doubt whatsoever.

In an instant the atmosphere between them changed from supportive intimacy to hostile confrontation.

'I'm a hell of a lot of things, Jax, but I ain't a liar!' he hurled back at her, eyes blazing.

She was backing away from him, stumbling on the tussocky grass. 'You can't bear it that Raymond is straight and honest and high-principled, can you? It just does your head in, doesn't it? You want me to believe bad things about him in order that you'll look better – in order that you won't seem quite so flagrantly dishonest, quite so unscrupulous! Well, it isn't going to work. All I want from you, Johnny, is that you stay out of my life! I don't want you interfering in it. My relationship with Raymond is my affair, not yours. Do you understand?'

Without waiting for a reply, tears now raining freely down her face, she twisted clumsily round on her heel and began to run.

He didn't run after her. There was no point. When Jackie got a bee in her bonnet no power on earth would shift it. He rammed his fists deeper into his bomber jacket pockets. For her sake, because she wanted it that way, he'd stay away from Pulfer for the time being. He wouldn't stay away from him for good, though. One day he'd get the bastard – and when he did, it would be an occasion DCI Raymond Pulfer wouldn't forget.

Jackie didn't stop running until she reached the edge of the heath and Prince of Wales Road. Her shock when Johnny had called out her name and she had turned and seen him so unexpectedly had been enormous and, hard on the heels of her shock, had been overwhelming relief. He was, after all, family – and her loneliness for her family had been intense. Why, why, *why* had he spoiled everything by making such a malicious and patently untrue remark about Raymond?

Dashing the tears from her face she walked swiftly out

of Prince of Wales Road and into the private road that led to Lavender's house. The instant the thought came into her head she corrected it. It wasn't Lavender's house. It was her and Raymond's house. One thing her meeting with Johnny had done for her was to clarify things. She hadn't wanted Johnny making things worse between herself and Raymond. She didn't want their marriage to reach a point of no return. She wanted things to become better and they *were* going to get better. She simply wasn't going to accept any alternative.

The minute she entered the house she heard the telephone ringing. It was a rare event. Raymond never rang her from work or, for that matter, at any other time. Dismayed and bewildered by Rosamund's illegitimate pregnancy, and aware that Rosamund's involvement with the father had stemmed from her friendship with Kelly and Jackie, Lavender now never rang her either.

'Hello . . .' As she was speaking she was shrugging herself out of her coat.

'How's it goin'?' Kelly's voice, fizzing with the joy of life, made it the most welcome telephone call she had ever received.

'Things are fine, Kel.' She was too happy that Kelly had at last got in touch with her to care about the mega size of her lie. 'How are you? I understand the new boyfriend is pretty tasty. How are Mum and Dad and Ros? Is Ros showing yet? She must be about three or four months now.'

Kelly's throaty laughter was music to her ears. 'Ros is heavily into Laura Ashley pinafore dresses and could be carrying a ten-ton truck without it showing. As for Dexter, he's absolutely wicked, utter cream. I've just found out I'm expecting a baby and I'm going to be the most super mum, Jackie! I'm going to be the best mum *ever*.'

Jackie had been perching on the arm of a sofa. Now she slid down onto the sofa cushions giving a squeal of disbelief. 'You! A mum! I don't believe it!'

It was just like old times when they had forever been exchanging girlish secrets and giggling fit to bust.

'I know! It's incredible! Aunty Lil has been telling me the most way-out old wives' tales. According to her if I eat nothing but meat from now to next June the baby will be a boy and if I stick to fruit and veg it'll be a girl.'

Jackie, who such a short time ago had felt as if her world was coming to an end, cracked with laughter. Just the fact that Kelly was speaking to her again made her feel miles better.

'Finding out about the baby made me realise how wrong I'd been not getting in touch,' Kelly was now saying. 'I don't understand your obsession with being straight – it seems mental to me – but we're sisters and when it comes down to it I need you, Jackie. Ros is magic but she doesn't really know where I'm coming from, d'you know what I mean? It's you I want to talk to about the baby. I thought I might come over. Uncle Albie's trying to get rid of a lorryload of Dutch bulbs and though it's too late to put daff bulbs in, Flo says if lily bulbs are planted now they'll come up a treat in the summer. How about I bring some over and we do some gardening?'

'You, gardening? Now I really know you're pregnant! And how come Aunty Flo knows about planting lilies?'

Kelly's infectious giggles reverberated down the telephone line. 'You ain't been down to Sheppey lately, have you? Flo's patch looks like Kew Gardens. I'll see you in half an hour then. Put the kettle on, but I don't want any of that Lapsang Souchong rubbish Lavender was always trying to pour down my throat. A mug of no-nonsense Tetley's is about as up market as I'm prepared to go.'

'You're on.' With the connection severed Jackie walked towards the kitchen, her mood barely recognisable from the one she'd been in an hour or so ago.

She and Kelly were back on good terms again and, hopefully, she'd soon be back on good terms with her mum and dad, too. As for the nasty row that had taken place between her and Raymond that morning – considering the stress Raymond was under she'd totally overreacted to it. Where their relationship was concerned perhaps the answer was for her to become pregnant. It would certainly focus their thoughts positively instead of negatively, and there was something very satisfying about the prospect of her and Kelly and Ros having babies all in the same year.

As for Johnny ... She filled the electric kettle and plugged it in. She wouldn't think about Johnny – especially not Johnny in his forties bomber jacket, his corn-gold hair tumbling low over his eyebrows, his grey eyes full of heat. Her hand was a little unsteady as she lifted a tea caddy from the shelf. Thinking about Johnny was too dangerous an exercise. Thinking about Johnny would do her no good at all. Not now. Not ever.

Chapter Sixteen

'So we planted about fifty of Albie's knocked-off lily bulbs and edged the entire lot with Kevin's reserve stash of Brinks-Mat gold!' Kelly said to Dexter, her voice thick with giggles. 'I painted all six ingots with putty-coloured mortar paint before taking them over there and I bought a bag of toning garden gravel as well. Jackie never even blinked. She just accepted that I thought it would be fun to tart up her garden. And it was.'

'Christ, Kel! You're taking a risk, aren't you?' Dexter didn't know whether to laugh until he choked or be appalled. 'What if Pulfer decides to do a bit of gardening too? He might decide putty-coloured brick edging isn't too hot and bin them all! What is it all worth? Thirty thou? Forty?'

'About fifty, I think.'

They were naked and in bed in Dexter's Deptford flat. A half-full bottle of Louis Roederer Cristal stood within hand's reach on the floor, and pale afternoon sunlight was spilling into the room on to the rumpled sheets.

Kelly moved slightly as she straddled him, enjoying the warm flush of post-coital satisfaction and the feeling of him stirring slightly as he slowly subsided within her, happy in the knowledge that it wouldn't be long before he would once again begin to harden.

'Kev said every bar is what is known in the trade as "four nines gold",' she said, small beads of sweat on her high full breasts, her tousled hair a fox-red halo. 'Which means its pure gold containing 999.9 parts of gold to the 1000.'

Dexter lay with his hands behind his head, loving the look of her creamily pale skin as she moved seductively on his dark flesh, loving everything about her; her amazing looks, her fizzing buoyancy, her quicksilver mind.

'And each four nines gold one kilo bar is worth about ten thou?'

'According to Kev and, knowing him, he'll have done his homework.'

Dexter's grin split his face. 'And £50,00 of it is in a Met DCI's garden?'

Kelly nodded, gurgling with laughter. 'It couldn't be anywhere safer, could it? And all I have to do when Kevin wants it retrieved is offer to do a little more gardening for Jackie.'

Dexter was no longer indecisive about whether to be amused or appalled. Kelly's bare-faced effrontery in using a high-ranking copper to act as unsuspecting keeper of loot taken in the biggest haul in British criminal history was absolutely priceless; the most side-splittingly funny piece of cheek he'd ever come across in his life. He began to laugh and once he'd started he couldn't stop. Kelly, still astride him, was laughing so hard she nearly fell off him.

'What if Pulfer is put on the Brinks-Mat case?' Dexter finally managed to gasp. 'How will we ever keep shtumm about it?

Kelly couldn't answer him. She was laughing so much her rose-pink-nippled breasts were bouncing like ripe fruit in a high wind.

The laughter in his eyes was replaced by one of heat. God, but she was beautiful – she was the most beautiful thing ever to happen to him; the most beautiful thing he'd ever had in his life and he was never going to let her go.

'Give me your mouth,' he said huskily, his hands on her hips.

She leaned down to him, her nipples brushing his chest. 'I love you,' she said simply, laughter forgotten. 'I love you with all my heart, Dexter.' He groaned with desire, lifting her and rolling her beneath him in a swift, fluid movement. 'Oh yes!' he panted, beginning once more to move hard and deep inside her, all thoughts of the Brinks-Mat forgotten. 'Now, baby! Now!'

Eddie Burns hadn't forgotten about the Brinks-Mat. Ever since he had first suspected that Kevin and/or Johnny might have been involved in it he'd thought of little else.

As far as he was concerned he understood now why Jock had been so anxious to have him out of the family firm. The cunning old bastard had known the Brinks-Mat had been pending and he hadn't wanted to have to cut him in on any of it. The nig-nog Kelly was shagging was in on it, though. He was bound to be. And he, Eddie, wasn't.

He spun the black leather director's chair he was seated in round so that he was facing the window, and rammed a Gucci-booted foot against the low window-bottom. He just *knew* that Kev had been in on the gold raid. He could feel it in his water. Why else would Kev have disappeared so completely from the scene? Johnny wasn't away on his toes but that didn't necessarily signify. As for the nig-nog ... He'd nearly done for him years ago in the snooker hall and he wished now that he'd done for him good and proper.

The thought of Dexter Howe benefiting in any way whatsoever from the Brinks-Mat had him grinding his teeth and clenching his knuckles until the bones were white. He'd have that black bastard! The prospect gave him such an orgasmic lurch in his groin that he decided not to postpone the pleasure. The chair creaked as he rose abruptly to his feet. He'd take a couple of sidekicks with him but only because he now never went anywhere without them. Dexter Howe he was going to sort personally – and he was going to enjoy every pain-inflicted minute.

*   *   *

'Is Dexter with you?' Kelly's voice on the phone to Johnny was cross. They were supposed to be going for a Chinese meal and he'd said he'd pick her up from Creek Row eight o'clock-ish. It was now nine o'clock and there was still no sign of him.

'Nope, sorry, Kel.' Johnny's voice was slurred and disinterested. He was alone in the Tower Hill flat, thinking of Jackie and drinking heavily. 'He's probably at the Becket.'

Kelly already knew he wasn't at the Becket because she'd already had a word with the Becket's landlady, a woman she could trust to be straight with her. There was no point in telling Johnny, though. Not when he was obviously half wrecked.

She severed the connection and looked at her Rolex. It was 9.45 p.m. Crossness turned to angry indignation. Whatever the business that had sidetracked him he could at least have telephoned her. Despite the fact that it was the depths of winter she was wearing a cropped citrus-lemon halter top, black leggings and snakeskin boots. Now, resolving to go kill a couple of hours at the snooker hall and then to go out clubbing even if it meant going out clubbing by herself she yanked off the halter top and, bra-less, replaced it with a semi-transparent glittery Vivienne Westwood number.

By eight o'clock next morning, standing in the doorway of Dexter's resoundingly empty flat, her anger and indignation had fused into deep anxiety. Not for one minute did it occur to her he might be with another woman. Dexter was as unlikely to be unfaithful to her as she was likely to be unfaithful to him. What they had between them was too deep and true. So where was he and why hadn't he got a message to her?

'Dexter?' Rosamund's weary voice was puzzled. 'Why would Dexter have rung me, Kel?'

'I've been clubbing all night. He wouldn't have been able

to get in touch with me. I thought he might have rung you to ask if you knew where I was.'

'No. No one's rung me.' Especially not Kevin, she wanted to add, but didn't. Kelly would only tell her that of course Kevin hadn't rung her for it was Kelly's belief that the family's telephone lines were being hooked up. She, Rosamund, found the very suggestion that Rice and Sweeting phone lines were being tapped by the police utterly incredible but no one else in the family did. It was something they simply took for granted.

'Shit,' Kelly said succinctly and rang off.

Rosamund took a deep, steadying breath. It failed to do the trick and, succumbing to morning sickness, she ran for the bathroom. Moments later, on her knees and with her head over the lavatory bowl, she heaved up bile and the dry toast she had eaten half an hour earlier. When she could trust herself to do so she leaned back on her heels, wondering if the reason she suffered from morning sickness and Kelly didn't, was due to the fact that she was miserably unhappy and Kelly was radiant.

Her unhappiness, now that Raymond had got her off the hook about the stolen car, though her name was still on police records, was all down to Kevin. It was bad enough that they were separated, but the inequality of their separation was more than she could bear. She was pregnant and in Bermondsey and Kevin's friends and family regarded her, and treated her, as if she were Kevin's wife. At one point this would have made her deliriously happy but now, because of the behaviour expected of her, all it did was emphasise her loneliness.

'Well, you can't go out clubbing now, can you?' Lil had said to her. 'Not with our Kev on the run. Fer one thing, word would get back to 'im and then there'd be 'ell to pay and fer another, 'is mates wouldn't like it – especially not seein' as 'ow you're in the family way.'

When she had complained that it wasn't very reasonable

to expect her to stay indoors when Kevin was whooping it up on sun-kissed Jamaican beaches Lil had really laid into her.

'There's a bundle of unwritten rules and regulations when you shack up with blokes who live outside the law,' she had said flatly. 'From what Kel told me I thought you understood 'em all but it don't seem as if you do. Number one, what you don't do when he's away – whether he's away in nick or away on his toes – is to put yourself in situations where you could be accused of lookin' fer a bit o' male company. It always causes a right ruckus. You've 'eard the expression "'er indoors"? Well, that's a villain's wife when 'e ain't around. There's no use complaining about it, that's just the way it is.'

Lil had popped a peppermint in her mouth, leaned against her kitchen sink with her arms folded, and got really in her stride. 'It ain't much better when he's out and at 'ome,' she had said bluntly. 'Wives play no part at all in crims' social lives. When 'e and 'is mates pull off a nice tickle they'll celebrate at some club or other but wives are definitely out of the picture at these jollies and it's a fair bet any females present are of the obliging variety – which is somethin' every wife knows and 'as no option but to put up with.'

It had been an even grimmer scenario than the one Jackie had once painted for her and, far worse, it was one she recognised as being true. Flo and Lil and Pearl were never seen in the Connoisseur, nor were any other wives she could think of. The girls in the Connoisseur, were young, pretty, impressed by villains and all out for a good time.

She heaved herself to her feet and ran herself a glass of water from the tap. She had no doubt at all that Kevin loved her and neither did she have any doubt that, if they were together, everything would be simply ace between them. But they weren't together. Kevin, loaded with Brinks-Mat dosh, was living it up in Montego Bay and she had seen the photographs Dexter's parents had sent to Dexter. The same girl, young and black and incredibly beautiful, had been in every picture – and in every picture she had been standing in suspiciously close proximity to Kevin.

Rosamund sipped at the water, her heart bleak. She knew Kevin. He might very well be missing her and wishing she was with him but, as she wasn't, it would never occur to him to keep his pecker in his pants – especially not when faced with the kind of temptation he was meeting with in Jamaica.

All she wanted was to fly out there and be with him but Jock and Johnny were adamant she shouldn't do so.

'The rozzers may not be shouting Kev's name from the rooftops but they've got him fingered as having been in on the Brinks-Mat,' they had said. 'You're tabbed as being his common-law wife, Ros. Show up with your passport at Heathrow or Gatwick and all you'll be doing is leading the filth straight to him.'

And so, because that was the last thing in the world she wanted to do, she continued with her limbo-like existence, envying Kelly her blatantly joyful relationship with Dexter and even envying Jackie, for at least Jackie knew that Raymond would be coming home to her each evening.

'Dexter?' Jackie's voice was even more bewildered than Rosamund's had been. 'But why would Dexter ring me, Kelly? He barely knows me . . .'

'He knows you're my sister and if he was in trouble and couldn't contact anyone else he might contact you.'

'Trouble? What kind of trouble? Is there a warrant out for him?' For Kelly's sake Jackie tried to drum up concern but she was so sick at heart that it was a near-impossible task. Dexter would turn up in an hour or so and Kelly's present anxiety and distress would be history. Her own distress was of another category entirely and was so deep she didn't think she would ever recover from it.

The previous evening, as they had been having dinner together, Raymond had coolly told her that he wanted a divorce. Spearing a mushroom with his fork he had told her he preferred not to wait for a divorce granted on the ground of mutual incompatibility but would be admitting adultery. 'That way things will be finalised quicker,' he had said, slicing through a broccoli floret, 'and the quickest divorce possible is necessary because of Melanie's desire to be married on her twenty-first birthday, which falls in August.'

'Melanie?' Jackie had felt as if she was falling through space. '*Melanie*?' It was the first she had heard of any Melanie. It was the first she had heard of any woman in Raymond's life other than herself.

'Melanie is Deputy Commissioner Laing's great-niece.' He had folded his napkin with mind-numbing neatness and risen to his feet. 'I'm sure you will agree that the sooner the farcical shamble of our own marriage is relegated to history the better it will be for both of us.'

Anger had rocked through her. Pushing her chair away from the table she had stumbled to her feet with such violence her wine glass had toppled over, Frascati soaking into the tablecloth and dripping onto the polished wood floor. 'Don't talk to me as if I'm a public meeting!' she had shouted, her voice cracking with rage and disillusionment and despair. 'And don't presume to speak for me! *I* don't want to consign our marriage to history! I've been *working* at it, or hadn't you noticed? I've been working at it as hard as I've ever worked at anything!'

'You've been wasting your time.' He hadn't even said the words regretfully. He'd said them on a sneer. 'This particular party is over, Jacqueline. And don't think for one moment you will receive half the value of the house because you won't. Not over my dead body.'

True to form, instead of staying to shout or argue the matter out, he had then made a speedy exit from the house, slamming doors behind him as he did so. It was now one-thirty in the morning and he still hadn't returned.

She had waited up for him till after midnight and had then gone to bed. She hadn't slept. Instead she had lain awake facing deeply painful home truths. The most significant one – and the one she found the most difficult to accept – was that Raymond had been right when he had called their marriage a shambles. It *was* a shambles, but not for the reasons he believed it to be. It was a shambles because, no matter how much she admired Raymond's lifestyle and his integrity and his ideals of public service, she didn't love him as she should love him. She wasn't *in* love with him – not in the utterly besotted way Rosamund was in love with Kevin and that Kelly was in love with Dexter.

Now, putting the telephone down on Kelly, she knew she had inadvertently nearly ruined Raymond's life and the distress she felt for having done so was deep. She could think of only one way in which to make amends and that was by causing no difficulties whatsoever over the divorce. What mattered was that Raymond's career should suffer no more harm.

That decision made, her thoughts were all for Kelly. Wherever Dexter had disappeared to she hoped he'd turn up soon. Kelly wasn't used to being given grief and, if ever she met with real grief, Jackie doubted if Kelly would be able to cope.

'Poor bastard.' Detective Chief Inspector Mottam didn't usually expend sympathy on victims of gangland killings because it could be taken as read that the victims would be criminals themselves. This victim, however, had taken a real pounding and then, as if that hadn't been enough, like a gruesome picture he'd been nailed spread-eagled to the wall of the warehouse he'd been found in.

'No one cared about how soon he was found and there's

been no attempt to hide his identity, guv,' his young detective sergeant said, avoiding looking at the blood-smeared wall and the congealing pools on the concrete beneath it. 'The warehouse doors were left wide open and his wallet was in his jacket pocket. No money left in it – natch – but there were membership cards of a couple of serious gyms. His name is Howe. Dexter Howe.'

'I want him down from that wall the minute Conrad's had a look at him.' Mottam hunched his shoulders deeper into his overcoat. The warehouse faced out onto the Thames and the temperature was icy. 'Bloody Forensics. By the time they answer a call-out the victim's suffering from rigor bloody mortis.'

'Christ All-bleedin' Mighty!' Johnny gripped the Manley Arms telephone receiver hard and whirled round to where Jock and Albie were seated at their usual table, enjoying a quiet pint. 'It's the Becket's landlady! Dexter's been croaked!'

Albie put his glass down so suddenly beer slopped all over the table. Jock sucked in his breath, his face draining white, his first thought being Kelly. 'When?' he rasped, surging to his feet. 'Where? How? *Why?*'

'*Why?*' Rosamund demanded, holding on to the newel post to steady herself as she took Johnny's telephone call.

'Christ knows . . . It was gangland, though. It wasn't a tidy street accident. Someone has to tell Kelly. Jock thought she might be with you.'

'No.' Rosamund could feel her legs buckling and knew if she didn't sit down soon she would fall down. 'She phoned early this morning asking if I'd seen him.'

'Try Jax then. I'm going down the Becket to see what news I can pick up.'

He rang off and Rosamund sank down onto the bottom stair step, the telephone receiver still in her hand. Dexter dead. It didn't seem possible. Next to Kelly he was the most alive person she knew. She thought of Kelly and the baby Kelly was carrying. She couldn't be the one to break the news to her. She couldn't do it. Johnny would have to do it himself. Or Jackie.

'*Why* would anyone kill Dexter?' Jackie demanded in near-hysterical disbelief, taking the telephone call in her sterile cream-and-white-decorated drawing room. 'If it's gangland, is Johnny's card marked as well? Is this the reason Kevin's not been around for so long? Is he in Jarrow because there's a contract out for him?'

'No . . .' Rosamund's head was spinning. She'd forgotten that Jackie didn't know of Kevin's involvement with the Brinks-Mat or that Kevin wasn't in Jarrow but was in Jamaica. How on earth did Johnny and Kelly manage never to become confused by all the secrets and lies they constantly lived with? 'I don't think it's anything like that, Jackie.' There was raw uncertainty in her voice. Until Jackie had suggested it she'd never even dreamed of such a possibility but then, until Johnny's telephone call and the subsequent ones he had made to her from the Becket it had never ever occurred to her that anyone she knew would be murdered in such a hideous manner.

'You have to tell Kelly, Jackie. I can't do it. I just can't. What about the baby? She's only a few weeks pregnant. What if she miscarries? What if –'

'Where is she now?'

'I don't know. Out looking for Dexter. She's bound to be back home soon.' A fresh thought occurred to her, even more terrible than all her other ones. 'What if whoever killed Dexter is after Kelly as well? What if . . .'

It was obvious Rosamund was on the verge of a complete breakdown and Jackie, thinking of Rosamund's own pregnancy, didn't blame her one little bit. Breakdowns, though, were something none of them could indulge in. Not when

Kelly still had to be told. Not when Kelly had somehow to be supported through the nightmare that lay ahead.

'Stay at the house, Ros,' she said, her own incipient hysteria now tightly under control. 'I'll be with you in fifteen minutes.'

Kelly's reaction, when Jackie broke the news to her, was to scream and to continue to scream. No one could stop her. Not Jackie. Not Johnny. Not Pearl nor Jock.

'Phone for the doctor!' Pearl said urgently to Jock. 'If she ain't tranquillised soon she's goin' to lose the baby!'

Later – much later – the entire family, with the exception of Kelly, who was deep in a valium-induced sleep, and Eddie, who hadn't been round to Creek Row since his big fallout with Jock, sat together around the table in Pearl's kitchen.

'Why?' Jock said again. 'Why and who? That's what I fucking want tae know.'

'Someone obviously had a grudge against him.' Johnny straddled a kitchen chair, tension in every line of his body. 'Perhaps it was the Turks. Let's face it, none of us know what Dexter was up to before he came in with us. He could have crossed anyone. It might even be boxing-related.'

'Nah.' Albie nursed a pint pot of steaming tea. 'He was a straight goer in the fight game. I 'ave that as a fact from a mate dahn the Becket. And 'e wasn't into anythin' 'eavy before 'e came in with us. I remember Kelly tellin' me so.'

'Kelly may not have known.' Johnny was far more disturbed by Dexter's brutal death than he was letting on. What if Dexter had been into something really heavy? The grapevine was well aware he was now running with them. What if there were repercussions?

'Perhaps it was a straight mugging?' Rosamund desperately wanted the conversation to veer back to something resembling normality. 'He's been carrying an awful lot of money around on him ever since Ports –.'

Several pairs of eyes shot her quelling looks. Awkwardly Rosamund fell silent. She had forgotten that, as Jackie was with them, discussing Portsmouth was a no-no. It wasn't because anyone thought she'd grass to Raymond but it wasn't fair putting her in a situation where, with a DCI for a husband, she knew about live jobs.

'Muggers don't do what was done tae Dexter,' Jock said grimly.

At the thought of what had been done to Dexter Pearl began sobbing noisily yet again and Rosamund bit hard into her lip. What had been done to Dexter was unspeakable. Kelly still didn't know the details and no one was volunteering to be the one to tell her.

'I think I'd better go to Catford and speak to the Turks,' Johnny said, painfully aware of Jackie's nearness. It was the first time she had been back home since the hideous scene that had taken place between her and Jock. Now, thanks to Jock's sincere remorse for what had happened and Jackie's inability to hold a grudge where her dad was concerned, all that was forgotten. 'Sorry, hen,' Jock had said awkwardly when Jackie had stepped into the house. 'The way I lost ma rag wi' ye was way out o' order. Will ye forgive your old dad fur being such a stupid fucker?'

Jackie hadn't answered him. She'd merely hugged him tight and afterwards Jock had blown his nose hard, his eyes suspiciously bright. Witnessing the scene, Johnny had wished with all his heart that his own angry words with her on the heath could be forgiven and forgotten as easily.

'It ain't the Turks who now rule Catford.' The speaker was Smiler. It was such an unexpected interruption that everyone looked towards him. 'It's my Eddie.'

'Only till Halide finishes his stint for the cannabis job.' Albie took a deep slurp of his tea. 'Yer know it went to appeal, don't yer? He ain't doin' nine years now. He's only doin' two.'

'Does Dexter have family in London?' The last thing Jackie wanted to hear about was the doings of south-east London's major 'face'. 'Will they be organising the funeral or will we?'

'His kid brother is back in Kingston at the moment with the rest of his family and so I reckon organising everything is going tae be down to us.' Deep lines grooved Jock's gnarled face. 'The Coroner's Office may not release his body till someone's been collared for killing him and, if they don't, the funeral could be months away.'

'Christ, I hope not.' It was the first time any of them had ever heard Jackie blaspheme. 'Kelly couldn't cope with knowing Dexter's body was lying in a pathology drawer! She'd have a mental breakdown.'

'Then let's pray the funeral is soon, hen,' Jock said, putting an arm around her shoulders and hugging her hard against him.

'Kelly's boyfriend's funeral is next Friday,' Jackie said to Raymond three weeks later. 'I shall be going to it. Under the circumstances I thought I'd better tell you.'

'The circumstances being he was a gangster tortured to death by other gangsters and half of London's gangland will be there paying their respects?'

Jackie took in a deep steadying breath. She'd long ago accepted that their marriage was over but what still shocked her – and still hurt – was the depth of his venom towards her. There was absolutely no need for it – not when she was being as accommodating as possible over the divorce.

That she was still living in the house was all down to Lavender. It had been Lavender who had insisted that Raymond didn't file for divorce until after Easter. 'At least then you will have been married for nearly six months,' she had said, heartsick at the thought of her son's marriage ending so soon and so disastrously. 'And the two of you may well come to a fresh understanding and decide not to divorce after all.'

Jackie knew there wasn't a hope of that but was still far too fond of her to tell her so.

'You may suspect Dexter was a gangster but you don't *know* he was a gangster,' she flared back at Raymond now. 'He didn't have any form.'

'He was at it.' Raymond spoke with positive certainty. 'And if there's even one single journalist or photographer at Howe's funeral you leave straight away, understand?'

'There won't be,' she retorted tightly. 'There won't be anyone there but a handful of friends and family.'

She was very, very wrong. When she and Rosamund stepped into the small chapel at the crematorium it was to find it packed to capacity with Dexter's boxing friends and colleagues.

It was a racially mixed gathering with far more black faces than white and lots of mixed-race gradations in between. Their own family group was seated in the first two rows of pews on the left-hand side of the short aisle. Albie and Smiler were barely recognisable in black suits that hadn't seen the light of day since Smiler's father had died in 1979. Her own dad, who never went in for a suited and booted look, no matter what the occasion, was sombrely dressed in dark pants and dark jacket, a borrowed black tie emphasising the whiteness of his shirt.

Even though Flo and Lil barely knew Dexter, they had both come up from Sheppey in order to swell the family ranks. Pearl, who had quickly recognised that in Dexter her daughter had found a true soul mate, was clutching a tear-sodden handkerchief, her eyes red-rimmed from crying.

As for Kelly . . . Jackie's heart hurt as she and Rosamund stepped into the front pew and she saw the stricken grief on

Kelly's face. Dressed in a knee-length black coat obviously bought for her for the occasion, a black frock embossed with tiny red roses peeping from beneath it, she was barely recognisable. Her face was bone-white; her eyes so dark with grief it was impossible to tell iris from pupil. Their dad had his arm around her shoulders and she leaned against him, tears rolling mercilessly down her cheeks and dripping on to her coat.

Suddenly the tension became acute. Even though it was to be a nonreligious service the vicar on call stepped forward, motioning them to rise. Music began to play. Taped music. The opening riff of a track Dexter had loved and that everyone present associated with him.

'*Sittin' on the dock of the bay . . .*' Otis Redding sang in his rich, black, laid-back voice as Johnny and five of Dexter's boxing mates began carrying his coffin down the aisle, '. . . *watching the tide roll in.*'

It was too much for nearly everyone present. It was certainly too much for Kelly. She gave a long low cry, hugging her breast as though holding herself together against an inner disintegration, weeping tears torn from her heart.

Jackie dug her nails deep into her palms. She hadn't known Dexter, but even without the pain she felt on Kelly's behalf she would have found it impossible not to be moved by the atmosphere in the tiny chapel. Dexter Howe had been a young man with a lot of friends in the boxing fraternity and their bewilderment at his hideous murder, their anger and their grief, were raw.

Things became no easier when, after the short, informal service, a fleet of cars returned to Creek Row. Within seconds of the wake getting under way Kelly collapsed and an emergency doctor had to be telephoned for. Aware that Kelly was pregnant and in danger of losing the baby, none of Dexter's friends objected to Johnny's suggestion that the wake be moved to the Becket.

'I'm not going,' Jackie said to Rosamund, feeling completely emotionally drained. 'I'm going to Blackheath to collect a few clothes and then I'm coming back here to be with Kelly.'

Rosamund's eyes flew wide. 'But what about Raymond? He's not going to like you being in Creek Row, no matter what the circumstances are.'

'What Raymond likes or doesn't like doesn't matter any more.'

Jackie's voice was bleak and Rosamund's eyes widened even further.

Seeing the expression on her face Jackie lifted her shoulders in a shrug that spoke a thousand words. 'It's all over between us, Ros. Raymond married me without having a clue as to who my family were. The minute he found out, everything more or less died between us.' She pushed a long smooth wave of shoulder-length hair away from her face. 'As far as his career is concerned I think he's been pretty good on the damage limitation front and there've been no comebacks as yet – or not that I know of. That situation, however, isn't likely to last long and so it's goodbye Jacqueline, hello Melanie.'

'Melanie?'

They were standing in the tiny hallway and a crowd of mourners squeezed between them on their way to the front door, the cars and the Becket.

When their conversation could be continued, Jackie said, 'Melanie is the new woman in Raymond's life. She's Deputy Commissioner Laing's great-niece so I don't think she'll have any skeletons rattling in her cupboard, do you?'

Despite her flippancy, her hurt was obvious, and Rosamund said awkwardly, 'I'm so sorry, Jackie. I thought you, of all of us, had things worked out.'

'So did I.' Jackie's voice held a bitterness Rosamund had never heard in it before. 'A wonderfully straight husband in a wonderfully straight job. A whole new way of life with no secrets and no lies. It's come as quite a shock to realise that straight men in straight jobs can be just as morally dishonest as out-and-out crims.'

She began fastening up her dark mulberry-coloured coat as if she were suddenly cold. 'Melanie has obviously been in the picture almost from day one – and I'd no idea that your mother had transferred the house into Raymond's name on the condition that he married me. That only came out by accident when she was urging the two of us to wait a little longer before seeking a divorce. Somehow I can't help feeling your mother's little bit of blackmail might have influenced Raymond's decision to propose to me, can you?'

Rosamund's embarrassed silence spoke volumes.

Jackie pulled her coat-collar up. 'Sorry about the sarcasm, Ros. And sorry for off-loading all this on you today of all days. I didn't intend to. I'm going now. When Mum comes downstairs from sitting with Kelly tell her I'm coming back and that I'll be staying here for a while.'

Abruptly she turned, walking out of the house before her hard-won composure deserted her. Though she hadn't woken up that morning intending it to be so, today was going to be the last day of her life with Raymond; of her life in Blackheath. When she returned to his house she wasn't merely going to pack enough for a few days away, she was going to pack everything, and when she left to return to Creek Row in order to be a supportive presence to Kelly she would be leaving for good.

When she reached Jamaica Road she didn't stand in line at a bus stop. Instead she kept on walking, her leather-gloved hands deep in her coat pockets, her collar pulled high against the biting wind.

It was a long walk, cutting south through side streets into the Old Kent Road and walking down the Old Kent as far as New Cross. From there she crossed Deptford Bridge into Blackheath Road, climbing Blackheath Hill. By the time she was on the heath she was frozen through and through.

A hot drink, she thought as she entered the private road leading to the Pulfer home; a hot drink and then I'll pack everything into one case and be gone.

The instant she neared the house her heart sank. Raymond's Toyota Cressida was parked in the driveway. He was hardly likely to raise any objections to her packing her bags and leaving, but he was also equally unlikely to keep his thoughts to himself whilst she did so.

Taking a deep steadying breath she entered the house, grateful for the surge of warm air that greeted her in the large square hallway.

If it hadn't been for the car parked outside she would have thought the house was empty. There was no sound of movement in any of the downstairs rooms but, as Raymond's study was a converted bedroom that wasn't too surprising. He was obviously upstairs and working.

She began to take off her gloves, seeing, as she did so, that the phone was off the hook. It wasn't an unusual occurrence. Raymond often took phone calls downstairs and then, needing to refer to paperwork, went upstairs, continuing the conversation in his study where he had all his paperwork to hand.

Stuffing her gloves in her coat pockets she walked across to the small Regency table that was home to the telephone and picked up the receiver in order to replace it.

Eddie's voice was loud and arrogant and unmistakable.

'So yer reckon the date is absolutely foolproof, Ray? I don't want to set up something this big and the timing ter be all up the fucking creek.'

'Trust me.' Raymond's voice was taut. 'My informant says it's logged in for the tenth of next month. The South Africans are as rigid about dates and times as the Germans.'

'Then go over it fer me one more time.'

There was nothing deferential in Eddie's voice. At first,

stupefied by shock at hearing Raymond in conversation with her cousin, Jackie had leaped to the conclusion that Eddie was on the phone to him because he was grassing on someone. Now, however, she just couldn't make out what on earth was going on. 'Ray' Eddie had called Raymond. Ray! *No one* called Raymond 'Ray', not even his family! Her fingers tightened on the receiver, her heart slamming against her breastbone.

'The tenth of Feb courier, a Mr Van de Naude, has full diplomatic immunity,' Raymond said with authoritative certainty. 'Which means he isn't checked or searched, not even cursorily. He's on a regular South African Government run.'

'And the runs are legit?'

'Usually.' Raymond's voice was edged with impatience. It was a tone of voice Jackie knew well. Raymond hated explaining anything twice.

She was leaning against the wall now for support, beads of sweat gleaming on her forehead. What seemed to be happening couldn't possibly be happening. There was going to be an explanation for all this. Perhaps Raymond was in conversation with Eddie as part of an undercover operation designed to entrap Eddie. Perhaps . . .

'This time, however, it won't be.' Raymond's voice was categorical. 'This time, because of UN sanctions, the courier will be carrying diamonds.'

'Great, but I still don't get it.' Eddie's voice was petulant. He was certain that, if he'd been Kevin or Johnny, Pulfer would have been sketching in all the political background.

Raymond sucked in his breath, audibly hanging on to his patience. 'Because of sanctions the South African Government can't pay for arms and oil through legal channels. In order to establish credit for what they need they're going to use diamonds and, in order not to bring attention to this highly irregular transaction, on arrival in London the courier carrying them will be met only by an embassy car. There will be no police escort. My information is absolutely rock solid as to that. Now have you got it?'

'Yeah. It's a beauty. An absolute peach. So what are we goin' to need? A dummy embassy car and driver and a fake police motorcyclist?'

'Yes. All of which is down to you.' There was a slight pause, as if Raymond were transferring the telephone receiver from one ear to the other, and a slight rustling of paper.

'Right,' he said, and Jackie could imagine him pulling a notepad closer to the telephone. 'Just before entering the boundaries of Heathrow I want the legit embassy car to be flagged down by what the chauffeur will believe is a police motorcyclist. Got it?'

Eddie grunted affirmation.

'The "policeman" will inform the chauffeur that the courier he is to meet has had his flight diverted to Gatwick. With the genuine embassy car speeding off towards Sussex, a lookalike car with dummy South African insignia and containing two of your heavies – one uniformed as the chauffeur, the other city-suited as an escort – will await Van de Naude's arrival at Heathrow. Once the unsuspecting Van de Naude is in the car and the car is on its way to London a gun will have to be pulled on him while the car veers off onto a minor road. You then relieve him of his precious cargo, truss him up, load him into the boot and transfer to a waiting getaway car. If everything goes to plan – and it had better – your men will be back in the heart of London long before the genuine chauffeur even realises he's been duped.'

Eddie gave another grunt – this time of extreme satisfaction. 'And there's no heat on me over the nig-nog?'

'Howe? Not as yet.' Raymond's voice was full of icy distaste. 'It's already being spoken of as being drugs-related. You shouldn't have said a word to me about it.

When it comes to your nasty little private gangland vendettas I simply don't want to know.'

Eddie laughed. It wasn't a pleasant sound. 'I thought in this instance you would – seeing as how he was the spade who got my cousin in the family way and seeing as how my cousin is your sister-in-law.'

'Don't push me, Eddie.' Raymond's voice came through gritted teeth. 'And let me know when you've got everything set up for the tenth. This is a big number. *The* big number. Once it's over, so is our relationship. Understood?'

'Yeah?' There was something very like a jeer in Eddie's brutal voice. 'Yer might not be able to do without me as easy as yer think, Ray. You've got quite a reputation for nailing high-profile villains but you wouldn't 'ave 'ad if I hadn't set 'em up fer you and fed 'em to you on a plate. Halide and his henchmen were all down to me. It's something yer need to remember.'

'Piss off, Eddie,' Raymond said succinctly and severed the connection.

Luckily, Eddie must have done so too almost immediately, for a disconnected dialling tone hummed in Jackie's ear. There was no other sound – only the ceaseless hum and her raw, ragged, agonised gasps as she tried to suck air into her lungs.

Chapter Seventeen

Only the sound of Raymond's footsteps crossing from his desk to his study door galvanised her into movement. He couldn't find her standing in the hall, the telephone receiver clutched in her hand. If he did . . . If he knew that she knew . . .

She blocked the thought from her mind. She couldn't deal with it now. She couldn't deal any of the thoughts she was going to have to face. She could only deal with the one realisation dominant over everything else. Raymond hadn't to know she had overheard his conversation and the minute he came downstairs and found her in the house he would remember he had left the hall phone off the hook and he would know she had overheard him. She simply wasn't a good enough actress for him not to know. She had to move. She had to force her limbs out of their shocked paralysis. She had to lay the telephone receiver back down on the table. She had to get to the door. She had to leave the house . . .

There came the sound of Raymond's study door opening. From the door to the top of the stairs – where he would have a clear view of her standing in the hall – was only a matter of three or four yards.

She wasn't going to be able to reach the front door in time. She was going to have to bluff it out. She was going to have to pretend she had only that moment entered the house.

Shaking violently she lowered the telephone receiver to the marquetry-topped table. Another door upstairs opened. He was going into the bathroom. God was being good to her. Somehow she reached the door. Somehow she slipped the Yale's catch and opened it. With the bathroom door closed he wouldn't hear her leaving the house and, as the bathroom window looked out over the rear garden, he wouldn't see her headlong flight down the front path to the gate.

Her chest hurt so much she thought she was going to faint. Somehow, no matter how hard she tried, she couldn't draw air into her lungs. Realisation after realisation was slamming into her so hard she felt as if she was being physically assaulted. Eddie had murdered Dexter. Raymond was a bent copper. Not only was Raymond a bent copper in the sense of doing favours to a villain and receiving favours from one, he was a criminal in the full old-fashioned sense of the word. He wasn't merely going to turn a blind eye to a major heist, *he* was the one who was setting it up and planning it! And, as if that indescribable unbelievable horror weren't enough, *Raymond knew Eddie had murdered Dexter and quite obviously had no intention of doing anything about it*!

She was on the heath within yards of the pond. She made for the nearest tree, hugging the rough bark for support. If she hadn't heard every fatal, terrible word for herself no one on earth could have made her believe the truth she was now facing. All her life she had tried to escape secrets and lies and all her life she had, knowingly or unknowingly, been embroiled in them. These, though, were the worst. The obscenity of them – that Eddie had murdered Dexter and that Raymond was a disgrace to the uniform he wore – had her vomiting as if she, like Rosamund, were suffering from morning sickness.

There were no witnesses. No small boys were sailing boats. No lone walkers were out with dogs.

Giddily she continued to cling to the tree for support. She would go to the police, of course. She would inform on both Eddie and Raymond. Eddie would face a murder charge and Raymond would be booted out of the Met, losing everything he held dear.

A pale winter sun gleamed on the still waters of the pond. Both Eddie and Raymond would deny everything. Raymond would say she was emotionally unbalanced, so distressed by his having instigated divorce proceedings against her that she was making wild accusations against him in the hope of gaining some kind of revenge.

Perhaps if she waited until after Eddie had pulled the Heathrow heist she would have more proof to substantiate her allegations? But if she waited until then, Eddie might have skipped the country with a fortune in diamonds.

The tree's bark was rough beneath her palms and her cheeks were stinging with cold. Deputy Commissioner Laing would believe her, surely? If she went now, immediately, to him then he would deal with everything; sort everything; ensure that justice was done.

For a few seconds merciful certainty flooded through her. It didn't last. Although she was 99.9 per cent sure that Laing was as straight as the proverbial die she couldn't *know* that he was straight. Someone, somewhere, had leaked information to Raymond concerning the transfer of diamonds from South Africa to Britain. What if it had been Laing? Remote as the possibility was it was a risk that couldn't possibly be taken.

She pushed herself away from the tree, nauseous no longer. What she was, now, was angry – bitterly, burningly, *murderously* angry. Somehow, some way, she was going to make Eddie and Raymond pay for their monstrous acts. How, though, if simply making a statement to the police was not going to be enough?

She began walking towards the road, intent on either catching a bus back down to Bermondsey or flagging down a cruising taxi. Kelly, obviously, had to be told who it was who had been responsible for Dexter's hideous death.

Rosamund, too, needed to be told about Raymond. He was, after all, her brother.

A black cab rounded the corner opposite the church, speeding down towards the pub and the pond. She stepped into the road, waving it to a stop.

'Creek Row, Bermondsey' she said, opening the passenger-side door and stepping into an atmosphere of stale cigarette smoke.

If she didn't trust the police to take proper action against both Eddie and Raymond – and she didn't – then she would have to go to Johnny. Johnny would know how best to deal with Eddie. What about Raymond, though? How could Johnny possibly ensure Raymond's career as a policeman came to a swift, sudden and ignominious end?

The cab veered left into Shooter's Hill Road, heading towards New Cross. The answer was that he couldn't. She put a hand to her aching head, her thoughts whirling chaotically. What on earth was Kelly's reaction going to be when she was told it was Eddie who had murdered Dexter? She wasn't going to want to leave retribution up to Johnny. She was going to want to go out and kill Eddie herself and, if she did so, her baby would most likely be born in prison. As for Raymond, even if the Heathrow job went ahead, she couldn't be certain of gathering enough evidence to implicate him in it. If she didn't – if no one believed her allegations about him – there was a possibility of his both remaining a high-ranking police officer *and* having untold dosh stashed away from his proceeds from the heist.

Unless . . . unless . . . The cab swung right into the Old Kent Road. What if Eddie and Raymond were cheated of the Heathrow heist? That would be a retaliation that would really hit where it hurt most. Eddie would still have to be brought to book for Dexter's murder and Raymond would still have to be publicly disgraced but how much sweeter it would be to extract that revenge if they had first had a fortune whipped from under them.

The cab swung right, negotiating the side streets that cut across into Jamaica Road. Jackie closed her eyes tight, fighting a sudden return of nausea. How *dare* Raymond have taken his holier-than-thou attitude where her family was concerned when he was every bit as bad? She mentally corrected herself. He wasn't as bad – he was far, far worse. Her family didn't pretend to be anything other than they were. Raymond's criminality was carried on behind the shield of his Met police badge and that, as far as she was concerned, was far more shameful.

As the cab turned into Jamaica Road she changed her mind yet again about her immediate intentions. She couldn't, today, tell Kelly that it was Eddie who had murdered Dexter. Kelly was deeply tranquillised and would be that way for quite some time. Even when she was no longer sedated, she would need several days in which to recover from the trauma of the funeral – and during those several days she, Jackie, was going to be busy. She was going to be very busy indeed.

Early next morning she left number 28 dressed in a pair of grey flannel slacks, a grey cashmere turtle-necked sweater, black leather hip-length jacket and black leather gloves, her hair wound into a sleek knot in the nape of her neck.

Driving Kelly's Jaguar, her first port of call was the garage her dad, her uncles and her cousins all used when they wanted hooky numberplates making up. Then she drove to Nunhead Cemetery and spent nearly two hours wandering between the gravestones, a notebook in hand.

When she returned to the parked Jaguar it was nearly lunchtime. Instead of heading back towards Creek Row she made straight for the Elephant & Castle roundabout, crossed the Thames via Westminster Bridge and, twenty minutes later, was speeding out on the A4 towards Heathrow Airport.

*　　*　　*

For the rest of that week her family barely saw her.

'Is Jax still here?' Johnny asked Pearl, his voice studiedly casual. 'Is she staying until Kelly is completely back on track again?'

'Kelly *is* back on track again.' Pearl crushed a half-smoked cigarette out in a saucer – the nearest available receptacle. 'She has to be, ain't she, when she has the baby to consider? As for how long she's goin' to be here – who knows? I don't. All I know is, she's here. She ain't showing any signs of returning to the family rozzer and none of us ever see a sign of her. She borrowed Kelly's Jag the day of the funeral and poor Kel ain't had her hands on it since.'

Jackie sat in the parked Jaguar, a leather-gloved finger tapping her lips, deep in thought. The car park at the back of the pub was large and secluded but was it secluded enough? Sod's law being what it was, there was always the chance another car would drive in just when it would be disastrous for it to do so. She looked at the street map spread open beside her on the passenger seat and then, another decision made, slid the Jaguar into gear. Twenty minutes later she was parked outside a house-letting agency in nearby Feltham.

'Why don't you go back to Sheppey?' Jackie said to her mother a few days later. 'Kelly's no longer in any danger of losing the baby and I'm not going back to Blackheath. As long as I'm here and Ros is next door Kelly will be all right.'

'Well, I must admit I wouldn't mind being down at Sheppey for a bit.' Pearl slammed an iron down on one of Jock's shirts. 'I miss all my little luxuries when I'm away for too long, plus it's a damn sight more lively than Bermondsey is these days. The Manley Arms is as dead as a doornail. We have karaoke now in the club down at Sheppey. It's a right laugh. Your Aunty Flo has Anne Shelton off to a T.'

Jackie didn't know who Anne Shelton was and didn't much care. What she wanted was for her mother to join her dad at the Sheppey house in order that she could have her long-postponed discussion with Kelly and Rosamund.

'And what d'you mean you ain't going back to Blackheath?' Pearl demanded, continuing to iron Jock's shirt with punishing vigour. 'D'you mean you ain't goin' back this week? Or you ain't goin' back this month? Or you ain't goin' back ever?'

'I'm not going back ever.'

Pearl spat on the iron and breathed a hefty sigh of satisfaction. 'Well, thank God for that. It's the first bit of good news I've had in yonks. What will you do? Will you go back to St Martin's?'

'No. I'm going to do something different. Something that will make dad proud of me.'

Pearl hooted with laughter. 'Blimey, gel!' she said at last when she was able to speak. 'You'd have to pull a job as big as Brinks-Mat to do that!'

Jackie didn't smile. She hadn't smiled since she had overheard the terrible conversation between Raymond and Eddie. She nearly smiled, though. The Brinks-Mat warehouse was a Heathrow security warehouse and the men who had raided it had probably spent just as much time as she had sussing out the area around Heathrow and the roads in and out of it. Her mother's wild remark wasn't, in fact, so wild after all.

The morning Pearl left for Sheppey Jackie made a huge pot of coffee and set it on the kitchen table cheek by jowl with a bottle of Rémy. Dressed in a scarlet silk blouse, a white arrow-straight skirt and gold mules she put coffee mugs out, brandy glasses, a big fat notebook and a handful of felt-tip pens. Then, taking a deep breath, she telephoned Ros.

'Could you get round here, Ros? More or less straight

away? You and me and Kelly are going to have a meet.'

Rosamund, who had been sipping coffee after another tedious bout of morning sickness, blinked. 'A *meet*? You're beginning to sound like Kevin and Johnny! You mean you want me to pop round for a chat?'

'No.' Jackie's voice, usually so attractively soft, was utterly businesslike. 'I mean I want you to come round for a meet. Five minutes, Ros. No later.'

Next she went upstairs into the bedroom she and Kelly were again sharing.

'I need to talk to you, Kelly,' she said in a gentle but firm voice to what was apparently a mound of bedclothes. The duvet-covered mound moved slightly and there was a glimpse of fiery-red hair. 'It's important, Kelly. Ros is on her way round and there's fresh coffee in the pot.' She paused for a moment and then, as there was no further sign of movement, said, 'I want to talk about Dexter's murder,' and turned and left the room.

Kelly hurtled downstairs so fast after her that she was almost in the kitchen before her.

'What about Dexter's murder?' she demanded fiercely. 'What have you heard? What's being said?' She was naked apart from the Mickey Mouse T-shirt that served her as a nightie. 'Have the cozzers been in touch? Has Johnny called?'

'I know this is going to be near impossible for you, Kel, but I need you to be patient . . .'

The front door crashed open and Rosamund stepped into the hall. Like Kelly she was still in her nightclothes, though her mules and white towelling dressing gown were a little more practical than Kelly's T-shirt. 'What the heck is this all about, Jackie?' she asked, bewildered. 'A papal summons would have been less urgent. Is that coffee I can smell?'

'It's something to do with Dexter, Ros.' Kelly's cat-green eyes were feverishly bright. 'What is it, Jackie? For Christ's sake, *what is it*?'

Jackie had intended waiting until Kelly and Rosamund were well fortified with coffee and brandy before she told them of Raymond and Eddie's telephone conversation. Faced with Kelly's desperate urgency it was an intention impossible to keep.

'I know who killed Dexter,' she said simply, knowing there was no way of dressing up the hideous truth; no way of softening the blow. Her throat was tight, her lips dry. 'It was Eddie.'

Rosamund gasped, her eyes rounding to the size of a marmoset's.

Kelly simply stared. 'Eddie?' she said blankly. 'Eddie who?'

'Let's sit down, Kelly.' Jackie took hold of Kelly's arm, propelling her out of the hall and into the kitchen. 'Sit down, try and stay calm, and I'll tell you everything.'

At the sight of the brandy bottle on the table, the notepad and pens, Rosamund sucked in her breath. Jackie hadn't been joking when she had said they were going to have a meet – and she knew with instinctive certainty Jackie hadn't been joking or relaying dodgy information when she had said that Eddie had killed Dexter. Eddie was capable of killing anyone. She, and everyone else in the family, had known that for a long time.

'Eddie?' Kelly said again as Jackie pressed her down onto a chair. '*Eddie?*'

Jackie nodded, sitting down beside her, taking hold of her hand and clutching it tightly. 'I'm going to tell you about a telephone conversation I overheard. A long telephone conversation. I know this is going to be near impossible for both of you but if you could stay in control until I've finished –'

'*Eddie murdered Dexter?*' Kelly's eyes were no longer green. They were black pits in a chalk-white face. '*Eddie murdered Dexter and you expect me to stay in control?*'

She sprang up from the table and Jackie jumped up with

her, holding her fast by the wrist. 'You have to listen to me, Kelly!' she said with such urgency Rosamund's scalp prickled. 'If you want to make Eddie pay for what he's done – without suffering yourself and having the baby suffer – *you have to listen to me*!'

Kelly stood rock-still, her breath coming fast and shallow. 'Does Johnny know about this? Does Dad?'

'No. And when I've told you everything you'll know why. Now sit down again, Kel. Have a coffee. Have a large brandy. The same goes for you, Ros. This is going to be no easier for you than for Kelly.'

Rosamund reached out for the coffee percolator with an unsteady hand. This Jackie, grim-faced and firm and utterly decisive, was a Jackie she barely recognised. It was as if Jackie had undergone a complete metamorphosis. As if, almost overnight, she had turned into a different person.

'It was the day of Dexter's funeral,' Jackie said succinctly as Kelly, her eyes burning hers, sat down once again at the table. 'You were in bed sedated. You, Ros, had gone down to the Becket with the funeral party. I'd gone home.'

Rosamund had finished pouring the coffee and Jackie hooked her fingers around her steaming coffee mug.

'I knew Raymond was in the house because his car was parked outside and the minute I stepped into the hall I knew he must be upstairs in his study because the phone in the hall was off the hook.'

Rosamund was familiar enough with her brother's habits to know what that signified. Kelly didn't know and didn't care.

'I picked the telephone receiver up to replace it,' Jackie's eyes held Rosamund's, 'and I heard Raymond talking to Eddie.'

Rosamund gave a strangled disbelieving cry.

'They were talking about a job, or rather Raymond was *telling* Eddie about a job – a job he wanted Eddie and his heavies to do for him.'

'No!' Rosamund pushed her chair back away from the table. 'I don't believe it! You've misunderstood things, Jackie! Raymond is pompous and self-satisfied and . . . and *tedious*. But he isn't bent! He doesn't take bribes! He doesn't –'

'The job was a diamond heist,' Jackie continued implacably. 'Raymond knew about a delivery being made from South Africa through diplomatic channels by a man named Van de Naude. His plan was that Eddie and his men would kidnap Van de Naude and relieve him of his cargo.'

Rosamund made a gagging sound and clapped a hand over her mouth, certain she was again going to be sick.

'Raymond said that Eddie and his men would be back in central London before anyone even realised there'd been a heist and then Eddie said . . .' Even though she'd had over a week to come to terms with the horror she was about to relate, Jackie could hear her voice crack. 'Eddie said, "And there's no heat on me over the nig-nog?" and Raymond said, "Howe? Not as yet . . ."'

Both Kelly and Rosamund erupted from the table like wild things.

'*This isn't true!*' Rosamund was gasping for breath, her eyes dilated. '*You can't say such vile things about Raymond, Jackie! Whatever you heard you misunderstood!*'

'*No I didn't!*' Jackie was on her feet, aware she was very possibly going to have to slap Rosamund's face in order to stop her hyperventilating but knowing she had to deal with Kelly first.

Kelly was at the kitchen door, yanking it open, and Jackie knew exactly what her little sister was about to do. She was going to throw on a pair of jeans, hurtle out of the house and drive off in her Jag in search of Eddie. And when she found him she would kill him – or try to.

Coming from behind Kelly she threw her weight against the half-open door, crashing it shut.

'No!' she shouted. '*Listen* to me, Kel!'

'*I'm going to kill him! He killed Dexter ... He killed my baby's father ... and I'm going to kill him, Jackie! I'm going to do for him ...*'

'And go to prison? Have Dexter's baby born in Holloway?' Jackie grasped her shoulders so hard that Kelly cried out in pain. 'Yes, you're going to do for Eddie! We're *all* of us going to do for Eddie – and Raymond – but we're going to use our brains about it! Come back to the table, Kel. Have a brandy and for Christ's sake and the hundredth time *listen* to me!'

Kelly sucked in a lungful of air but made no further move to try to open the door. Behind them there came the sound of Rosamund clattering the brandy bottle clumsily against the rim of a glass. Jackie let out a deep ragged breath of relief. The worst was over. They'd both been told and they were about to listen to her at last. Now the three of them could really get down to business.

'We'll all have one of those,' she said to Rosamund as she propelled Kelly back to the table.

'I still don't think it's true.' Rosamund's voice was as unsteady as her hand as she slopped Rémy into another two glasses. 'I'm going to listen to you, Jackie, but I still don't believe it's true.'

'It's true all right.' Jackie legs were shaky as she seated herself once more at the table but they weren't shaky with distress or shock. They were shaky with relief. After over a week of living with the burden of her terrible knowledge the relief of sharing it was monumental.

'Right,' she said as Kelly spilled open a packet of cigarettes. 'At the end of the conversation Raymond told Eddie that after the diamonds were lifted their relationship would be over. Eddie asked Raymond how he thought he would be able to manage without high-profile villains being handed to him on a plate.' Her eyes held Kelly's. Kelly would realise the full significance of what she was next going to say far more than Rosamund would. 'It was Eddie who was responsible for Halide going down, Kel. His exact words were, "Halide and his henchmen were all down to me. It's something you need to remember."'

'Cousin Eddie. A murderer and a grass.' Kelly's voice was as brittle as glass. 'So how are we going to sort him, Jackie? How are we going to sort both him and Raymond?'

'Where Eddie is concerned – and for the baby's sake – we're going to keep our hands squeaky clean. We're not going to murder Eddie – we're simply going to visit Halide and let him know who his prison sentence is down to. Halide's family will then make sure Eddie is sorted. It will follow as easily as night follows day.'

Kelly pushed her chair abruptly away from the table. 'Then let's do it now. Today. Where is Halide? Winson Green? Parkhurst?'

'Winson Green – but we're not going there today, Kelly. We have other things to plan today.'

'Other things?' For the first time the huge change that had taken place in Jackie – her steely determination and ruthless decisiveness – impinged on Kelly's consciousness. Slowly she again sat down. 'What sort of other things?'

Jackie sent a notebook skittering across the table towards her. 'Start taking notes, Kel. We're going to see that justice is done where Eddie and Raymond are concerned but, as it will be Halide's men who will take care of Eddie and a police tribunal that will deal with Raymond, I thought, before that happens, a more personal kind of revenge would be in order.'

Rosamund took a deep swallow of brandy. Kelly's eyes widened. Was this *Jackie* making such a suggestion? Jackie, who had always been so prim and proper and ultrastraight and mind-bendingly respectable?

Jackie's eyes met hers, cool and clear and utterly in control. Aware that, where she and Jackie were concerned, the status quo had changed entirely and possibly for good, Kelly picked up her pen. 'Such as?' she asked tautly.

Jackie hooked her crossed ankles around the leg of her chair and leaned across the table slightly, resting her weight on her arms. 'I thought we could pay the two of them back in their own coin with the added satisfaction of letting them know we had done so.'

Kelly nodded, her thoughts so full of Dexter and the hideous way he had died that she couldn't trust herself to speak.

Rosamund looked bewildered. 'How?' she asked, still struggling to come to terms with the realisation that Raymond wasn't merely a bent copper but that he was mega-bent.

Jackie tapped a cigarette from Kelly's packet of Benson & Hedges and lit it. Neither Kelly nor Rosamund had ever seen her smoke before.

'I thought we could hijack their diamond heist,' she said simply.

Kelly gasped. Rosamund stared at her, goggle-eyed.

'It can be quite easily done.' Jackie slewed her notepad around so that they could both read what was written on it. 'Number one,' she read. 'Raymond's plan is for one of Eddie's men to dummy up as a police motorcyclist and for him to intercept the car that is to meet the diamond-carrying Mr Van de Naude at Heathrow. The chauffeur will be told that, as the courier's flight has been diverted to Gatwick, he has to reroute. Well, we don't need to interfere with that part of Raymond's plan at all. The official car will head off towards Gatwick and a duplicate car, containing either two of Eddie's heavies, or Eddie himself and one of his heavies, will take its place en route to Heathrow.'

'And then?' Kelly's eyes were fiercely bright. It was obvious to her what Eddie and Raymond then planned to do. The unsuspecting Van de Naude would be greeted by the man acting as the escort in the duplicate car. He would be shepherded into the car and then, once out of Heathrow, would have a gun pulled on him and be relieved of his cargo. How, though, could they hijack such a plan? They couldn't very well ambush the duplicate car. Not only would the 'escort' be armed, the pseudo-chauffeur would be armed as well.

'Number two. Eddie's duplicate car will park up, complete with South African flag and insignia, and wait for Van de Naude to emerge from Arrivals. He has diplomatic immunity, remember? He won't be going through Customs.'

'I'm sorry, Jackie, I don't understand.' Rosamund felt as if she were floundering in quicksand. 'Are you suggesting that we – you and me and Kelly – *rob* someone?'

'Yes.' Jackie had no intention of beating about the bush with Ros. Ros now knew the score. The robbery was one her brother – a high-ranking police officer – had set up. Either she was in with them or she wasn't. And if she wanted to be reunited with Kevin before he became permanently involved with someone else, then she'd be in with them.

'But . . . but that's *criminal*.' Rosamund knew exactly how wet she was sounding but she couldn't help it. She'd never done anything criminal in her life. She remembered how near she had come to being charged with possession of a stolen vehicle and mentally corrected herself. She had never *knowingly* done anything criminal.

'Yes, it's criminal,' Jackie said calmly, 'but when you threw in with Kevin you embraced a life of criminality, didn't you? There's more ways of being criminal than being *actively* criminal. You can be passively criminal – and living with a criminal and enjoying his ill-gotten gains with him is being passively criminal. I'm not condemning you for it, Ros. I'm just pointing it out to you. You made certain choices when you committed yourself to life with Kevin and, those choices made, you can't keep shillyshallying between being a gangster's moll and being Miss Outraged of Tunbridge Wells.'

For a long tension-filled moment neither Jackie nor Kelly knew if Rosamund was going to remain at the table and, if she didn't, they knew they and Kevin would never see her again.

'I . . . can't believe you're talking to me like this.' Rosamund's towelling dressing-gown was gaping open at the neck and her breasts were rising and falling as if she had been running.

'And I can't believe your brother would have been tempted into marrying me merely because your mother then signed your family home over to him or that, having discovered my dad was a crim, he would immediately begin divorce proceedings when all the time *he* was criminally involved with Eddie,' Jackie flared back, her patience at last beginning to snap. 'I can't believe a man with all Raymond's advantages would stoop as obscenely low as he has stooped. I can't believe that, knowing Eddie murdered Dexter, he would still continue having dealings with Eddie!'

Her passion-filled words vibrated around the room and then there was a long, long silence.

Kelly twisted round on her chair so that she was sitting on one leg while the other swung free.

Rosamund's face was ivory-pale.

'What's it to be, Ros?' Jackie asked at last. 'A heist that will turn the tables on Eddie and Raymond and will show Kevin that you're loyal to the family, by his side for ever, or are you going to wait in the hope that Kevin will eventually send for you, enduring the mortification of Raymond's public disgrace whilst you do so.'

'I'm in with you.' Rosamund's voice was quiet but perfectly steady. 'We're family, after all, aren't we? And I don't want the diamond heist to be successful for Eddie and Raymond. What if Eddie should leave the country with his share of them before Halide's men catch up with him? What if Raymond manages to salt his share of the diamonds away? Even if he's booted out of the Met it won't be much consolation if he's able to hot-foot it to a life of luxury with Melanie.'

'We're on then.' Kelly grasped hold of one of Rosamund's hands and Jackie followed suit making the clasp three-handed.

'So how do we fuck up Eddie and Raymond's plans?' The prospect of planning and carrying out such a heist – and doing so with her big sister – was the best antidote to her grief that Kelly could imagine.

'Whilst Eddie's duplicate car is waiting outside Arrivals *our* dummy car will be waiting elsewhere. One of us, probably me, will be in British Airways uniform. Before Mr Van de Naude even reaches the Arrival's area I will approach him, inform him his car is waiting for him and escort him to it. Kelly will be at the wheel in chauffeur's livery. You, Ros, will be suitably dressed as a PA. The two of you will zip off with him and take a B road off the A4 towards Feltham. The instant you do so he will, of course, know he's been had and Ros will pull a gun on him.'

'A *gun*! I can't pull a gun on anyone! I've never even *held* a gun . . .'

'You're an actress, aren't you?' Kelly snapped, irritated at the interruption. 'You can *act* as if you know what you're doing with a gun.'

'Feltham is mere minutes away,' Jackie continued, 'and I've rented a house there under a dummy name on a three-month let. Kelly will drive straight in the garage – there's an electronic up-and-over door – and then, while Ros continues to hold the gun on Van de Naude you, Kelly, will gag him and manacle him to an immovable object. You then break into his attaché-case, remove the diamonds and hot-foot it back on to the street where a getaway car will be parked up.

'You drive back to the airport with one of you inserting the diamonds into tubes of toothpaste. I will have changed out of my uniform and will be waiting to meet you. We'll have tickets for somewhere in the sun and we'll be travelling on false passports.'

She slipped three birth certificates still with St Catherine's House receipts attached to them from out of the back of her notebook.

'I trolled round Nunhead Cemetery the other day. These three women were all born the years we were born. I can't say I relish becoming known as Joanna Winterbottom or Tracey Dunwell, which are the choices Ros and I have but the name Miranda Cash is going to suit Kelly down to the ground –'

'What about the first car, the car that will pick the courier up from the airport?' Ros interrupted, determined she wasn't going to be dumped with the name Tracey. 'Won't Mr Van de Naude be immediately suspicious if it doesn't have the right kind of numberplates and some sort of insignia?'

'The car Kelly will be chauffeuring will have *exactly* the right kind of numberplates on it.' For the first time since they had seated themselves around the table a wide smile of amusement split Jackie's face. 'For a family that's been ringing cars for as long as this one has, arranging for a legit-looking diplomatic limousine is going to be the easiest piece of the job.'

'And Mr Van de Naude?' It seemed to Ros that if she were the one who was going to have to terrorise him with a gun she should at least be making quite sure of his eventual safety.

'We make a last-minute phone call from the airport to the letting agents telling them there's an urgent problem at the house that needs their attention.' Jackie's satisfaction was palpable. 'Then off we go with a fortune in diamonds. There are still some details that have to be sorted but broadly speaking that's the plan. It's simple and straightforward, and providing we don't lose our nerve it will work like a dream.'

'It's blinding,' Kelly said, her eyes ablaze with anticipation. 'What are the details that still need to be sorted?'

'The gun.' Both Jackie and Kelly ignored Ros's quick intake of breath. 'I thought I'd leave that up to you, Kel. If I started poking round the family slaughter, Dad or Johnny would be immediately suspicious. No one will take any notice if you do it. Another important detail I still haven't sorted is the air stewardess uniform. I thought you might be able to help there, Ros. When you did the end-of-term play *Boeing Boeing* last year you had to have an Air France uniform, didn't you? Is there any chance of getting a British Airways one from the same source?'

'From Wardrobe? I could try. Stuff like that, for plays, is nearly always out of date, though, or suspiciously shabby.'

'Then it'd be no good,' Jackie frowned. 'A uniform like that would be a bigger giveaway than no uniform at all.'

'I have a friend at RADA who has a sister who is a stewardess with British Airways. Perhaps if she thought it was for a one-night play I was doing she would lend me it.'

'But when news breaks about the job she might just connect the oddity of such a loan – especially when the only way of returning the uniform would be by post – and share her concerns with the police. That way, even though you'd be out of the country, the police would have your card marked. It's an untidiness we could do without.'

'Dad will know of someone who provides pseudo-uniforms.' Kelly said. 'Do you remember years ago when he did the Barclays? A Barclays staff uniform was used, wasn't it? I'll just have a general old chitchat with him and find out. You're going to need an identity tag as well and possibly a security pass. All it will take to get them is cash and I have plenty of that.'

'You have?' Jackie's sleek eyebrows rose slightly.

Kelly hugged a naked leg to her chest and came very near to grinning. 'I was in on a big job with Dad and Johnny only a few weeks back. The Isle of Wight-to-

Portsmouth ferry haul. It's how I bought the Jag. And while we're all being completely open with one another it's about time you knew that Kevin is in Jamaica, not Jarrow.'

'He was in on the Brinks-Mat,' Rosamund said, determined not to leave the punchline to Kelly and feeling a stab of satisfaction as Jackie's eyebrows shot nearly into her hair.

'Bloody hell!' Jackie rarely swore but then, before today, she'd never smoked either.

'And just in case it turns out to be hard to prove that Raymond has been in cahoots with Eddie, the Brinks-Mat will nail him absolutely.'

Both Jackie and Rosamund stared at Kelly in blank incomprehension.

Kelly's cat-green eyes were dancing. 'Kevin left a little souvenir of the Brinks-Mat before he high-tailed it off to Jamaica. He left six gold bars with me all beautifully stamped and instantly identifiable as being from the Brinks-Mat raid.'

'Oh God . . .' Jackie, so composed a few moments ago, was fast becoming a quivering wreck. 'You're sitting on Brinks-Mat gold, Kelly? It's here, in the house?'

'No.' Even though her heart was broken over Dexter's death and even though she knew she would grieve for him for a long, long time, Kelly knew now that her life wasn't over. An hour ago she had thought her life would never have fun in it ever again. She had been wrong. It was fun now. Terrific fun. 'No,' she said again, wanting to explode with laughter. 'It's not hidden in this house. It's hidden at your house.'

Jackie's scream of disbelief was loud enough to have been heard at London Bridge.

'It's in the garden,' Kelly continued, wishing she had a camera to capture the moment. 'Remember that fake stone edging we put down when we put the lily bulbs in? They were Brinks-Mat ingots painted with stone-coloured paint.'

Jackie now had both hands clapped over her mouth and Rosamund's eyes were out on stalks.

'So . . .' Kelly wriggled into a more comfortable position on her chair, this time hugging both her knees to her chin. 'Nailing Raymond as a bent copper is going to be easy, and I reckon it will be worth the expense. We simply let the powers that be know that he's harbouring stolen gold. He'll try and talk his way out of it, of course, but together with the other evidence we're going to gather in the next two weeks – I'm going to put a bug on Eddie's phone and hopefully get taped evidence – I think it will put an end to his career, don't you?'

'Oh God . . .' Jackie was no longer blaspheming in horror. She was choking with laughter.

Rosamund began to giggle and then to splutter with mirth. By the time Kelly reached for the bottle of Rémy and began pouring generous measures into the brandy glasses she was laughing as hysterically as Jackie.

'Here's to us then.' Kelly raised her brandy glass high. 'We're going to shaft Eddie and Raymond and fly off with a fortune.'

'And we're going to fly to Jamaica,' Rosamund said with new-found bouncy assertiveness. 'Kevin's had things his own way for too long. From now on our relationship is going to be on a very different basis . . . and his Jamaican girlfriend will have to find another hunk with dosh to latch on to.'

'Poor Kevin . . .' Jackie succumbed to a fresh gale of laughter. 'Can you imagine his face when Ros trolls up to him on Montego Bay beach having pulled a heist almost comparable to his own? He'll never be the same man again.'

Kelly tapped her notepad with her felt-tip pen. 'Enough frivolity girls,' she said in mock seriousness. 'Let's get down to business again. We need to apply for the passports, buy return tickets for Kingston –'

'Return!' Ros stopped giggling so suddenly she hiccuped. 'But we won't be coming back so why do we need return tickets?'

'We're just three lone women holidaymakers, remember?' Jackie's voice was still thick with laughter. 'Return tickets will cause no interest whatsoever whereas single tickets just might.'

'We need to get a limousine and to check out what kind of numberplates it should be carrying,' Kelly continued, writing the list of things to do in a surprisingly neat hand. 'Most important of all we need to get our hands on a British Airways ground staff uniform and have the security pass and identity card made up.'

'And Jackie needs to do some dummy runs wearing the uniform around Heathrow,' Rosamund said, viewing the ground staff part of their plans as she would a role in a play. 'She has to both feel and look comfortable in the uniform and she certainly has to know her way around the relevant part of the airport like the back of her hand.'

'And is toothpaste the best way of taking the diamonds out of the country?' Kelly asked, her head cocked enquiringly to one side. 'Wouldn't it be safer to put them in Durex and either swallow them or stuff them up our fannies?'

'You can do what you like with yours,' Jackie said as Rosamund again collapsed into giggles, 'but I'm opting for the toothpaste. It will be absolutely safe. There's no reason why we should be searched extra thoroughly, is there? We're not travelling in or out of Amsterdam or Caracas and our passports will be virgin –'

'It's the only thing about us that will be!' Rosamund said through a fresh bout of giggles.

'And Johnny.' Kelly looked across at Jackie. 'Is he going to know about this?'

Jackie kept her eyes firmly on her notepad. 'No. This a female-only operation.'

'And afterwards?' Kelly persisted.

'Afterwards . . .' Jackie knew perfectly well what Kelly was driving at, but what happened afterwards, between her and Johnny, was something she dare not even begin to speculate about. 'Afterwards we'll wait and see,' she said, her voice nonchalant, her heart racing as fast as an express train.

Chapter Eighteen

'Wait? Wait for what?' Johnny was standing at the open door that led from number 28's kitchen into the hall passageway. He was dressed in a T-shirt and jeans, his biceps bulging, his hands on his hips. His whole attitude was one of angry confrontation and Jackie hadn't the slightest idea how she was going to deal with it. 'I'm in love with you.' His eyes burned hers. 'You know that, Jax. You've always known it. You've left Pulfer. You're back home. What the hell is all this wait and see rubbish?'

'I need time . . .' It was a lie. She didn't need time at all. She was so confounded by desire for him that it was taking more willpower than she'd ever known she possessed not to fly into his arms.

She thought of the heist. It wasn't just a robbery. It was far, far more. And it was something she and Kelly and Ros had to do for themselves. If she and Johnny became lovers now she couldn't possibly keep the heist a secret from him – and once he knew of it male machismo would kick in and the heist would be out of their hands.

He moved swiftly. So swiftly she couldn't have escaped him even if she'd tried. '*I* don't need time!' he said harshly, pinning her against the wall. 'I need you!' His mouth came down on hers, hot and sweet and hard.

She didn't try to push him away. There wasn't willpower in the world enough for that. Her arms flew up around his neck, her mouth opening willingly beneath his. As his body pressed hard against hers and desire overcame her completely she clung to one last fierce resolve. She wasn't going to tell him about the heist. She wasn't going to tell him about the ticket for Jamaica now in her purse. She would tell him afterwards – by telephone from Kingston. If he wanted her for life, as she wanted him, then he would know where to find her.

'I love you,' she whispered, her voice breaking with emotion as he swung her up in his arms. There was no one else in the house. Ros was down at Petty France picking up her Joanna Winterbottom passport. Kelly was timing a practise run from Heathrow to Feltham. 'I love you with all my heart, Johnny.'

Carrying her with ease he strode out of the kitchen and down the passageway to the foot of the stairs. He loved her too – and in a few more minutes, when her bedroom door had closed behind them, she would at long last know how very, very much.

Kelly jotted on a small notepad the timing of the run she had just made and slipped the notepad into the side pocket of her fake-leopardskin-trimmed black leather jacket. Despite the variability of the traffic every run she made was panning out the same to within three or four minutes.

Her shoulder bag was on the seat beside her and she flipped its flap open. The micro-sized recording bug and gizmo lay snugly on top of her make-up bag. She turned the key in the ignition, sliding the Jaguar again into gear. Putting the gizmo in place was going to be a high-risk factor but it wasn't going to be the hardest part of what she was now about to do. The hard part was going to be facing Eddie and not allowing any of her burning hatred for him to show.

Though she and Ros and Jackie now knew it was Eddie who had murdered Dexter none of them knew *why* he had murdered him. They'd had a good try at guessing, though, and they'd all guessed the same thing. Eddie had murdered Dexter for no other reason than out of pique. He'd done it because Dexter had been taken into the family firm at a time when he, Eddie, had been judiciously dropped from it. And he'd done it because Dexter was black and he hated blacks and didn't want his cronies knowing that his youngest cousin had a black boyfriend.

She motored back into London at a speed so sedate it set her teeth on edge. It was a tedious but necessary precaution. The last thing she needed was to be pulled over for a motoring offence when the heist was only days away.

She was heading towards Eddie's lair above one of the clubs he now ran in Catford and when she reached it she was going to behave towards him just as she'd always behaved. She had to, for everything depended on Eddie and Raymond having not the slightest glimmer they'd been rumbled.

'Hiya,' she said breezily forty minutes later to a suited and booted lump who had been posted at the club's relatively discreet side entrance. 'Is Eddie at home?'

The lump's eyes narrowed. He knew who she was. She was one of Sweetie-pie Sweeting's girls and family to Mr Burns. The question was – was Mr Burns going to want to see her? If he didn't, and she was allowed in, there was going to be trouble with a big T. And if he did, and he refused her entry, there'd be even bigger trouble in store.

'You expected?' he asked, trying to strike a note that couldn't be taken the wrong way no matter what the circumstances.

'Chill out, why don't you?' Kelly retorted crushingly, zipping past him without checking her hip-swinging stride for so much as a second.

She ran lightly up a flight of creaky wooden stairs, knowing exactly what she would find when she entered the large room they led to. Eddie would be lounging in an executive-type swivel chair, his feet on a massive Biedermeier desk. There would be at least six other men in the room, possibly more, and all would be slickly suited and booted.

With a black Emanuel miniskirt skimming her bottom, tarty high-heeled shoes, her jacket open to reveal a spangly scarlet boob-tube and her bag slung carelessly over her shoulder she mounted the last step and, without troubling to knock, sashayed into the lion's den.

'*What the bleedin' hell* . . .?' Eddie's feet crashed from the desk to the floor.

'It's only me,' Kelly said before his heavies went for their guns. 'A family visit. How's things?'

She dropped her shoulder bag to the floor and perched on the corner of the desk, revealing honey-gold silky smooth thighs.

The tension that had filled the room at her abrupt and unexpected entry was replaced by a different kind of atmosphere entirely.

Eddie gave a wolfish grin. His little cousin was quite the business – and now she was no longer fucking a nig-nog he could flash her in front of his soldiers with justified pride.

'Business is great boys, ain't it?' He stood up, sending his chair rolling back a foot or so. There were rumours that Kelly was now doing high-profile wheelman work. He wondered if they were true and, if they were, he wondered if he could poach her. His little cousin Kelly was about the only woman in the world he'd ever even come close to liking. He slipped an arm around her shoulder, giving her a hug. He'd done her one hell of a favour when he'd croaked her blackie boyfriend. A girl like Kelly should be taking a leaf from his own book. She should be travelling alone.

With Eddie's big brutal paw hugging her close and the scent of his distinctively sweet aftershave in her nostrils Kelly found herself, for the first time in her life, praying hard. She had to maintain iron self-control. She mustn't let her thoughts dwell on Dexter and on what Eddie had done to Dexter. If she did she would end up trying to kill

326

him then and there and, with all his stooges present, failing miserably. There would be no sweet revenge then in taking a fortune from him and probably no final revenge. Once he knew his card was marked for Dexter's death he'd be so extra careful about his personal safety that even Halide's soldiers might find it impossible to take him.

'So this guy's waving a tool around like crazy . . .' one of Eddie's suited and booted lumps said, breaking the silence and continuing the conversation that had been taking place before Kelly had walked in on them. 'He tries to dodge past me to get to the door and I leap on him and gave him it twice in the chest.' He began laughing, his eyes on Kelly's legs. If she moved just a fraction he'd be able to see the colour of her panties – that is he would if she was wearing any. 'He went down like a sack . . . there was blood everywhere.'

'Serves him right.' Eddie was quite unperturbed at such a conversation being continued in front of Kelly. 'It'll teach him not to take liberties. He was getting to be a right pain in the colon.'

Kelly prayed harder. She prayed so hard she thought she was going to explode. And she forced her face to split in a dazzling smile. 'It sounds like there's not much peace and quiet round here,' she said in a careless manner. 'How are the clubs doing? Word is you're building quite an empire, Eddie.'

While Eddie began bragging about his ever-expanding network of clubs Kelly's eyes were on the phone and the phone wiring. Her plan had been to empty the room of Eddie's henchman by asking Eddie if they could have a few minutes on their own to discuss a family matter. She'd then been going to spin him some story about Johnny and, whilst doing so, had intended looking out of the window and making out that she could see Raymond Pulfer in the street. Her hope had been that Eddie would then leave the room in order to check out what the hell was going on and that, while he was fruitlessly looking for Raymond, she would be able to do the necessary where the phone line was concerned. Now, however, she was aware of just how implausible her plan had been.

The mini tape recorder was going to have to be somewhere completely unspottable and there was nowhere completely unspottable. What was needed was for the line to be tampered with from the telephone junction box and that, accessible only to British Telecomm workmen, would be somewhere down on the street.

'Reliable? That eejit? He couldn't reliably be entrusted with a supermarket trolley.'

The speaker was Eddie. The conversation had obviously taken another shift. Kelly joined in with the laughter, her brain still working furiously.

She needed a skilled bellman. A bellman would be able to gain access to the junction box as easy as her dad could gain access to a safe. Once in it he would be able to hook a line from Eddie's telephone line to an empty line . . . an empty line in an unoccupied house. That way there'd be no risk of Eddie tumbling to the fact that his phone calls were being recorded.

'Don't go belly-aching to me about it . . .'

Eddie, his arm still draped around her shoulders, was responding to something someone had just said though what it was Kelly hadn't the faintest idea. With Eddie's reputation now so fearsome there wasn't a bellman in south-east London who would take on such a job.

She sucked in her breath sharply. Eddie assumed it was in admiration at his words. It wasn't. She had just thought of a bellman who would do the job with no questions asked. Albie. She'd have a word with her Uncle Albie and, Albie being Albie, she wouldn't have to explain a thing. Albie had become disenchanted with Eddie years ago. Albie would do the job for her sweet as a nut and with no questions asked.

'Cunt!' Eddie said with explosive savagery, his entire manner changing. 'He said that about me? You sure?'

The henchman whose snippet of news Eddie was reacting to so extremely nodded.

Eddie ground his teeth, his eyes like chips of granite. 'I'm goin' to have him! I'm goin' to rip his nuts off and ram them down his throat!'

Kelly slid away from him, picked up her shoulder bag and slung it over her shoulder. In a few days' time, when the Heathrow heist had been carried out, Eddie's reign of torture and murder would be over. Halide's men would deal with him and they would do so in a far more satisfactory manner than she could ever hope to do.

'Bye, Eddie,' she said, strolling towards the door, uncaring of the several pairs of eyes on her quality cleavage and her tantalisingly near-visible crutch. 'See ya.'

'Mother, I want you to go for a walk,' Raymond said dictatorially. 'The conversation I'm now going to have with Rosamund is one that would only distress you.'

'But I don't *want* you having a conversation with Rosamund that would cause me distress,' Lavender protested, knowing she was being bullied and not liking it one little bit.

'I think it would be better if you do as Raymond asks.' Rosamund's voice was low and not quite steady. She was visiting her mother for what she knew was going to be the last time for a long, long while. The heist and her flight to Jamaica were only three days away. That Raymond had chosen the same day and time to make a visit was, as far as she was concerned, a catastrophe of the highest order. It meant she wouldn't be able to say goodbye to her mother in the manner she had hoped to do and it meant she was face to face with Raymond for the first time since knowing the sickening truth about him.

Overcome by a feeling of absolute inadequacy Lavender

looked from her son to her daughter and then, aware that neither of them wanted her presence, reached for her walking stick and with an exceedingly heavy heart left the room and, a long minute later, the flat.

'Yes?' Rosamund said tautly when the front door had closed behind her mother. 'What is this conversation you want to have with me?'

If she hadn't been an instinctive actress – and a RADA-trained one – she would have found the confrontation unendurable. She and Raymond had never been close, even as children. There had been the age difference and the gender difference. He had gone away to school as a boarder whilst she had been educated locally. It hadn't helped to form a bond between them. When they had been thrown into each other's company, on family holidays for instance, she had always found him irritatingly patronising and excruciatingly autocratic. On his part he'd never had any time for her and had never pretended otherwise. She had not expected the day to come, though, when she would passionately despise him.

'It's about the house. About money.'

It took every ounce of self-control she possessed not to ask why he was worrying about money when the diamond heist he had planned was so imminent.

'Yes?' she said again, not having the slightest pang about the fact that he would soon be facing a disciplinary hearing.

His eyes flicked from her face to her belly. Her pregnancy was now just about discernible.

'I'm selling the Blackheath house,' he said, returning his gaze to her face, his expression one of open contempt. 'Melanie has no desire to live south of the river. When we marry we shall be setting up home in Putney.'

'Really?' Rosamund wondered if Deputy Commissioner Laing's great-niece would stand by Raymond when he was publicly disgraced and kicked out of the Met. It was as unlikely as pigs flying.

'Your behaviour has been so disgusting, so unforgivable, such a total betrayal of the way you have been brought up and of everything Father stood for that I think even you would agree with me that you've forfeited the right to any family money.'

Rosamund was aware of a new feeling – a feeling of sick fascination. 'This disgusting, unforgivable behaviour being my friendship with the Sweetings and my love affair with Kevin Rice?' she asked, regarding him as if he were something that had crawled out of a pit of slime.

'The Sweetings are Bermondsey trash criminals and Rice is a gangster.' His voice was a whiplash that didn't pain her in the slightest.

'The Sweetings may be criminals but in their personal relationships they have a code of honour you'd do well to emulate,' she said, wondering how on earth she was biting other words back. 'And Kevin isn't a gangster. He's a bank robber. There's a world of difference, as I'm sure you know.'

He made a jeering sound and as he faced her, tailor's dummy neat in a beige sweater and beige flannels, his light-coloured hair slicked neat and close to his head, she could contain herself no longer. 'A gangster is a heavy villain who is in the business of hurting people,' she said, her eyes holding his, wanting to see the expression her next words would bring. 'Eddie Burns is a gangster. If I were consorting with him then you'd be quite correct to say that I've betrayed everything Father stood for. But I'm not. I'd go to my grave before associating with such a psychopath.'

The expression that flared through Raymond's eyes came and was suppressed with such speed it was impossible for her to categorise it.

'The topic under discussion is family money,' he said cuttingly. 'Money you are no longer morally entitled to. The house is mine entirely – I'm under no obligation to even inform you that I intend to sell. The money that would have been coming to you – the money that is held in stocks and shares and bonds – will not now be doing so. Mother feels as I do. Your behaviour and choice of lifestyle has effectively severed your relationship with us. You're no longer part of this family, Rosamund.'

'Where you are concerned, Raymond, I no longer want to be!'

She strode towards the door knowing she had to get out of his presence immediately, that if she didn't she would hurl at him everything she knew about him.

As the door crashed after her she heard his short, satisfied laugh. She began to stride so quickly for the road that she was nearly running. She would have the last laugh – and it was one she'd be sharing with Jackie and Kelly.

She yanked open the door of the car Johnny had loaned her. As for what Raymond had said about her mother's feelings, she didn't believe him. Her mother was deeply distressed by everything Raymond had told her about the Sweetings and about Kevin and she was utterly anguished at the prospect of becoming grandmother to a baby who was, as far as she could discern, going to be born illegitimately, but Rosamund didn't for one minute believe Lavender wanted to sever all ties with her. What was clearly obvious, though, was that Raymond intended bullying her in that direction.

She turned the key in the ignition, pressing her foot down on the accelerator and revving the engine. With a little luck on the hard evidence front Raymond was soon going to have the self-satisfied smirk wiped off his face.

She crashed the car into gear and pulled away from the kerb. Three days. That was all that were left until the heist. Jackie's British Airways uniform was hanging in the wardrobe at number 28 thanks to the services of the specialist who had, long ago, provided Jock with a Barclays Bank uniform. All the necessary gear for the heist had really simply come down to a shopping list. With money

– which thanks to Kelly's involvement with the Portsmouth job they had in plenty – everything and anything was possible.

The limousine, complete with insignia and correct numberplating, was in a lock-up adjacent to Creek Row. The getaway car – a ringer – was already parked outside the house Jackie had rented in Feltham and three packed travel bags were stowed in its boot. Jackie had already done three dry runs up at Heathrow, dressed in uniform, and hadn't been challenged.

Kelly knew the route from Heathrow to the Feltham house like the back of her hand. They were all in receipt of their new fake passports. They all had tickets for the same Kingston flight – a flight that departed exactly two hours after Mr Van de Naude's flight arrived from South Africa. She, Rosamund, had spent long hours handling a 9mm Smith & Wesson Model 940 until she could do so as if she knew exactly what she was about. She had also spent hours practising how to snap handcuffs on an unwilling subject.

'You'll need to cuff him almost the same instant you draw the gun on him,' Jackie had said. 'Otherwise he might wrestle you for the gun and turn the tables on both of you. Stick the gun beneath his ribs with your left hand and while he's frozen with shock, or fear, or whatever it is that takes him, snap the handcuffs on him with your right hand. After that you need to force him down between the seats for the rest of the journey and for that you'll have to have the gun to his head.'

It had sounded horrific to her but practice, Jackie taking the part of Van de Naude whilst Kelly drove down the A4 at high speed, had given her confidence. So far preparing for the heist had been, for her, like preparing for a dramatic role.

Now, she drove through Blackheath Village, taking a right-hand turn towards Lewisham at the top of Lee Road.

'A successful heist is made up of three equal components,' Jackie had said to her. 'One part planning, one part nerve, and one part luck.'

She cruised down Belmont Hill to the traffic lights at Lewisham's clock tower. Their planning had, as far as she could tell, been immaculate. Where nerves were concerned she had been the only weak link but she was so no longer. Her unexpected confrontation with Raymond had filled her with iron-strong resolve.

'Which only leaves luck,' she said aloud to herself as she headed out of Lewisham in the direction of the Old Kent Road. Even though she was driving, she crossed her fingers. They were going to need luck, too, where the bug and tape-recording of Eddie's telephone line was concerned. Kelly had taken to sitting by the tape recorder in the deserted house Albie had hooked a line to so that she heard every conversation on Eddie's telephone line the instant it was made. So far Raymond hadn't been among Eddie's callers and time was fast beginning to run out. Halide, too, still hadn't been told about Eddie's duplicity. Jackie had visited his family and told his cousin she needed to visit him and asked if he'd OK it. The cousin had rather cautiously agreed and tomorrow, which was the first possible visiting day, Jackie was going to drive up to Winson Green with him.

She began slicing through side streets towards Jamaica Road. With the heist all set and with only two other loose ends to tie up, she would soon be heading for Jamaica itself – and Kevin.

Her heart tightened within her chest. He didn't know, of course, how very soon they were going to be reunited. '*Please* don't let me find you with another girl in your bed,' she whispered passionately to herself as she turned into Jamaica Road. '*Please* be glad to see me, Kevin! Please *please* let everything work out ace!'

*   *   *

'You goin' to tell me for why you want to see my brother?' Kemel Sestos was driving fast out of London, Jackie his only passenger. 'I have rights to know, don't I?'

He had but Jackie didn't want Kemel then taking everything out of her hands. It was important that *she* was the one who broke the news to Halide that Eddie had shafted him.

'You'll know soon enough,' she said with cool composure. 'Fifteen minutes with Halide is all I need, Kemel. Just fifteen little minutes.'

The rest of the drive was conducted in near-hostile silence. Jackie was unruffled. She was doing this her way just as she was doing everything else her way. Despite her totally focused state of mind her tummy muscles tightened a little as they reached Birmingham and turned off on to the road leading to the prison. Winson Green held bad memories for her; memories of being taken as a child to visit her father when he'd been serving time there.

She beat them firmly to the back of her mind. Those days were gone and she was a child no longer.

Armed with the necessary visiting order Kemel parked up and, walking a little apart from each other, they entered the prison.

It was just as Jackie remembered. There was the same unmistakable odour of cheap soap; the same faint aroma of boiled cabbage, the same institutionalised smell of Jeyes Fluid. The visiting room was just as she remembered it as well. Sitting across small tables from their menfolk were tired women all wearing the same brave expression on overly made-up faces. Some had children with them. The sense of urgency, of making the most of what little time they were being given, was profound.

As she sat beside Kemel, waiting for Halide, Jackie was wryly aware that in her navy suit, sheer navy tights and suede navy court shoes she looked more like a visiting probation officer than a family visitor. She fingered the collar of her white shirt-blouse wishing she'd worn something a little brighter.

Even though she had never previously met him, she recognised Halide the minute he walked into the visiting room. He was a huge man – a mountain of a man, his neck so thick the nape was lost in rolls of fat.

'What the fuck we got here then?' he asked, looking only at Kemel as he lowered his bulk on to a perilously flimsy-looking chair. 'A fucking new girlfriend or an official fucking prison visitor?'

'She's cousin to the Rice brothers.' Kemel clasped and unclasped his hands uneasily. If Jackie Sweeting proved to be nothing more than a gangster-groupie hoping to link her name to Halide's the shit was really going to hit the fan.

Halide grunted and condescendingly turned his attention to Jackie. 'You want speak with me? Your cousins have a message for me?'

'Yes, I want to speak to you. No, my cousins have no message for you.' Jackie leaned forward a little, her eyes burningly intense. 'This stint you're doing, Halide . . . you were set up.'

Halide's eyes narrowed. He said nothing – merely waited for her to continue.

Jackie's mouth was dry. She had no proof to show Halide whatsoever. All she had was her sincerity and it occurred to her that Halide would have little experience in gauging sincerity.

'I'm married to a DCI in the Met.' Beside her Kemel Sestos sucked in his breath sharply. Halide's fleshy face remained as impassive as ever. 'I overheard a telephone conversation of his . . . a telephone conversation he was making to Eddie Burns.'

There was a gleam in Halide's eyes now. A gleam that indicated a long-held suspicion was about to be confirmed.

'Eddie Burns is my cousin . . . if you know Johnny and

Kevin Rice are also my cousins then you'll know that. In the conversation I listened in to, Eddie referred to a murder he'd done. He was asking my husband if he was under any sort of suspicion for it.'

'A murder?' Halide's voice was soft but with warders nearby that was understandable. 'Whose murder?'

Jackie, too, was keeping her voice as low as possible. 'Dexter Howe's.'

An expression very like bewilderment flickered across Halide's fleshy face. Jackie had never believed Dexter's death had been gang-related, but that belief had been based only on instinct. Now she knew it for a fact. Dexter's name meant nothing to Halide and Kemel. Eddie's reason for murdering Dexter was one known only to himself.

'Dexter was my sister's boyfriend,' she said, and then paused as a warder walked near to their table. 'It's why I'm here,' she continued when the warder was out of ear-shot again. 'It's why I'm telling you all this. My husband told Eddie he'd nothing to worry about where Dexter's death was concerned and said that he was thinking of ending his relationship with him. It was then that your name was mentioned.'

Halide's hooded eyes sharpened yet again.

Jackie leaned her arms on the table, her hair, held away from her face by ivory combs, swinging forward slightly. Eddie said, "Yeah? You might not be able to do without me as easy as you think. You've got quite a reputation for nailing high-profile villains but you wouldn't have if I hadn't set them up for you and fed them to you on a plate. Halide and his henchmen were all down to me. It's something you need to remember."'

'Did he? Did he indeed?' Halide looked across to his cousin. 'Do you think we believe this, Kemel? Or do you think we think we're being stirred up for no good reason?'

'Considering how Eddie's set himself up as virtual king of the manor, *your* manor, I think we believe it.'

'Yeah.' Halide's piggy eyes held Jackie's long and hard. She returned the look unflinchingly. 'Yeah,' he said again. 'I think we believe it.'

'And you'll act on it?'

Halide grinned, showing a mouthful of gold teeth. 'What do you think?' he said, beginning to heave himself to his feet.

The interview was obviously over. She had said what she had come to say and she had been believed. There was only one more little detail that needed to be covered.

'I have a surprise of my own in store for him on the tenth of February and so . . .'

'And so nothing will be done until after that date,' Halide said.

She, too, rose to her feet. Everything that needed to be done had been done. 'I'll go home by train,' she said to Kemel. 'I want to be on my own for a while.'

Kemel shrugged. Despite the length of her legs he hadn't particularly enjoyed being seated so close to her on the journey from London to Birmingham. Her navy suit had made him feel he was in the company of a QC.

An hour and a half later, drinking coffee on a London-bound train, Jackie mentally ran through the list of tasks still to be completed. There were very few. She needed to deposit a change of clothes in a locker at Heathrow and she needed to hand the letter she had made in the presence of a solicitor, a letter detailing what she knew of Raymond's relationship with Eddie, to Deputy Commissioner Laing. Kelly was the one who had opted for the pleasure of making an anonymous telephone call, tipping Laing off as to the presence of Brinks-Mat bullion in the Pulfer garden.

She frowned. Without the incontrovertible proof of a taped, incriminating conversation between Raymond and Eddie, there was little more be done where Raymond was oncerned. Her uncorroborated allegations would carry very little weight and Raymond would say – with indisputable sincerity – that he knew nothing about the gold and that she, with her criminal connections, was the one obviously guilty of hiding it in what had been, at the time, their family home.

At the thought of Raymond wriggling off the hook she felt a surge of intense frustration. There was, however, nothing further that could be done. What was needed was for Raymond to telephone Eddie and to talk to him as incriminatingly as he had in the conversation she had overheard. That way he'd never be able to talk himself out of the Brinks-Mat connection.

As the train slid into Euston Station she felt a tightening of her tummy muscles. Two more days. That was all the time left now until the day of the heist. Two more days and all that was needed, in order for everything to be beautifully sewn up, was one last little piece of luck.

Thirty minutes later, as she walked into number 28 and Kelly danced down the stairs towards her, a sizzling grin splitting her face, she knew that Lady Luck had come up trumps.

'We've got him!' Kelly said fizzingly, a tiny cassette held high in her hand. '*We've got him!*'

Chapter Nineteen

'The flight is on time.' Jackie's voice was as taut as a draw
bow. It was 7.30 a.m. on Friday, 10 February and it wa
all systems go. Jackie was already pin neat in her Britis
Airways uniform, her security pass prominently displayed
She slid her arms into a navy tie-belted coat. 'Keep to tim
and keep your nerve,' she said, drawing on a pair of leathe
gloves. 'Nothing is going to go wrong.'

'What if Mr Van de Naude isn't on the morning flight?
Rosamund already had a tighteningly giddy sensation i
the pit of her stomach. It wasn't surprising – not whe
beneath her fashionably baggy jacket she was wearing
shoulder holster with a revolver tucked into it.

'You know what happens.' Jackie's voice was crisp a
she picked up a roomy shoulder bag containing only
clipboard. When it really came down to it Ros had th
most nerve-racking role of all of them. All she, Jackie, ha
to do was to have the cool to carry out the most enormou
bluff. Kelly's part – being the wheelman – was one that wa
second nature to her. Ros was the one who was armed. Ro
was the one who was going to have to intimidate Van d
Naude successfully and handcuff him. Ros was the one wh
had to make quite, quite sure Van de Naude didn't wrestl
the revolver from her grasp. 'If he isn't on this morning'
flight we do a rerun when the evening flight arrives. OK?'

To her relief Ros nodded, not asking further questions
Further questions, at this stage, would have indicated tha
Ros was beginning to lose her nerve.

'OK,' she said again, this time as a statement. 'I'm off
The next time we meet will be when I hand Mr Van d

Naude into your loving care. Keep cool and good luck.'

'You're the one that needs the luck.' Kelly's titian Afro was tamed into the kind of neat bob that befitted a chauffeuse. 'You're the one who has to successfully waylay Van de Naude in the first place.'

'Thanks for that reminder, little sister,' Jackie said drily. 'See ya.'

She walked briskly out of number 28's kitchen and out of the house. She was travelling to Heathrow on public transport: a bus for the short journey to the Elephant & Castle underground station; a short hop on the Bakerloo line to Piccadilly Circus underground and then, from there, all the way to Heathrow on the Piccadilly line. It was a journey she'd taken many times over the last few days. She knew exactly what variances in time could occur and, setting off at the time she had set off, knew she didn't have to worry about them.

She felt completely at ease in her uniform. Ros's advice, that she should wear the uniform often in the days leading up to the heist, had been good. She didn't feel as if she was guised up in any way – and so didn't look as if she were.

Her gloved hands were clasped lightly in her lap as the train thundered in and then out of Green Park station, Hyde Park Corner station and Knightsbridge. Johnny thought he was seeing her that evening. At the thought of Johnny her hands tightened and her heart began to slam. What on earth was his reaction going to be when he learned of the mammoth job she, Kelly and Ros had pulled? Was he going to be furious he hadn't been let in on it? How was he going to feel about her high-tailing it off to Jamaica without so much as a word? What if he made no suggestion at all about joining her there?

The train skimmed to a halt at Earls Court. Johnny loved her as she loved him. As she had always loved him. They were an item. A couple. Soul mates. He would understand why it was so important that she, Kelly and Ros carried out this particular heist alone. He would be absolutely staggered at their having pulled it, but he would understand – and as soon as he could do so undetected, he would fly out to Jamaica and join them.

The train was whizzing along furiously again. Baron Court, Hammersmith, Acton Town.

All she had to worry about now was Mr Van de Naude being on the morning's flight from Johannesburg into Heathrow. If Van de Naude were not, after all, the designated courier, then the heist was off. She had no way of being able to detain any first-class passenger other than by name. And if he didn't choose to accept her self-appointed task of acting as his escort to his waiting car . . . ?

The train doors wheezed open. They were now at Osterley and nearly all the remaining passengers were laden with luggage and quite obviously Heathrow-bound.

Van de Naude was an international courier. He might brush her offer aside. He might insist the car was waiting for him at the usual place it waited for him. With all his experience of airport staff he might take one look at her and sense instinctively that she was a fake.

Hounslow Central. Hounslow West. It was all open countryside now. They were nearly at Heathrow. She glanced down at her watch. She had an hour in hand. It was enough. Too much leeway in time would not be an advantage; not when, at any moment, there was the risk of a member of airport staff cottoning on to the fact that she was a rogue. In and out, that was how it had to be played.

When the train slid to a halt she alighted with purposeful briskness. The main trick in successfully carrying out the kind of masquerade she was now attempting lay in utter certainty of manner and movement. One minute's hesitation as to which way to go or what to do, coupled with the fact that her face was not known, and she would immediately arouse suspicion.

She breezed into the international terminal making straight for a ladies' loo. There, having stuffed her gloves

n her pocket, she shrugged herself out of her coat, hung
t on the back of the loo door where, until taken to Lost
Property, it would remain, and removed her clipboard from
her bag. She stood for a second, breathing deeply. Apart
from having a passenger's left luggage locker key in her
skirt pocket she was to all intents and purposes a member
of British Airways ground staff.

She exited from the public loo, banking on the fact that
anyone seeing her do so would assume she'd been called
in it to attend to a passenger, and walked swiftly through
the Arrivals Hall. The monitors showed that the Johannesburg flight was due to land in twenty minutes.

She knew the route through to the far side of Customs
and Passport Control and, her security badge around her
neck, took it unchallenged as she had taken it on her
familiarising practice runs.

Ten minutes. She checked with a member of the ground
staff as to which gate the South African flight was coming
in at and then walked briskly towards it, quickening her
speed as she reached the actual disembarkation ramp. Kelly
and Ros would be in position now. As would Eddie and
his henchman. What if Eddie saw Kelly and Ros? What if
it was proving impossible for Kelly to park where it had
been planned she would park?

'Hi,' she said in a relaxed manner to a male ground staff
member standing at the bottom end of the ramp. 'I've been
detailed to meet a diplomat.'

Too late she wondered if her phraseology would immediately label her a fake. There was probably an acronym for
passengers travelling on diplomatic immunity passports.
She should have got Ros to check with her airline hostess
friend at RADA.

'They'll want their bottoms wiping next,' he said, too
instantly intrigued by her superb bone structure and wide-
spaced gentian-blue eyes to worry about the fact that he
didn't know her by sight.

Her mouth curved in an encouraging smile. If all she had to do to survive the next few minutes was to flirt, then she could do that with ease.

A stewardess came down the ramp pushing a wheelchair and looked questioningly at her.

'I've been asked to escort a Mr Van de Naude,' Jackie said, her clipboard held in a business-like manner. 'He's a diplomat in first-class. We're not doubling up on each other, are we?'

The girl shook her head. The aircraft was not only down now but was trundling into position for disembarkation. 'No. My charge is female and at least ninety years old.'

The ramp was in place and the aircraft doors were being opened. Jackie adjusted the clipboard in her hand so that the sheet of paper uppermost on it could be read clearly. MR VAN DE NAUDE was printed on it in large block letters. She was going to ask one of the cabin crew to direct him to her, of course, but just in case there was any slip-up she also wanted to be holding a sign no disembarking passenger could miss.

'Would you tell Mr Van de Naude, travelling in First Class, that I've been detailed to escort him to his car, please?' she asked the steward who had manually operated the aircraft doors. 'His priority disembarkation is a matter of some urgency.'

'Three ticks and he'll be right with you.'

Jackie wondered if the noise in her ears was her blood beating or the sound of the aircraft's passengers slamming overhead lockers shut. Any minute now . . . Any minute . . .

'Goodbye, sir,' she could hear a stewardess aboard the aircraft saying. 'Thank you for flying with us.'

It was Van de Naude. Even before the steward standing at the aircraft's open doors spoke to him as he left the aircraft Jackie knew who he was. First off the aircraft, he was middle-aged, not very tall, sun-tanned, immaculate dressed and he was carrying a leather carryall and a leather attaché case.

'Mr Van de Naude?' she lowered her clipboard as he stepped away from the steward. 'Welcome to Britain, Mr Van de Naude. I hope you had a pleasant flight. I've been detailed to escort you through the airport to your waiting limousine.'

Accustomed to such personal attention Van de Naude nodded. It was only as they were walking at a brisk pace up the disembarkation ramp that Jackie felt a stab of pure panic. What if Passport Control sussed her presence as being odd? What if . . . ?

They were at the desk. Van de Naude had his distinctive passport at the ready.

'Your passport please, sir.'

One glance was enough to announce his special status. No one even looked at her.

'This way, sir,' she said to him smoothly as he began showing every intention of marching straight towards the VIP exit where, if Eddie's pseudopolice motorcyclist had done his stuff, Eddie and his henchman would be waiting with the pseudodiplomatic limousine. 'Your car is waiting at the far end of the concourse. We're having a little problem at the moment with the main automatic doors and it's causing a traffic-flow problem.'

Not slowing her brisk pace down for a second she steered him left, away from the main doorway. The exit they would leave the terminal by was a side staff exit, but a man like Van de Naude would, she hoped, be quite used to by-passing the common herd – especially if the common herd was likely to be facing irritation of any kind.

'England is enjoying beautiful weather for this time of year,' she said pleasantly, marching him through one set of doors and then another. No one stopped her. No one asked her what she thought she was doing or where she thought she was going.

With her heart slamming so powerfully in her chest she thought it was going to explode she stepped out into the February sunshine. The limousine was there, a small South African flag fluttering on the bonnet's nose. Kelly was at the wheel. Rosamund, in PR mode, was standing at the rear nearside door waiting to great him.

'Good morning, Mr Van de Naude.' Right on cue Rosamund stepped forward, a welcoming smile on her face. 'My name is Jane Delaney. If you have any letters or memos you wish to dictate on the journey into town I shall be only too happy . . .'

'A secretary? I have no need of a secretary.' As Kelly stepped out of the car in order to open the rear door for him Van de Naude came to an abrupt halt. 'I certainly didn't request a –'

'It's a new service, sir.' Rosamund smiled winningly, looking every inch a Sloane Ranger, her fair hair held away from her face by a black velvet Alice band, her jacket cream slubbed silk, the sleeves pushed high, her accent cut-glass. 'I also have details with me of the latest shows and events and will immediately arrange any tickets you may require, or . . .' she paused slightly, her dark-lashed eyes holding his, '. . . any escorts.'

The tension that had been discernible in Van de Naude's shoulders ebbed. The prospect of driving from Heathrow to the centre of London with Rosamund for a companion was becoming, apparently, a pleasant one.

'I need to be on my way,' he said cursorily.

'Of course,' she said as Kelly opened the door for him. 'Traffic is light this morning, Mr Van de Naude. It should be a quick trip.'

For one brief, emotion-charged moment her eyes flicked away from his to Jackie's and then she was walking around to the far-side rear door. Seconds later she was slipping into the rear seat beside Van de Naude and Kelly was in the driving seat sliding the limousine into gear.

Fighting the temptation to stand watching it until it had not only drawn away from the kerb but had disappeared from sight, Jackie turned and walked smartly back inside the terminal.

All she had to do now was remove her travel bag from its locker; visit a ladies' loo yet again and change her clothes.

She couldn't do it, though. She couldn't do anything. Her legs had turned to jelly and she was shaking as uncontrollably as if she had malaria. Kelly would be speeding down towards the turn-off point where Ros was going to draw the revolver. What if anything went wrong? Dear Christ, what if there were a fatality?

'Excuse me, young lady, but could you tell me where to find a lavatory?' an anxious elderly lady was asking her.

With tremendous effort Jackie resumed her efficiently brisk ground staff manner.

'I can do more than that,' she said, aware she could have no better cover for her last few minutes in British Airways uniform than to be seen to be escorting a passenger. 'I can take you to one.'

There were no side doors or staff-only doors to negotiate this time. At a slow but steady pace they entered the terminal by the main door. Parked as near as possible to it was a limousine with diplomatic plates and a South African flag fluttering on the nose of its bonnet. A man she didn't recognise, in chauffeur's uniform, was at the wheel. Eddie, looking every inch a professional bodyguard, was standing by the rear door facing the Arrivals Hall exit.

The South African flight had only landed a mere fifteen minutes ago and Eddie would be well aware that the majority of its passengers were still filing in line at Passport Control or waiting for their baggage. As yet it didn't seem to have occurred to him to be overly anxious about the nonappearance of Mr Van de Naude. He soon would be, though. He would soon be very anxious indeed.

'Would you excuse me for just one moment whilst I

retrieve something from a left-luggage locker?' Jackie said to her elderly companion, aware that once again she had a perfect foil as, dressed as a member of staff, she removed a travel bag from a public locker.

Minutes later her charge was gratefully entering a cubicle in the ladies' and Jackie slipped into an adjoining one. Hat, blouse, skirt and tights were whipped off and stuffed into one side of the bag. From the other she took out a blackberry-coloured turtle-necked sweater, a white noncrease skirt and a scarlet lightweight jacket. She dressed swiftly and then, sitting down on the loo seat, gave herself up to a crippling attack of nerves. Ros would have drawn the revolver on Van de Naude by now. The whole heist was already a success or an abject failure – and if it were a failure all she could do was pray to God no one had been hurt.

'And the escort side of the theatre-booking programme?' Van de Naude was asking in a studiedly casual manner as Rosamund sat close to him in the back of the limousine.

Rosamund shot him a seductive smile. 'Only exceptional young women are employed, Mr Van de Naude. Accompanying diplomats and international businessmen to the opera and ballet or whatever corporate function they may be attending is really just another aspect of the PA work they do.'

Her knee lightly brushed his, her loose-fitting jacket disguising all signs of her early pregnancy. Her skirt was short. Her skin was English Rose perfection. Her features were flawless and she smelled enticingly of Patou's *Joy*.

'You act as an escort yourself?'

Ros felt as if her chest was about to explode. Though her attention was flatteringly fixed on Van de Naude she was registering landmarks out of the corner of her eye. They were nearing the junction. The fraction of a second when Kelly turned off the main road on to it was make or break time. Immediately the limousine diverted from the straight route into the centre of London Van de Naude would be on his guard, querying the deviation.

The revolver had to be pulled on him whilst he was still totally unaware of there being anything odd about anything. The surprise had to be total – and she had to get the handcuffs on him fast. Going over the route they were now travelling Jackie had sat in for Van de Naude time and time again, going through every permutation of reaction they could think of as Ros had dug the revolver in the side of her ribcage and handcuffed her.

The practice runs were the reason she had arranged things so that she was seated to the left of Mr Van de Naude. The revolver, the barrel only 2 inches long, was in a shoulder holster beneath her right arm.

'It's the most compact model Smith & Wesson make,' Kelly had said to her reassuringly when she had first handed it to her. 'It only weighs 23 ounces.'

It hadn't felt compact to Rosamund then and it didn't do so now. It felt as big and heavy as a lead cannon. 'Yes,' she said now in answer to his question. 'Escort work is part and parcel of my job description.'

Van de Naude smiled, his eyes crinkling at the corners. He was an attractive man, his sun-bleached hair lightly touched with grey at his temples, his teeth a triumph of expensive cosmetic dentistry.

From the front of the limousine Kelly cleared her throat loudly. Rosamund knew why. They were at the junction. Kelly was already signalling to make the left-hand turn. It was now . . . *now*!

As the car swooped into the turn Rosamund sent a fervent prayer to heaven and leaned hard against Van de Naude and, as she did so, dived her right hand beneath her jacket, drawing the revolver and jabbing it into his side with a swiftness that had been practised hard.

'Don't move! *Don't move*!'

'What the . . . ?' For a merciful moment Van de Naude

didn't cotton on to what was happening. He'd been looking at her legs when the car had lurched and assumed the hard object now digging into him was, perhaps, a handbag.

'Cuff him! *Cuff him!*' This time it was Kelly who was doing the shouting.

Rosamund didn't need any telling. As her right hand had been moving for the revolver her left hand had been seizing hold of the handcuffs in her left-hand jacket pocket.

The expression on Van de Naude's face changed from one of pleasurable sexual anticipation to one of disbelieving horror. 'NO!' he bellowed, wrenching himself backwards, away from her.

Rosamund sprang on him and this time he saw the revolver clearly. As he did so – as he was still registering his predicament – Rosamund cuffed him on one wrist. '*Struggle you bastard and I'll shoot!*' Even as she shouted the words Rosamund couldn't believe she was uttering them. An image of her father, resplendent in the uniform of a deputy commissioner, flashed through her brain and then, as she successfully closed the second cuff around Van de Naude's wrists, was gone.

'*Get down!*' she yelled at him as Kelly sent the limousine speeding in the direction of Feltham. '*Get down and don't move!*'

With a revolver rammed hard against his side and his wrists handcuffed Van de Naude had little option but to comply. As he shifted himself down into an undignified position between the seats, and as Rosamund lifted the revolver away from his side so that it was, instead, pointed down at him, he let loose a stream of filthy Afrikaans words.

Rosamund, nearly sobbing in relief that the worst was over, was indifferent. He could call her names in any language he pleased. All that mattered to her was that her main role was now over and she hadn't fluffed her part in any way.

'How long till we reach the house?' she asked Kelly urgently as Van de Naude's continued to shout and rave.

'Five minutes. Maybe four.'

'Can't we go any faster?'

Compared to Kelly's usual breakneck method of driving the speed they were travelling was excruciatingly sedate.

'And get pulled over? *Keep him down!*'

Van de Naude was trying to heave himself up onto the seat. If he did so, keeping a gun on him in a manner unnoticeable to passing traffic, would be near impossible.

'*Down!*' she yelled at the hapless Van de Naude, the gun aiming at his head. 'And stop swearing! They're not your diamonds! They're not family heirlooms! They're your government's diamonds and they're being used as crooked currency –'

'A police car!' Kelly said suddenly. 'Jesus sweet Christ.'

Van de Naude made a strangled sound in his throat and for one terrifying moment Rosamund thought he was going to put her to the test and lurch up onto the seat beside her. If he did, if he raised his handcuffed wrists to the window as the police car passed by . . .

'I'll shoot,' she threatened him in a voice not remotely recognisable as her own.

The nightmare was that, despite all her pleas to the contrary, Jackie and Kelly had insisted on the revolver being loaded. 'An unloaded revolver always *looks* unloaded,' Kelly had said. 'It's something that can be sensed. The revolver has to be loaded, Ros. The fact that it is will transmit itself to Van de Naude and that way he'll be good as gold.'

Van de Naude's eyes, full of hate and fury, met hers.

She had both hands on the revolver now. The grip was hard in her hands. 'I'm not joking,' she said, willing him to believe it. 'This isn't a rehearsal. It's for real.'

The remark had Kelly snorting with laughter. 'You're priceless, Jane Delaney,' she said as she made a sharp right-handed turn into a tree-lined road and began to slow the limousine down fast.

Twenty miles an hour. Fifteen. Ten. Then, to Rosamund's unspeakable relief, Kelly was swinging off the road and into the driveway of a semi-detached house. There was a garage at the end of the drive and its electronic door slid open.

Seconds later, as Van de Naude continued a litany of what would happen to them when they were caught, Kelly slammed open her door and, a split second later, wrenched open the rear door nearest to where Van de Naude was crouching.

'Out,' she ordered. 'And no funny business.'

'*White trash*!' Van de Naude spat at her as he uncoiled himself. '*Bitch! Whore!*'

As he eased himself out of the car Rosamund edged after him, the revolver's grip clammy in her perspiring hands. 'It's called an Uncle Mike's Boot,' Kelly had said to her of the hand grip when first familiarising her with it. 'Funny kind of name, isn't it?'

It was a funny kind of name but Ros wasn't amused by it at the moment.

Standing up was proving difficult for her. It was as if her legs simply wouldn't do what her brain was commanding.

'Into the driver's seat,' Kelly ordered Van de Naude. 'And don't look for the keys because I'm not so silly.'

'You'll never get away with this! Never!' Van de Naude was literally spitting with fury. 'My government never allows itself to be made a fool of! Our secret police will track you down no matter where you run to or where you hide!'

'That's what I like,' Kelly said drily, 'fighting talk. Now get into the driving seat, Mr Van de Naude.'

Still volubly raving he did as he was ordered. Kelly reached into the glove compartment and removed a second pair of handcuffs and a roll of gaffer tape.

'I don't like using this tape,' she said as she manacled his handcuffed wrists to the steering wheel, 'but if it's good enough for our and your security forces to use then it's good enough for us.'

Ros, able to stow the revolver at long last, took the roll of tape from her and plastered a broad section of it across Mr Van de Naude's mouth.

'We're nearly there!' Kelly was exultant. 'Get the attaché case from the limo. It's time to get down to business.'

Rosamund did as she was asked, wondering how many other names she was going to have to become accustomed to. Joanna was the name she would be using long-term. Jane was only for the duration of the heist. She was supposed to be referring to Kelly as Claire . . . or was it Christine? Not being able to remember she'd merely made quite sure she didn't call her anything.

She placed the case on the workbench, watching in fascination as ignoring the locks, Kelly began slicing the leather with a lethal-looking Stanley knife.

Van de Naude skittered his handcuffed wrists backwards and forwards on the steering wheel like a chained animal. Rosamund avoided his blazing eyes, wondering exactly which branch of the government the diamonds had been destined for. Van de Naude had said the South African Secret Police would hunt them down. What if men from MI5 were also soon on their tail?

Over on the workbench the attaché case was yawning wide enough for a hand to be slid it into it.

Dry-mouthed, Kelly eased out its only contents – a padded Jiffy bag. 'We'd best check it's what we hope it is,' she said to Rosamund, picking up the knife again. The bag ripped, puffs of fibre stuffing flying free. A leather pouch fell out on to the workbench. For a charged second neither Kelly or Rosamund was capable of movement and then, her hands shaking slightly, Kelly began to undo the laces fastening it.

Rosamund forgot all about worrying about secret policemen and secret servicemen. This was it. The prize was truly in their hands at last. Inside the leather pouch a fistful of gems glittered and sparkled.

Rosamund gasped and Kelly let out her breath on a long, low whistle. When Rosamund could finally speak she said in a voice that was a croak. 'How many do you think there are? Fifty? Sixty?'

'I don't know.' Kelly was already feverishly retying the laces. 'All I know is that there are enough. Come on. Let's say our goodbyes and get out of here.' She thrust the pouch into Rosamund's hand. 'The minute we're in the car you do your stuff with them, OK?'

Rosamund nodded. She was holding a fortune in her hands. A buzz of euphoria swamped her in orgasmic intensity. Now she knew how Kevin felt when he'd successfully pulled a job. Once enjoyed, it was a feeling to which nothing else could possibly come close.

'It's been a pleasure knowing you,' Kelly was saying cheekily to Van de Naude. 'Don't panic. There's no need. The cavalry will be with you in an hour or so.'

Van de Naude's gagged reaction was almost apoplectic. Neither Kelly nor Rosamund cared. Kelly was slamming the garage door down and then, with wings on their heels, they sprinted up the driveway to the street and the waiting Vauxhall Cavalier that was their getaway car. Kelly opened the boot and hoisted out three zip-up travel bags.

'Here,' she said, thrusting them towards Rosamund. 'It doesn't matter how you divide the stones up. And when you've done it, drop the revolver and holster into a carrier bag. There's a couple stuffed down one of the side pockets.'

As she was talking she had been getting into the car. Now, as Rosamund scrambled into the rear seat, plonking the bags down at her side, she turned the key in the ignition. 'Last lap,' she said exultantly, her eyes meeting Rosamund's through the mirror. 'One more hour and we'll really have liftoff. Liftoff to Jamaica!'

She slid the car into gear and pressed her foot down on the accelerator.

Rosamund dropped the leather pouch in her lap, took off her gloves and began unzipping the bags, taking out a toilet bag from each. The giant tubes of toothpaste were all only half full. As Kelly surged out of the quiet residential street Rosamund took a pair of eyebrow tweezers and an orange stick from one of the toilet bags and began the delicate task of inserting gem after gem into the toothpaste tubes.

'How's it going?' Kelly asked as they sped down yet another side road. 'Are they fitting in or are we going to have to use the face-cream pots?'

'They're fitting in ... just.' Rosamund tapped the diamond she had just inserted down to the middle of the toothpaste tube with the orange stick. 'How are we doing for time, Kel? Are we on schedule?'

'Nearly to the minute. Checking-in started twenty minutes ago.'

Rosamund continued working with swift dexterity. She had been right at the guess that they were fifty to sixty diamonds in the pouch. The actual number was dead on sixty. As Kelly zipped on to the A4 she twisted the cap back on the first packed toothpaste tube and put the tube back into one of the toilet bags.

'They look blue,' she said in a worried voice as the diamond she next picked up in the tweezers sparkled from dozens of perfectly cut facets. 'Do you think that means there's something wrong with them? Some zircons are blue, aren't they?'

'They are, but those aren't zircons, sweetheart.' Kelly made the turning for the airport. 'And diamonds come in all colours. Yellow. Pink. Blue. If these are blue they'll be even more valuable than plain old white. Do you reckon

Eddie is still kicking his heels outside Arrivals? Shall we zoom past and have a deck?'

'No!' The last thing Rosamund wanted was to waste even a second of time before checking in on their flight and she certainly didn't want to see Eddie again – not ever. She twisted the cap back on the toothpaste tube and, as Kelly zoomed into the airport proper, began frantically stuffing the remaining diamonds into the last lot of toothpaste.

'Passports, tickets, diamonds,' Kelly said, making straight for short-term parking. 'I think we've got everything, don't you?'

'We have to phone the letting agents.' Rosamund sucked a blob of toothpaste from her finger. 'And how are we going to make quite sure they go round to the house immediately? Wouldn't it be safer to phone the police?'

'God, but you're a worry-bucket.' In affectionate exasperation Kelly slid the Vauxhall into a parking space. 'The worst that can happen to Van de Naude is that he has an overfull bladder by the time he's cut free but yes, if you feel happier tipping off the police as well, do so – only don't for Christ's sake give them your name and address!'

Rosamund giggled, on such a high she didn't know how she was ever going to come down. She tossed the last toothpaste tube into the last unzipped toilet bag, zipped it smartly and tucked it deep down in the bag it had come from. There was only the gun to see to now. She took a Marks & Spencer carrier bag from the side pocket of one of the bags and then slipped her arms out of her jacket. With her gloves back on she then unfastened her shoulder-holster and stuffed it, together with the revolver, into the green plastic carrier.

'Ready?' Kelly asked as she switched off the engine.

Rosamund nodded. In eight hours, maybe even less, she would be with Kevin again. Of course she was ready. She'd never been more ready in her life.

She got out of the car with all three bags and the carrier, and handed one of the travel bags to Kelly. 'I could get quite used to being an international diamond thief,' she said as they began walking away from the car and towards their terminal. 'All it needs is a lot of front.'

'And inside information,' Kelly said drily. 'Don't forget that little detail, will you? We've Raymond to thank for this and where he got his info from we'll probably never know.'

Rosamund gave a little shudder, wishing she hadn't inadvertently led the conversation on to the topic of her brother. Deputy Commissioner Laing was now in possession of a letter from Jackie detailing all she knew about Raymond's dealings with Eddie and, even more importantly, the vital cassette tape of Eddie's satisfyingly incriminating conversation with him.

Kelly, in the last few minutes before leaving number 28, had made the anonymous telephone call tipping the police off as to where they could find six bars of Brinks-Mat bullion. Where Raymond was concerned it was all that could be done and all of them were dubious as to whether it was going to be enough. If it wasn't and if he remained a serving police officer then the heist they had just pulled would be all the sweeter. Raymond would know he had been foiled of a fortune – and his fury would probably be life-long.

Jauntily they swung into the Departure Hall. Jackie, seated where she could see every passenger entering the terminal, erupted from her seat, her face radiant. Kelly had primed all of them on the dangers of allowing emotion to take over at this moment. 'No whoops of triumph,' she had warned sternly. 'Nothing that is going to draw attention to us. Got it?'

'Everything went sweet as a nut,' she now said briefly as Jackie hugged her tight. 'All that's left is to off-load the carrier bag and arrange Van de Naude's rescue.'

Jackie looked up at the nearest monitor. Their flight was beginning to board. 'I'll put the bag in the locker,' she said, taking both the carrier bag and one of the travel bags from Rosamund. 'You get on the phone, Ros. We're boarding at Gate 10. Get your baggage checked in and meet me there.'

As she swiftly made her way towards the left luggage lockers she wanted to punch the air like a triumphant boxer. They'd done it! Over in the Arrivals Hall, frantically buttonholing ground staff with queries as to why Van de Naude hadn't yet emerged from Passport Control or Baggage Reclaim, Eddie would be a man demented. Raymond, when Eddie telephoned him with the news that Van de Naude had disappeared into thin air, soon would be, too.

She bundled the carrier bag into a locker. Then she took a stamped addressed envelope from the pocket of her jacket and slipped the key inside it. The envelope was addressed to Johnny. The accompanying letter asked him to retrieve the contents of the locker and dispose of them. It would be the first he knew of the heist and what his reaction was going to be she couldn't even begin to imagine. She knew one thing, though: he wouldn't let her down.

'Will passengers flying on flight WI454 for Kingston please make their way to Gate 10 where boarding has now commenced,' a Tannoyed announcement intoned.

Jackie picked up the travel bag and made directly for the check-in, to all intents and purposes just another holidaymaker seeking to escape Britain's chill February weather.

'Smoking or nonsmoking?' she was asked as she was checked in and a label was slapped on her bag.

'Smoking,' she said, fairly sure it was what both Kelly and Rosamund would have asked for.

'And you have only hand luggage?'

Jackie nodded.

The ground staff stewardess smiled. 'Thank you, Miss

Dunwell,' she said, handing her documentation back to her. 'Enjoy your flight.'

Passport Control was just as trouble-free. With the travel bag slung easily over her shoulder she strode briskly towards Gate 10. The chauffeur of the original limousine detailed to collect Mr Van de Naude would most probably by now be well aware he had been hoaxed. Whether he had, or hadn't, made no difference now to her and Ros and Kelly. They were now Tracey Dunwell, Joanna Winterbottom and Miranda Cash and no one could possibly suspect them of anything.

As she strode to Gate 10 she saw Kelly and Rosamund ahead of her. There were only minutes to go now. Only minutes and they would be clear away.

There was a final documentation check and then, Kelly and Rosamund still ahead of her, the last brief walk down the ramp to the plane.

The aircraft was full with far more black faces than white. As she squeezed down the aisle to the rear of the plane and the smoking section she felt a pang of grief on Kelly's behalf. This was a flight Kelly should have been taking with Dexter. If Eddie hadn't so brutally murdered him perhaps Dexter would have taken Kelly on a visit to his family for their honeymoon. Even if he hadn't done so then he would most certainly have done so when he'd had a son or a daughter to introduce to his parents.

She was in an aisle seat as, she saw, was Kelly. From two rows behind her Kelly shot her a sizzling grin. Rosamund had a window seat one row behind Kelly. Jackie stowed her bag and its precious cargo into the overhead locker and sat down. Ms Joanna Winterbottom, Ms Tracey Dunwell and Ms Miranda Cash were on their way. Nothing could stop them now. Nothing.

The engines started up and the plane began to taxi down the runway. She wondered what her dad's reaction was going to be when he learned of the stunt she and Ros and

Kelly had pulled. She would phone him – though only on a line she could be quite sure was safe – just as soon as she arrived. With the diamonds safely out of the country she needed his help in knowing how to fence them. Compared to the heist itself fencing the diamonds was going to be a minor problem. Her dad would know of someone – probably someone in New York. Whoever it was, for a haul such as theirs, the fence would come to them. They wouldn't have to go to him.

'Would you like a drink?' a stewardess was asking her. 'Fruit juice, red wine, white wine or champagne?'

'Champagne, please.' From now on, for her and Johnny, it was going to be champagne all the way.

As the champagne bubbles fizzed she held her glass high and turned to look to where Ros and Kelly were seated. Kelly's chauffeuse's neat hairdo had been tousled into its usual Afro frizz and she had taken her jacket off to reveal a gaudy Bob Marley T-shirt. Rosamund was looking as contented as a cat that had swallowed cream. Both of them were grinning from ear to ear and both of them had glasses of champagne in their hands.

Jackie's grin matched theirs. They'd done it. They'd shafted Eddie and Raymond and, to a lesser degree, Kevin. From now on, in her relationship with Kevin, Rosamund would be calling just as many shots as he.

She leaned her head back against her headrest.

For a girl who had never previously indulged in even a criminal thought, let alone a criminal action, she had done a very good job indeed of robbing two governments of a fortune in diamonds. In bone-deep satisfaction she began to drink her champagne, aware, as the plane soared towards the stratosphere, that she was very much Sweetie-pie Sweeting's daughter after all.

Chapter Twenty

In the hot sun the Jamaican rum punch was ice cold. It was April. The mango trees were in blossom and in the gardens surrounding the azure waters of the swimming pool wax-white orchids rioted against a backdrop of purple and crimson bougainvillaea.

Jackie adjusted her white-framed Armani sunglasses and, reclining on a comfortable lounger, gave a cat-like stretch. Lady Luck had been with them when they had carried out the heist and she hadn't deserted them since.

Reports of the robbery in the *International Daily Herald* had stilled Rosamund's worries about Mr Van de Naude. The police and the letting agent had arrived at the house simultaneously and Van de Naude had been released from his handcuffs the same moment their Kingston-bound flight had left the ground.

He hadn't, however, reported that he'd been robbed of a million-pound fortune in diamonds. According to the *Daily Herald* he'd been carrying no valuables of consequence and it was being assumed that his kidnappers had mistaken him for a much wealthier traveller.

'And we know why he's keeping shtumm about the diamonds, don't we?' Kevin had said when he had read the report. 'It's because if he admitted to what he'd been carrying, lots of questions would be asked. Questions which would put both the South African Government, and ours, on the spot.'

He'd been sitting by the pool in swimming trunks, his hard, well-muscled body slicked with sun oil, a serious gold chain around his neck, a Rolex on his wrist. Even without the ingots he'd left in Kelly's care his Brinks-Mat whack was going to see him in comfort for a very long time. As for Kelly's cavalier decision to forfeit his 'souvenir' stash in an attempt to stitch up Raymond – he'd howled in anguish at first but hadn't done so for long.

'I can overlook him being bent,' he had said, handing round mint juleps as Rosamund watched his every movement adoringly, 'but not his continuing an association with Eddie when he knew Eddie wasn't a straight crim but a torturer and a murderer.'

'Was,' Jackie had quietly corrected, and the conversation had come to an end. No one wanted to talk about how Halide's men had put paid to Eddie. It had been a gangland killing carried out in gangland style.

Kelly's voice, coming from the house, broke in on her thoughts. 'Is there any of the stewed guava with coconut cream left?' she could hear her asking Violet, their cook-housekeeper. 'And if there isn't, could you please make some more?'

The corners of Jackie's mouth tugged into a smile. Now five months pregnant Kelly's addiction to guava and coconut cream had become a standing joke. Wearing a sizzling pink bikini, proud of her burgeoning belly, she ate it like a child eating sweets.

'Me hear of some funny addictions when yah carry baby,' Dexter's mother had said in indulgent amusement, 'but me neva hear of anyone eatin' guava till it a come outa dem ears!'

Dexter's parents were regular visitors. Kevin would send a car for them and they would travel out of Kingston on the spectacular Junction Road, spend the whole day, and often several days, with them.

From the far end of the pool there came the clink of cutlery being set. Jackie took off her sunglasses and looked across to where, beneath a yellow and white striped awning, the house staff were setting a long table for a formal meal. Starched white napery gleamed; glasses shone. It was to be a very special meal – a wedding breakfast. Dexter's parents were due to arrive mid-afternoon accompanied by a vicar from the Anglican Church in Kingston, together with a registrar.

The wedding was going to take place at the poolside and Rosamund, her belly even more burgeoning than Kelly's, was insisting that she and Kevin didn't meet that day until the time came to exchange their wedding vows.

As Jackie swung her legs from the lounger and rose to her feet Rosamund stepped out of the marble-floored house dressed in an azure silk peignoir, her hair in jumbo curlers.

'Isn't it time you were on your way to collect our special guest?' she asked as she walked around the poolside to where the lounger was positioned against a backdrop of tulip trees.

Jackie nodded, picking up the copy of the *International Daily Herald* she'd been reading earlier. The short news report, tucked away on page four, wasn't one Rosamund was likely to get round to reading on her wedding day, but the risk, if the newspaper was left lying around, was there.

'I'm going now.' She was wearing a mauve skirt, a turquoise blouse, gold sandals and not much else. The blouse, carelessly fastened with only one pearl button, was knotted beneath her breasts exposing her sun-tanned midriff. Her long golden legs seemed to go on and on for ever and her hair, much longer now than she had ever previously worn it, fell in a smooth wave to her shoulders, pushed away from her face on one side with a single gardenia-decorated comb.

She picked up the cream leather purse that held her car keys and replaced her sunglasses, hardly able to contain the excitement spiralling through her. The special guest she was meeting was very special indeed; so special that the mere thought of him striding towards her at the airport had her heart feeling as if it would burst.

Johnny had known of the heist ever since he had received the left-luggage locker key and her accompanying letter. It had taken until now, though, for him to be able to fly out and join her without the risk of leaving a trail anyone could follow.

'I'm in Amsterdam,' he had said on the telephone two days previously. 'And I'm travelling under the name Carl Hemmings. Turn down the sheets, sweetheart. I'm on my way!'

The broderie-anglaise-edged sheets on her vast double bed had been turned down with immaculate care. There were fragrant sprays of frangipani in a vase on the dressing table and an ice-bucket stood near the bed, ready and waiting for a chilled bottle of Louis Roederer Cristal.

The mere thought of their reunion had her dampening in anticipation and it was only with the greatest effort that she dragged her thoughts to the present moment.

'By the time I get back with Johnny you'll be all in your glory,' she said to Rosamund who, despite her obvious pregnancy, had bought the most gorgeous white wedding dress she'd been able to lay her hands on. 'Don't forget to wear the blue garter for the "something blue" and Kelly's St Christopher for the "something old".'

Tears of happiness glittered in Rosamund's eyes. 'I love you, Jackie,' she said. 'I'm so glad I'm going to be your cousin-in-law.'

'Lord, Ros! Don't start the waterworks now – wait till the wedding proper!'

Hugging her tight, knowing that at any moment she, too, would be giving way to emotion, Jackie kissed her on the cheek. 'If I don't leave for the airport now, Ros, Johnny won't be here in time to be best man.'

Rosamund nodded. Even if Jackie and Johnny were late she wouldn't marry Kevin before they arrived but she didn't want them to be late because she didn't want to wait a second longer than was absolutely necessary before she became Mrs Kevin Rice.

Jackie walked towards the carport. The Mercedes was low and sleek and open-topped and, after retrieving her car keys, she tossed her purse and the newspaper carelessly on to the passenger seat.

The news she had wanted to keep from Rosamund, at least for today, was that Raymond was to face a disciplinary hearing. The short report hadn't been solely about Raymond, of course. It had been about corruption in the London Metropolitan Police Force in general but Raymond's name had been there, coupled with that of another moderately high-ranking officer.

The expulsion of an officer from the force, on the grounds of corruption, was a long process and the hearing Raymond was to face was only the first step. It was a vital step, though. It meant Deputy Commissioner Laing wasn't corrupt for, if he had been, the letter and cassette tape she had sent him would have been binned – and if Laing wasn't corrupt and was convinced that Raymond was, then the eventual outcome of the charges against Raymond was almost a foregone conclusion.

She swung the Mercedes out on to the perilously high coast road towards Oracabessa, thrusting Raymond to the back of her mind, thinking only of Johnny. He had already asked her if she would marry him and she had said yes to him on the telephone and would soon be saying yes to him in his arms. Like Kevin and Rosamund they would marry by the poolside in the frangipani-scented garden.

There were ravishing, dizzying views on her left-hand side as the hillside slid at times almost sheer away into the sea. Looking at them as she drove her heart sang. Johnny was going to love Jamaica.

She turned inland, heading across to Kingston through a range of densely foliaged hills. The New York-based jewel fence her dad had contacted for them had already made two profitable trips to see them. As far as Jackie was concerned, as she finally neared Kingston and the airport, God was in his heaven and all was right with the world.

As she parked the Mercedes she saw a KLM plane on the tarmac, the luggage aboard being unloaded. Aware that Johnny would be travelling light and wouldn't be held up waiting in the Baggage Reclaim Hall, she picked up her purse and scrambled out of the car, setting off at a run for the airport's entrance.

The breeze on the long drive had whipped at the sheets of the *International Daily Herald*. The top sheet had blown away completely, a second was fluttering in the passenger-seat well and other sheets had simply blown over. On the page now exposed was a Late News column. Under the section for London news the bulletin read: 'Detectives investigating the murder of Mafia-style gangland boss, Eddie Burns, have released a statement confirming that the body found in the Thames is not that of Mr Burns. Police investigations are continuing.'

Happily heedless, Jackie ran into the welcome air-conditioned coolness of the Arrivals Hall. Hand-baggage-only passengers from the KLM flight were just beginning to file through. There was a clutch of Jamaican businessmen no longer wearing the jackets to their suits but carrying them jauntily slung over one shoulder, the top buttons of their shirts already undone, their ties pulled loose.

Her heart was slamming, her pulse pounding. Where was Johnny? *Where was he?*

And then she saw him. There was no mistaking that swift purposeful stride. Everything about him was the same as it had always been. His hair, his eyes, his mouth. Vaguely she was aware of the passengers still behind him at Passport Control: a Jamaican woman carrying a baby; a well-built European man, ginger-haired, bespectacled and tweed-jacketed. A black teenager moving to the beat of the music being played on his Walkman.

Her heart stopped slamming; seemed to stop completely. His eyes burned hers and then she was running. Running for the airport exit, running for her car, running for her life.

She had a few seconds' start but it wasn't enough. As she yanked her car door open, praying, praying, praying, she could hear the thunder of his feet behind her. Frantically she spilled her purse open, grabbing at her car keys. She had to get away. She couldn't allow herself to be caught. Not for Kelly's sake – for Ros's – for anything in the world.

She slammed the key into the ignition and turned it. The engine roared into life but not fast enough. As she feverishly let out the clutch his hand was on the passenger-side door. 'No!' she screamed. 'No!'

It was an involuntary protest, utterly useless.

As she roared out of her parking place, tyres screaming, Eddie vaulted over the passenger-side door, slithering down into the seat beside her.

'*Got you, you bitch*!' he snarled, whipping a flick knife out of his jacket pocket and ramming the hasp deep into her side.

One slight movement and flick of his thumb and she knew the blade would be slicing into her flesh, into her kidneys, and that she would be bleeding to death.

'You grassed me up, you cunt!' He was panting, not from his sprint to catch her up but from sheer explosive rage. 'You went to Halide, didn't you? You went to Halide so that he'd do the dirty for you!'

What to do? What to do? What to do? Like a rat in a cage Jackie's mind raced in frenzied circles. She couldn't stall the car now and jump for it because she would never make it. He'd plunge her without a second's hesitation. She couldn't hare off towards the Junction Road and Oracabessa hoping to God an opportunity for escape would present itself because she would only be driving him closer and closer to the villa.

They were out of the airport now and on a road that by-passed Kingston. Dimly she was aware of one of the airport taxis being hard on her heels but of what use was that? Whatever signals she made to the white driver he couldn't possibly help her. No one could help her. All she could do now was to ensure Eddie never reached the villa.

'And it was you who shafted me and Pulfer over the diamonds.' He was seated sideways on towards her, one arm on the back of her seat dangerously close to her neck, the other gripping the haft of the knife as he pressed it even harder beneath her ribcage. 'Ros Pulfer wouldn't have had the bottle and Kel wouldn't have had the knowledge. You was the one who sussed out what Ray and me was up to. You was the one who put the others up to it.'

She didn't know where she was driving. Desperately she tried to recreate a map of the island's roads in her head but it was impossible. She only knew the route across the island from Kingston and the roads on the North Coast.

'And you needn't think we're going to waste time on a wild-fuckin'-goose chase either.'

With the hand that had been behind her neck he reached into his inside jacket pocket and took out a driver-sized map of the island, shaking it open. 'You've always thought I'm bleedin' stupid but I ain't. What I want is a little talk with you and Kel and the Pulfer bitch. So get us on the right road. Stop poncing around.'

They were nearing a turn-off for Junction Road. She was going to speed straight past it, keeping to the south of the island and driving, if necessary, into the sea.

Dextrously Eddie changed the knife from one hand to the other and then, with his free hand, scooped up the contents of her purse that had spilled into the foot well and began rifling through them.

There was perspiration on her forehead and trickles of perspiration on her back. What had she had in her purse? The car keys, a lipstick, a small amount of money . . .

Eddie triumphantly waved a receipt for a roll of film she'd left to be developed at a chemist's in Port Maria. 'Miss Tracey Dunwell.' Eddie read the pharmacy assistant's pencilled scrawl with ease. 'Grand Vista, Oracabessa.' His wolfish grin was as demonic as it had always been. 'I think we're going the wrong way, Jackie. I think you need to double back and take that last turn-off you passed.'

She had absolutely no option but to do as he said. In a cloud of dust she swerved the Merc around. They might be heading back for Junction Road but there was no way she was going to take Eddie to Grand Vista. She would sooner drive the two of them over a cliff edge.

'So the three of you have been holed up here in luxury ever since Feb?' Eddie said conversationally. 'I have to give it to you, Jackie. You did well. And you stitched up that old man of yours like you was an old hand at it.'

Now on Junction Road Jackie's grip on the steering wheel tightened. 'The *three* of you,' Eddie had said. Her and Kelly and Ros. *Which meant he still hadn't cottoned on to the fact that they were with Kevin.*

As she drove into the hills her brain was working furiously. Was there any way she could lead Eddie into a trap at Grand Vista? If Kevin could be aware of Eddie's arrival without Eddie being aware of Kevin's presence then Kevin would be able to take him by surprise. Or could if he was there. As it was traditional that the bride and groom didn't meet on their wedding day until they came to exchange their vows, Ros had insisted that Kevin make himself scarce. He hadn't been at the villa when Jackie had left it and might very well still not have returned.

She decreased speed, playing for time, trying to think of an alternative plan.

'I don't think so,' Eddie said nastily, jabbing the hasp

beneath her rib cage as a reminder to her of its presence. 'I've waited a long time and come a long way for this little meet and I don't want to waste time in getting to it.'

Reluctantly she pressed her foot down a tad harder on the accelerator. There was quite a lot of traffic on the road but she couldn't think of a way of making use of it. A flash American car was immediately behind her and, a little way behind that, the taxi that had followed them out of the airport. The scenery was growing more and more spectacular by the moment but both she and Eddie were indifferent to it.

Where was Johnny? Had he been on the same flight as Eddie and at the rear of the plane, not the front? Was that why Eddie had passed through Passport Control and Customs whilst Johnny had, presumably, still been waiting in line at them?

Never before had she crossed the island in what seemed to be so little time. Eddie, the map wedged on his knee, gave her not the slightest opportunity of haring off down the coast in the wrong direction. As she took the first of the high hairpin bends her thoughts were frantically fixed on Johnny. He knew the name of the villa and that it was between Port Maria and Oracabessa. When he realised she wasn't at the airport to meet him he would make his own way to Grand Vista.

On their right-hand side the land fell steeply away down to a sea that merged from azure to indigo to jade. He wouldn't do so immediately, though. He would simply assume she had been delayed or had confused the time of the flight and he would wait for her. There were almond trees on one side of them now and, seawards, glimpses of small coral beaches with lint-white sand.

How long would he wait? She was driving on automatic pilot now, changing gears and taking corners without a conscious thought for the road. If she could stall Eddie somehow ... delay their arrival at the villa ...

'Let's talk,' she said abruptly as Port Maria came into view. 'You're quite right in thinking that the heist was basically down to me. It was. That being the case I'm the one to trade with. Kelly and Ros don't have a say in anything. They're merely passengers.'

'You've become quite the business, ain't you?' The sneer in his voice and on his face was even more unpleasant than his grin had been. 'Quite the boss-lady.'

'We have a fence – a New York dealer. He's taken a dozen of the stones but he doesn't know the number that are left.'

She began scooting around Port Maria. Eddie, too, wouldn't have a clue as to how many diamonds Van de Naude had been carrying. 'There are eighty left,' she lied, overtaking a refrigerated lorry that was delivering food to the string of luxury hotels scattering the hillside between the road and the shore. 'Let's come to a deal, Eddie. If you don't front Kel and Ros I'll do a fifty-fifty split with you.'

Eddie snorted in derision. 'You're in no position to be stating terms, Jackie. I'm here to take the fuckin' lot.'

There was blinding pain behind Jackie's eyes as she took the final stretch of road for Oracabessa. If the diamonds were all that Eddie was after, as far as she was concerned, he could have every last one of them. Only it wasn't just the diamonds. It was revenge – and revenge of any sort meant only one thing to Eddie: torture and death. She thought of Kelly and Ros and of the babies they were carrying. Eddie mustn't reach Grand Vista. If he did the slaughter would be a copy-cat to the killing of Sharon Tate and her friends by Charles Manson and his drug-crazed followers.

She was on the last steep curve of the road before it began sweeping down to Oracabessa. At the top was a magnificent lookout point from which could be seen headland after headland stretching away to the horizon in the general direction of Cuba.

'I'm going to stop the car,' she said, beyond caring if he shifted the knife away a little and flicked the notch on the hasp, plunging the blade into her side. If he did, it was hardly a wound from which she would die instantly. She would be able to speed the car across the lookout point and over the cliff edge and she would die in the happy knowledge that he would die also and that Ros and Kelly would be safe.

It was what she intended doing anyway. Yes, she would talk to him first, playing for time and for a miracle. But when the talking was over and time had run out she was going to put no trust in any promises he might give. It wasn't just Ros and Kelly's lives that were at stake. It was the lives of the babies they were carrying. When it came to moving away from the lookout and motoring down to Grand Vista she wouldn't reverse back onto the road; instead she would drive at full tilt for the cliff edge.

It was only when she had swung the Mercedes off the road and halted it on the small lookout plateau that she realised it had all been too easy. Eddie had made not the slightest objection. He had wanted her to stop the car short of Grand Vista. She wasn't leading him to his doom. He was leading her to hers.

'Out,' he said. Through the driving mirror she could see the Cadillac that had been behind them zoom past the lookout turning, continuing in the direction of Oracabessa. Of the taxi that had been with them ever since the airport there was no sign. Coming from the opposite direction a bright yellow hotel minibus whizzed round the corner and was gone. The air was hot, the silence profound.

'Out,' Eddie said again. This time, with the flick knife's hasp still bruising her side he wrenched her arm behind her back. The turquoise silk ripped beneath her armpit as, holding her arm at a cruel angle, he forced her out of the car.

He meant to kill her then and there. She knew it instinctively. He'd never wanted to talk with her. He'd never wanted to have a meet of any sort with her and Ros and Kelly. He simply wanted to slaughter all three of them and, now he was on the doorstep of Grand Vista, he was going to take her out first.

A wooden rail protected sightseers from standing too close to what was a virtual precipice dense with tropical vegetation. At the bottom of the dizzying drop was a half-moon beach and gentle, creaming waves.

He forced her so near to the rail that it pressed hard against her legs. 'So . . .' he said, in the thick brutal voice she had long ago come to hate with all her heart. 'It's goodbye time, Jax.'

'*Don't call me that! Don't ever call me that!*'

He laughed, genuinely amused. 'Why? Because it's Johnny's name for you? A fat lot of use Johnny is to you now. He'll be down the Connoisseur, shooting his mouth off and with a bird on either arm.'

As he continued to hold her fast, her arm so high up her back it was nearly out of its socket, he was so close she could feel the hardness of his erection.

Somehow or other she had to twist free of him and get the knife from his grasp, but how? Even if she succeeded in hooking a foot around his ankle and throwing him off balance it would do her no good. The instant she made any such attempt he would flick the blade deep into her gut. Talking was her only chance; her only hope. He thought Johnny was still in south-east London. If she could keep him talking long enough Johnny would pass the look-out point in either a hired car or a taxi.

Any driver now seeing the two of them from the road would assume from their stance that, standing with her back against him, she was resting her head on Eddie's chest and that he had his arms lover-like around her. Johnny wouldn't assume that, though. If Johnny drove past and recognised Eddie – and even from a distance and from the rear Eddie's massive physique was distinctively recognisable – Johnny would instantaneously read the situation correctly.

That is, he would if he wasn't driving so fast he never even glanced towards the lookout – but for all she knew he might not be driving the road at all. He might still be at the airport waiting for her to show.

'You've been very quick on the uptake about a lot of things, Jackie, but then you always were, weren't you?' He rammed her arm yet another half-inch higher. 'You didn't latch on to everything, though.' He sniggered, enjoying himself hugely. 'You didn't latch on to the fact that it was your other half who asked me to sort out the photographer bloke who did your wedding pictures for you.'

It was a moment of horror so total Jackie thought she was going to die then and there.

'Duggan had been a bit too clever fer his own good,' Eddie continued, moving the knife away from her side and flicking it so that the long, hard blade shot free. 'He'd recognised your surname, Jackie. Not many Sweetings about, are there?' He put the knife against her throat. 'And then he did what Ray didn't do. He put two and two together. Poor Ray. You have to feel a bit sorry for him, don't you? There he was on his wedding day, Laing and half the top boys in the Met swanning round at his reception, and he finds out he's married one of Sweetie-pie Sweeting's daughters! Even worse, he finds out he's now my cousin-in-law!'

Jackie didn't care that he was laughing. She cared only that she was about to die without being able to shout the names of Micky Duggan's murderers from the rooftops.

She closed her eyes tight as the blade nicked her skin and a trickle of blood ran hotly down her neck, dripping on to her blouse. It was then that she heard it. A sound so quiet and so stealthy that at first she thought it was her imagination. A footstep on dry earth. It wasn't a sightseer

374

approaching. A sightseer inadvertently about to crash in on her murder would be walking with a much different tread. Why, though, would anyone else be approaching them in such a manner? No one, approaching from behind them, would know that Eddie had a knife at her throat and, even if they did, who was likely to take on an armed man in a one-to-one confrontation? Especially an armed man built as Eddie was built.

It had to be Johnny. It *had* to be Johnny!

As Eddie, still laughing, braced himself in readiness to draw the blade across her throat the arm that shot out, hooking him around his neck from behind, was not that of a man dressed as casually as Johnny would have been dressed. Instead it was incongruously tweed-jacketed.

Eddie was making a gargling sound. The knife had dropped from his hand and Jackie dropped to her knees, scrabbling to retrieve it. By the time her sweat-soaked palm closed on the handle Eddie and her rescuer were locked in a battle that could only end in death, and – from what she had glimpsed of her rescuer as she scrambled back up off her knees – it would be his death, not Eddie's.

How could an ordinary law-abiding traveller take on a professional killer like Eddie in a fist fight? And her rescuer, ginger-haired and bespectacled, was obviously very much an ordinary traveller. It was the man who had been in line at Passport Control a little behind Eddie. The man who, she now realised, had been at the wheel of the taxi that had been behind them on their drive across the island.

She had the knife, though. She had the knife and the minute there was an opportunity for her to use it – an opportunity when there was no chance of Eddie wresting it from her grasp – she was going to do so.

'Oh my God,' she sobbed sharply as Eddie head-butted and punched and kicked in a manner that would have wiped out a Mr Ordinary in minutes. 'Oh my *dear* God!'

Her ginger-haired saviour was proving to be not

remotely ordinary. He was proving to be not at all the man he had seemed to be.

As they rolled and brawled and kicked and struggled he was giving as good as he got. Suddenly his fist shot out in a powerful left hook, slamming into the nerve centre below Eddie's ribs. Eddie hurtled backwards and his opponent was on him, crashing the heel of his hand upwards into Eddie's nostrils with such force that the bone in Eddie's nose broke, splintering back into his skull, blinding him instantly.

For ever afterwards Jackie believed it was then that Eddie died. His attacker, though, was taking no chances. As Eddie sagged senselessly, he was hauled upright by a tweed-jacketed arm and then another punch, this time to his jaw, sent him sprawling backwards with full force into the wooden rail at the edge of the precipice. It creaked and cracked but didn't break. That didn't save Eddie. The momentum with which he had crashed into to it was so strong that he toppled backwards over it, arms splayed, mouth gaping. Then there was nothing. No sound. No cries. Only, finally, the distant thud and spatter as his body made contact with the lint-white beach.

'Oh God! Oh Christ!' She was still holding the knife in her hands its blade spotted with blood from where it had pierced her neck. Tears were streaming down her face. Tears of delayed shock. Tears of relief. Tears of gratitude.

He had been looking down to the beach and the body that lay motionless on it and now he turned towards her, blood oozing from a cut above his eye, one arm of his jacket ripped off completely, his spectacles somewhere on the ground, smashed beyond repair.

'Oh but I love you!' she gasped, dropping the knife and hurtling into his arms. 'Oh, but I love you so!'

Johnny grinned. 'So I should hope,' he said, his mouth coming down in unfumbled contact on hers as he held her close against his thudding chest.

Later, much later, still standing on the plateau, she looked up into his handsome hard-boned face and said, 'It never occurred to me you would be travelling in disguise. I knew you were flying in as a Mr Carl Hemmings but even Kelly didn't think to warn me you wouldn't look like you.'

'Your dad would have known,' he said, beginning to walk her away from the scene of Eddie's death and back towards the curving, almond-tree-edged road. 'It was Jock's advice I was following. Always 'guise up when you don't want anyone hard on your tail. He's drummed it into us since we were kids.'

They had reached the road. A Mini-Moke full of noisy laughing teenagers swept past them. 'When did you know Eddie was on the plane?' she asked, her arm around his waist, her head resting against his shoulder as they walked across to her Mercedes, the taxi he had driven now clearly in evidence some twenty yards or so down the curving road. 'And how come you were at the wheel of a taxi? Where is its rightful owner?'

'I didn't know Eddie was on the plane until I saw him striding out ahead of me in the Arrivals Hall and I saw you turn and run.' At the mere memory of the moment his voice held a note so raw her tummy lurched. 'By the time I reached the concourse you were speeding away and Eddie was sliding down into the seat beside you. I thrust a wad of notes fit to choke a pig at the first taxi-driver in the rank and the rest, as they say, is history.'

They had reached the Mercedes and as he opened the driver's door for her she said in an unsteady voice. 'And Eddie? What's going to happen when Eddie's body is found?'

His eyes held hers. 'Not much, I should think. With a bit of luck he'll simply be written off as a tourist who walked a little too near the edge for his own safety.'

'Then there's nothing to worry about?'

He paused for a moment. The afternoon heat was coming out of the ground in waves and the scent of wild hibiscus was thick as smoke in the sunlight.

'If Eddie knew where to find you, the chances are that Pulfer will know as well,' he said at last. 'It's something I'm not too happy about but then again, I'm not too trashed about it either. What about you?'

His eyes continued to hold hers, grey and gold-flecked and vibrantly alive.

'No,' she said truthfully. 'As long as we're together I shall never be afraid of anything.'

He shot her a familiar, loving, down-slanting smile. 'Then let's be on our way. We've a wedding to attend. Do you think this cut is going to stop bleeding by the time I act as Kev's best man?'

She giggled, loving him with all her heart, knowing they would be together for the rest of their lives; knowing they would never again argue over the kind of lifestyle they would lead; knowing that there would never be any secrets between them and never any lies.

'I doubt it,' she said, sliding into the drivingseat as he vaulted into the seat beside her. 'Come on, lover.' She gunned the engine into life. 'We've people to see. Places to go.'